Praise

"Inspiring and heartwarming."

—*RT Book Reviews* on *Her Texas Ranger*

"Her expressive narrative gives her seemingly ill-fated couple substance and makes their love story palpable. Talented storytelling keeps readers absorbed and makes the first kiss unforgettable."

—*RT Book Reviews* on *Her Rugged Rancher*

"A wonderful read, rich in conflict and plenty of sparks. Stella Bagwell will steal your heart."

—*RT Book Reviews* on *Just for Christmas*

Praise for *USA TODAY* bestselling author Barb Han

"Great connection and chemistry between the main characters give the book a perfect blend of action and romance."

—*RT Book Reviews* on *Texas Takedown*

"A thrill a minute...sexual tension, suspenseful danger and fast-paced drama."

—*RT Book Reviews* on *Gut Instinct*

"*Witness Protection* starts off with a literal bang and doesn't let up as the on-the-run action sequences keep the story's momentum going."

—*RT Book Reviews*

HOME ON THE RANCH:

COWBOY'S HONOR

USA TODAY Bestselling Authors

STELLA BAGWELL

BARB HAN

HARLEQUIN® HOME ON THE RANCH

Recycling programs for this product may not exist in your area.

ISBN-13: 978-1-335-02041-3

Home on the Ranch: Cowboy's Honor

This edition published by arrangement with Harlequin Books S.A.

For questions and comments about the quality of this book, please contact us at CustomerService@Harlequin.com.

Printed in U.S.A.

CONTENTS

After writing more than eighty books for Harlequin, **Stella Bagwell** still finds it exciting to create new stories and bring her characters to life. She loves all things Western and has been married to her own real cowboy for forty-four years. Living on the south Texas coast, she enjoys being outdoors and helping her husband care for the horses, cats and dog that call their small ranch home. The couple has one son, who teaches high school mathematics and is also an athletic director. Stella loves hearing from readers. They can contact her at stellabagwell@gmail.com.

Books by Stella Bagwell

Harlequin Special Edition

Men of the West

His Badge, Her Baby...Their Family?
Her Rugged Rancher
Christmas on the Silver Horn Ranch
Daddy Wore Spurs
The Lawman's Noelle
Wearing the Rancher's Ring
One Tall, Dusty Cowboy
A Daddy for Dillon
The Baby Truth
The Doctor's Calling
His Texas Baby
Christmas with the Mustang Man
His Medicine Woman
Daddy's Double Duty
His Texas Wildflower
The Deputy's Lost and Found

The Fortunes of Texas: All Fortune's Children

Fortune's Perfect Valentine

Visit the Author Profile page at
Harlequin.com for more titles.

A TEXAN ON HER DOORSTEP

STELLA BAGWELL

To my brother Lloyd Henry Cook, who always insisted I could be anything I wanted to be. And to my brother Charles Cook, who pushed me to send off my first manuscript. Without either of you, I wouldn't be a writer today. I love you guys, and thank you for believing in your sister.

Prologue

The worn, yellowed envelopes bound with twine had been placed on Phineas McCleod's kitchen table more than an hour ago; yet he'd not touched them. Nor had his brother, Ripp. Both men had skirted around the stack of papers as though they were a coiled rattlesnake.

For the past several months, Mac, the nickname everyone called Phineas, and Ripp had searched for any trail of their mother, Frankie, who'd walked out on the family nearly thirty years ago. And up until yesterday, when Oscar Andrews, an old family acquaintance of the McCleods, had appeared on Ripp's doorstep with letters addressed to his late mother, Betty Jo, their searching had gone in vain.

Now, because of the letters exchanged between Betty Jo and Frankie, the brothers had more than clues. They had an address, a definite place to look for Frankie

McCleod. Yet strangely neither of them was eager to race to the spot or even read the letters. Doubts about the search for her had settled like silt in the bottom of a wash pan.

Now, as Mac roamed aimlessly around his modest kitchen, he glanced over at his younger brother. Since Ripp had arrived an hour ago, he'd done little more than stare out the window. Obviously, learning about the existence of Frankie's letters had shaken him. Hell, it had done more than shake Mac; it had practically knocked him to his knees. Two deputy sheriffs, who'd faced all sorts of danger, were now jolted by the idea of seeing a woman who had been out of their lives for twenty-nine years.

"One of us has to go to this ranch and meet with her, Ripp, and it should be me," Mac said. "You have a family now. A wife, a son and a baby daughter. They need you at home. I don't have anything to hold me here, except my job. And Sheriff Nichols will give me time off. Hell, I've got so much sick leave coming to me I could take off a year and still not use it all up."

Ripp's snort was meant to sound humorous, but it fell a bit short. "That's because you're too mean to get sick." His expression dry, he looked over his shoulder at Mac. "But who knows—after this you just might need a good doctor."

Ripp didn't have to explain that "this" meant finding Frankie McCleod. After all this time without her, Mac couldn't think of the woman as their mother. Not in the regular sense of the word.

Mac said, "Well, we both decided after Sheriff Travers told you that story about Frankie calling Dad, asking to come home, that maybe we should try to find her.

See if his story was true and what really happened back then. Are you having second thoughts?"

Groaning, Ripp turned away from the window. "Hell yes! I keep thinking that maybe not knowing about her is better than learning that she really *didn't* want us."

Mac thrust a hand through his dark hair as he stared at the stack of letters. Each one had been written by Frankie Cantrell and mailed to Betty Jo Andrews, who'd lived in Goliad County all her life until she'd died three months ago from a massive stroke. Her son, Oscar, had been going through her things, getting her estate in order, when he'd discovered the letters in an old cedar chest. Frankie's last name had changed from McCleod to Cantrell, but Oscar had glanced through one of the letters and spotted Mac's and Ripp's names. As a result, he'd thought the brothers would be interested to see them.

Interested? The existence of the letters had stunned them. Betty Jo had certainly kept her correspondence with Frankie a deep secret. If anyone else had known about it, they'd not disclosed it to Mac or Ripp.

"I don't agree," Mac finally replied. "The not knowing is bad, Ripp. Besides, if it turns out she didn't want us, then it will be easy for me to say good riddance and put the matter out of my mind once and for all."

"That's cold."

Mac let out a long breath. "I can't help it, Ripp. I remember watching her pack up and drive away. That does something to a ten-year-old kid."

Walking across the room, Ripp placed a comforting hand on his brother's strong shoulder. "We don't have to do this, Mac. We'll always have each other. If that's enough for you, then it's enough for me."

Mac's throat tightened as he looked in his brother's eyes. While growing up, the two had clung to each other more than most siblings. And down through the years that closeness hadn't wavered. Mac didn't have to think twice about his brother's love. Ripp would always be there for him, no matter who or what came and went in their lives.

"We both deserve to know the truth, Ripp. And I'm gonna find it." Mac gestured to the letters. "I'll take one of those with me for evidence. You can read the rest while I'm gone."

Ripp shook his head. "We'll read them together. Once you get back."

"We might not want to read them then," Mac countered soberly.

"Find the woman first, Mac. And then we'll make a decision about her."

Chapter 1

"Dr. Sanders, if you have a moment could you come to the nurses' station? There's—someone here who I think you need to see."

Ileana Sanders frowned slightly. It wasn't like Renae to sound evasive. In the few years that Ileana had known her, she'd been an excellent nurse who didn't waste time playing guessing games.

"I'm working on a chart, Renae. Who is it? Do they need medical attention?"

"No. He—looks pretty healthy to me." There was a pause on the phone, and when Renae's voice returned, Ileana could barely hear her whisper. "Get down here now, Doc. If you don't, I'm not sure I can keep him out of Ms. Cantrell's room!"

"I'll be right there."

Dropping the phone back in its cradle, Ileana grabbed

a white lab coat from the back of her chair and left the little cubicle she used as an office while making her hospital rounds.

From the internal medicine wing of the building, Ileana had to walk down a long, wide corridor, then make a left turn and walk half that distance again to reach the nurses' station.

Along the way, she met several of the more mobile patients walking the hallway. They all spoke to her, and she gave each one an encouraging smile and a thumbs-up on their progress. One of the perks of working in a smaller town, she thought, was knowing most everyone who walked through the hospital doors.

But the moment Ileana turned the corner and peered toward the nurses' station, she definitely didn't recognize the tall man standing at the counter. Even though it was exceptionally cold outside, he was without a jacket, making it possible for her to see that he was dressed all in blue denim. A chocolate-brown cowboy hat was slanted low over his forehead and covered hair a shade darker than the felt. And in spite of the lengthy distance, she could see he was a walking mass of lean, hard muscle.

He must have heard the hurried click of her heels on the shiny tile, because he suddenly turned in her direction, and for one brief moment, Ileana felt her breath catch, her heart jump. His features were chiseled perfection, his skin burned brown by the sun. Authority was stamped all over him, and she knew, without being told, that he was a stranger to Ruidoso. There was a subtle edginess about him that was different from the locals.

Instinctively, Ileana's steps slowed as she tried to

regain her composure, while to her left, Renae swiftly walked from behind the counter to intercept her.

"Dr. Sanders, this is Mr. McCleod. He's traveled all the way from Texas to see Ms. Cantrell."

His dark brown eyes were sliding over Ileana with a lazy interest that left her uncomfortably hot beneath her lab coat; yet she did her best to appear cool and collected as she stepped up to the man and thrust out her hand.

"Nice to meet you, Mr. McCleod," she said with a faint smile.

His big hand closed around hers, and Ileana was acutely aware of warm, calloused skin and firm pressure from his fingers.

"Call me Mac," he said. "Are you Ms. Cantrell's attending physician?"

The easy smile on his face was a tad sexy and a whole lot charming. As Ileana drew in a deep breath, she realized she'd never met this man. Because he was clearly unforgettable.

Inclining her head, she hoped she didn't look as awed as she felt. Which was really a quite ridiculous reaction on her part. She'd lived on the Bar M Ranch all her life. She'd been around rugged men throughout her thirty-eight years, and some of them had been darn good-looking with plenty of rough sex appeal. Yet none of them had grabbed her attention like this one. This was one striking cowboy.

"Yes, I'm Ms. Cantrell's doctor. Are you a friend of hers?"

Beneath his dark tan, she watched a hint of red color work its way up his throat and over his face. His embarrassed reaction wasn't the norm, but Ileana had certainly contended with worse. Everyone reacted differently when a friend or loved one became ill. Some got downright angry, quick to blame the doctor, even God, for the misfortune. She'd learned to take it all in stride.

The aim of his brown gaze landed somewhere near her feet rather than on her face, making her curiosity about the man go up another notch.

"Uh—not exactly," he said.

His face lifted, and Ileana couldn't help but notice the faint, challenging thrust of his chin, the resolution in his eyes. She shivered inwardly. For all his smooth manners, she instinctively sensed Mac McCleod had a very tough side to him.

"Nurse Walker tells me you're not allowing Ms. Cantrell to have visitors right now."

"That's right," she said, then feeling she needed to keep their conversation private, Ileana touched a hand to his arm and gestured to a waiting area several feet away from the nurses' station. "Why don't we step over here, and I'll explain."

He didn't say anything as he followed her over to a small grouping of armchairs and couches covered in green and red fabric, but once they stood facing each other, he didn't wait for her to speak.

"Look, Dr. Sanders, I've traveled a considerable distance to see Ms. Cantrell. At the Chaparral Ranch, I was told by a maid who answered the door that she was hospitalized, so I drove straight here. All I'm asking is a few short minutes with the woman. Surely that couldn't hurt," he added with a persuasive little smile.

Even though he seemed pleasant enough, there was something about the way he said "the woman" that left Ileana uneasy. Besides sounding a bit disrespectful, there was no warmth, no fondness inflected in the words. Had he and Frankie had a falling-out over something? Did he actually know her?

"I'm very sorry, Mr. McCleod. Perhaps you should have called before you made the long drive. Ms. Cantrell isn't up for visits. Presently, her condition is very fragile. The only people I'm allowing into her room are her son, daughter and father-in-law."

For one brief moment his jaw hardened, but just as quickly a smile transformed his face, and Ileana felt certain he was deliberately trying to charm her into letting him enter Frankie's room. The idea was very odd and even more worrisome.

"What about her husband?" he asked.

This brought Ileana's brows up. Clearly he wasn't a close acquaintance of Frankie's. Otherwise, he would have known that Lewis, her husband, had passed away a little more than a year ago.

"I'm sorry if you didn't know. Ms. Cantrell is a widow now. Lewis died about a year ago."

His expression suddenly turned uncomfortable, and Ileana was relieved to see that the man did have a streak of compassion in him.

"Uh—sorry. No, I didn't know."

"Have you spoken with Quint or Alexa, Ms. Cantrell's children? Perhaps they can help you," she said.

Quint and Alexa. Mac mulled the two names over in his mind. If Frankie Cantrell was Mac's missing mother, and from every indication it appeared that she was, that would make Quint and Alexa his half siblings. The idea knocked him for a loop. For some reason all these years, he'd never considered the idea of Frankie having more children. A stupid, infantile idea to cling to, he supposed. But if she'd not wanted to be a mother to Mac and Ripp, why would she have had more children?

"No. I've not spoken to either of them," he told her. "I—I'm not sure there were any family members at home when I visited the ranch."

"Well, both of Frankie's children have their hands full with trying to watch over their mother and keep up with their jobs, too. Alexa works in Santa Fe at the state capitol, and Quint runs the ranch here in Ruidoso. I expect he'll be around later tonight. If you'd like to wait. Or contact Abe Cantrell, her father-in-law."

Frustration made him want to howl, but he kept the reaction to himself. This woman wouldn't understand. And frankly, she was looking at him as though he were one of those criminals he often locked behind bars. Which was a strange reaction for Mac, who was used to women sidling up to him with a warm, inviting smile on their faces. He liked to flirt but hadn't gotten serious in a long time.

Hell, Mac, she's a professional. She isn't going to be flashing you a sexy smile or flirting with you.

She was a doctor. And from the looks of her, she'd never heard the words *sex* or *glamour.* She was plainer than vanilla yogurt and appeared to be one step away from a convent.

Except for a pair of deep blue eyes and naturally pink lips, her round face was pale and devoid of any color. Dark, reddish-brown hair was brushed tightly back from her forehead and fastened in a long ponytail at her nape. The starched stiff lab coat hid her clothing, along with the shape of her body. Even so, Mac sensed she was as slender as a stick and as fragile as the petal of an orchid.

"I'm not sure I can wait," he told her. "You see, I was planning on talking to Ms. Cantrell about an— urgent matter." Besides, Mac wasn't ready to meet the man who might be his half brother. He'd only arrived in Ruidoso, New Mexico, a few hours ago. He'd driven straight out to the Chaparral Ranch in hopes of finding Frankie and putting the whole matter of her disappearance to rest. Now it looked as though there wasn't going to be any meeting or answers of any sort.

Dr. Sanders—Ileana, he'd heard the nurse call her—shook her head. "I'm sorry," she said again. "But I'm only allowing family members to enter Ms. Cantrell's room and even they are only allowed five minutes with her."

"Is she in the intensive care unit?"

The woman's shoulders drew back, as though remembering privacy laws for patients. He wondered just how well this doctor knew the woman. Maybe Frankie had been a patient of hers for a long time, but that didn't necessarily mean Dr. Sanders knew all that much about Frankie's personal life.

"Not exactly. She's in a room where she's monitored more closely than a regular room. That's why I made the decision to limit her visitors to relatives only. People can be well meaning, but they don't realize how exhausting talking can be to someone who's ill."

Mac's visit hadn't meant to be well meaning or anything close to it. Maybe that made him a hard-nosed bastard, but then in his eyes, Frankie had been more than callous when she'd walked out of Mac's and Ripp's lives. She'd promised to come back, but that promise had never been kept. Two little boys, ages eight and ten, had not understood how their mother could leave them behind. And now that they were grown men, ages thirty-seven and thirty-nine, they still couldn't understand how she could have been so indifferent to her own flesh and blood.

Mac's gaze settled on the doctor's face, and Frankie McCleod was suddenly forgotten. Plain or not, there was something about Ileana Sanders's soft lips, something about the dark blue pools of her eyes that got to him. Like a quiet, stark desert at sunset, she pulled at a soft spot inside him. Before he realized what he was doing, his glance dropped to her left hand.

No ring or any sign of where one had once been. Apparently she was single. But then, he should have known that without looking for a ring. She had an innocent, almost shy demeanor about her, as though no man had ever woken her or touched her in any way.

Hell, Mac, her sex life or lack of one has nothing to do with you. Plain Janes weren't his style. He liked outgoing, talkative girls who weren't afraid to show a little leg or cleavage and drink a beer from a barstool.

Yeah. Like Brenna, he thought dourly. She'd showed him all that and more during their brief, volatile marriage. Since then he stuck to women who knew the score.

Sucking in a deep breath, he tried again. "I guess you'd say I'm more than a visitor, Dr. Sanders. I—well—you might consider me…a relative."

Even if Renae hadn't told her that the man was from Texas she would have guessed. Not just from the casual arrogance in the way he carried himself, but the faint drawl and drop of the *g* at the end of his words were a dead giveaway.

"Oh? I didn't realize Frankie had relatives living in Texas."

"We haven't been together—as a family—in a long time. And we just learned that she was living in New Mexico."

Totally confused now, Ileana gestured to one of the couches. "Let's have a seat, Mr. McCleod. And then maybe you can better explain why you're here in Ruidoso."

Without waiting for his compliance, Ileana walked over and took a seat. Thankfully, he followed and seated himself on the same couch, a polite distance away.

As he stretched out his legs, her gaze caught sight of his hands smoothing the top of his thighs. Like the rest of him, they were big and brown, the fingers long and lean. There was no wedding ring, but then Ileana had already marked the man single in her mind. She doubted any woman had or ever could tame him. He looked like a maverick and then some.

With a sigh she tried to disguise as a cough, she turned toward him and said, "Okay. Maybe you'd better tell me a little about yourself and your connection to Frankie. None of this is making sense to me."

He glanced over to a wall of plate glass. Snow was piled against the curbs and beneath the shade of the trees and shrubs. It was as cold as hell here in the mountains, and being in this hospital made Mac feel even colder. At the moment, South Texas felt like a world away.

"I imagine right about now you're thinking I'm some sort of nutcase. But I'm actually a deputy sheriff from Bee County, Texas. And I have a brother, Ripp, who's a deputy, too, over in Goliad County."

Ileana inclined her head to let him know that she understood. "So you're both Texas lawmen who work in different counties."

"That's right. So was our father, Owen. But he's been dead for several years now."

"I'm sorry to hear that. And your mother?"

His gaze flickered away from hers. "We're not certain. You see, my brother and I think Frankie Cantrell is our mother."

If a tornado had roared through the hospital lobby, Ileana couldn't have been more shocked, and she struggled to keep her mouth from falling open.

"Your mother! Is this some sort of joke?"

"Do I look like I'm laughing?"

No, she thought with dismay. He looked torn; he looked as though he'd rather be anywhere but here. And most of all, he appeared to be genuine.

"What makes you think she's your mother?"

Clearly uncomfortable with her question, he scooted to the edge of the cushion. "It's too long a story to take up your time. I'd better be going. I'll—come back later. When you—well, when you think it'll be okay for me to talk to her."

For a moment, Ileana forgot that she was a doctor and this man was a complete stranger. Frankie and her family had been friends with the Sanderses for many years. In fact, Ileana's mother, Chloe, was worried sick praying that her dear friend would pull through. If this man had something to do with Frankie, Ileana wanted to know about it. She *needed* to know about it, in order to keep her patient safe and cocooned from any stress.

Grabbing his arm, she prevented him from rising

to his feet. "I've finished my rounds, Mr. McCleod. I have time for a story."

He glanced toward the plate glass windows surrounding the quiet waiting area. "There's not a whole lot of daylight left. I'm sure it's time for you to go home."

"I can find my way in the dark," she assured him.

Her response must have surprised him, because he looked at her with arched brows.

"All right," he said bluntly. "I'll try to make it short. When I was ten and my brother eight, Frankie McCleod, our mother, left the family." Reaching to his pocket, he pulled out a leather wallet and extracted a photo. As he handed the small square to Ileana, he said, "That was twenty-nine years ago, and we never heard from her again. At least us boys never heard from her. We can't be certain about our father. He never spoke of her. But a few days ago, we found out that Frankie Cantrell had been corresponding through the years with an old friend of hers in the town where we lived. She has to be Frankie McCleod Cantrell."

Dropping her hand away from his arm, Ileana took the photo from him and closely examined the grainy black and white image. Two young boys, almost the same height and both with dark hair, stood next to a young woman wearing an A-line dress and chunky sandals. Her long hair was also dark and parted down the middle. If this was Frankie Cantrell, she'd changed dramatically. But then, nearly thirty years could do that to a person.

"Oh, dear, this is—well, my family and I have been friends with the Cantrells for years. We never heard she had another family. At least, I didn't. I can't say the same for Mother, though." She handed the photo back to him, while wondering if it was something he always carried with him. "The woman in the picture—she's very beautiful. I can't be sure that it's Frankie. I was only a small child when she first came here. I don't recall how she looked at that time."

He lifted his hat from his head and pushed a hand through his hair. It was thick, the color of a dark coffee bean and waved loosely against his head. The shine of it spoke of good health, but Ileana wasn't looking at him as a doctor. No, for the first time in years she was looking at a man as a woman, and the realization shook her even more than his strange story.

He released a heavy breath, then said, "I wasn't expecting to run into this sort of roadblock—I mean, with Frankie being ill. I'm sure you're thinking I should have called first. But this…well, it's not something you can just blurt out over the phone. Besides, if I'd alerted her I was coming, she might have been…conveniently away."

Ileana didn't bother to hide her frown. "Not for a minute. Frankie isn't that sort of woman."

He looked at her. "Do you know what kind of woman she was thirty years ago?"

The question wasn't sharp, but there was an intensity to his voice that caused her cheeks to warm. Or was it just the husky note in his drawl that was making her feel all hot and shivery at the same time? Either way, she had to get a grip on herself and figure out how best to handle this man. If that was possible.

"No. But I hardly think a person's moral values could change that much."

Mac McCleod rose to his feet. "A person can change overnight, Doctor. You know that as well as I."

Not the human heart, she wanted to tell him. But

singing Frankie's praises to this man wouldn't help matters at the moment. She wasn't sure what would help this cowboy or how to provide it—other than to let him see Frankie, which at this point was out of the question. If this man was Frankie's son, the shock of seeing him might send her patient into cardiac arrest.

Rising to her feet, she said, "What are your plans? Do you have a place to stay?"

As soon as the questions slipped past her lips, she realized they were probably too personal. Yet she was moved by his plight.

"I have a room rented at a hotel here in town." His dark gaze landed smack on her face. "The rest depends on you."

The man would be leaving the hospital in a few minutes. Her heartbeat should have been returning to its normal pace; instead it was laboring as though she was climbing nearby Sierra Blanca.

"I'm not sure I understand, Mr. McCleod."

A grin suddenly dimpled his cheeks, and she felt like an idiot as her breath caught in her throat.

"I have a feeling we're going to get to know one another very well, Doc. You might as well start calling me Mac."

Ileana cleared her throat. "All right—Mac. Why do your plans depend on me?"

He folded his arms against his chest as his gaze lazily inspected her. For the first time in years, Ileana was horribly aware of her bare face, the homeliness of her plain appearance.

"I can't leave town until I see Ms. Cantrell, and right now it looks as though you're calling the shots as to when that might be," he said.

Ileana not only felt like an idiot but she needed to add imbecile to the self-description. Normally, her mind was sharp, but this man seemed to be turning her brain to useless gray pudding.

"Oh—uh—yes." Hating herself for getting so flustered, she threw her attention into digging a prescription pad and pen from her lab coat pocket. "Do you have a phone number you can give me? Just in case Ms. Cantrell's condition changes."

He gave his cell phone number to her, then asked, "Are you expecting her to improve in the next day or two—at least, enough for visitors?"

As Ileana folded the piece of paper with the phone number, she carefully chose her words. "Honestly, no. And that's if no complications pop up."

"You do expect her to survive, don't you?"

There was a real look of concern on his face, and Ileana tried to imagine what he must be going through at this moment. He'd traveled hundreds of miles to search for a woman who might be his mother, only to find her desperately ill.

She reached across the small space separating them and folded her hand around his. "I'm doing all I can to make sure she does."

Was it surprise or confusion she saw flickering in his brown eyes before he glanced away? Either way she could see he wasn't nearly as cool as he wanted her to believe. The idea drew her to him just that much more. She knew what it was like to try to hide her emotions, to not allow people to see that she was hurting or troubled.

"Thank you for giving me your time," he murmured. "I'll be checking back with you."

Dropping her hand, she stepped back. "You're very welcome."

"Goodbye, Ms. Sanders."

He cast her one last look, then turned and strode quickly toward an exit that would take him to the parking lot.

As Ileana watched him walk away, she wondered why he'd called her Ms. Sanders. Everyone, even those who had known her for years, didn't think of her as a woman. She was Doc or Doctor. A physician and nothing more.

"Who was *that?*"

At the sound of Renae's voice, Ileana turned her head to see the nurse had walked up beside her. Both women continued to watch Mac McCleod as he disappeared through the revolving door.

Ileana bit back a sigh. "*That* was trouble. A big dose of it."

Chapter 2

"Ripp, I must have been crazy when I told you to stay home and let me come out here," Mac said into the cell phone. "Nothing is going right."

Two hours had passed since Mac left the hospital, and during that time, he'd continually tried to call his brother back in Texas. But Ripp, and the majority of the sheriff's department, had been on a manhunt most of the evening for a hit-and-run driver. Subsequently, Ripp had just now found time to return his call.

"What do you mean?" Ripp asked. "Did you find the ranch okay?"

"I did," Mac answered as he sat on the side of the hotel bed, his elbows resting on his knees. "A maid was the only person I talked to. She informed me that Ms. Cantrell was in the hospital in Ruidoso."

"Hospital?"

The shock in Ripp's voice mirrored Mac's feelings. That Frankie might be in ill health or dead was something that neither brother had really wanted to consider. After all, if this Frankie were really their mother, she would only be about sixty years old. But a relatively young age didn't always equal good health.

"Yeah. I drove back to Ruidoso and went to the hospital thinking I could talk to her there. No such luck. Her doctor says she's too ill to see me."

"What's wrong with her?"

"The doctor wouldn't tell me much. I was so damned aggravated at the moment that I can't remember everything she said regarding Frankie's health."

"She?"

"Frankie's doctor. It's a woman. And from what she told me, her family and the Cantrells have been friends for years. She—uh—told me that Frankie has a son and daughter. Quint and Alexa, I think she called them."

"Oh." Several long moments passed as Ripp digested this news, and then he finally asked, "Did this doctor know anything about Frankie's past?"

Ripp's question caused the image of Dr. Sanders to parade to the front of Mac's mind. She'd been as plain as white flour. The type of woman he normally wouldn't glance at twice. Yet her gentleness had touched him in a way that had been totally unexpected.

Clearing his throat, he said, "I asked. She doesn't know anything about it. From what she says, Frankie is a respected woman. That ought to tell you the doctor is in the dark."

Ripp sighed. "We don't really know what Frankie is, Mac. That's why you're there. To find out. So when did this doctor think you might be able to see Frankie?"

"Several days, at least."

"Oh. Well, you might as well come home, Mac. There's no use in you hanging around Ruidoso for that long. Or do you think you ought to see her children?"

"And say what?" Mac asked sarcastically. "Hi, y'all, I'm your half brother?"

Ripp growled back at him. "What the hell is the matter with you, Mac? You're nearly forty years old! It's not like you're that ten-year-old little boy, staring out the window with tears on your cheeks. We're not going to let the woman keep hurting us, are we?"

Mac shoved out a heavy breath. His brother was right. He had to get a grip on his emotions and view this whole thing as a man, not that little boy who'd had his heart ripped out so long ago.

"I tell you, Ripp. The news that she had a son and daughter knocked my boots out from under me. I just never imagined her having other babies. Did you? I mean, if she didn't want us, why the heck would she have had more children? Doesn't make a lick of sense to me."

"We don't know that she didn't want us, Mac. Dad told Rye that she wanted us."

"Hell," Mac muttered. "Rye was probably just trying to make you feel better. You'd been stabbed with a butcher knife at the time, remember? He probably thought you couldn't handle any more pain."

Ripp chuckled under his breath. "I can handle anything you can take and more, big brother."

In spite of his frustration, a smile tugged at Mac's lips. If anyone could make him forget his troubles, it was his brother. And even though they were sometimes as different as night and day, there was a bond between them tougher than barbed wire.

"Yeah, you probably can," he told him as he glanced at the digital clock on the nightstand. He was getting hungry. Besides that, the small hotel room was beginning to close in on him. "Look, Ripp, I'm gonna go out and find something to eat. It's been a hell of a day, and I'm beat. I'll call you tomorrow—after I find out more."

"So you're not coming home?"

"No way. I've started on this journey and I don't mean to cut it short. I'm going to camp in the hospital until Dr. Sanders gets her belly full of me. She'll have to give in sooner or later."

"Poor woman. She's not going to know what hit her," Ripp murmured more to himself than to Mac. "Just try to be your charming self, Mac. We don't want anyone out there thinking we're a pair of arrogant Texans."

Mac chuckled. "Why not—we are, aren't we?"

"Go eat. I've got to go help Lucita. Elizabeth is having a squalling fit about something. I'll call you tomorrow."

His brother cut the call, and Mac closed the instrument in his hand. Ripp had a beautiful wife, a twelve-year-old son and a baby daughter. His family adored him. He had something to live for, something to come home to at night. He was blessed. And Mac was happy for him.

Yet there were times that Mac looked at his brother and wondered what it would feel like to have those same things. Oh, yeah, he'd had a wife once. But Brenna hadn't been a wife in the real sense of the word. She'd been more like a permanent date. Someone to go out with for a night of fun. Someone to have sex with. Giving him children had not been in her plans. And giving him love, the sort that came from deep within a person, was something she'd been incapable of. But then, Mac couldn't put all the blame on Brenna for their failed marriage. At first he'd gotten exactly what he'd wanted—a party girl. And for a while he'd been perfectly content with their life together. Then as time went by, the partying had begun to wear thin, and his life and marriage started to look more and more shallow. He'd begun to yearn for something more lasting and meaningful. Like raising kids in a real home. Brenna hadn't married him under those terms, and when he'd asked her to change, she'd laughed all the way to the office of a divorce lawyer.

Now, after that humiliating lesson, he felt like a fool for ever thinking a good timin' guy like him had once dreamed he could be a father to a house full of kids. Now he told himself it was better to simply enjoy women on brief, but frequent, occasions and forget about ever having a family.

Several miles east of Ruidoso, smack in the middle of the Hondo Valley, Ileana shifted down her pickup truck as it rattled across the low wooden bridge that crossed the Hondo River. The truck was old, and the speedometer had rolled over so many times that she'd lost count. For the past two years her father, Wyatt, had pestered her to buy a new one. After all, she had heaps of money and not a lot to do with it.

But Ileana didn't want a new truck. What would be the use of shaking it over a dirt road every day? she'd argued. Besides, why did she need a new vehicle when the only place she ever went was to work and back home?

She was a practical person, and when something worked as it should, she didn't see any point in changing it.

Across the river, the dirt road made a gradual climb into open meadows dotted with ponderosa and piñon pine. On either side of the road, cattle and horses stood at hay mangers, chomping alfalfa in the falling twilight of a late February day.

The Bar M Ranch had been Ileana's home for all her life and her mother's before that. Her grandfather, Tomas Murdock, had built the place from the ground up and turned it into one of the most profitable ranches in southern New Mexico.

But the Bar M hadn't been her grandfather's only interest. He'd been a gambler and a bit of a womanizer, the result of which had produced illegitimate twins. The babies had been left on the doorstep of the Bar M Ranch house, and for weeks no one had known who'd parented them. It had been a shocking event that had rocked all of Lincoln County.

So Ileana wasn't a stranger to odd stories, and the one that Mac McCleod had told her this evening—well, it sounded like more than an odd circumstance to her. Could he possibly be a son from Frankie's past life? And if he hung around like he'd promised, how would the woman react to seeing him again?

The questions had been stewing in Ileana's head ever since Mac had left the hospital, and now she decided she couldn't go home to her little place on the mountain until she stopped by the main ranch house and had a talk with her mother. If anyone might know about Frankie's past, it would be Chloe.

Five minutes later, she parked the truck behind the pink stucco hacienda and entered a gate that opened to a center courtyard. In the summer months, her parents were always having barbecues and other parties. Her brother, Adam, and his wife, Maureen, often brought their family to join in the fun. So did her sister, Anna, and her husband, Miguel. Even Ileana's aunts, Justine and Rose, made frequent trips to the Bar M with their grandchildren. The crowd of family and friends made the oval swimming pool and courtyard a lively place. But this evening, a cold wind was whipping through the bare garden and ruffling the plastic cover over the pool. The lawn chairs were stacked beneath the covered ground-level porch that followed the square shape of the house.

When Ileana stepped inside the kitchen, she found Cesar, her mother's longtime cook, laying out plates and silverware on a round pine table.

The old cowboy looked up and smiled as he spotted Ileana. "Good evenin', Doc. You stayin' for supper?"

Ileana walked over to the tall, wiry man and kissed his leathery cheek. From the time Cesar had been fifteen years old, he'd worked on the Bar M. After forty years of dealing with fractious horses and several broken bones to show for it, Chloe had relegated him to the kitchen. Now after twenty years of stirring up ranch grub, he could safely be called a hell of a good cook.

"I hadn't planned on it, Cesar, but if you have plenty, I will. Where's Mother? Is she in from the barn yet?"

"She came in a few minutes ago. You might find her in the den."

"Thanks," Ileana told him, then quickly left the kitchen.

The den was quiet and so was the living room. Ileana

eventually found Chloe in her bedroom changing into clean clothes.

"Hi, honey!" Chloe said with a bright smile. "You must have stopped by 'cause you knew I'd be lonely tonight."

Ileana sat down on a cedar chest positioned at the foot of a large, varnished pine bed. "Lonely? Isn't Dad here?"

The petite woman finished the last button on her blouse and reached up to whip the towel off her wet hair. Chloe had been a horse lover since she was old enough to sit in the saddle, and she'd made a life breeding and training racing stock. The job was physically strenuous, and now that Chloe was sixty-two, Ileana was beginning to wonder how long she could keep up with the demands of the business. But though she might be small in stature, Chloe was an iron lady. Ileana figured, God willing, her mother would still be working up into her eighties.

"Sanders Gas Exploration has just purchased a competing company, and your father has gone to Oklahoma to tie up all the loose paperwork."

Ileana was incredulous. At a time when her father should have been slowing down, he seemed to be going hell-bent for leather. "He's expanding? Again? Mom, when are you two going to retire and travel the world?"

Chloe laughed as she briskly rubbed her short auburn hair. "Honey, don't ever look for your parents to go galloping around the world for any length of time. Maybe a short vacation now and then. We have too much we want to do."

"But it's work," Ileana complained.

Chloe settled a pointed look at her daughter. "And isn't that what your life is all about?"

Ileana certainly couldn't argue that point. Most every waking hour she spent at her private medical clinic or at the hospital. Even if she wasn't a workaholic, traveling and socializing wasn't her style.

"Okay. So I can't make that argument. But as a doctor I can tell you to slow down."

Chloe laughed. "And as your mother, I can tell you to quit being so fussy." She hung the damp towel on a door hook and began to run a comb through her hair. "So are you going to have dinner with me tonight? Cesar has made goulash and corn bread. He knows I love goulash and your father hates it, so he makes it for me whenever Wyatt is gone."

Chloe started toward the door, and Ileana slowly rose to her feet to follow her out of the bedroom. "I suppose I can stay long enough to eat, but then I've got to get home and go over several test results. I…actually, I stopped by to talk to you about something."

"Oh?" Chloe tossed her a look of concern as the two of them walked along a hallway. "Has something happened? Are you feeling okay?"

"I'm tired. That's the only thing wrong with me, and I'll tell you all about it when we get to the kitchen."

"You've intrigued me now," Chloe said with a smile. Then with a happy groan, she reached over and curled her arm tightly around her daughter's shoulders. "I love you, sweetie. I'm glad you stopped by. No matter what the reason."

Her mother's display of affection was as commonplace as breathing, but Ileana never took it for granted. She'd seen too much suffering in her life to know that there were plenty of unloved people in this world. They marched through her office complaining of one malady after another when their real problem was loneliness.

The idea had her wondering about Mac McCleod's life and what he must have gone through if the story he'd told about his mother was true. It was hard for Ileana to imagine growing up without her mother's love, her constant hugs and kisses. Had the tough cowboy with the sexy brown eyes missed out on being cuddled and praised, or had a stepmother given him and his brother those things? she wondered.

That part of Mac McCleod is none of your business, Ileana. Just stick to the facts and concentrate on keeping your patient away from any undue stress.

The little voice of warning continued to pester her until the two women entered the kitchen and seated themselves at the small dining table.

"Okay, honey, what's this thing you wanted to discuss with me?" Chloe asked as she spooned a hefty amount of goulash onto her plate. "I hope you haven't stopped by to tell me that Frankie's condition has gotten worse."

"No. Actually, I think she's slightly improved from yesterday, but her lungs still have a long way to go before I can pronounce them clear."

"Damn woman," Chloe muttered. "She should have had heart surgery a year ago when you advised her to."

Ileana sighed. Frankie wasn't the first stubborn patient she'd encountered. Over the eleven years she'd been a practicing physician, Ileana had run into her fair share, and when a patient refused treatment it always left her feeling frustrated and helpless. "That's true.

Her lungs are going to keep giving her problems if she doesn't get her heart sound. But she's afraid."

Chloe frowned. "Well, aren't we all afraid of medical procedures? But if we're smart, we do them, because we want to be well and at our best. Life is too short to simply exist. I want to live my God-given days to the fullest."

Ileana thoughtfully stirred sugar into her iced tea. "Yes, but you have lots to live for. I'm not sure that Frankie views life the same as you, Mother. Losing Lewis has devastated her. Just like it would devastate you if Daddy died."

"Of course losing Wyatt would crush me! He's the love of my life. But I'd have to go on doing the very best that I could. To do any less would be dishonorable to Wyatt and you children."

Yes, her mother would see it that way, Ileana thought. But Chloe was a scrapper. As very young women, she and her two sisters had struggled and sacrificed to keep the Bar M going when others would have given up. Frankie didn't have that same fighting spirit. Could her past life be some of the reason for her lack of grit? Ileana wondered.

"Mother, speaking of children, have you ever heard Frankie mention that she had other children?"

Across the table, Chloe's fork stopped midway to her mouth. "Other children? What kind of question is that?"

"It's not some sort of joke, if that's what you're thinking. Besides, you know I don't joke."

Chloe rolled her eyes. "Unfortunately, I do know. But let's not get into that now. What are you getting at? The idea of Frankie having other children is preposterous."

Ileana reached for a piece of cornbread. "You wouldn't be saying that if you'd met Mac McCleod."

Her expression puzzled, Chloe repeated the name. "I've never heard the name. Who is he? Where did you meet him?"

"He's a deputy sheriff from Bee County, Texas. He showed up at the hospital wanting to see Frankie."

Her expression full of concern now, Chloe leaned forward. "You didn't allow him to see her, did you?"

Her mother's sudden anxiousness was suspicious. "You know I'm not allowing anyone in to see her except Quint, Alexa and Abe."

Chloe glanced down at her plate but didn't attempt to resume eating. Ileana could tell that her thoughts were whirling.

"Was it official business?" her mother asked.

"No. Personal." Ileana stabbed a piece of macaroni with her fork. She didn't like giving people she loved bad news. And she had a deep feeling that Mac McCleod's appearance was going to shake up more than a few around here. Especially Alexa and Quint. What would they think about having two half brothers? "He—uh—he says he thinks Frankie might be his long-lost mother. In fact, he seems almost certain of it."

"My God, Ivy! You can't be serious!"

She couldn't remember the last time her mother had called her Ivy, the nickname her father had given her shortly after she'd been born. He'd considered Ileana too long and formal for a tiny baby girl. But by the time she'd reached high school age, Ileana had outgrown the nickname. Now, the only people who sometimes called her Ivy were her father and her brother, Adam. Apparently, her mother was completely distressed tonight.

"Yes, Mother. It seemed incredulous to me, too. But the man isn't a flake. Far from it. He seemed more than legitimate and very determined. He showed me an old snapshot of him and his brother and his mother before she'd left the family. If you took off thirty years, the woman did resemble Frankie."

"An old photograph doesn't prove anything. What was this man like? Did he look like he could be related to Frankie?" she asked, then shook her head with disgust. "What the hell am I doing asking that question? There's just no way. No way at all that Frankie had other children. She would have told me."

Just conjuring the image of Mac in her brain was enough to leave Ileana's mouth dry, and she quickly reached for her tea. "He's a tall, very handsome guy. A cowboy type. A typical Texan," she added, even though there had been nothing typical at all about the man, she thought.

Ileana took several sips of tea while her mother sat in silence. Chloe was either stunned or scared, and Ileana couldn't figure which.

"What's wrong, Mother? You do know something, don't you?"

"You can't let this man see Frankie," she suddenly blurted. "At least, not until we find out more about him."

"Well, I'd already planned on that. Why?"

With a heavy sigh, Chloe went back to eating but not with the same gusto as when they'd first sat down at the table.

"Look, Ileana, when I first met Frankie, almost thirty years ago, she was just traveling through the area. She'd left Texas and a husband behind. He was making some frightening threats against her, and at that time she was in the process of getting a divorce and was going by the name of Robertson. She said she'd reverted back to her maiden name."

Ileana's thoughts were spinning. She'd not even known that Frankie had been married before. Apparently that was a part of her life she didn't want others knowing about, and if that was true, she probably wanted to keep other things secret. Like two more sons? The whole idea was shocking.

"When you first met her, did she ever mention what her married name was while she'd lived in Texas?" Ileana asked.

Chloe shook her head. "No. She didn't tell me. And I wasn't about to ask. I only knew that she needed a friend. I could tell that she was a bit traumatized, but what woman wouldn't be? The man had threatened to kill her. And he was a farmer, a respected member of the community, or so she'd said. She'd run because she'd figured if she'd tried to get help, no one would have believed her complaints."

Ileana thoughtfully pushed the goulash around her plate. "Mac didn't mention anything about farming. He said his father had been a sheriff. Maybe Frankie isn't the woman he's looking for. But most of the things he said adds up, Mother."

"How old was this—Mac—as you call him?"

Color instantly bloomed on Ileana's face. Now why had she come out with his first name, as though she knew the man on a personal basis? "My age, I think. He told me his mother left the family when he was ten and his brother eight. And that she's been gone twenty-nine years."

"Oh, dear."

Looking across the table, Ileana spotted tears in her mother's eyes.

"No matter how hard I try, Ileana, I can't imagine Frankie doing such a thing. She loves her children more than her own life. In fact, I've always told her that she smothered them too much. While they were growing up, she was frightened to turn her back for one instant in fear that something would happen to them."

"Well, it's hard to speculate what might have taken place in Texas. Could be that Frankie didn't have much choice," Ileana said thoughtfully. "If the man was threatening her, she might have been forced to leave her boys."

Chloe shook her head emphatically. "But she would have gone back for them. Somehow, someway, she would have gone back."

"Obviously she didn't," Ileana countered. "In fact, she's never mentioned them to you. Doesn't that seem odd?"

"Odd? Hell, no. It seems downright mean," Chloe shot back, then with a weary sigh, she reached across the table and covered Ileana's hand with hers. "Honey, when will you be seeing this man again?"

Ever since he'd disappeared through the hospital door, Ileana had been asking herself that same question. A huge part of her was thrilled at the idea of seeing him again, but the practical side cowered at the very thought. Mac McCleod was hardly the sort of man she would ever dream of consorting with. As if a man with his striking looks would ever think of giving her the time of day, she thought wryly. Everything about the man said he liked fast, showy horses and his women just the same. And Ileana was as far from that category as one could get.

"Tomorrow. Or so he said. I do have his telephone number."

Chloe heaved out a breath of relief. "Good. I want you to give him a call and invite him to the ranch tomorrow night. For dinner."

"Mom! Have you gone daft? I'm not going to do such a thing! I've just now met the man!"

"Look, Ivy, this is crucial!" Chloe pleaded. "You don't want anything happening to Frankie, do you?"

What about your daughter? Ileana wanted to ask. Being around Mac McCleod was difficult on her heart. She wasn't sure it could withstand the strain of being in his company for a whole evening.

"Of course I don't want anything happening to Frankie. She's my patient and a friend."

"All right then." Chloe gave Ileana's hand one last pat and then leaned back in her chair. "I need to talk to this man and find out what's really going on."

"If you have a notion that you can change his mind about seeing Frankie, forget it. I doubt the man has ever uttered the word *surrender.* Unless he was yelling it at a fleeing criminal."

Seeming not to hear Ileana's warning, Chloe continued. "Quint and Alexa don't know anything about this yet, do they?"

"No. But I suggested that he talk to them."

"Oh, God, what is this going to do them?" Chloe mumbled worriedly. "They believe their mother is a saint."

Across from her Ileana picked up her fork and tried to muster up the hunger she'd felt earlier this afternoon.

The day had been long and exhausting, and she'd hardly had time to eat three bites of a dry turkey sandwich. But now all she wanted to do was go home and get this telephone call to Mac over with.

Back in Ruidoso, Mac had just returned to his motel room after a meal in a nearby restaurant. As he stretched out on the bed and reached for the remote control, the ring of his cell phone caught him by surprise. He'd not expected Ripp to call again tonight.

Pulling the phone from his jeans pocket, he was surprised to spot a local number illuminated. No one here had this number, except Dr. Sanders!

"Hello. Mac McCleod here."

"Uh… Mac—this is… Dr. Sanders calling."

His heart began to hammer with anticipation, or did a part of the adrenaline spurting through his veins have something to do with hearing her voice? After all, it was a sweet, husky sound. The kind that would sound perfect whispering in his ear.

Damn, Mac, leaving Texas soil has done something to your brain.

Snapping himself to sudden attention, he said, "Yes, Dr. Sanders. Has something happened?"

"If you mean Ms. Cantrell's condition, no. I just spoke with her nurse. She's resting comfortably. I'm calling for an entirely different reason."

There was hesitancy about her words that put Mac on guard. Without thinking, he sat up on the side of the bed and stared expectantly at the floor. "You've changed your mind about allowing me to see her?"

"Uh—no. I'm…well, I'm calling to ask you to dinner tomorrow night," she said, then rushed on before he could make any sort of response. "I live on a ranch in the Hondo Valley—my parents' ranch—the Bar M. My mother thought you might like to visit with her. Since she's known Frankie for nearly thirty years, she might be able to fill in some pieces of information for you."

Mac hesitated for several seconds before he finally asked, "And why would she want to do that? I got the impression that you and your family want to shelter Frankie at all costs."

He could hear her long sigh, and he was suddenly wondering how she might look with all that dark hair spilling around her pale face, with a sultry little smile on her lips and a sensual glint in her blue eyes. Was it possible he could ever see her like that?

"I do—we do. But we want to consider your side of this thing, too. Besides, Cesar is an excellent cook. If nothing else, you'll get a nice meal."

"And what about the company? Will you be there, too?"

There was a long pause, and Mac could very nearly imagine the blush that was creeping across her face. She reminded him of the timid, high school librarian who'd pursued him a few months ago. Once he'd gotten her in the dark, she'd been shy but sweet and eager. If he played his cards right, he might get lucky and discover that behind her lab coat and sturdy shoes, Dr. Ileana Sanders was just as sweet.

"Yes. I'll be there," she said.

"Great. What time and how do I get there?"

"Meet me at the hospital tomorrow evening at six," she told him. "You can follow me out to the ranch from there."

"Count on me being there," he told her.

"Fine. Good night, Mac."

"Good night, Ms. Sanders."

She cleared her throat. "Please call me Ileana."

A lazy smile spread across his face. "You can count on that, too—Ileana."

She blurted another hasty good-night to him, then ended the call. Mac leaned back on the bed and stared thoughtfully up at the ceiling. Maybe hanging around here in New Mexico for a few more days wasn't going to be as cold and lonely as he first feared.

Chapter 3

The next evening, a few minutes before six, Ileana managed to wind up the last of her hospital rounds and hurriedly changed from her work clothes into a royal-blue sweater dress and a pair of tall, black suede boots. The dress had only been worn once, two years ago, when she'd attended a charity dinner with her parents. Ileana rarely bothered to vary her wardrobe from slacks or professional skirts and mundane blouses. No one bothered to look at her sideways. And if they did, it was because she was a doctor and they wanted to hear what she had to say about a patient or ailment.

But this morning, she'd grabbed the dress from her closet and convinced herself that her mother would be pleased if she dressed for their dinner guest tonight.

Shutting the door on her private workspace, Ileana hurried down the hallway toward the nearest hospital exit. She was almost past the nurses' station, when Renae called out to her.

"Dr. Sanders, is that you?"

Stifling a sigh, Ileana paused and looked back at the nurse. "Yes, it's me, Renae. I'm on my way home. Was there something you needed before I leave?"

The tall nurse with wheat-blond hair and bright blue eyes stepped out from behind the high counter. "No. Everything is quiet." Her gaze ran pointedly over Ileana's dress and boots. "My, oh my, you look—so different! I've never seen you dressed this way! And you're wearing lipstick!"

A faint blush warmed Ileana's cheeks, making them match the shell-pink color she'd swiped over her lips. She felt incredibly self-conscious. Which was absurd. She was thirty-eight years old. She could wear what she wanted, whenever she wanted, she tried to reassure herself. "I break out of my rut once in a while, Renae."

The other woman smiled. "Well, you should do it more often, Doc." Renae's expression turned impish. "You wouldn't want to tell me what the occasion is, would you?"

Renae would be the first one to admit that she did her share of contributing to the hospital gossip grapevine. But Ileana certainly didn't have anything to hide. Her personal life was as flat and uninteresting as a cold pancake.

"Mother is having a dinner guest, and she doesn't like for me to show up in wrinkled work clothes."

Renae started to reply but paused as the sound of approaching footsteps caught both women's attention. Ileana looked around to see Mac McCleod striding directly toward them. He was wearing a jean jacket with a heavy sheepskin collar, and his cowboy hat was pulled low over his forehead; but the moment he neared the two women, he tilted it back and smiled broadly.

"Good evenin', ladies."

Renae gave him one of her sexy smiles, and Ileana thought how perfect a companion the young nurse would be for the Texas cowboy. She was full of life and nothing—not even a man like Mac McCleod—intimidated her. Whereas Ileana felt like Little Red Riding Hood standing next to the big scary wolf.

"Good evening, Mr. McCleod," Renae greeted him. "Fancy seeing you here again."

He glanced briefly at the nurse before settling his eyes on Ileana. The direct gaze heated her body more than a huge shot of whiskey ever could.

"Yes," he said to the nurse. "Dr. Sanders was kind enough to invite me to dinner."

The sound of his voice was low and sultry. Or at least it seemed that way to Ileana. But she could be overreacting. Either way, she was ready to leave the hospital and break the odd tension that had suddenly come over her.

"Oh, how nice," Renae responded while casting a shocked glance at Ileana.

"We'd better be going, Mac. Or we'll be late." Ileana quickly grabbed him by the arm and urged him toward the exit. To Renae, she tossed over her shoulder, "See you tomorrow."

As the two of them headed down the wide corridor, he asked, "What's the rush? Afraid I'm going to pester you to see Frankie before we leave the hospital?"

"No," Ileana replied. "It wouldn't make any difference how much you pestered me. The answer would still be no. At least for today."

"So she's still too ill for visitors?"

Now that they were away from Renae and nearing a revolving door that would take them outside the hospital, Ileana dropped her hand from his arm and purposely put space between their bodies. Even so, she was intensely aware of his spicy scent, the sensual swagger of his posture and the pleasant drawl to his voice.

"I'm afraid so."

"Are you sure she's getting everything she needs at this hospital? Maybe if you sent her to Albuquerque or Santa Fe? I mean, I'm not doubting your ability as a doctor, but she might need to be in a more high-tech facility."

Ileana paused to pull on the black coat that was draped over her arm, but before she could swing it around her shoulders, he took the garment from her and graciously helped her into it. Ileana couldn't remember the last time a man, other than a relative, had done such a personal thing for her. It made her feel awkward, yet sweetly cared for at the same time.

She'd never been really hurt or abused by any man, but her natural shyness and private nature had kept them at bay for years. Now it was a habit she couldn't seem to break out of. Everyone thought of her as a plain old maid, and she couldn't seem to change her own opinion of herself. But seeing her in this stranger's eyes was giving her new hope.

Looking up at him, she smiled. "I'm sure you mean well, Mac. But there is no high-tech machine that can cure Frankie right now. And even if there were, our hospital here has up-to-date equipment. No, the only thing that can help Frankie is medication and total rest."

He let out a long breath, and she could clearly see that

he was frustrated, but his demeanor changed as quickly as the snap of two fingers. Once again he was smiling down at her. For a moment Ileana forgot that they were standing to one side of the door and that people were coming and going behind them. She was momentarily mesmerized by the subtle glint in his brown eyes, the faint dimples bracketing his lips, the dent in his chin.

"Well," he said softly, "that just means I'll have to stay here in Ruidoso longer and get to know you a bit better."

Dropping her head, she cleared her throat as she tried to gather herself together. "Um…we'd better go. It's a fairly long drive to the Bar M," she told him.

Out in the parking lot, a north wind was whipping across the asphalt, rattling the bare limbs of the aspens and shaking the branches of the blue spruce trees. Ileana huddled, shivering inside her coat, as she gave him general directions to the ranch, then climbed into her truck and waited for him to do the same.

Soon a dark, fairly new-looking pickup truck pulled directly behind hers. She steered her own vehicle onto the street while carefully watching in the rearview mirror to make sure he was following. After a maze of turns and several traffic lights, they hit the main highway that would take them east to the Hondo Valley.

The Bar M was nearly thirty miles away and in the daylight, a beautiful drive through the mountains. But night had fallen more than an hour ago. As she drove, Ileana's gaze switched from the white line on the highway to the headlights following a respectable distance behind her, while her thoughts raced faster than the speedometer on the dash panel.

What was the man really trying to do? There was no

reason for him to flirt with her. In fact, the whole idea seemed ridiculous. But he had flirted, she mentally argued with herself. At least, it had felt that way to her. So why? Was he still thinking he could charm her into letting him see Frankie?

Yes. That had to be the reason. A man like him didn't look twice at a woman like her for romantic reasons. And during the evening ahead, she was going to do her best to remember that.

Since Mac McCleod was a guest who had never visited the ranch before, Ileana purposely parked in front of the house so that they could enter properly through the main entrance.

When he joined her on the small stone walk leading up to the long porch, he paused to look around at the area lit by a nearby yard lamp.

"This is quite a beautiful place. I'd like to see the ranch and the drive up here in the daylight sometime."

"Yes. Even though it is my home, I never take the scenery for granted," she replied, then gestured toward the house. "Shall we go in? It's very cold this evening."

"It's damn—sorry—it's darn cold to me," he said as he followed her to the door. "It gets cool where I come from but not anything like this. We're lucky if we see a frost, much less snow."

"Oh, come June and July we'll get some very warm weather," she told him. "But with the high altitude the nights remain cool."

She opened the door and gestured for him to enter, but he shook his head and smiled.

"I'd never go before a lady. You lead the way."

Even though Mac's mother had left the family, he'd obviously been raised with manners, Ileana thought.

And a whole lot of charm. Something she needed to ignore. But everything inside her was so aware of the man, so pleased to be in his presence. And the reaction made her feel more foolish than she'd ever felt in her life.

As they moved from the foyer into the long living room, Ileana was relieved to find her mother sitting on the couch. The moment Chloe spotted them, she rose to her feet and quickly joined them.

"Mac, this is my mother, Chloe Sanders. Mother, this is Mac McCleod," Ileana promptly introduced.

"Mr. McCleod, I'm very happy you decided to join us tonight," Chloe told him as she reached to shake his hand.

He took her hand, but rather than shake it, he simply held it in a warm, inviting grip. As a smile dimpled his cheeks, Ileana could see her mother succumbing to the man.

"It's my pleasure, ma'am. Having you two ladies for company sure beats the lonely meal I had last night."

Chloe chuckled softly. "Eating alone isn't much fun. But my husband sometimes travels so I have to do it at times. Are you married, Mr. McCleod?"

Mac gave her a lopsided grin. "No. I'm a single man. And call me Mac, ma'am. Ileana already does."

Chloe's brows inched upward as she glanced over at her daughter. Ileana smiled awkwardly as her mother's gaze swept over her sweater dress and her stacked heel boots.

"Does Cesar have dinner ready yet?" Ileana asked quickly.

"I think it will be a few more minutes," Chloe said, then looped her arm through Mac's. "Come along, Mac, and make yourself comfortable. I was just having a small glass of wine. Would you like to join me?"

"Only if Ileana will share one with us," he said.

"Usually Ileana doesn't drink anything but water," Chloe said. "But maybe she'll make an exception tonight—for you," Chloe added.

Ileana didn't know why her mother was speaking in such a coy manner or why Chloe expected her to drink a glass of wine when she knew her daughter didn't like alcohol. But then, this whole issue with Mac McCleod was strange. His presence must be rubbing off on her mother, too, she thought.

"Only a very small glass," Ileana told her.

Mac took a seat in a stuffed armchair situated a few feet from the fireplace, which at the moment was cracking and hissing with a roaring fire. Ileana took a chair across from him and crossed her legs. Then realizing she didn't feel comfortable, she rested both feet flat on the floor and folded her hands in her lap.

Across the room, at a small wet bar, Chloe asked, "So have you been in Ruidoso for long, Mac?"

"Only since yesterday, ma'am."

"How do you like this area?" she asked, as she handed him a glass of wine.

He thanked her, then said, "It's very beautiful. But it's not Texas. No offense, ma'am."

Chloe laughed softly. "I know what you mean, Mac. Texas is your home, so nothing could compare."

"Yeah," he agreed. "That pretty much says how it is."

Chloe handed Ileana a glass with a very short amount of red liquid in the bottom, then took a seat on a nearby couch.

Ileana said, "I'm sorry my father couldn't be with us tonight, Mac. He's away on business right now."

"Is he a cattleman?" Mac asked.

"No. Daddy knows about cattle, but he's mainly an oilman," Ileana explained.

"Wyatt owns and runs a natural gas exploration business," Chloe added. "He was doing that when we married—oh so many years ago."

Mac looked back and forth between the two women. These people were well off financially. Even more than he'd initially thought. "This ranch, do you run stock on it?"

"Oh, yes," Chloe answered. "It's been a working ranch for nearly seventy-five years. For the most part, we raise horses, and I train them for the racetrack."

He looked intrigued now, and Ileana wasn't surprised. Her mother lived and worked in mostly a man's world, at an exciting sport. Whereas Ileana worked at a job that was oftentimes depressing and complicated. Men were rarely drawn to her occupation.

"Thoroughbreds or quarter horses?" he asked Chloe.

"Both."

Mac looked over at Ileana and was struck at how lovely she looked with her face bathed in a golden glow from the fire and the tail of her simple ponytail lying against one shoulder. There was a quiet dreaminess about her expression that was both soothing and inviting at the same time, and he found himself wishing he was going to have dinner with her alone.

"What about you, Ileana? Are you familiar with horses?"

"Ileana is an excellent horsewoman," Chloe spoke

up before her daughter could answer his question. "But she rarely takes the time to ride."

"Keeping others well is important to me, Mother."

Chloe smiled, but Mac got the sense that there was sadness behind her expression. As though she didn't quite approve of her daughter's lifestyle.

"Yes. And I'm very proud of you, darling. You know that."

The room went quiet after that, and it suddenly dawned on Mac that he'd been so caught up in conversation with Ileana and her mother that Frankie, the reason for this visit, had totally slipped his mind.

"Ileana tells me you're from Texas, Mac. What part?" Chloe asked.

"South Texas, ma'am. About forty miles north of Corpus Christi. I'm a deputy for Sheriff Langley Nichols in Bee County."

She nodded slightly. "I have a brother-in-law and nephew who both served several terms as sheriff here in Lincoln County. We know all about the dedication you men put in your jobs. You're to be commended."

"Thank you, ma'am."

Ileana's mother smiled. "Call me Chloe."

At that moment, an older man, tall, with a thick head of salt and pepper colored hair, appeared in an open doorway of the room. He politely inclined his head toward Mac, then turned his attention to the mistress of the house.

"Supper's ready, Chloe."

"Thank you, Cesar. We'll be right there."

The two women rose to their feet, and Mac followed behind Ileana as they left the living room and entered an adjoining room to their right. The rectangular space was furnished with a long cedar table that seated ten. The top was made of board planks while the legs had been roughly hewed from small cedar post. The matching chairs were worn smooth from years of use. Above the table, a lamp fashioned like a kerosene lantern hung from a low ceiling and cast a dim glow over the dining area. Across the way, heavy drapes were pushed back from a double window. Beyond the blackened panes, Mac could make out the tall branches of a spruce tree whipping in the cold wind.

In the past year, his brother had married a ranching heiress, a daughter of one of the Sandbur Ranch families. Since then, Mac had had the pleasure of visiting the huge ranch, and he could safely say that this house was nothing like the huge, elaborate homes there. This Bar M Ranch house was much smaller in scale and far more rustic in furnishings and appearance. As Mac helped both women into their chairs, he decided the Sanders family was only concerned with two things. Comfort and practicality.

After Mac took a seat directly across from Ileana, the man called Cesar served them a salad that was full of ripe olives and bits of corn chips. The concoction was so tasty Mac forgot that he didn't like salads.

"Ileana tells me that you've come to Ruidoso to see Frankie Cantrell," Chloe said, once all of them were eating.

Mac hadn't expected her to bring up the subject so bluntly, but he was quickly seeing that Chloe wasn't bashful about speaking her mind.

"That's right. I—we—that is, my brother and I didn't have any idea she was ill. If we'd known I would have put off the trip to a later date."

Chloe thoughtfully chewed a bite of food, then said, "So Frankie didn't have any idea you were coming to New Mexico?"

"No. Ripp and I didn't want to write or call. This matter is something that needs to be dealt with in person. Face-to-face."

Silence settled over the table, and Mac could feel Ileana's gaze settle on him. When he looked across the table at her, there was a shy smile on her face. The sweetness of it caught his attention far more than a wicked wink would have, and he wondered if the high altitude of these desert mountains was doing something to him. Right now they were probably more than seven thousand feet above sea level. Maybe he was getting altitude sickness. Something was definitely making him dizzy.

"I've told Mother about your concerns—that you believe Frankie might be your mother. I hope you don't mind me sharing the information."

"Of course I don't mind," he said. "It's hardly something I'm trying to keep a secret. I can't find answers without asking questions. And questions require explanations."

"Well," Chloe began, "I'll be honest, Mac. Your story floored me. I've known Frankie Cantrell for nearly thirty years. I've never heard her mention having other children. I mean, children from her past."

Mac told himself not to let this morsel of information get to him. A good lawman always gathered all the evidence he could find before he took action. Even when he might be the victim.

"Maybe she wanted to forget she had other children," he suggested.

With a long sigh, Chloe put down her fork and faced him directly. Mac studied her closely, and as he did, he found himself comparing the woman to Ileana. The two didn't match in looks or demeanor, so he assumed Ileana must have taken after her father.

"I'm being honest with you now, Mac. The Frankie Cantrell I know just wouldn't forget her children. It's unfathomable. She's been the most loving, caring mother I've known. She's a good and decent woman. If she is your mother, something dire must have happened in her past to make her leave."

Everything inside Mac went still. This woman knew something. Probably more than she was saying. But he honestly didn't want to hear it from her. For years now, all he'd gotten about his mother was secondhand words and phrases. He wanted to hear it directly from Frankie herself. Otherwise, it wouldn't have the same meaning.

"What makes you say that?" he asked quietly. "Do you know about my mother's past? Where she came from?"

Chloe shook her head. "Only that she came from somewhere in Texas. I've never asked. And she's never told me more."

"So you don't know what her name was before she married Lewis Cantrell?"

"She told me it was Robertson, and I never thought it could be anything else."

Mac shook his head. "Well, that wouldn't have been our mother's married name or her maiden name, which was Anderson, but everything else seems to fit. My brother and I have just learned that Frankie Cantrell had been corresponding with a friend's mother through the years. That's a bit too much of a coincidence."

Concern marred Chloe's face, but whether it was for her friend or for Mac, he had no idea. Most likely the former. Friendship was oftentimes thicker than kinship.

"Have you questioned this woman?"

"Unfortunately she passed away a couple months ago. Our friend, her son, was trying to organize her things and ran across the letters. That's how we happened to find out about them."

"Oh. I'm sorry your friend's mother is no longer with us," Chloe said.

"Mac, this might be too personal," Ileana spoke up, "but have you read the letters? Did they give you any clues?"

His mouth twisted. Now that the sweet doctor had put the question to him, the fact that he and Ripp had refused to inspect the letters sounded inane. They should have scoured every line, every word. Instead, they'd both been reluctant to discover what, if anything, Frankie might have said.

Looking down at his salad, he said, "No. I couldn't bring myself to look at them. Neither could my brother. We wanted to see what Frankie had to say first, before we let things that had been written in the past sway our feelings. But we do know that both of us are mentioned in the letters."

"I can certainly understand you being reluctant to read them," Ileana said softly. "You have no idea what you might find. Things that could be heartbreaking."

"Well, frankly, I'm not as understanding as my daughter," Chloe said firmly. "Reading the letters might have answered everything for you."

He looked directly at the older woman. "You think

so? Reading a letter would be the same as talking in person to your mother? I don't think so."

"I can't speak to my mother, Mac. She died when I was twenty-three and so did my father."

If Chloe expected him to apologize she was going to be disappointed. She was the one who was guilty of speaking out of turn. Especially when she didn't know what sort of life he'd had or anything about his family. She couldn't guess the devastation that Frankie's leaving had caused the McCleod home. His father had never been the same, and as for Mac and Ripp, well, he supposed they'd never been the same either.

"We've all lost family," he said politely.

Chloe suddenly smiled. "Sorry if I sounded harsh, Mac. I didn't intend to. In fact, I think I'm beginning to like you. I'm just concerned about my friend. Surely you understand."

"I do. And for what it's worth, I'm not here to cause Frankie Cantrell any sort of grief. Or to harm her in any way. My brother and I aren't interested in any sort of monetary gain, whether that be from money, property or anything else. The only thing we're interested in is knowing if our mother is alive—if this woman could be the same Frankie."

Chloe nodded in a way that said she understood but still found the whole matter worrisome. "And you can't be a hundred percent certain of that until you finally speak with her, will you?"

Mac looked across at Ileana. "That's true. And Ileana has the final say over that."

Even in the dim light, he could see a faint pink color stain her cheekbones. The blush brightened her otherwise pale face.

"Frankie needs to improve greatly before I allow such a meeting." She looked directly at Mac. "Why don't you show Mother your photo, Mac? She might be able to recognize if the woman is Frankie Cantrell."

He glanced hesitantly toward Chloe. "I'm not sure your mother wants to see the photo."

Chloe put down her fork and held out her hand in an inviting way. "Of course I want to see it. Whatever you might be thinking, Mac, I can't hide from the truth. No more than you can."

Mac forgot about the food in front of him as he fished the photograph from his wallet and handed it over to Chloe. The woman studied it for long agonizing moments before she finally lifted her head.

"When I first met Frankie she had naturally black hair. Was that the color of your mother's hair?" she asked him.

Mac tilted his head to one side as he allowed himself to remember. "I guess you'd call it that. It looked black until she got out in the sun, and then it had a fiery sort of glow to it. I thought she was the prettiest woman who ever walked the earth."

Chloe's smile was gentle. "I expect we all think that of our mothers." She handed the ragged photo back to Mac. "I can't be for certain, but the woman in the photo looks very much like Frankie Cantrell."

Mac and Ripp had already pretty much come to the logical deduction that the two women had to be the same person. Still, it was a jolt to hear this woman actually say it. Even so, he did his best to remain casual as he stuffed the photo back in his wallet.

"Well, I guess that answers one question," he said quietly.

"But there are so many more questions to come," Chloe stated wisely. "And I have to admit, Mac, that I'm just as anxious as you are to hear them."

Mac agreed, while wondering if he and his brother would be better off if he simply packed his things and headed back to Texas. In all likelihood he'd found Frankie McCleod. She was in ill health but alive. She owned a ranch and had other children. What good would it do now to appear in her life, in her children's lives?

I promise, boys, I'll be back for you. No matter what, Mommy loves you, and I'll come back.

That hastily spoken promise had haunted Mac and Ripp for nearly three decades. If anything, they deserved to know why she'd not kept it.

After a few awkward moments of silence passed, Chloe turned the conversation to other things, and before Mac knew it, he was relating some of the more colorful incidents he'd experienced since becoming a lawman. In turn, Chloe and Ileana recounted stories about their relatives who had spent years in the capacity of sheriff.

Eventually, when the meal was over, Cesar served them coffee and dessert in the living room, but after a few short minutes, Chloe excused herself saying she needed to make a few important phone calls.

The woman's exit left Mac and Ileana alone, with nothing but the sound of the crackling fire and the cold north wind whistling through the spruce trees outside the window.

Mac ate the last bite of cake from his dish and placed it and his empty cup on a nearby coffee table. Then he walked over to the fireplace.

With his back to the flames, he looked pointedly at

Ileana. "Your mother knows more about Frankie than she's saying."

Ileana rubbed her palms nervously down her thighs, then rose to her feet and walked over to stand in front of him. She'd only met him yesterday, yet she felt connected to him in an odd sort of way. Maybe it was because he'd shared such personal troubles with her. Or maybe it was because he'd seemed to look at her. Really look at her.

"I probably shouldn't be saying anything. But Mother told me that when she first met Frankie, she was running from an abusive husband. Is that in character with your father?"

The expression on his rugged face didn't change, but she could see surprise flicker in his eyes and then a shutter lowered and blocked any inkling of his feelings.

"No. Once our mother left, Dad refused to speak of her. But while we were still a family, I never saw him lift a hand to her in any way. Neither did Ripp, or he would have told me."

"There are other ways of abusing a person," she dared to say.

His eyes suddenly softened, and as they settled on her face Ileana felt her insides turning as mushy as a hot chocolate bar.

"That's true," he murmured. "And it's true that two young boys wouldn't know what went on with their parents behind closed doors. But my father was a good man. He loved us and raised us without any help from friends or relatives. And the people in the county liked and respected him. In fact, he was never voted out of office. His failing health finally forced him to retire after fifteen years of service to his community. Does that sound like an abusive man?"

Making people feel better was the very thing that Ileana had dedicated her life to. And more often than not, she couldn't stop her emotions from getting involved. But there was something about Mac that made her feel more deeply, made her ache to give his heart ease. What did that mean?

She sighed. "No. And I only told you what Mother said because I know that you need answers. If you can hang on a few more days, Frankie will be well enough to give them to you."

The wry smile on his lips deepened to a seductive grin, and Ileana's breath lodged somewhere in the middle of her chest.

"Hang on?" he repeated softly. "With you for company I won't have any problem at all hanging on in New Mexico for a while."

The suggestive implication of his words shocked her, but she tried her best to keep a cool mask on her face. The last thing she wanted to do was let him know just how inexperienced she was with men like him—any man in general. And she especially didn't want him knowing that her knees were threatening to buckle beneath his charm.

"Mac, I—"

Before she could form any sort of sensible response, he shocked her further by stepping forward, until the small space separating their bodies had disappeared and she could smell his scent, feel the heat radiating from his body.

"From the first moment we met, I've been wondering something about you," he drawled in a low, sultry voice.

She tried not to shiver as his gaze made lazy trails over her face. "What is that?" she asked, unaware that her own voice had dropped to a husky whisper.

"How you would look like this."

With one smooth movement, his hand moved to the back of her head and released the barrette holding her hair. Once he pulled the clasp away, the silky tresses spilled onto her shoulders and tumbled against her cheeks.

She tried to make herself step away, to admonish him for being so forward and impertinent, but all she managed to do was stand paralyzed and breathless as his long fingers pushed into her hair, combed the loose curls against her collarbone.

"You—you've lost your mind."

Her strangled words were said with more awe than accusation, making the grin on his face a slash of satisfaction.

"Not yet. But I will if I don't do this."

Before she could ask what *this* was, his face dipped to hers, and then she could see nothing but a glimpse of hard jaw, flared nostrils and a perfectly chiseled mouth descending toward hers.

The shock that he was going to kiss her short-circuited her senses. Even if she'd wanted to run, she was helpless, caught in his spell like a horse against a tight rein.

Softly, his lips settled over hers and then running was all but forgotten as the wild, forbidden taste of him swirled her to a place she'd never been.

Chapter 4

Mac was totally lost in the taste of Ileana's kiss, the feel of her soft body next to his, when the faint sound of a throat being cleared suddenly jarred his senses.

Like a kid being caught with his finger in the Sunday dinner dessert, he thrust himself away from Ileana and glanced across the room to see Chloe standing in an open doorway, then back to Ileana's shocked face.

Oh, hell, what had he done?

He opened his mouth to try to make some sort of apology to Ileana, but before he could muster a word, she whirled and ran from him, nearly crashing into her mother along the way.

The urge to run after her was about to push Mac's boots off the hearth, when she disappeared into the foyer and then the sound of the front door slamming told him his efforts would be wasted. Ileana was leaving without a word.

"It looks as though I've interrupted something," Chloe said with faint surprise as she glanced at him then to the foyer where her daughter had made a quick exit.

Knowing his face was red, he said sheepishly, "I don't know what to say. Except that I'm sorry. We were talking and—well, I… Your daughter is a lovely woman and I…got a little carried away. Please forgive me. You were both so kind to invite me to dinner this evening. Now I've made a mess of everything."

Walking deeper into the room, Chloe smiled at him as though nothing was wrong. "Nonsense. My daughter is a grown woman. A little kiss isn't going to hurt her. At least, not your brand."

Relief poured through him. Although he wasn't exactly sure why Chloe's opinion of him should matter that much, it did. She was Ileana's mother, and he didn't want to offend either woman.

"It doesn't look like Ileana feels that way," he said dismally. "I doubt she'll want to speak with me again."

Chloe shook her head. "Ileana never harbors bad feelings toward anyone. If she's angry, she'll forgive you."

Regret fell on his shoulders like a lead weight. Ileana had raced out of the room like the devil himself was on her heels, he thought. If anger hadn't been pushing her, then fright had and to Mac that was equally bad. He was a protector at heart. He didn't want a woman fearing him for any reason.

Wiping a hand over his face, he turned an apologetic smile on his hostess. "Well, I think I've done enough damage for one night. I'd better be going. Thank you for the great dinner. And your hospitality."

Mac started to move past her, but she quickly stepped in his path.

"Not so fast, Mac. I'd like to talk to you before you leave." She gestured toward the couch. "Why don't you have a seat? I don't want you to bolt out on me like my daughter just did," she added wryly.

Trying to hide his surprise, Mac moved over to the couch and took a seat at one end while Chloe eased down in an armchair opposite him.

"Is this something about Frankie Cantrell?" he asked with a puzzled frown.

Smiling wryly, she said, "I guess you could say so. In a roundabout way. You're here to see my friend, and I feel like the least I can do is offer my home to you while you're waiting for her to get well."

Confusion puckered his brow. "Your home?"

Nodding, Chloe used one hand to gesture about the room. "Yes. This house. The Bar M. I'd like for you to stay with us. And—" she added quickly as he opened his mouth to protest "—please don't dismiss my invitation before hearing me out. You'll be far more comfortable here than you would be in a stifling hotel room."

To say that he was shocked would have been a mild understatement. "I don't doubt that. But I wouldn't want to be an inconvenience to you. Besides that, I'm not sure how my staying here would look to your family and friends."

She chuckled softly. "Mac, my husband will be home tomorrow evening. And even if he weren't, it would hardly matter to him. He welcomes all my friends to the Bar M."

"But you hardly know me," Mac pointed out.

He could feel her gaze sizing him up, and something about her keen scrutiny told him she was a woman who rarely missed a beat about people and situations. So what was she really thinking about him? That he was actually a liar or a con man looking for money from Frankie? Lord, the woman's money or things weren't what he wanted.

"I know you well enough to know that I'd like to help you."

"What about Frankie? She's your friend. If I stay here, it might cause hard feelings between you and her family."

Chloe was quick to reply. "I appreciate your concern, Mac. But Quint and Alexa are open-minded people. You staying on my ranch is hardly going to cause a rift between our families. Frankie has been a good friend for many years. I want to help her, too. And you being here just might do that. And anyway, it looks as though the Cantrells might have to get ready for some new relatives in the family...whether they want them or not."

If Frankie hadn't wanted to see him and Ripp for twenty-nine years, he could hardly imagine her being thrilled at his appearance in her life. As for her two children, Mac couldn't imagine what they were going to think when they discovered they had two half brothers in Texas. At the moment, it was almost more than his brain could process.

"I'll be honest, Chloe. The idea of staying here on your beautiful ranch sounds a heck of a lot nicer than holing up in a hotel room. But I'm not used to—"

"Accepting people's hospitality?"

Opening one's home to a stranger was far more than

hospitality, Mac thought. He couldn't remember anyone ever offering him such a personal invitation. Even his ex in-laws had never invited him and Brenna to spend much time in their home. Their visits with the Phillips had been brief and a bit uncomfortable. But then, Brenna's parents had always believed that Mac had ruined their daughter by turning her into a party girl. He'd never bothered to defend himself against the accusation. There'd been no point in hurting them further by revealing to them that Brenna had never been the innocent wife who stayed home, baked cookies and planned a nursery.

"I guess you could say that."

She smiled at him. "Well, this will be a good time for you to start."

"But what about Ileana? I don't think—"

"Ileana no longer lives here in the main house with us. Her schedule is oftentimes hectic, and she likes her solitude. She lives on up the mountain in her own house."

Mac hadn't expected that. He'd already pictured Ileana as the homebody sort. The type who wouldn't leave her parents unless it was necessary. But then, as a deputy he'd learned that first impressions could be off base. There could be other things about Ileana Saunders that he'd gotten wrong. But her kiss wasn't one of them. He'd be safe in saying it had been the softest, sweetest thing he'd ever tasted.

"Oh. She didn't tell me that."

"Ileana doesn't do much talking about herself."

Maybe no one had ever asked her to, Mac thought. And he suddenly realized he was a bit disappointed in hearing that Ileana lived elsewhere. Having her company around this place would have been nice.

He rubbed his fists down his thighs, then awkwardly rose to his feet. "All right, Chloe. I accept your invitation. And hopefully Frankie will be well soon and you won't have to put up with me for long."

Leaving her chair, Chloe accompanied him to the door. "Trust me, Mac, you won't be a burden."

Pausing at the door, Mac turned and shook Chloe's hand. "Thank you, Chloe. I'll be out with my things tomorrow afternoon."

She patted the top of his hand in a reassuring way. "Come at any time you'd like. If you need me, I'll probably be down at the barn. Otherwise, Cesar will be around, and he'll make sure you have everything you need."

Mac thanked her again and then bade the woman a good-night.

Outside, as he walked to his truck, cold wind whistled through the canyon and shook the nearby fir trees. But this time the cold didn't turn his wishful thoughts to the warm climes of South Texas. Instead, he looked toward the mountain rising up behind the Bar M Ranch house and wondered how soon he'd be able to see Ileana again.

The next afternoon at Murdock Family Clinic in Ruidoso, the private health center Ileana established several years ago, she peered into the ears of an elderly gentleman sitting on the edge of the examining table, then stepped back to give him her diagnosis.

"Mr. Hanover, how long have you been having trouble hearing?"

The frail man with snow-white hair frowned blankly at her. "Huh?"

Ileana deliberately raised her voice several decibels. "Your ears are going to be fine. I'm going to write you a prescription, and I want you to use it every day for the next week. Then I want you to come back here to the office, and I'll wash your ears out."

He pointed an accusing finger at her. "Why can't you wash 'em out today? You gonna make me come back so you can get more money out of me?"

Ileana didn't know whether she wanted to laugh or sigh as she used the next few minutes to explain to her patient that his ears were full of wax and that she couldn't safely remove it until it was softened.

"I won't charge you for next week's visit, Mr. Hanover," she assured him as she helped him out of the examining room. "You just make sure you keep the appointment that Evaline gives you at the front desk."

Out in the hallway, Ada, her longtime assistant, immediately appeared to take Mr. Hanover off Ileana's hands. The registered nurse was close to Ileana's age and divorced. For the past ten years she'd helped Ileana build the clinic up to the busy place it was today.

"Let me take care of this, Doc," she said to Ileana. "You go grab a bite to eat."

"Thanks, Ada. I'll be in my office if you need me." She turned, then paused as another concern crossed her mind. "Oh, Ada, did you give Tommy those sample inhalers? His mother is having a hard time making ends meet, and I want to make sure he keeps his asthma under control."

"Sure did," Ada assured her. "Two of them."

Ileana gave her assistant a grateful smile, then

turned and headed on to her office. From the moment she'd stepped into the clinic this morning, Ileana had been working nonstop. With cold weather still hanging on, the flu season was lingering with it. Patients with coughs, fevers and runny noses had been in and out of the examining rooms all day. She'd hardly had time to drink a whole cup of coffee, much less eat the thermos of soup she'd brought for lunch.

Her private office was small but nicely furnished with a large cherrywood desk, leather chairs and small matching couch. Along the outside wall, a bay window framed a partial view of Sierra Blanca. The area had gotten a record snowfall this year, and vacationing skiers had been coming into town in a steady stream to enjoy the fresh powder on the slopes. Ileana often found herself treating a myriad of injuries relating to the snow sports that went on in the nearby mountains, but so far today there had been no sprains, cuts or bruises, only systemic illnesses.

She'd just sat down at her desk and reached for the lunch she'd left waiting more than an hour ago when Ada suddenly appeared in the doorway.

"Ileana, I'm sorry to bother you again."

The odd look on the woman's face caused alarm bells to clang. Had something happened to a patient? "What's wrong?" Ileana asked as she started to rise to her feet.

Immediately, Ada motioned for her to sit back down. "No. It's not an emergency. Although, he sorta looks like one to me," she added coyly, then smiled. "There's a cowboy in the waiting room. With a bunch of flowers. He told Evaline he was here to see you. She pointed out that he didn't have an appointment, so he told her to put him down as a walk-in."

Mac! What was he doing here at the clinic—and with flowers? Was he planning to take them over to the hospital to Frankie? No. She couldn't allow that. The woman would want to know where they came from, and Frankie was still far from being strong enough to hear that her estranged son was in town. *If* he was her son, Ileana reminded herself.

Ileana twisted the plastic lid back on the fat thermos. "I'll deal with this, Ada. Please send him back here to my office. And hold everything else. Even my calls."

She could see questions rolling across Ada's face, but her assistant innately knew when to keep them to herself. Instead, the nurse simply nodded.

"Will do," she told Ileana.

Once Ada disappeared down the hallway, Ileana drew in a deep breath and passed a shaky hand over her face. How could she face the man after that kiss he'd given her? After she'd raced out of there like a complete idiot? Long after she'd fled the ranch house and even after she'd gone to bed, the man and her overwhelming reaction to him continued to dominate her thoughts. The only time she was able to dismiss him from her mind was when she was examining a patient. For that much, she supposed she should be thankful.

Down the corridor, a few feet from the open door of her office, she could hear his boot heels tapping against the red and white tile. The anticipation of seeing him again made Ileana's heart pound, then settle into a rapid flutter. Thank God she wasn't hooked up to an EKG. Her colleagues would take one look at the reading and suspect she had heart trouble. And maybe she did.

Quickly, she cleared her throat and smoothed a hand over her hair. By the time Mac and Ada appeared in the doorway, she was sitting ramrod straight, her face quietly composed.

"Here's your new patient, Doc. I'll be in the drug room whenever you're ready to see Mrs. Talbot."

"Thank you, Ada. I'll be there in a few minutes," she told the nurse.

Ada disappeared, and Ileana forced herself to focus on Mac. As he sauntered casually over to her desk, she noticed he was dressed in jeans and a hunter-green shirt. His cheeks were ruddy from the cold wind, and the scent of sage and spruce had followed him indoors. Tall. Tough. Sexy. The three images whammed her, tilted her off kilter.

"I hope I'm not interrupting too much," he said with a little half grin as he swept off his hat. "Your nurse said you weren't that busy. But I could see the waiting room was full. So I won't keep you long."

A huge bouquet of fresh cut flowers wrapped in red cellophane was cradled in the crook of his arm. When he extended them out to her, Ileana stared at him in confusion.

"What's this?" she asked inanely.

A dimple appeared in his left cheek, and Ileana felt the flutter in her heart leap into a gallop.

"These are for you," he said huskily. "I hope you'll accept them and my apology for my ungentlemanly behavior last night. I'm very sorry if I upset you."

Upset her! It was more like he'd sent her into upheaval, Ileana thought. But she wasn't about to let him know that. To do so would be admitting that his kiss had nearly made her swoon and turned her thinking on a one-way track—to him.

Struggling to keep her hands calm, she reached for the flowers. "Your apology is accepted, Mac."

Deliberately keeping her eyes on the flowers, she folded back the cellophane. Her throat thickened at the sight of the yellow rosebuds mixed among pink carnations and blue asters. Other than her father and brother, no man had ever given her flowers. To think that a sexy cowboy like Mac was the first seemed incredible to Ileana.

"I hope you like the flowers," he said lowly.

She had to swallow before she could speak. "They're beautiful. But unnecessary." Lifting her head, she forced her gaze to meet his. "I should apologize, too, for racing out of the house without a word. I— It was just so embarrassing with Mother finding us… Well, you know."

She sounded like a flustered teenager rather than a mature woman and a doctor at that. But the man did something to her that she couldn't seem to control.

He smiled gently. "Yeah. I know," he agreed quietly, then let out an uncomfortable little cough. "I think I should tell you, just in case you haven't spoken with your mother, that I'm moving my things out to the Bar M later on. Chloe has invited me to stay at her home until this thing with Frankie Cantrell gets resolved."

Ileana was already floored just by him appearing here at the clinic with an armful of flowers. But this! Had her mother lost her mind? Only two nights ago, she'd been expressing her concerns about Mac's appearance ruining Frankie's life. Now Chloe had invited him into the ranch house as though he were an old friend!

Yet her mother could be very unpredictable, she thought, especially when it came to the needy. Chloe had often gone above and beyond to help people she'd never met before. This had to be one of those times, Ileana thought.

"I don't know what to say," she told him. "You and Mother must have had quite a discussion last night after I left."

He shrugged as though nothing earth-shattering had taken place. Ileana fought the urge to groan. She could only imagine her mother's response to witnessing their heated kiss. Oh, God, she could only hope that Chloe hadn't pointed out that her daughter was a lonely spinster in need of male companionship. That would be more humiliation than Ileana could bear.

"I tried to tell her that me staying on the Bar M might cause trouble with the Cantrells, but she doesn't seem to think so. I hope she's right. I've not come here to cause trouble."

Maybe he hadn't. But trouble was certainly brewing inside of Ileana. She could feel it coming on like a bad fever with no medical relief in sight.

"How did you find out about my clinic?" she asked. "Did Mother tell you?"

He shook his head. "No. I went by the hospital hoping to catch you on rounds. But the nurses said you'd already left. They told me where to find you."

"Oh. You didn't try to persuade any of them to let you into Frankie's room, did you?"

His grin was a tad wicked. "No. Do you think I could have?"

Ileana wanted to roll her eyes. Instead she pursed her lips with disapproval. "Not unless one of them wanted to lose her job."

His expression turned serious as he absently ran his thumb and forefinger around the brim of his hat. "How is Mrs. Cantrell today?"

"I ordered new X-rays of her lungs this morning, and they showed slight improvement. I'm feeling optimistic about her recovery."

"That's good." His gaze wandered over to the bay window and the view of the mountain. "I guess…you didn't mention anything about me."

Ileana felt something deep inside her stir—something far more than just empathy for his difficult situation. The raw need she saw on his face reminded her of her own disappointments and lost dreams.

"No," she answered. "I'm not sure how she'd react. I can't take that chance. Not yet."

Shrugging, he looked back at her. "I'm not sure how she's going to react, either."

He obviously had moved beyond wondering if Frankie was his mother. He seemed resigned to the idea that Frankie Cantrell and Frankie McCleod were one and the same.

He suddenly smiled and shook his head. "But I'm not here to talk about her. Will you be coming back to the ranch house this evening?"

The idea of repeating what had happened between them last night shot a thrill from the soles of her feet to the top of her head. She'd be lying to herself if she tried to pretend the man didn't excite her. But something told her if she expected to keep her peace of mind intact, she needed to give him a wide berth.

She gripped the stems of the flowers as though they were the last handhold at the edge of the cliff. "Not this evening. I have tons of work to do."

"Chloe tells me your father will be back home tonight. I'm looking forward to meeting him."

How could she resist him when he seemed so nice

and unpretentious? Should she even bother trying to resist? "I'm sure you'll like Dad," she said. "He's an easygoing guy."

He awkwardly cleared his throat. "Well, maybe I'll see you tomorrow at the hospital."

She gave him a brief smile, while wondering why she didn't have the courage to tell him she'd stop by the ranch tonight, that she'd like to spend time with him.

Because men don't want those sort of signals from you, Ileana. You're plain and boring. A few minutes with you is all it takes to make them uninterested. Haven't they always dropped you after one date? Isn't that enough to convince you you're a disaster with men?

Doing her best to ignore the hateful little voice in her head, she said in the most professional tone she could muster, "Yes. I'll be doing my rounds in the morning and tomorrow evening."

"Okay," he said stiffly. "I'll try to catch you then."

She didn't make any sort of reply, and after a few more awkward moments, he gestured toward the bunch of flowers in her hand. "You'd better put those in some water. And I'd better let you get back to work."

Planting his hat back on his head, he quickly slipped out the door. Ileana looked down at the flowers and wondered whether she should cry or smile.

The next evening, after another long, arduous day, Ileana prepared to leave the hospital. On her way out, she stopped by the nurses' station to write out last-minute patient instructions.

As she quickly scribbled across the bottom of a chart, she said, "Renae, I want Mr. Tinsley's blood pressure to be checked every hour. And make sure his family doesn't sneak donuts or anything in to him tonight. I can't get it through to them that his diabetes will be fatal if he doesn't take care of himself."

"Doc, they think they're treating him when they bring him sweets."

She handed the chart to Renae. "Yes, well, I'm the only one who's supposed to be *treating* him," Ileana said firmly.

"What about Ms. Cantrell? Anything extra for her?"

"No. Just make sure she doesn't try to get out of her breathing treatments. I understand they exhaust her, but they must be done."

Her expression curious, Renae picked up the chart. "You haven't changed your visitor orders for her, have you?"

"No. Only Quint, Alexa or Abe. And only five minutes at a time. They understand why I'm doing this."

"Yes. But does he?"

Frowning, Ileana asked, "What are you talking about?"

Renae motioned with her head toward the waiting area. "The cowboy. The Texan. He's over there right now. I was expecting him to try to sneak down the hallway to Ms. Cantrell's room or something, but he says he's here to see you."

Ileana's heart picked up its pace as she looked down the wide corridor to where a glass wall separated family and visitors from the hustle and bustle of hospital traffic. From her position, she couldn't see Mac, but she had no doubt that Renae had spotted the man. Yesterday in her office he'd mentioned that he would try to catch up to her while she was on rounds. She'd not seen him this morning, and by this evening, she'd figured he would think it too late to drive all the way in from the ranch.

"Has he been here long?" Ileana asked.

"Maybe thirty minutes." Renae's eyes narrowed in a calculating way. "Just what sort of connection does he have to Ms. Cantrell, anyway?"

Leave it to the nurse to ask personal questions, Ileana thought irritably. Renae was mostly well meaning, but she loved to gossip. The last thing Ileana wanted was for the news of Mac's presence to travel through the staff and be repeated to Frankie.

"He used to know her. And I'd appreciate it, Renae, if you didn't repeat this to anyone. And that especially goes for Frankie."

Renae looked properly insulted. "You don't have to tell me to keep my mouth shut, Doc. I can keep secrets."

Secrets. If Mac's story was true, then it appeared that Frankie had been keeping some very deep, dark secrets, Ileana thought. The whole idea still stunned her. Almost as much as the man himself.

Shouldering her handbag, she said, "Thanks, Renae. I'll see you tomorrow evening. Unless I'm needed back here tonight."

"Let's hope that doesn't happen." The nurse's smile turned sly. "Are you going to drop by the waiting room to see the cowboy?"

Ileana bit back a sigh. "Renae, I'm sure if you'll look, you'll find you have plenty of work to do."

The nurse scrunched up her nose and giggled. "Okay, Doc. You don't have to say anything else. Have a nice night."

Ileana left the nurses' station and as she headed toward the waiting area, she unconsciously smoothed a hand over her hair. Normally she wore it pulled tightly in a ballerina's knot or clasped at her nape, but for some reason today, she'd allowed the dark, reddish brown tresses to flow freely around her shoulders. The unrestricted hairstyle had gotten several looks from her coworkers and Ileana suspected they were all trying to figure out what had come over her. Even if they had questioned her, she wouldn't have had a sensible reason for the change in her hairstyle. She didn't know what had come over her, either.

Mac was just ending a call to his brother when he spotted Ileana striding toward him. The first thing he noticed was all that burnished hair lying loose and shiny on her shoulders, and then his gaze caught the fatigue on her face. Apparently her day had been long and draining, and he could only wonder why a woman who was financially secure chose to work at such a demanding job.

Because she's a caring, giving woman, Mac. Because life holds a deeper meaning for her than it does for those women you've associated yourself with.

Irritated at himself for even comparing Ileana Saunders to his former girlfriends, he shoved the thoughts away and rose to his feet to greet her.

"Good evening, Ileana. Did the nurse tell you I was waiting to see you?"

She nodded, and like yesterday, Mac found his gaze going straight to her lips. He'd kissed many a woman in his time, and some of the exchanges had been sexual mindblowers. But none of them had affected him the way that Ileana's sweet lips had. The feel of her, the taste of her had continued to go over and over in his head like a vinyl record hung in one spot. He wanted to repeat the kiss. He wanted to see for himself if the whole experience had simply been magnified in his mind. If she was just a distraction from his other worries.

"Yes," she answered. "I'm surprised to see you. When you didn't show up this morning, I figured you had changed your mind about coming by the hospital."

An odd sort of excitement seeped through him, causing his lips to spread into a sheepish grin. He couldn't understand why this quiet, modest woman made him feel so very young, so happy to be alive. None of it made sense. But then, Mac wasn't going to try to figure it out. For tonight he was simply going to enjoy these unexpected feelings.

"Actually, I had selfish reasons for driving in from the ranch this evening," he told her. "And it wasn't to pester you about seeing Ms. Cantrell. I wanted to see if you were free tonight. To have dinner with me."

Her eyes widened, and Mac could see that his suggestion had taken her by surprise. The reaction made him wonder if she ever had social evenings with a man. Or did she put being a doctor first and a woman last?

"Dinner? With me?" she repeated.

"Yes. As good as Cesar's cooking is, I thought it would be nice to try one of the restaurants in town. And for us to share a little time away from your family."

She glanced away from him, while her fingers fiddled nervously with the leather strap across her shoulder. "I'm afraid I have to decline, Mac. I have lots of work to do tonight."

Mac wasn't used to being turned down, and Ileana's refusal chopped a hunk right out of his ego. But more than that, it disappointed him greatly.

"Do you work every night?"

"Almost."

"Then you don't take time to eat?"

She looked at him with faint annoyance. "Of course I take time to eat. I'm a doctor. I know I need nourishment to keep my body going."

He smiled broadly. "I'm glad you do. So it's settled.

You have to eat anyway, so it might as well be with me. I've already told your folks I won't be back."

Shaking her head with surrender, she looked down at herself. "I'm hardly dressed for dining out."

The gray woolen slacks and thin black sweater could only be described as practical rather than glamorous. But they draped her slender figure becomingly. In fact, in an odd way, the high neck of her sweater was more provocative than a plunging neckline. It teased his imagination and made him long to see what she was hiding.

"You look just fine to me."

She sighed. "All right. But it will have to be a short dinner."

Smiling happily, he took the coat she had tossed over her forearm and helped her into it. "Surely you don't want us to dine on fast food. That wouldn't be healthy."

Ileana could have very nearly laughed. Who was the man kidding? She doubted he'd ever had a second thought about anything he'd eaten. He was the sort of man who satisfied his wants, whether they were good for him or not.

So why was he inviting her to dinner? To think he actually wanted to be with her was crazy. She wasn't beautiful or interesting. She wasn't exciting or sexy. And as soon as Mac realized she was nothing but plain and practical, he'd disappear like mountain snow in mid-July.

"Since when have you been concerned about your health?"

Grinning, he eased his arm around the back of her waist and urged her toward the nearest exit.

"Since I met a doctor with pretty auburn hair and blue, blue eyes."

Don't get caught up in this, Ileana. The man has an agenda, and it isn't romance.

Chapter 5

Ten minutes later, as Mac drove them to the north edge of town, Ileana was still trying to convince herself that nothing about this evening was romantic. But it felt like that and more as Mac turned in to a small, rustic-looking restaurant built against a steep mountainside.

"I didn't know this place existed. How did you find it?" Ileana asked curiously as he helped her out of the cab of his truck.

For tonight the wind had disappeared, leaving the night air crisp and still. Mac's hand remained against her back as they walked across the graveled parking lot. She tried to tell herself that he was simply being a gentleman, but still the casual touch was creating havoc with her senses.

"I was driving around earlier this evening," he said, "trying to spot a nice place for us to have dinner. This one caught my eye. It's a simple little hideaway. But from the packed parking lot, I have a feeling the food is good."

So he'd already picked out a restaurant before he'd even asked her to have dinner, she thought. Did he think she was that eager for a date? That she'd be that willing to agree to his plans?

This isn't a date, Ileana. You haven't been on a date in years.

The little voice in her head had Ileana asking herself why she'd even want to go on a date anyway. The few times she'd attempted to find a compatible companion, she'd endured dates spent in boring silence, or she'd ended up exhausted from listening to her date drone on and on about himself. But she wasn't going to think about those times. This was different. She was simply having a meal with an acquaintance and nothing more, she reminded herself.

Inside the restaurant, a hostess promptly ushered them to a small table tucked in an out-of-the-way corner. After helping Ileana take off her coat and into a wooden chair, Mac took a seat directly across from her.

"I'm starving," he said as he slipped off his hat and shoved it beneath his chair. "I hope you brought your appetite with you tonight. I don't want to be the only one eating too much."

Earlier, before she'd finished her rounds at the hospital, Ileana had felt so hungry she'd been tempted to raid the vending machine and chomp on a candy bar between patients. But now food was nothing but an afterthought. Her whole body was buzzing, trying to digest the fact that she was sitting across from Mac in a cozy restaurant. Soft music was playing in the background, and he was looking at her as though he really wanted to be here.

"I'll try to down my fair share," she said with a faint smile.

He settled comfortably back in his chair, and as Ileana cast surreptitious glances his way she was reminded all over again at how muscular, rugged and sexy he was.

"So how was Frankie today?" he asked.

"Slightly improved. Her heart problem greatly slows her progress at getting well, though."

The idea that his mother might have a very serious heart condition left Mac uncomfortable. All these years she'd been away, he'd envisioned his mother as a vibrant, healthy woman. The way she'd been when she'd left their home. It was hard to imagine that same woman with thirty years added on to her age and in declining health to boot.

"Exactly what is wrong with her heart?" he asked curiously.

Her soft smile was apologetic. "I'm sorry, Mac. I can't discuss the details of a patient's condition. But I'm sure Alexa or Quint would be glad to explain it all to you."

Mac was about to tell her that he had no definite plans to speak with Frankie Cantrell's children, when a waitress arrived with menus. After she'd taken their drink orders and left the table, he said, "Can you tell me whether Frankie's condition can be fixed?"

Ileana picked up her menu, yet she kept her gaze directly on him, and Mac realized he liked her polite attentiveness. Whenever they spoke to each other, she made him feel as though she was really listening, as though what he had to say was important to her. He couldn't remember any woman who had done that to him.

"Her problem can be fixed. But she refuses treatment."

Mac frowned. "Why is that? In this day and age,

medical procedures are a heck of a lot easier to deal with than they used to be."

"Frankie understands that. But I'm not sure what's behind her thinking. Losing Lewis, her husband, last year pretty much took her will away. But I shouldn't be saying this much to you about her health situation."

She dropped her eyes to her menu, and Mac decided not to push the issue. Sooner or later he'd meet Frankie Cantrell face-to-face and then he'd find out for himself what the woman was about. Or would he? Even if she turned out to be his mother, that didn't mean she'd want to speak with him, much less spend time explaining anything to him.

Dear God, what if that happened? He'd spent years trying to get over Frankie's rejection. How could he live through a second one? How could he go back to Texas and tell Ripp that their mother refused to allow them into her life?

Because you're a grown man this time, Mac. Because you've got a tough hide and an even tougher heart. You're not going to let any woman hurt you again.

Clearing his throat, he picked up his own menu and turned his thoughts to the list of meals.

A few moments later, after the waitress had served them wine and left with their orders, Mac said, "I met your father last night. I really liked him. He was nothing like I expected."

She warmed to his compliment. "What were you expecting him to be?"

He shrugged. "I'm not sure. More of a stuffy businessman, I suppose. He's very down to earth."

"I do have a wonderful father. Even though he has a stressful job, he's always put his family first. What about your father, Mac? Did you two get along well?"

For a moment Mac was taken aback by her question. Not because it was personal but because he'd never had a woman ask him such a thing. The women he often dated never initiated conversations about family relations. Their chatter was limited more to the latest movies, fashions or material things like cars or technical gadgets. At the deepest, the local town gossip was discussed. This sort of talk, especially with a woman, was very different for Mac, and he wasn't sure just how to go about it.

"We got along good," he said after a moment. "Owen was a very tough man in many ways, but he was devoted to my brother and me. All the years while we were growing up he worked as a farmer, raising corn and cotton. He taught us both all about making things grow from the ground and what it took to make a living from such a job."

So Mac's father was a farmer, Ileana mused. And from what Chloe had told her, Frankie's ex had been a farmer, also. The facts had to be more than coincidental. Her expression curious, she asked, "What caused him to leave farming and become a sheriff?"

"When I was sixteen, we went through a really rough period when the price of corn plummeted and cotton wasn't much better. Add a drought onto that and it nearly wiped us out financially. That's when Dad decided he needed a more stable income and a friend talked him into running for the county sheriff's position. Once he won the election and became certified as a law officer, Dad seemed to take to the job. Besides having a knack for solving crimes, he treated everyone fairly, and I think that's why he kept getting reelected."

"So you and your brother took to that side of your

father, the law official part of him rather than the farming," she mused aloud.

Mac nodded. "Seems that way. Although my brother Ripp still likes to make things grow. And he's good at it. Now that he has a family I wouldn't be surprised to hear him say he's putting away his badge and going back into farming. But me, no. That's too mundane for me."

She took another tiny sip from her wineglass, then placed it on the table. "So you need excitement in your life," she said more as a statement than a question.

Shrugging, Mac wondered why her comment made him feel just a tad shallow. There wasn't anything wrong with wanting excitement. Everyone needed a little dose of it, didn't they? Otherwise life would be boring.

"If you want to put it that way," he said. "I guess I'd have to say I'd rather be shot at than sit in a tractor for twelve to fourteen hours a day."

Mac expected to see a flash of disapproval in her eyes and was surprised when he didn't.

"We all have a different calling," she said. "And yours is being a lawman just like mine is being a doctor. We can't make ourselves be something we're not."

The waitress arrived with their salads, and while she served them, Mac wondered if Ileana was really as understanding as she seemed or if she was simply being diplomatic. Once the waitress headed off to another table, Mac said, "Being a deputy is not a macho thing with me, Ileana. I like the notion of serving the public, of helping my fellow citizens remain safe in their homes and on the streets. If that sounds corny, I can't help it."

Across the table, Ileana forced an interest in the crispy romaine lettuce. But that was difficult to do when all she wanted to do was gaze at him, listen to his soft drawl and watch the subtle expressions move across his features. Being with the man was intoxicating, she realized. He made her forget who she was, what she was.

"I don't think it's corny. I think it's admirable. Remember, I've had relatives in law enforcement, too." She forced herself to chew and swallow. "So what exactly happened to your father? He must have died a fairly young man."

He grimaced. "Dad died when he was only fifty-six years old. He developed emphysema—a bad case. Probably from all the dust and herbicides he inhaled when he was young. That was before he could afford a tractor with a cab."

"That's so unfortunate," she said. "Especially when his illness could have probably been prevented."

"Yeah. But he did the best he could with what he had. And I admire him for that. Especially when I know he was working hard to put food on the table for his family."

The idea of this big, strong man losing so much, hurting so much, touched Ileana deep inside. Especially when she could see that he'd had the inner strength to go on and make something worthy of himself. "I can't imagine what it must be like to lose both parents."

He looked across at her. "When Dad died Mom had already been gone for twenty-odd years. Ripp and I had long gotten used to not having a mother."

Her heart winced as she tried to picture Frankie Cantrell, or any woman for that matter, deliberately leaving two sons behind. If by some wild chance Ileana ever had children, she'd make them the center of her world. Nothing and no one could separate her from them.

"So your father was farming when your mother left the family?"

Mac nodded. "My brother and I were both in high school when he became sheriff. And we thought having our dad as the sheriff was pretty neat. Until he got in a shoot-out with a bank robber and then we were scared that something would happen to him." His face was suddenly touched with a mixture of pride and irony. "We didn't know something else was going to happen to him and that it would have nothing to do with a bullet."

The waitress arrived with their main courses. Ileana promptly dug into the grilled salmon on her plate, while from the thick veil of her dark lashes, she watched him slice into a rare rib eye steak.

His strong, brown hands evoked all sorts of images in Ileana's mind, most of them so erotic that she was shocked at herself. Men had touched her body before, and though some of their touches had been pleasant, none of them had ever elicited pure desire in her, the kind that made a person lose all control, the kind that she'd felt in Mac's kiss.

Oh, God, she prayed, don't let me think about that. About the way she'd wanted him.

Clearing her throat, she asked, "So now it's just you and your brother?"

"That's right. Our father's parents both passed away about the time Ripp and I graduated high school. Mom's parents, the Andersons, never kept in touch. Mom never talked about them, and Dad once told us that his in-laws had disapproved of Frankie marrying him, so they'd always kept their distance. We never met them, so it's impossible to say whether they're still living or not." His face grim, he sliced off another bite of beef. "I had a wife once, too. But that only lasted a couple years. Now I'm content to let my brother be a husband and father."

The fork full of salmon she was about to put in her mouth paused in midair. "You were married once?"

A cynical grin twisted his lips. "Yes. Does that surprise you?"

Everything about him surprised her, Ileana thought. "Yes, it does. You—don't seem the sort."

"My ex didn't think so in the end either," he said wryly.

The idea that he'd once thought of one woman enough to marry her intrigued and bothered Ileana. In a fantasy world, she wanted to think Mac had never loved a woman before. That he would never love one in the future, unless that one was her. But she was a doctor, and she didn't deal in fantasies.

"If she didn't think you were the husband sort, then I'm curious as to why she married you," Ileana told him.

He chuckled, but the sound didn't hold much amusement. "Because she thought it would be fun for us to be husband and wife."

"Fun?" Ileana parroted. "Is that all?"

"Well, I think Brenna halfway loved me until I tried to make the marriage serious. You see, she wasn't ready for settling down and raising children, so she cut out."

Ileana gripped her fork. "What about you? Did you love her?"

His gaze dropped evasively to his plate. "I married her when I was twenty-five because I liked her a lot and we had fun together. I thought that was enough. It was a heck of a lot more than some of my friends had. But after a while I got tired of all the going and partying. I thought if we settled down and had children that it would change both of us for the better. I thought it would make me love her and she love me. I was young and green. I didn't really understand what marriage meant. It ended after two years."

"Well, we all live and learn," Ileana said. "And you seemed to realize the mistakes you've made, so why haven't you ever remarried?"

A grin touched his mouth. "It would take a hell of a woman to make me go down that road again. And so far I haven't found her."

And he wasn't hunting one, either, Ileana thought with a measure of foolish disappointment. Those soft, attentive looks he'd been giving her were probably practiced. If he even suspected she was thinking of him in a romantic way, he'd probably laugh himself silly. Only he'd keep his laughter inside so as not to offend her. He couldn't afford to do that when she held the entry key to Frankie Cantrell's room.

Feeling like an idiot for letting the man turn her head, even for a minute, she reached for her wine and took a grateful sip. Normally she never needed extra fortitude for any reason. But tonight Mac was shaking her up in ways she'd never imagined.

Lifting another bite of salmon from her plate, she said bluntly, "I know why you brought me to dinner tonight, Mac. And frankly, I should tell you that you're wasting your time and money."

His brows shot upward at the sudden change in her. "Really? I'm enjoying my meal. Aren't you?"

How could he insult her even more by appearing so innocent? she wondered.

"The food is good," she agreed, then her mouth twisted with sarcasm. "But you know what I'm talking about. I'm talking about your attempt at making it appear as if we're on a date or something. And the flowers yesterday—you don't have to do that sort of thing as a way to see Frankie. I intend to let you meet with her just as quickly as I think it's safe for her health."

Frowning now, he placed his fork down beside his plate. If any other woman had been saying these things to him he would probably be getting angry right about now. But this woman was different. She was like a hurt little kitten, hissing pitifully to ward away his advances.

"Look, Ileana, I don't know what brought this on. But you have me all wrong. This meal isn't some sort of charm tactic! It's insulting to me that you think it is! And I gave you the flowers because I wanted to. Because I'd hoped that you would like them."

Her head was bent, but Mac could still see the torn expression on her face. Clearly, she was fighting a war with herself as to whether to believe him, and he wondered why. True, she didn't know him that well. But as far as he could tell, he'd not given her any reason to mistrust him. Had some man deceived her, hurt her?

"If that's true…then it was a nice gesture," she finally mumbled.

Mac sighed as he wondered why this woman's feelings even mattered to him. "Ileana, have you ever been married? Or had a serious relationship?"

Her head jerked up, and she stared at him in stunned silence.

"I'm sorry if you think I'm getting too personal," he told her. "But turnabout is fair play, isn't it?"

Glancing down at her plate, she absently pushed her fork at a morsel of fish. "I suppose. But I don't know why that sort of thing about me would interest you."

Something in the middle of his chest was suddenly aching. It was an odd feeling that was totally new to him. He didn't know why the pain was there. Only that it had something to do with the woman sitting across from him and his need to make her feel better about herself, to make her smile.

"Why? Because you think no man could be interested in you? If that's what you're thinking then you're wrong," he said softly. "I'd like to know why you're still single."

The corners of her mouth turned downward, and Mac could see the expression of disapproval was aimed more at herself than him.

"Why? Because I'm thirty-eight and well-off?" she asked.

"No. Because you're a nice, lovely woman, and I can't figure out how you've escaped marriage for all these years. That's what I'm wondering."

A splash of color suddenly painted her cheeks, and Mac found himself enchanted by her modesty. Had Brenna or any of his dates ever blushed? But then Mac had usually associated himself with bold, thick-skinned women. They were easier to handle, easier to keep at an emotional distance. He didn't have to worry about their feelings, because there weren't many feelings involved. Ileana's fragility was something very new for him, and he felt like a clumsy-footed horse carefully trying to avoid stepping on a violet.

Her eyes met his, and he could see all sorts of doubts swimming in the blue depths.

"I'm sorry, Mac, if I sounded skeptical, but you see, I…well, I'm not used to getting attention from men."

She let out a nervous little laugh, and Mac could see the color on her face deepen even more.

She went on. “I mean…your sort of attention. I’m just a doctor, and that’s the only way men ever look at me.”

“Always?” he urged.

She slowly shook her head. “Well, I’ve had a few dates when I was much younger. But none of them turned into anything lasting.”

“Did you want them to?”

A soft yearning flickered in her eyes, and Mac found himself desperately wanting to reach across the table for her hand. He wanted to fold it in his and let the pressure of his fingers tell her that he understood, that he knew what it was like to be rejected and humiliated.

“I don’t know. I never got the chance to know any of them that well. I guess I’m not exactly an exciting date. I’ve always been a little shy, and becoming a doctor took years of schooling and training. I kept myself buried in my studies and my focus on a medical career. I felt confident and at home in a chemistry lab, but at parties I was a boring clam. After I finally accepted the fact that I was different from most women, I never bothered trying to catch a guy’s attention.” She gave him a hopeless little smile. “When God passed out brains he handed me a pretty good one, but I missed out on the beauty and personality.”

“Who says?”

She shrugged, and he could tell his question embarrassed her even more. “Mac, my sister, Anna, and my mother are very beautiful women. Next to them I feel I’m lacking. But that doesn’t matter. All I’ve ever wanted to be was a doctor. And I’m good at my job. That means everything to me.”

Then why didn’t she look happy and content? he

wondered. Why was he seeing sad shadows come and go in her eyes?

"You've never wanted a family of your own?"

She glanced away from him. "I have my moments. Especially when I see my brother and sister with their families. But I would never want to marry just for the sake of being married. I want someone to really care about me. The way my dad cares for my mom."

When Frankie had married Owen, had she been looking for that same sort of love? During those years as a young boy, Mac had always thought of his mother as being kind, gentle and loving. She'd never raised her voice to her boys or her husband. But apparently she'd been unhappy. Had Owen not loved Frankie enough? Or had she simply not wanted to raise two rowdy boys? To Mac, either choice was not a pretty one.

Suddenly he couldn't stop himself from reaching across the table and folding his fingers around hers. "Ileana, beauty comes in all shapes and sizes. And I think those guys you dated needed eyeglasses."

Her cheeks were rose-colored as she demurely lifted her gaze to his and gave him a grateful smile. "Thank you for saying that, Mac."

Mac forked the last bite of steak to his lips while wondering what in hell was coming over him. It wasn't like him to be so protective of a woman's feelings. It wasn't like him to be so open and honest with a lady just because he had her out to dinner. Yet, he'd been telling her the truth when he'd said he had no agenda behind asking her out this evening. At least, not the sort of agenda she was thinking. He knew that Ileana was point-blank honest. If she said she would allow him to see Frankie soon, then she would. He didn't doubt that. And he wasn't trying to charm her into moving the meeting date forward. So what was he doing having dinner with her tonight?

Face it, Mac. You like the woman. She's soft and gentle and doesn't grate on your nerves. She knows how to have a conversation. And there's something about the fresh loveliness of her face that gets you, that makes you dream of quiet nights with her lips whispering in your ear, kissing you with love.

From out of nowhere he felt his throat tighten, making his reply little more than a husky murmur. "You're very welcome, Ileana."

Later, after coffee and dessert, Mac drove the two of them off the mountain and back through town to where Ileana had left her truck in the hospital parking lot.

As they traveled through the sparse traffic, Ileana was completely amazed at herself. For the life of her, she couldn't figure out what had made her open up to Mac like she had. Why had she admitted to him that she'd always been a shy geek, that she wouldn't be able to turn a man's head even if she had him hobbled and bridled?

But, oh, God, the answers to those questions were nothing compared to the feelings rushing through her at the moment, the wild excitement bubbling just beneath the surface of her veins. She could feel her body longing for the touch of his hands, her lips aching to press themselves against his. This had never happened to her before, and she didn't know what to do, how to make it all stop or even if she should try to make it stop.

By the time they reached her truck, which was parked in one of the slots allotted for physicians, the parking lot was mostly deserted. Mac pulled up alongside her Ford, then cut the motor.

In spite of the wine she'd had with dinner, her heart suddenly started to pound.

"There's no need for you to wait around to see if my truck starts. It never fails. Besides, I can always find a maintenance man inside the hospital to help me."

Resting his arm along the back of the seat, he turned toward her. Streetlamps shed dim light inside the cab and caused shadows to slant across his strong face. She couldn't see exactly where his hand was lying, but she could feel its presence near her shoulder. The idea that he was so close to touching her left her feeling faint and foolish at the same time.

"I'm not worried about your truck. I only want to make sure you know how much I enjoyed this evening," he said.

Ruidoso hadn't seen a warm day in months, yet everything inside Ileana was melting as though he'd just yanked her into bright sunshine.

"I'm glad," she admitted softly. "I enjoyed it, too."

His dark eyes continued to roam her face, and Ileana unconsciously licked her lips.

"I don't suppose you're planning on stopping by your parents' house this evening," he said.

Her neck felt stiff as she wagged her head back and forth. "No. I have several charts to update before I head back to work tomorrow morning."

He grimaced. "Don't you have someone to do that for you?"

Ileana had never thought she suffered from claustrophobia, but the walls of the truck cab seemed to be shrinking around the two of them. His spicy scent was filling her head, his nearness making her breathing erratic.

"I could dictate comments and have someone else do it for me. But I prefer to do it myself. The well-being of my patients is *my* personal responsibility, not some person filing charts and records."

In spite of the dark interior, there was enough lamplight to see a look of appreciation flash across his face, and the sight pleased Ileana far more than it should have.

"Your dedication is to be admired," he said. "But it brings me to another question. Why do you want to be a doctor? Seems to me you're always working—even when you're home. Doesn't that get old?"

"Everyone gets tired—even at a job they love. I'll bet once in a while you even need a break from being a deputy."

He nodded in agreement. "The hours are crazy, and the pay is low. Not to mention the danger. And sometimes it gets so hectic that I ask myself if I'm crazy for hanging on at the job."

"But you keep on doing it, because, like you said earlier, you want to help people. It's the same way with me, Mac. I want to be a doctor so that I can help people."

He leaned toward her, and Ileana's gaze zeroed in on the lopsided grin on his face.

"Well, right now I wish you'd forget about being a doctor," he said softly. "There's still plenty of evening left. If you stopped by the ranch house, we could—"

"Mac," she gently interrupted, "I have to go home. Really."

His hand came up and stroked the side of her hair. "I was only going to say that we could—talk."

Ileana swallowed as her heart pounded wildly in her chest. "We've already done a lot of talking tonight."

His fingers left her hair to slide gently along her jawline before coming to a rest beneath her chin. "You're right," he murmured. "We have. And I've learned a lot."

Her lashes fluttered as her gaze sought his. "What have you learned?"

"That I want to kiss you again," he whispered as his mouth inched toward hers. "And I think you want to kiss me, too."

She tried to counter his words, but all she could manage to do was breathe his name, and even that one tiny sound was swallowed up as his mouth covered hers.

Her full lips were soft, softer than anything he'd ever tasted. But it was their vulnerable quiver that got to Mac and urged his arms to circle around her shoulders. And it was the sweet surrender of her mouth that caused him to groan deep in his throat and press her close against him.

In a matter of moments he was lost in her gentle response, and then he was struggling, fighting the urge to deepen the kiss, to acquaint his hands with every inch of her body. In the pit of his belly coals of desire stirred to flames and heated his blood.

Knowing he was close to losing control, Mac jerked his mouth from hers and drew in a long, ragged breath. Beneath his hands he could feel Ileana trembling, her back rising and falling as she struggled to regain her breath.

Mac was stunned. He'd never expected to want this much, feel this much. Especially from a woman who could possibly still be a virgin, an innocent waiting for the man of her dreams.

He couldn't, in good conscience, be the man who burst those dreams. More than anything, even more than assuaging the desire simmering in his loins, he wanted her to remember him as a gentleman.

"I… I think we'd better head for home," he said with heavy reluctance.

"Yes—you're right," she said in a choked voice.

Avoiding his gaze, she reached to the floorboard for her handbag. While she retrieved it, Mac hurriedly left the cab and walked around to the passenger door to help her to the ground.

Once she was standing in front of him, Mac clung to her hand while his gaze snatched hungry glances at her face.

"I'll drive behind you until we get to the ranch," he told her.

"Okay."

She didn't make any sort of move toward her own truck, and Mac finally realized he was still holding her hand in a firm grip.

Quickly he dropped it and smiled sheepishly. "Would it do me any good to come here to the hospital tomorrow?"

"I doubt it. But miracles do happen."

He stuffed his hands in his pockets. "I'll be here then. Good night, Ileana."

To his surprise, she rose up on tiptoe and kissed his cheek. "Thank you, Mac, for the lovely dinner. Good night."

As he watched her climb into her truck, Mac figured he had a goofy look on his face. Had any woman ever kissed him there before? Maybe. If one had, she'd not meant it. Not in the genuine way that Ileana had.

What the hell was coming over him, he asked himself as his gaze followed her retreating taillights. Since when did he let a woman end a date with a kiss on the cheek?

Since he'd met Dr. Ileana Sanders.

Chapter 6

The next afternoon, Mac was exploring the Bar M racing stables when he spotted Chloe on a nearby dirt track, exercising a big, steel-gray Thoroughbred.

After three circles in an easy gallop, she pulled up the horse and, after sliding to the ground, handed the reins over to a groom.

"Put him on the walker for ten minutes, Manuel, then shower him," she told the young man, who was using all his might to keep the energetic horse under control.

"Yes, ma'am."

Manuel led the horse up a slight hill to a big barn with a connecting row of stables. Mac continued to stand with his forearms propped on the board railing surrounding the racetrack, until Chloe came within reach. Then he turned and tipped his hat politely.

"Good mornin', Chloe."

She was bundled in a red plaid jacket and her jeans were stuffed in the tops of her riding boots. The cold air had nipped her face with color, and the smile she wore as she walked over to him was one of exhilaration.

"Good morning, yourself," she replied. "What did you think about Rebel? Does he look like he's ready for the big track?"

Mac chuckled. "I'm the last person to be asking. I own a couple of horses, but they're quarter horses that I use to herd cattle. But from what I could see of Rebel he looked great."

She reached over and fondly patted Mac's arm. "I hope you're not getting too bored here on the ranch, Mac. I'm sure it's nothing like being home, but it has to be better than hanging around a hotel."

Mac shook his head. "I haven't been bored at all. The ranch is beautiful, and I enjoy watching all the horses."

Her expression turned keen. "Have you spoken yet to Ileana today? I'm wondering if there's any change in Frankie."

"I haven't spoken to her today. But last night she told me that Frankie had slightly improved. That's all." Mac hadn't told Ileana's parents that he'd taken their daughter out to dinner last night. He wasn't sure why he'd kept the information to himself. He didn't think they would frown upon it; he just considered his time with Ileana private. "I plan to go to the hospital this evening and maybe catch up with her as she does her rounds."

Chloe frowned. "Why do that when you can catch up to her at her house?"

Mac realized that Chloe was merely being practical, but he wasn't at all sure that Ileana would appreciate him showing up on her doorstep. Even after that kiss she'd given him last night. "I don't think it would be a good idea to intrude on Ileana's privacy."

"Mac," Chloe gently scolded, "Ileana wouldn't consider you an intrusion. My daughter was born to help others. And I know she wants to help you resolve this issue with Frankie."

Help him? It wasn't exactly help he wanted from Ileana. When he'd decided that, he didn't quite know. He only knew that spending time with Ileana had somehow become more important to him than meeting Frankie Cantrell.

He was trying to think of a nice way to dismiss Chloe's suggestion when he caught the sound of approaching footsteps directly behind him.

As Mac turned to see who was joining them, Chloe said, "Quint, how good of you to come this morning."

The dark-haired man was dressed like Mac, in hat and boots and worn jeans. He was tall with broad shoulders and at least twelve years younger than Mac, but his rugged features implied a maturity that belied his age.

Quint. As Mac rolled the name through his head, it suddenly struck him as to where he'd heard it. This man was Frankie Cantrell's son! This man could possibly be his half brother! The notion nearly paralyzed Mac.

With an easy smile, the young man assured Chloe, "No trouble."

As her gaze swung guardedly from one man to the other, Chloe took Quint by the arm and turned him toward Mac.

"Quint, this is the man I wanted you to meet. Mac McCleod. Mac, this is Quint Cantrell, Frankie's son."

The whole situation felt totally surreal to Mac as he

thrust his hand out to the younger man. "Nice to meet you, Quint."

"Same here," Quint replied.

Mac cleared his throat, yet the effort did little to ease the lump of emotion that had suddenly lodged behind his Adam's apple.

"I didn't realize Chloe had invited you here to the ranch this morning," Mac candidly admitted.

Quint tossed a fond look at Ileana's mother. "When this lady calls, I usually come running."

Well, Mac thought, Chloe had taken the question of whether to talk to Frankie's children out of his hands. With Quint here, he could hardly avoid talking about his mother—their mother. Oh, God, could this be any worse for both of them?

Yes, Frankie could be dead and then no one would know what really happened thirty years ago.

"Now that you're here, Quint," Chloe spoke up, "I have horses to tend to. If you men will excuse me, I'll get out of your way so you can get acquainted."

Both men watched the woman make her way back to the barn. Once she was totally out of sight, awkward silence settled in until Quint finally suggested, "Would you like to walk to the other side of the track? Down below this shelf of mountain there's a pasture full of yearlings you might like to see."

Grateful that the young man was making an effort to be friendly, Mac nodded. "Sure. It's kind of cold just standing here, anyway."

Quint smiled briefly. "Chloe tells me you're from South Texas. I guess this mountain air does feel chilly."

"I'm getting a bit more used to it," Mac admitted.

With mutual concession the two men turned to the

right and began strolling along the outside rail of the exercise track. As they walked Mac was acutely aware of the younger man's presence, and for some odd reason it suddenly struck Mac that he was far, far from Texas, from everything familiar, from Ripp and home.

"I really don't know what to say," Quint said after they'd walked a few yards in silence. "The whole story that Chloe told me sounds rather fantastic."

"You're right. It does," Mac said soberly.

"Chloe says you have letters from my mother and that they were mailed to a family friend of yours."

"I didn't know Chloe planned to say anything to you," Mac admitted. "I wasn't sure—I didn't want to concern you or your sister if this turned out to be untrue. But now that Chloe has let you in on part of it, you might as well hear everything."

Quint nodded. "I'd appreciate that, Mac. This whole thing is...well, it's pretty much shaken my sister and me. Hell, it's more than shaken us—we're both in a daze! And we don't know what to think...except that we've got to find out the truth about all this."

Mac let out a breath of relief. At least this man wasn't accusing him of being a crackpot or threatening legal action to keep him away from Frankie. Apparently, he must have recognized a thread of truth to Mac's story.

Mac said, "We only learned about the letters a little over two weeks ago. My brother and I were both shocked when Oscar Andrews, Betty Jo's son, brought the letters to us. You see, we...well, for thirty years we haven't known whether our mother was alive or dead."

Pausing on the rocky ground, Quint looked at him squarely. "And you think Frankie, my mother, is that woman?"

"I can't think anything else. In the letters she mentions my brother and me by name. How else would she have known us?"

The younger man sighed as he shook his head back and forth in disbelief. "I don't know. It doesn't make sense. She's mentioned that she used to live in Texas when she was young and that she still had a few friends there. But she never went to visit. And she certainly never talked about being married before or having children. It's like—"

"She wanted to forget she ever had us," Mac finished for him.

Quint's jaw dropped, and Mac could see that the young man felt badly for him. Mac didn't want his sympathy. After all, they'd both been misled and the way he viewed it, Quint was just as much a victim as he.

Looking down at the toes of his boots, Quint said, "I didn't want to say it like that, but I guess it does look that way. I can't believe that Mother would just go off and leave two sons behind. She's not that sort of woman. She's always been dedicated to my sister and me. She—well, at times she can even be too clingy to her children. Does that sound like a woman who could walk away from two sons?"

Quint Cantrell's gaze was direct and forthright. But Mac was noticing far more than that about the man. His eyes were blue, the same azure color as Mac's mother. The notion struck him, crushed him with all the implications of having siblings he'd not known about. Of not having his mother's love while this man had been showered with her affection.

"From a law officer's standpoint, I'd have to agree with you. It sounds totally out of character."

Quint jammed his hands in his pockets, and Mac realized the other man wasn't wearing gloves or a jacket. Maybe that's why his face was pinched, his shoulders shivering.

"I guess Ileana has told you all about Mom's illness," he said.

"A bit. She believes in protecting her patient's privacy. But she made it clear that Frankie is too fragile to discuss this yet. And I respect her decision."

Quint regarded him thoughtfully. "I'll be honest with you, Mac. Mom's health is precarious at best. She needs heart surgery, but she won't discuss it. Ever since Dad died, it's like she wants to die, too."

"Have you tried to change her mind about the surgery?"

"Oh, yes. Alexa and I have tried. When we talk about it, she only gets angry. You see, when Dad died, my parents had been married for twenty-eight years. They were very close, and I don't think she's ever recovered from his death."

"My father died, too. About six years ago," Mac told him. "It's been hard not to have him around. Although, I can't imagine what he would think about his sons going on a search for their mother. He was very bitter about Mom's leaving. He practically forbade us to mention her name."

Quint looked at him curiously. "Why was that? I've heard of sour divorces, but that was carrying things a bit too far, wasn't it?"

Mac shrugged. "From what my brother and I can glean from acquaintances, when Frankie left her family, she moved in with Will Tomlin, a man who owned a tire business in town. We're not exactly sure how long she lived with him before she left for parts unknown. Only a few weeks, we think. Will moved away from Goliad County not long after Frankie did, and no one around town could give us information as to his whereabouts now. Anyway, back when all this was happening, Dad had to try to hold his head up while his wife flaunted an affair with a local townsman. It was rough on him."

Quint looked around him as though he needed to find a place to sit down. Mac understood the other man's feeling all too well.

"God, this is— It just can't be the same woman, Mac. The one appears to be exactly opposite of the other. My mother has always been a good, honest woman. It's impossible to believe anything else."

Feeling utterly terrible, Mac reached over and squeezed the other man's shoulder. "I understand, and I'm sorry about this, Quint. Maybe when your mother gets well, we'll find out that she never was Frankie McCleod."

Quint's expression was anything but hopeful. "Yeah, maybe. But I don't believe so. All I ask, Mac, is that whenever you do finally get to see Mother…be as gentle as you can be."

That terrible lump had suddenly returned to Mac's throat. "I'd never planned to be any other way."

Later that day at the Saunders Family Clinic, Ileana worked through the last of her patients, then made her way over to Sierra General to wind up her workday. It was Friday, and this coming weekend she would not be on hospital call. Thankfully, a fellow physician would be handling her rounds for her. So barring some horrible emergency, Ileana's time would be free for the next two days.

Because her Friday patient list had been short, it was still daylight when she drove across the ranch, then up the mountain to where her log house was perched on a shelf that overlooked the Hondo Valley.

Eight years ago, when Ileana had turned thirty, she'd had the house built for herself. Up until that time, she'd lived with her parents in the main ranch house. And even though she'd always gotten along very well with her parents, she'd wanted to give them and herself more privacy.

Compared to the main house, the log house with its green tin roof was modest in size. But with Ileana living alone and with not much hope of ever having a family, she'd figured it had plenty of space for her.

Now, as she parked her truck and grabbed her handbag from the bench seat, she paused to gaze through the windshield at her home. The log structure sat snugly against the mountainside. Attached to the front, and shaded by one lone Aspen growing just to its left, a wide wooden deck with a waist-high rail ran the length of the structure.

Because of the steep terrain, there wasn't much of a yard. And since Ileana didn't have all that much time to devote to gardening, she'd left the rugged ground dotted with twisted juniper, yucca plants, choya cacti and clumps of blue sage.

Ileana figured the place would be too isolated and wild for most folks. Yet as she left the truck and climbed the steep wooden stairs leading up to the deck, she wondered what Mac would think of it.

The notion to invite him here had struck her several

times today, but each time she'd squashed the idea. Even though he'd kissed her again in the hospital parking lot, she didn't want to appear too eager for his company. After all, she was wise enough to know that a kiss, even two, was nothing to a man like him. He probably went around kissing women all the time. She doubted a day passed in his life when he didn't have a woman near him. Ileana was nothing new or special to him, and she needed to keep that thought in her head.

And yet, she couldn't help but feel a bit special, a bit hopeful about seeing him again. He'd implied that he might catch her on hospital rounds again today. But he'd not shown up, and she'd not waited around to see if he would. Renae had already been tossing sly questions at her about Mac. Ileana didn't want to add more gossip to the nurse's repertoire by sitting around the hospital, waiting for the man to appear.

She'd changed into a pair of jeans and a long-sleeved T-shirt and had just finished eating a bowl of stew when she heard a knock on the front door.

Figuring it was one of the family, or Cesar with a box full of leftovers from supper, she was totally surprised when she opened the door to find Mac standing alone on the other side of the threshold.

"Mac!" she softly exclaimed.

"I'm sorry if I'm interrupting, Ileana. I wasn't going to bother you like this. But your parents kept insisting you wouldn't mind. I just wanted to get an update on Frankie. I know I should have called—" Pausing, he grinned, then shrugged. "But I thought it would give me a good excuse to see your home."

Her heart beating fast, she pushed the door wider. "Of course, you're not bothering me. Please, come in."

He stepped past her, and Ileana quickly shut the door behind him. Then with her back against the wooden panel, she took a second to draw in a bracing breath and collect herself.

"Just when I thought it was going to get warmer today, the wind starts blowing," he said as he shrugged out of his jacket. "I don't know how you folks get used to the cold."

"When you're born into it, you don't know anything else," she said, then walking around him, she reached to take his jacket. "Here, I'll hang that up for you."

"Thanks."

He gave her his jacket and his Stetson, and Ileana hung both items in a closet not far from the door. Then ushered him down a short hallway to the living room. With each step they took, she caught his male scent, felt his presence wrap a blanket of excitement around her.

"I'm sorry to say that Frankie's condition hasn't changed all that much. A slight improvement but not enough."

"Well, at least she's not worsening," he said.

As they entered the living room, she started to invite him to take a seat in front of the crackling fireplace. But then she suddenly remembered it was dinnertime. "I just finished a bowl of stew. Would you like to eat something?" she asked politely.

"No. I had supper with your parents. Cesar is such a good cook that I couldn't down another bite. Unless it was dessert," he added impishly.

"In that case, we'll go to the kitchen," she told him. "I was just about to dig into a pecan pie."

Ileana guided him out of the cozy living room,

through an open doorway and directly into a kitchen that seemed even smaller with Mac in it.

"Have a seat," she invited, as she gestured toward a round pine table situated near a glass patio door. "Would you like coffee, too?"

"Coffee would be nice. Black will be fine."

Ileana went to the cabinet and began to pull down cups and saucers. While she gathered the coffee and pie, she could hear him taking a seat at the table. Just thinking about him being here in her house, so near and touchable, made her hands tremble, and she silently scolded herself as she fumbled the pieces of pie onto small breakfast plates.

As she placed everything on the table, she carefully kept a polite distance between them. Yet in spite of that, she felt breathless and terribly foolish for reacting so strongly to the man.

"I suppose I should reassure you that I didn't bake the pie," she said as she took a seat across from him.

He chuckled. "Why? Are you a bad cook?"

She wrinkled her nose. "Not exactly bad. The things I do know how to cook turn out pretty well. But I only know how to make a few dishes. Mother says I always had my nose stuck in a test tube instead of an oven, and I suppose she's right."

As Mac dug into the pie, he decided Ileana was much more animated tonight. It was good to see, he realized, and even better that she didn't appear to be annoyed by his showing up on her doorstep.

After last night, when he'd practically forced her into having dinner with him, he'd promised himself that he wouldn't barge in on her private life like this. But he'd desperately wanted to see her again, and all it had taken was a little nudge from Chloe and Wyatt to put him on the road to Ileana's house.

Mac forced his gaze away from her face and around the room. "I like your home. The outside is beautiful. And the inside is comfortable and homey."

Before he'd arrived here at Ileana's, he'd pictured her as having a modest brick or siding house with a neat fenced lawn that would grow flowers and green grass in the summer. He'd been shocked to see her home was nothing like that. Perched on the steep mountainside, the place was wild and untouched, yet simple and inviting at the same time. Exactly like Ileana.

Across the table, Ileana blushed at his compliment. "Well, it's nothing fancy. But I'm not fancy. Since it's just me I keep things the way I like them."

Her gaze flickered shyly up to his. "What is your home like, Mac?"

He swallowed down a bite of pie before he answered. "Nothing this fine. I live in an old farmhouse on a hundred acres. The furnishings are things that I gathered up at old estate sales, and the yard consists of one mesquite tree, two oleander bushes and a few patches of Dallas grass. Every acre I own is flat and the dirt black."

"Sounds like farmland. Is this the same home where you grew up?"

Mac shook his head. "No. After Dad died Ripp and I didn't feel comfortable around our old family home. Dad's last year there was pretty rough. Guess those images were too hard for us to shake. So we decided to sell it."

She smiled gently, and Mac wondered if there had ever been a mean bone in her body. He very much doubted it. He couldn't imagine her swatting a pesky bug, much less raising her voice to anyone.

"Well, I'm sure the place you have now is very nice," she replied. "Do you do anything with the acreage?"

He could see a true interest on her face, and the sight drew him to her just that much more. Which didn't make sense. Mac had always believed a set of flirtatious eyes and red lips were the things about a woman that caught his attention. How was it that Ileana's simple curiosity about his life made him feel so pleased and important?

"I have twenty-five mama cows with calves at side, one bull and a couple of horses. With my deputy job, that's about all the cattle I have time to care for."

She nodded with understanding. "So who's watching out for your livestock while you're here in New Mexico?"

"Well, where I live we're fortunate enough to have a warm enough climate that the grass stays year-round. So we don't have to feed much in the winter—just a few cattle cubes, a molasses lick and a bit of hay. But to answer your question, a fellow deputy is taking care of them for me."

"Oh." Her gaze dropped to her plate, as though she was embarrassed about asking him personal questions. "I can't imagine it not getting cold there. Does it snow?"

Mac chuckled. "Maybe once every forty or fifty years. Palms and banana trees and tropical plants like that grow where I live. Have you never been to South Texas?"

She shook her head. "No. I've been to Fort Worth to a medical convention but that's all."

Even though she'd shown a bit of interest in his life,

Mac realized he was far more curious about hers. Which was something that continued to surprise him. Normally he didn't want to dig deep into a woman's psyche. If she had a pleasant personality that was enough for him. He didn't want to know what drove her. He didn't want to uncover the deep longings in her heart. But with Ileana, he found himself wanting to know anything and everything about her.

"That's a shame," he gently scolded. "You need to come over and visit your neighbor once in a while."

She put down her fork and picked up her coffee cup. "I don't have much time for travel. I don't like leaving my patients for very long. What about you? Do you travel much?"

His smile was a bit guilty. "No. I've only been to New Mexico once before and that was when I flew to Albuquerque to pick up a prisoner who was being extradited back to Bee County. Normally, the most traveling I do is driving over to Goliad County to visit with my brother."

"It sounds as though neither one of us strays too far from home."

"Sounds like," he agreed.

Rising from the table, she carried what was left of her pie over to a trash basket positioned at the end of the cabinet counter.

As she raked the scraps from the plate, she said, "My sister, Anna, lives here on the ranch so I don't have to drive but about a half mile to visit her."

"I've met her husband, Miguel. He seems like a genuine guy."

"Anna is very lucky to have Miguel. He adores her and their children, a son and two daughters."

"What about your brother, Adam? Where does he live?" Mac asked.

"Only a few miles from here, but he comes to the ranch a lot. He and his wife, Maureen, have two sons."

Mac had been totally surprised to see her dressed so casually in jeans and a T-shirt. He would have never expected her to even own a pair of jeans, but now that he could see her in them, he was darn glad she did. The worn denim clung to her rounded bottom and shapely thighs, giving him a nice hint at the body beneath.

"Chloe mentioned something about your siblings being twins. Is that right?"

She placed her dirty plate in the sink, then rejoined him at the table. "That's true. Adam and Anna are twins. Did she also tell you that they're actually my aunt and uncle, too?"

Her question caused him to do a double take, and he shook his head in confusion. "Pardon me, Ileana, did I hear you right? Your brother and sister are also your aunt and uncle, too? How did that happen?"

A wry smile touched her lips. "It's a long story. So to make it shorter, I'll just say that my grandfather, Tomas Murdock, was a—well, a bit of a rounder. He got involved with a woman less than half his age. Only none of his daughters knew about it until my aunt Justine came home one evening and found baby twins in a basket on the doorstep."

"Oh, hell. That sounds like a movie or something."

Ileana nodded. "I'm sure it does to you. But it really happened. And because Tomas had died a few months before, no one knew he was the father. It took a while, but Justine's husband, Roy, who was sheriff of Lincoln County at the time, finally figured it all out. Turns out the mother of the twins was my father's sister, Belinda Sanders."

"Amazing. So were Chloe and Wyatt married then? How did they end up with the twins?"

"My parents weren't married, but while all of this was being sorted out, they fell in love and married. At that time, it was thought that Chloe would never be able to give birth to a child of her own, so she and Wyatt adopted the twins. Thankfully, I came along shortly after and proved that prediction wrong."

Finished with his pie, Mac picked up his coffee cup. "What about Belinda, the biological mother?" he asked with a thoughtful frown. "Didn't she want the babies?"

A sad shadow crossed her face. "Belinda had a substance abuse problem that caught up to her. She died not long after she left the babies at the ranch. Seems she became totally distraught after Tomas died. I suppose she wasn't emotionally strong enough to deal with losing him and caring for two infants."

"That's a hell of a story," Mac said, then immediately shook his head with regret. "I didn't mean that in a disrespectful way, Ileana, I just meant—it's rather incredible. I can't imagine what your family must have been feeling about the babies and your grandfather. Total shock, I suppose."

Ileana nodded. "It was a scandal that rocked the whole county for a while. But now—well, I don't bother explaining to anyone how my siblings came to be. I only told you because...you're trying to figure out things about your family in the same way that mine had to. I thought it might help you to not feel so alone."

He glanced at her. "I think you just explained why

your mother offered to help me that first night we met. Chloe must have understood how I felt."

"I believe you're right about that."

His gaze studied her face, and he suddenly realized that when he now looked at this woman the word *plain* never entered his head. True, she wasn't painted with bright makeup, a chic hairstyle or flashy jewelry. But she had a quiet beauty that filled him with pleasure, a loveliness that wouldn't fade with age. Because it was a loveliness that came from deep within.

"So why did you want to help me?" he asked.

Her gaze suddenly fell to the tabletop, and her fingers fidgeted with the handle on her cup.

"I'm a doctor," she said after a moment. "Helping people is my business."

Now why did that answer disappoint him? Hell, what was he expecting her to say? That she'd taken a sudden liking to him? That something about him had touched a compassionate note in her? It didn't matter, he told himself. When it came right down to it, Ileana's opinion of him meant nothing at all.

Liar, liar. You actually think you can make yourself believe that, Mac?

Feeling restless now, Mac rose to his feet and meandered over to the patio door. Beyond the glass it was mostly dark, but he could see enough to discern that the mountainside was only a few feet away. He could see juniper and sage whipping in the wind, and in that wind fat snowflakes were flying and smacking into the glass in front of his face.

"It's snowing!" he exclaimed.

Behind him, Ileana left her seat at the table and walked over to where he stood.

"I didn't realize snow was in the weather forecast," she said softly as she peered out the window. "Maybe by morning you'll get to see a heavy blanket."

Her flowery scent and close presence was more than enough to distract him from the snowfall, and as he gazed at her warm auburn hair he couldn't stop his fingers from tangling in the tresses or his body from moving closer.

"I'd rather look at you, Ileana," he said simply.

He heard a little gasp escape her lips and then her head turned toward his. He could see uncertainty in her eyes, but he could also see longing, which was enough to justify pulling her into his arms.

"Mac," she breathed his name as his head bent toward hers. "This is all so new to me."

His lips brushed against hers as he spoke. "It's all new for me, too, Ileana."

Her expression dubious, she pulled slightly back from him. "But, Mac, you—"

"Yes, I've had a wife," he reasoned. "And I've had other women in my life. But none of them have been like you, Ileana. You're sweet and special, and I don't even know how to behave around you, much less treat you. All I know is that I want you. And I think you want me, too."

She emitted a groan that sent a surge of triumph through Mac and then suddenly her hands were resting against the middle of his chest, her lips were tilting invitingly up to his.

Mac closed the distance between their lips and wondered why his heart felt like it was singing.

Chapter 7

A moment later, as the search of Mac's lips deepened against hers, the only thought in Ileana's head was that she was playing with fire. And if the flames got out of control, she didn't have a clue as to how to douse them. Or if she even wanted to end the consuming heat.

The warmth of Mac's body was seeping into hers, melting her in the most delicious sort of way. His lips were setting off tiny explosions that made her head buzz and her whole body tingle. Instinctively she snuggled closer while her mouth opened to the seductive prod of his tongue. When it slipped past her teeth and began to mate with hers, a moan of surrender vibrated her throat; her hands slid upward and curved around the back of his neck.

How had she lived so long without this man? Why had it taken *him* to wake up the woman inside her?

The questions were racing wildly through Ileana's mind when the ringing of her cell phone crashed through to her senses.

Slowly, reluctantly, she broke the contact of their lips and stepped back. "I—it's—my phone," she said in a strangely garbled voice. "I have to get it."

She raced out of the kitchen, and, gulping in a ragged breath, Mac raked a shaky hand through his hair.

God, what was he doing? If the telephone hadn't interrupted them, he might have been on his way to seducing her. Is that what he really wanted? To make her just another one of his bed partners?

He shoved the frustrating questions aside as he heard Ileana answer the phone and begin to speak.

"Yes, I'm here. No. I hadn't planned on it. Codeine? No. She's had a bad reaction to it before. She's coughing because— Yes, I understand. But her heart is too weak."

There was another long pause, and Mac was beginning to wonder if she was speaking to someone about Frankie Cantrell, when Ileana said, "Tell her I'll be there in thirty minutes. Yes. Don't apologize. She's my patient."

As she stepped back into the kitchen, Mac waited expectantly while she snapped the phone shut and jammed it into her jeans pocket.

"I'm sorry, Mac," she apologized. "I have to go into the hospital."

It took a moment for him to digest her words, and when he did, he walked rapidly over to her. "I understand you're a doctor and that you have emergencies, but this—I guess it caught me off guard. And I—I'm selfish. Our evening has just started."

Her gaze clashed with his then awkwardly drifted

to the floor. "I wasn't supposed to be on call tonight," she admitted. "But my stand-in is having trouble with Frankie."

The unease that raced through Mac took him by surprise. Whether Frankie Cantrell was actually his mother or not, he didn't want anything to happen to the woman. Not when he'd gotten this close. Not when his life and that of his brother's was on this precipice of uncertainty. And certainly not now that he'd met Quint. The man loved and needed his mother. For Quint's sake, Mac wanted her to survive.

"Is this something serious? Has she had a setback?"

"I don't believe it's anything physical. But I need to go just the same."

She turned and started out of the kitchen. Mac quickly followed on her heels.

"Of course," he said. "I'll drive you to town."

She tossed him a look of surprise. "That isn't necessary, Mac. I've made the drive at night hundreds of times."

Quickly, she opened the coat closet and pulled out a heavy woolen jacket. As she shrugged into the garment, she headed over to a small desk where she'd left her handbag and truck keys.

"I don't care if you've made the drive a thousand times," he said. "It's snowing, and I don't want you to make the trip alone."

She studied him for one brief moment, then held her palms up in a gesture of acquiescence. "Okay. If that's what you want."

"I do."

He grabbed his hat and coat, and they quickly left the confines of the warm house. Outside the snowfall had grown much thicker, and the ground was beginning to turn white.

Even though Mac wasn't familiar with driving in such weather, he insisted on taking his newer truck. Fortunately, the highway wasn't yet beginning to pack, and all he had to concentrate on was following the unfamiliar crooks and turns through the mountains.

Across the console, Ileana wrapped her coat tightly around her and tried to gather her scattered senses. She wasn't quite sure what had just taken place between her and Mac. One minute they'd been talking and the next she'd found herself in his arms, kissing him, holding him as though she'd done it many times before.

In the dimness of the truck cab, her face burned at the memory of how she'd responded to him. And it wasn't embarrassment that was heating her face. It was the coals of lingering desire that were still warming her blood.

Clearing her throat, she said, "This is very good of you to drive me to the hospital."

"I'm glad to do it."

Why? she wondered. Where was this protective side of him coming from, and why did it make her feel so cared for?

She was studying his face, trying to decide whether to bring up the subject of that heated scene in the kitchen when he glanced over at her.

"I met Quint this morning."

His blunt statement took her totally by surprise. "Oh. How did that happen?"

"Your mother invited him to the Bar M."

Ileana bit back a groan. "And let me guess, she didn't let you in on it until Quint was already there."

"That's pretty much how it was."

Sighing, she said, "I don't know why she takes it upon herself to interfere in other people's business."

His gaze remained focused on the dark highway ahead of them, and Ileana wondered what he was thinking about her, their kiss, her family, everything. Never before had she wanted to get inside a person the way she did Mac. Sometimes he seemed so serious, and at other times he appeared to treat life very lightly. She doubted he'd ever revealed the true man to anyone.

"Is that what she does with you? Interfere?" he asked. "Is that why you don't live in the main ranch house?"

Ileana looked down at her lap. "She is not really an interfering mother. She cares—sometimes too much. But I have my own home because I like the privacy. And my parents deserve to have their privacy, too. Especially after raising three children. But as to why she called Quint, that's just her way of saying I care and I want to help fix things. She doesn't stop to think that her meddling might not be appreciated at times."

Mac shook his head. "I don't mind. Now that it's happened, I'm glad I met Frankie's son."

"How did that go? What does Quint think about the situation?"

He shrugged as though the meeting wasn't a big deal, but Ileana figured deep down it had to have been rough on him and Quint.

"Naturally, he's shocked. He can't believe his mother might have kept a past life hidden. But he sees the evidence is a little too coincidental to dismiss. He wants to find the truth just as much as Ripp and I. I offered to let him read Frankie's letter that I brought with me, and he took it back to the ranch with him."

"What about his sister, Alexa? Does she know about this yet?"

He nodded solemnly. "Quint said he called her this morning. I got the impression that he didn't like giving her the news."

"Alexa is pregnant. I guess he didn't want to upset her unduly. But hearing that sort of thing from someone other than him would have been far worse," Ileana explained.

Frowning, Mac shook his head in regret. "I'm sorry, Ileana, about all of this. Sometimes—" Pausing, he glanced at her. "Sometimes I wonder if I've done the right thing by coming here. Sometimes I wonder if Ripp and I, and everyone involved, would have been better off if we didn't know the truth of the matter."

It was easy to see that he was agonizing over his decision to search for his mother. It was also obvious that he didn't want to hurt anyone along the way. As Ileana studied his strong profile in the darkness of the cab, she wished that things could have been different for him. She wished with all her heart that she could make it all better.

"Sometimes the truth hurts, Mac. But so does going through life with agonizing questions at every turn."

"Yeah. But it doesn't look as though there are going to be any winners here."

"I wouldn't say that," she pointed out. "You don't know what's going to happen yet."

He looked at her, and the faint smile on his lips tugged at the very center of her heart. "Well, one good thing has come out of this—I met you."

Another flash of heat spiraled through her, and she forced her gaze on the falling snow in hopes it would cool her thoughts of this man who merely had to look at her to charm her.

"That's sweet of you to say, Mac."

After that their conversation turned sporadic as Ileana forced her attention on the worsening weather and Mac focused his efforts on getting the truck safely down the highway.

Thankfully, fifteen minutes later, they arrived safely at Sierra General. While Mac took a seat in the waiting room, Ileana fetched a stethoscope and Frankie's chart from the nurses' station as Renae gave her an update.

"Earlier tonight she was very restless. Her cough was worse, and she kept asking the nurses if her son had been around. And Annette caught her trying to get out of bed by herself. I know she's your family friend, Doc, but the woman is difficult. No, I take that back, she's spoiled rotten."

Ileana's lips pursed to a grim line. "I understand, Renae. Just do the best you can. If she's not having some sort of setback, I'm going to allow her to sit up tomorrow. Maybe that will help matters."

After a quick conversation with Jerry Vickors, Ileana hurried down the hallway to Frankie's room.

When she entered the small space, the head of the bed was raised slightly, and the television that was fastened to the wall in one corner was flickering a black and white classic movie. The woman's eyes appeared to be closed, but she must have heard the door swish as Ileana opened it, because she immediately turned her head toward the sound.

"Ileana," she said weakly, "what are you doing here?"

Ileana quickly walked over to her patient's bedside and reached for the blood pressure cuff hanging on the wall. As she wrapped it around the woman's upper arm, she said, "Dr. Vickers said you'd been coughing up a storm. I thought I'd better check on you."

Frankie's thin hand lifted from the sheet to wave dismissively. "It's that breathing machine that does it, Ileana. I told Dr. Vickers that, but he doesn't listen—" She broke off as a spasm of coughs shook her thin shoulders. Ileana didn't make any sort of reply as she pumped up the arm cuff. After she'd read the slightly elevated pressure, she said, "You tried to talk him into giving you codeine. You know better than that, Frankie. Am I going to have to put signs on your door warning the nurses that you're suicidal?"

The woman with blue eyes and black hair threaded with only a few gray streaks, frowned up at Ileana. "Don't be silly. I only wanted something to stop this damned coughing."

Ileana stuck a thermometer in her patient's ear and waited for the instrument to beep. "You wouldn't be coughing in the first place if you'd taken care of your heart condition months ago. In fact, you wouldn't be here in the hospital at all. You'd be home with your son."

Frankie closed her eyes as if to tell Ileana she didn't want to discuss the matter, but this time Ileana wasn't going to let her get off so easily. Frankie was her own worst enemy, and she wasn't stopping to think of the grief her stubbornness was causing her loved ones.

Another spate of coughing hit Frankie, but this time it was brief and not nearly as deep. "Ileana," she said after she'd caught her breath, "this isn't like you to be so mean. I thought you came back to make sure I wasn't dying."

Ileana bit back a groan. "You're not dying. In fact,

I think you're doing better. Tomorrow I'm going to let you get out of bed for a while."

This news totally surprised her. "Oh, really? Is that why Quint didn't come to see me this evening? You told him I was better?"

So Quint hadn't shown up to see his mother, Ileana thought, and that explains why she'd been asking the nurses about him. Quint usually didn't let one day go by without seeing Frankie, and Ileana could only suppose his visit with Mac had left him too upset to face her. Dear God, it was going to be awful if Mac's appearance here in Lincoln County tore the Cantrell family apart. Especially when it wasn't his fault what happened thirty years ago; he'd only been a small boy.

"No," Ileana assured her. "I haven't spoken to Quint today. I'm sure he's very busy. The weather is turning bad, and he has plenty of cattle to care for."

Ileana warmed the end of the stethoscope in her hand, then placed it to her patient's chest.

"I suppose he gets tired of driving in to see his old mother every day," she whined with a bit of self-pity. "He's young and has better things to do."

As Ileana listened to Frankie's heart, she wondered if this woman had truly left Mac and his brother behind, and if so, had she thought of them, longed for them? The whole idea troubled Ileana greatly, yet she did her best not to let it slant her opinion of her patient. She also told herself not to think of the sexy man who was sitting just down the hall waiting for her.

Satisfied with Frankie's heartbeats, Ileana helped the woman to a sitting position and placing the stethoscope to her back, focused on her lungs. After having Frankie breath in and out several times, Ileana straightened and cast her a firm look.

"Maybe Quint's tired of having a mother who refuses to help herself. Have you ever thought of that?"

Frankie sniffed. "Well, if that's the way he feels then he needs to say it to my face," she said, then sighed. "But at least he does show up. I can't say the same for Alexa."

If the woman weren't so sick, Ileana would have given her shoulder a good shake. "Alexa is hardly in any condition to be running up and down the highway every day between here and Santa Fe. You do want your grandchild to be born safely, don't you?"

For the first time since Ileana had walked into the room, a semblance of a smile touched Frankie's lips. "I can't wait for the little darlin' to arrive. It's the only ray of sunshine I've had since Lewis passed."

Hiding a sigh, Ileana reached over and pushed the disheveled black hair from Frankie's forehead. Under normal circumstances the woman was always fastidious about her appearance. Even at the age of sixty, she was very attractive, and Ileana had no doubt the woman could easily find another husband if she so wanted. But since Lewis had died, Frankie had simply been languishing in grief, and her heart condition was only complicating the whole matter.

"I'm glad you're happy. Focusing on something positive will help you get well more quickly."

"My children are all I live for," she murmured faintly.

Ileana studied the woman's haggard face and compared each feature to Mac's. Was there a resemblance? The nose? The cheekbones?

Carefully choosing her words, Ileana asked as casually as possible, "Frankie, did you, uh, ever want to have more children?"

The woman's brows puckered together. "What a strange question from you, Ileana."

Ileana forced an easy smile to her face. "Oh, the subject of Alexa's baby made the question cross my mind, that's all. Mom has always wished she'd had another child after me. I thought—well, you might have had the same sort of regrets."

Frankie turned her head so that her line of vision was on the picture window. Presently, the heavy drapes that framed the glass were partially opened, and Ileana could see the snow was continuing to fall at a heavy rate. Yet she got the feeling that Frankie was hardly watching the weather.

"I've often thought of other children—other babies. But I didn't think it would be fair to Lewis. A woman can't expect a man to take on more than he can bear." She sighed, then looked back at Ileana. "Are you getting the urge to have a child, Ileana?"

Ileana blushed. "Of course not. How could I be? I don't even have a boyfriend."

She reached up and patted Ileana's hand. "A woman can always dream, honey."

A few minutes later, after leaving Frankie's chart and written instructions at the nurses' station, Ileana walked down to the waiting area to find Mac in friendly conversation with an elderly gentleman and a young boy.

When he spotted Ileana approaching, he bade the two of them goodbye and hurried over to where she stood.

"Can you believe it? I found some vacationing Texans. The boy's dad had a skiing accident. They think his arm is broken."

His hand curled around her upper arm in a totally familiar way, and Ileana realized she was getting used to being touched by this man. She was even expecting it, liking it. Oh, God, what was she getting herself in to?

"How was Frankie?" he asked.

She swallowed at the tightness in her throat. "She's doing okay. Just being a bit fractious."

I've often thought of other children—other babies. Frankie's words whispered through Ileana's mind, and along with them came a haunting suspicion. But Ileana kept the thoughts to herself. Now wasn't the time for speculation. Mac had already been hurt enough in the past. He needed concrete proof, not assumptions.

"So it wasn't a dire emergency?"

"Thankfully, no. Are you ready to start back home? I'm thinking we'd better leave before the weather gets any worse."

"I'm thinking you're right."

With his hand at her back, they hurried out of the hospital. By now the wind had picked up and was blowing the heavy snowflakes in a horizontal direction. As they made their way across the parking lot, Ileana put up the hood on her coat and clung to Mac's arm to help steady her footsteps on the slippery ground.

Before they left the parking lot, Mac put the truck in four-wheel drive and drove the thirty miles back to the ranch at a slow and steady speed. Once they'd gotten to the Bar M, Mac gestured over to the main ranch house where a few lighted windows could be seen through the snow.

"Should we stop here? Or do you think we can make it up the mountain?"

She grimaced thoughtfully. "I'd really rather get home if at all possible. But if you'd rather not try it, I'll understand."

He allowed the truck to roll to a stop in the middle of the dirt road, then looked at her.

"Ileana, you know more about the driving conditions. If you were in your own truck right now, would you drive it up the mountain?"

"Yes. Sometimes I have to stop halfway up and walk the remaining distance to the house. But it's not that far and I'm wearing boots."

Enjoying this surprising, adventurous side of her nature, Mac laughed. "I'm wearing boots, too. So we'll see how far we can get."

Ten minutes later, after a few slips and slides up the road to Ileana's house, Mac parked his truck safely to one side, and they hiked the last thirty yards. By the time they were inside, their coats were covered with snow, and they were both shivering from the cold.

"I'll stoke up the fire," Ileana told him, "after I hang our coats where they can dry."

"I can deal with the fire," Mac said as he shrugged out of his coat and handed it to her. "Just show me where you keep the firewood."

"Follow me," she said.

In the kitchen, on the opposite wall from the cabinets, Ileana opened a wooden door that led into a large mudroom equipped with a washer and dryer and a double sink. While Ileana shook the coats, and hung them on wall pegs, she said, "The wood is stacked in a little alcove just out that door over there."

Mac stepped through the door and found himself in a lean-to of sorts. Thankfully, the open side was facing the east, sheltering him and the stacked firewood from the driving snow. As he took a moment to glance out, he could see the mountain directly behind the house was now a white wall. Since he wasn't at all familiar with this sort of weather, he had no idea of how bad it might get, and he wondered if he'd be wise to hurry off the mountain or risk being stranded.

Who was he kidding? he thought, as he stacked several pieces of wood in the crook of his arm. If he was going to be stranded with anyone, he'd want to be with this sweet angel of a doctor.

Back inside, Mac carried the wood to the living room and, after removing the screen on the fireplace, carefully stacked it on the low burning coals.

He was using a poker to fire up the coals when Ileana appeared from another part of the house. She'd brushed her long hair and buttoned a thin sweater over her T-shirt. And if Mac was seeing right, there was a bit of new pink color on her lips. The idea that she might have used the lipstick for his sake made him glad. Which was totally ridiculous. Most women wore lipstick regularly. At least, the ones he knew.

But not Ileana. She wasn't the glamour, take-a-look-at-me sort of girl. He figured it had to be something special to make her put a bit of color on her face. And he wanted to believe *he* was that something special.

Smiling tentatively, she eased a hip down on the arm of a stuffed chair. "I'm sure you weren't planning on getting this much of a lesson about our bad weather," she said.

"That's all right. It'll give me a story to tell Ripp whenever I get home."

Home. Right now it was hard for Mac to picture the rooms of his house, to feel the emptiness that touched him each time he stepped through the door. It was different for him here with Ileana and her family. Just being around them made him feel as though he was a part of something. How could that be, he wondered, when he'd only known them for a few short days?

"You could call him," Ileana suggested. "He might enjoy hearing that you're in the middle of a snowstorm."

Mac shook his head. "I tried dialing him earlier. I guess the weather has knocked out the tower signal. I couldn't get anything to work."

Ileana gestured toward a telephone sitting on a table at the end of the couch. "There's the landline. You're very welcome to use it."

"Thanks," he said with a half grin, "but I'll call him later. It's not necessary right now."

She rose from her seat and picked up the television remote lying on a coffee table made of varnished cedar. "I'll turn on the weather, and maybe we can find a forecast to tell us how much more of this we can expect."

The fire had begun to crackle merrily, so Mac put the screen back into position, then turned to see her searching through the channels.

He thrust a hand through his hair, then wiped it over his face. "Ileana, I'm wondering if I should head down the mountain to your parents' house. Otherwise, I might be stuck here tonight."

Her eyes wide, she glanced at him and then a bright blush stole across her cheeks.

"Oh. I didn't realize you were planning on going back to the ranch house tonight. The weather isn't fit for any more traveling. You really should stay here with me."

Chapter 8

Utterly stunned by her comment, he took a few uncertain steps toward her. "When I drove you up here, I did it because I wanted to see you home safely. But I—well, staying here certainly hadn't crossed my mind."

She placed the remote on the coffee table, then straightened to face him. Mac was surprised to see her gaze didn't flinch shyly away from his when she spoke.

"Why not? I have a guest room. You should find it comfortable. Much more comfortable than traipsing through the snow again."

Mac could hardly argue that point. But staying here with Ileana somehow felt indecent. Maybe he felt that way because she was so prim and proper. Or maybe it was because his mind was drifting to places that were far from appropriate.

"I'm sure you're right about that." He rubbed his chin

with his thumb and forefinger. "But what about your parents? They're going to be expecting me to show up. They're probably already wondering why I haven't."

Not bothering to reply, she walked over to the telephone and quickly punched in a number. After a few short moments, she began to speak, "Mom, it's me. Yes. I…that was our lights… I had to go to the hospital. Mac drove me. No. Everything is okay there. I wanted to let you know that Mac is going to stay here at my place tonight. The mountain is getting icy. Yes, we will. Yes, I'll tell him. Good night."

Ileana hung up the phone and looked at him. "She thinks you're doing the smart thing. And the snow is supposed to level off by morning. If necessary, Dad will send up a tractor to help you get your truck off the mountain."

"It does make sense," Mac said more to himself than to her. "I just don't have anything with me. Not even a toothbrush."

"I have a new one that's still in its box. And if you're worried about clean clothes, my brother left a few of his clothes with me a while back to give to a charity in town, and I've never completed the chore. He's pretty much your size. In fact, there might even be pajamas if…you need them."

Mac grinned. "Thanks, Ileana, I might take you up on a pair of clean jeans in the morning. But as for the pajamas I wouldn't know what to do with them."

"It gets very cold up here on the mountain. As you'll find out tonight."

"I'll survive." Just thinking about her was enough to keep him warm, he thought.

She slid her palms nervously down the thighs of her

jeans, then rose to her feet. "Well, I'll go make us something warm to drink. Would you like more coffee or hot chocolate?"

"Hot chocolate would be nice," he told her.

She gestured to the couch. "Sit down. Make yourself comfortable. It won't take me long."

"I'll just keep you company in the kitchen. If you don't mind," he added.

The corners of her mouth tilted upward. "I wouldn't mind at all."

Mac followed her into the other room, and while she pulled out milk and fixings for the drink, he walked over to the patio door and looked out.

"I can hear the wind howling out there," he said. "I hate to think of the wildlife and livestock having to deal with this brutal weather. Does your mother care for her horses any differently when it gets this cold?"

She chuckled softly. "Believe me, Mac, Mother coddles her horses at all times. Right now they're snug in their stalls. They're all wearing blankets, a barn heater is blowing and a radio is playing music for them. They're happy."

He turned away from the glass door and walked over to where Ileana was working at the cabinet counter. Her head was bent slightly, making her dark auburn hair slide forward to curtain her face. The few times he'd touched her hair, the rich, shiny strands had been soft and silky against his hands, and he found himself wanting to bury his fingers in them again, to gather them in his fist and draw her close against him. What would she think? That he was a jerk? Or would she be glad to surrender in his arms? Usually Mac could read a woman. But he was learning that nothing about Ileana was the same as other women.

Jamming his hands in his pockets, he said, "How long has your mother been interested in racing horses?"

"Since she was a little girl. From the time she could walk, my grandfather would take her to the track with him. So she caught the bug early on. By the time he died, he'd already taught her most everything he knew about training racehorses. Mother says she's one of those people who have been blessed with getting to do a job that she loves."

Mac studied her thoughtfully as she stirred powdered cocoa and sugar together. "You're doing a job that you love, aren't you?"

One of her slender shoulders lifted and fell. "Yes. But I don't think I get quite the same enjoyment that Mother does from hers. When one of her horses finishes at the top, she's jumping up and down, laughing and yelling. She stays on a high for days afterward. Now me, when I see someone pull out of a serious illness I just feel glad inside. That's all."

"Hmm. Well, it makes you happy just the same, doesn't it?"

She glanced up at him, and Mac was smitten with the way her blue eye was playing peekaboo with the strand of hair resting on her brow. The woman was sexy, he realized. And she didn't even know it.

"I suppose."

"Is there anything that would make you happier than being a doctor?"

Her gaze quickly fell to mixing bowl on the counter. "I've never thought about it that much," she said softly. "Maybe…having a child. That would make me very happy."

Yes. He could see where this woman might long to be a mother. With her soft hands and gentle, nurturing ways, she seemed made for the part. Yet on the other hand, he couldn't quite imagine her making wild, passionate love to a man. Unless, maybe that man was him.

What the hell are you thinking, Mac? Ileana doesn't want to make love to you. And she sure as heck wouldn't want a child of yours!

Why wouldn't she want a child of mine? Mac asked the pestering voice in his head. What was wrong with him, besides being a little arrogant and selfish and a set-in-his-ways bachelor?

Don't bother answering those questions, Mac. You gave up wanting children long ago. When you mentioned having babies to Brenna and she laughed in your face.

Ileana poured the cocoa and milk in a large pot and carried it over to the gas range. As she adjusted the flame beneath it, she said, "I don't know if you're aware of this or not, but Mother first met Frankie at Ruidoso Downs."

Her statement grabbed Mac's attention and jerked his mind off his meandering thoughts. "No. I didn't know that. What was Frankie doing there?"

"Working in the concession."

"So she'd needed a job when she first arrived in Ruidoso," he said thoughtfully.

"I think so. I remember Mother saying that Frankie was pretty down and out. She helped her find an affordable place to live and eventually a better job as a file clerk in a local savings and loan."

Mac crossed the space between them and stood next to her at the stove. "How did she meet Lewis?"

"Through my parents. They were giving a party for some of the local ranchers, and Mother had invited both of them. I guess you could say the rest is history. They fell in love and got married not long after they met. Now Frankie is shattered over losing him."

She must have adored her second husband, Mac thought, whereas, she must have hated Owen. Why else would she have left his father? He couldn't answer that. Not until he knew whether the Frankie lying in the hospital bed was one and the same.

"This is almost ready," she said. "If you'd like, you can find two mugs over in the cabinet next to the sink."

Glad for the distraction, Mac fetched the cups. After Ileana filled them, they carried their drinks into the living room and took seats on the couch.

For the next hour, Mac urged her to tell him more about the Bar M and her family. Eventually she pulled out a scrapbook of photos and pointed out special places and occasions that had happened over the years.

Mac was surprised at how much he enjoyed hearing her talk about simple family things, at how much her voice soothed him, seduced him into thinking the two of them were in a world all their own.

But eventually, she put the photos away and announced she was tired and needed to retire for the night.

Mac could have easily sat next to her all night for no other reason than to simply be near her, but he understood she'd put in a stressful day at work, not to mention the long added trip of going into town to check on Frankie. No doubt she was exhausted.

Rising from the couch, he said, "I'm sorry I've kept you up so late, Ileana. I wasn't thinking."

Standing on the hearth, she looked across at him. "Don't be silly. I stayed up because I've enjoyed talking with you. This evening has been special for me."

Special. Yes, that word kept coming to Mac's mind, too. And wouldn't his brother's jaw drop if he could see him now, enjoying a quiet evening at home with a woman who considered her brain much more important than her looks? Yes, Ripp would be surprised at this change in his brother but not nearly as surprised as Mac himself. Getting to know Ileana was something very new for a man like him. And very special.

Something suddenly swelled in Mac's chest, but he did his best to ignore the feeling as he gestured toward the fireplace. "Should I put more wood on the fire tonight?"

Ileana shook her head. "Once the fire burns out, the central heating will take over." She stepped off the hearth and walked over to him. "Come along, and I'll show you your room."

Mac followed her out of the living room and down a short hallway. At the very end, she opened a door on her left and, after flipping on the light, motioned for him to enter.

"It's been a while since anyone has stayed overnight with me. But I'm certain the sheets are clean," she said as she trailed behind him. "If you should get cold there's more blankets in the closet, and behind that door in the corner is your own private bathroom. And while I think of it, I'll go get you that toothbrush."

She hurried out of the room, and Mac walked over to the standard-size bed covered with a patchwork quilt done in bright blues and yellows. The room was spacious and comfortably furnished with plain pine furniture, including a rocking chair and a small cedar chest at the end of the bed. More photos of horses, the Saunders family and areas of the ranch hung on all the walls.

No doubt she was proud of her heritage and her home. And no doubt she'd never be willing to leave it.

God, Mac, why would that thought ever enter your head? Ileana is just a nice woman that you're getting to know. That's all.

But it felt like so much more when she returned to the room and his gaze encountered her smiling face.

"Here you go. I brought a tube of toothpaste with it." She handed him the slender boxes. "Everything else you might need should be in the bathroom."

"I'm sure I'll be comfortable," he said. Then on second thought he asked, "Will you be going into town tomorrow for your hospital rounds?"

Reaching up, she ran a hand over her hair, and Mac could see that she was weary. The sight made him want to scoop her up and carry her to bed, to stroke and cuddle her and then in the morning make breakfast for her.

"Thankfully, I'm not on duty tomorrow. Dr. Vickers will be on call all weekend."

"What about Frankie? You made a special trip in for her."

"I don't plan on doing that again. I've left certain instructions for Dr. Vickers, and he's perfectly capable of handling her illness while I'm off."

"That's great!" Mac exclaimed, then figuring that didn't sound quite right, he added, "I mean, it's good that you'll have time off to rest."

"Yes." She smiled faintly. "Maybe we could do something special together tomorrow."

There was that word again, Mac thought. Then unable to stop himself, his hand reached out to settle on her shoulder.

"Ileana, I—"

Feeling more awkward than he ever had in his life, his words broke off and her eyes widened in question, then flickered with something that looked to Mac like longing. Or was that just a mirror of his own feelings?

He swallowed and tried again. "I just wanted to say that earlier—before we drove into Ruidoso—that kiss…it was, well, I'd not meant for it to get so out of hand. But I'm going to be honest and admit that I'm glad it did."

He could hear her soft intake of breath, and then her eyes softened in a way that melted his heart.

"I'm glad that it got out of hand, too," she whispered shyly.

The urge to jerk her into his arms warred with his silent vow to be a gentleman and the violent tug on his emotions was something he'd never experienced before.

His eyelids drooped as he gently trailed his fingers over her hair.

"I think we'd better say good-night," he murmured. "Or I might not let you out of this room."

Her bottom lip quivering ever so slightly, she looked at him for long moments. Then finally she let out a long breath and nodded.

"Good night, Mac."

Slowly, reluctantly, he released his hold on her shoulder, and she quickly turned and left the room. As soon as the door shut behind her, Mac eased down on the side of the bed and tried to gather his senses.

What in hell was happening to him?

When Ileana awoke the next morning, sunshine was streaming through the bedroom window, and the smell of bacon and coffee was filtering beneath the door.

The fact that Mac was already up and obviously cooking had her jumping quickly out of bed and racing to the bathroom. When she emerged a few short minutes later, she pulled a pink chenille robe over her gown and hurried through the house.

When she entered the kitchen, she found Mac standing at the range, turning sizzling bacon strips with a long fork. On top of the refrigerator, a transistor radio was playing sixties rock, while on the dining table two places were neatly set with plates, silverware and napkins.

To have a man in her kitchen doing such things was a shock to Ileana's senses, and for a moment she simply stood in the open doorway staring at him.

He must have sensed her presence, because he suddenly looked over his shoulder and smiled brightly at her. "Good morning, sunshine! Ready for breakfast?"

Shoving her tumbled hair off her face, she walked over to him. He was wearing the same jeans and shirt he'd been wearing last night, only he hadn't bothered buttoning the shirt, and it flapped open to show a tempting strip of skin and chest hair.

If having him in the house wasn't enough to shake her up, the sight of his bare chest was. "Yes, I think so. Are you always this chipper in the morning?"

"Depends on how many beers I have the night before," he teased.

She rubbed fingers over her puffy eyes. "Well, I'm a deep sleeper, so I apologize for looking and sounding so groggy."

"You look very pretty to me."

The man had to be legally blind and in desperate need of glasses, she thought. The mirror didn't lie and yet Mac had a way about him that made her feel pretty and attractive, and that was something she'd never experienced in her life before.

Clearing her throat, she said, "Did you find everything you needed?"

"Eggs, bacon and biscuits. If you have some jelly to go with them, that would be nice."

Her brows lifted as she looked at the back panel of the range to see that the oven was baking. "Biscuits? You know how to make biscuits?"

He laughed at her dismay. "I found your dry mix. It was easy."

"But you have to knead them, roll them out and cut them!"

Laughing, he held up a hand in defense. "Sorry. I'm not that good. I just dropped them from the spoon. But they'll be edible."

Just to look at the man, she figured the most he would know about cooking was to open a can of soup or slap a sandwich together. He'd totally surprised her. Something he'd been doing ever since she'd first spotted him in Sierra General.

"I can't wait to try them," she said.

She left him tending the meat, and after placing jelly and honey on the table, she opened the drapes to the patio. The mountain blocked out the sun, but the white coat of snow on the ground illuminated everything.

"Hey, that looks like a winter wonderland," Mac said as he placed the plate of bacon on the table. "Do you have a sled?"

"No."

"What about skis?"

She joined him at the table. "Yes. Put away in the attic. Do you know how to ski?"

He laughed. "Only on water. Remember, where I come from we don't ever see this stuff." He gave her a suggestive wink. "I'm trying to picture you as a little ski bunny with a stethoscope."

She laughed. "I put that away when I'm on the slopes. But it's been a long time since I've skied. I guess as a person grows older work starts to replace play."

"Unfortunately," he agreed as he pulled out a chair and gestured for her to take a seat. "Everything is ready, my lady. Just sit and let yourself be served."

Feeling ridiculously pampered, Ileana eased down in the chair and waited while he placed the rest of the food on the table, then served her a small glass of orange juice along with a cup of coffee. And all the while he moved about her, the only thing Ileana could think of was the way he'd kissed her last night, the way he touched her hair, the way he'd intimated that he wanted to make love to her.

Make love to *her!* The thought of it had kept Ileana awake long after she'd gone to bed and thinking of it now made every nerve inside her shiver. Would she be a fool for encouraging him? He would eventually be heading back to Texas. But, oh my, he was here with her now. And this might be her only chance to taste real love. To pass it up would be like closing her eyes to a beautiful sunrise.

They consumed the rich breakfast—and delicious biscuits—and then Ileana cleaned the dishes while Mac took a shower and changed into a set of her brother's old clothing.

He emerged into the kitchen just as Ileana was hanging a damp dish towel. The worn flannel shirt was just a bit snug, and she swallowed hard as her gaze traveled over his hard, muscular body.

"I'm all finished here," she said. "If you'll excuse me, I'll go get dressed, and then if you like we can walk down and check on your truck."

"Fine," he said. "While you're doing that, I'll stoke up the fireplace."

Hurrying to her bedroom, Ileana searched out a pair of jeans and a red, cable-knit sweater with a turtleneck. After jerking the clothes on and a pair of snow boots, she pulled her hair into a ponytail and swiped on a dab of lipstick.

Mac was waiting for her in the living room, and she fetched a barn coat and a plaid muffler from the closet before they headed outside onto the deck.

"Wow! This is spectacular," Mac exclaimed as they paused to lean against the railing and gazed out across the snow-covered mountains. "Too bad it isn't Christmas. I've never seen a white one."

Just having him with her felt like Christmas to Ileana. Excitement was surging through her, making her suddenly feel very young and carefree. She wanted to laugh and smile, the same reckless way her mother did whenever she won a derby.

She pulled on a red knit cap, then latched on to Mac's arm. "Come on," she urged, "let's walk down the mountain and see how bad the road looks."

The steep wooden steps were practically hidden beneath the deluge of snow, making their descent slow and cautious. Once they reached the ground, they discovered the depth of the white powder was over a foot deep and almost reached the top of Ileana's boots.

It took them a few minutes to make the trek from the driveway to Ileana's house, down the mountain road to where they'd left Mac's truck. When they finally reached the vehicle, they stared in amazement at the high drifts of snow piled around it.

"Do I have a truck under there somewhere?" Mac joked.

"I'm so sorry, Mac."

They were standing close together in the middle of the road, and now Mac glanced at her.

"Why should you be sorry?" he asked, amusement curving his lips. "You didn't make it snow."

The morning was perfect with bright sun and no wind. The snow acted like an insulator, buffering the sounds around them, except for one lone cry in the sky. Ileana glanced up to see a hungry hawk circling the valley below. She understood the bird's lonely frustration. She'd lived it for most of her adult life.

"No. But I caused you to get stranded. And now you can't get down to the main ranch house. Unless one of the hands brings a bulldozer up here after you."

His arm suddenly snaked around her back and edged her closer to him. "Why would I want to do that?" he asked lowly. "Don't you think this is where I want to be? With you?"

She began to shake and her trembles had nothing to do with the cold. "I… I don't know, Mac."

With his eyes locked on hers, he curled his other arm around her waist and pulled her forward against his chest. Her heart hammering, her head tilted back, she watched the smile on his face disappear, his gaze turn sober.

"Oh, Ileana, you don't know much about men, do you?"

Her head swung back and forth. "I know how to treat one whenever he has an illness."

"Then I'd better let you know that I'm sick—sick to have you in my arms. Hurting to make love to you."

Ileana was too stunned to form any sort of reply. But then words didn't appear to be what he wanted from her anyway. Like the hawk she'd spotted earlier, his lips swooped down on hers in a kiss that was rough and tender, shocking and delicious.

With a tiny moan of surrender, Ileana flung her arms around his neck and pressed herself against him. Mac's hold on her tightened as his lips slanted hungrily over hers, searching, prodding, asking her for things she'd never been asked for before.

If she opened her eyes, she felt the sky would be whirling around their heads, or was it the center of her being that was spinning out of control? She didn't know. The only thing she knew was that she wanted to get closer; she wanted this man in the most basic way a woman could want a man.

She couldn't have guessed how long the kiss went on. But by the time he finally tore his mouth from hers, she was gulping for air, and her knees were on the verge of collapsing.

"Oh, sweet angel," he whispered against her cheek. "I never expected to want you like this. I never expected to feel like this."

"Neither…did I." She tried not to groan out loud as

his nose nuzzled the stretchy fabric of her cap away from her ear and his teeth sank gently into the soft lobe.

His mouth nibbled at her ear, then tracked a moist trail back to her lips. After another long kiss that completely robbed Ileana of breath, she clung to his shoulders for support while her head tilted back and away from his tempting lips.

"Mac, we're standing in foot-deep snow! Don't you think we should go inside?"

For a moment he looked totally dazed and then a grin appeared and he began to chuckle. The sound was so warm and nice and infectious that Ileana immediately began to chuckle, too.

"I knew you had more sense than any woman I ever knew!" He grabbed her hand and began to tug her up the hill.

After several slips and falls that had both of them rolling and laughing like children in the snow, they made it onto the deck and into the house.

Once inside, they shed their wet boots and coats in the short foyer; then in silence, Mac took her by the hand and led her into the bedroom where he'd slept the night before.

Earlier this morning he'd straightened the bedcovers, and now he placed Ileana gently on top of the quilt and then stretched out beside her. As he gathered her to him, he could feel her trembling and felt his own heart hammering out of control.

"Are you cold?" he whispered against the top of her head. "Do you want to get under the quilt?"

She leaned her head back far enough to look at him, and Mac spotted something in her eyes, a forlorn plea that touched his heart, thickened his throat.

"I'm fine. I just...this is something I've never done before, Mac. I'm afraid I'll ruin everything. You'll be disappointed and—" Too choked to go on, she closed her eyes and pressed her cheek against his.

With a hand on her shoulder, he eased her back from him. "Ileana? My God, are you—are you telling me you're a virgin?"

A blush stung her face as her head barely moved in an up and down direction. Even though he'd suspected that Ileana had never had sex, he was still stunned by her statement, shocked to think she'd gone all these years without being physically connected to a man. And all he could do was stare at her as though he was seeing a different Ileana, one that was far too precious for him to touch.

"Please, please Mac. Whatever you're thinking—just don't laugh at me."

The anguish on her lovely face tore right through Mac. How could she ever think he'd want to hurt her in such a way? Had some other man insulted her innocence? If so, he wanted to kill him.

"Laugh? Oh, sweetheart, nothing about this is amusing. I'm—" He shook his head in wonder. "I'm thinking all these years—you've saved yourself for your husband."

Closing her eyes, she cupped her hands around his face. "In the beginning, when I was very young and romantic," she whispered. "Now, I—I've just been saving myself for the right man. And that's you, Mac."

Chapter 9

Mac had never felt so humbled or special in his life. Nor had he ever felt anything so valuable in his arms.

Groaning with misgivings, he said, "Ileana, sweet, sweet, Ileana. I don't have the right to do this. And later, after I'm gone, you'll have regrets—and I don't want—"

Before he could finish, she lifted her head and pressed kisses on his cheek. "Now is not the time for you to go all gentlemanly on me, Mac. The only regret I'd have is if you go without making love to me. I'm not in my twenties anymore. I've waited a long, long time for a special man to come along and look at me. You're here, and I don't intend to let you leave before we are together."

And he couldn't leave, Mac thought. Hell, it would probably kill him if he tried to get off the bed and leave her now. Just having her sweet voice in his ear, her soft little hands stroking his face was enough to cause explosions of desire beneath his skin. Besides, she needed him almost as much as he needed her. He could hear it in her voice, feel it in her touch. The knowledge filled him with a power that left him trembling.

"I'm not going anywhere, my lovely girl," he whispered against her ear, then with another hungry groan, he brought his lips on hers.

Over and over he kissed her until Ileana's senses were whirling, her body twisting into fiery, agonizing knots. Need began to consume every inch of her, dictating her every move.

Desperate for any sort of relief she could find, her fingers reached for the buttons on his shirt and fumbled until she had the two pieces of fabric pulled apart and his hard chest exposed for the pleasure of her exploring hands.

As her fingers skimmed his heated skin, she could hear the sharp intake of his breath, feel the tightening of his abs, and his reaction amazed her, pushed her reticence behind and emboldened her exploration.

Soon his hands were plunging beneath her sweater, sliding up her rib cage until his palms were cupping her breasts, his fingers kneading her nipples through the thin lace of her bra. But eventually the barrier of fabric became an offensive intrusion, and he broke the contact of their lips in order to lift the sweater over her head.

When her bra followed the garment onto the floor, Ileana had expected to be completely embarrassed by the exposure of her naked breasts. But there was such a tender, reverent look in his eyes that all she could feel was utter happiness, a need to give him more and more.

"You're so lovely, Ileana," he said huskily as his gaze

devoured the picture she made lying against the patchwork quilt. "So precious."

Bending his head, he placed a trail of moist kisses across her throat, along her collarbone, then down the valley between her breasts. Each patch of skin that his lips touched sizzled like water drops on a heated frying pan. But when his mouth finally settled over one budded nipple, the sizzles turned to outright explosions, and in a matter of moments she was writhing against him, silently begging him to make their connection complete.

When he finally lifted his head and looked questioningly down at her, she pressed her palm against the region of his heart. It was thumping rapidly against her fingers, almost as rapidly as her own heart was beating behind her breast. And once again, Ileana was amazed that she could have that much effect on this man. That she could actually fill him with that much excitement.

"Love me, Mac," she whispered breathlessly. "That's all I ask."

He drew in a deep, shuddering breath. "And that's all I want, baby. To love you."

She sighed, and then in a low, awkward rush, she quickly informed him that he didn't need to worry about birth control; she was protected with the Pill. "I—my GYN prescribed it for me—for reasons other than sex."

Smiling down at her, he reached for the zipper on her jeans. "Now you have one more reason for taking it," he said in a wickedly suggestive voice.

In a matter of moments he'd stripped away the remainder of their clothing, and as he rejoined her on the bed, their arms and legs tangled like a moonflower vine waiting to bloom in the dark.

Mac's hands and lips spread magic over Ileana's

body, stroking and touching, tasting and teasing. In turn, Ileana took her cue from him and used her own hands to express the needs that were crying out within her body. As her fingers explored the hard length of his muscles, raced over his feverish skin, she realized she didn't want to just receive pleasure. She wanted to give. She wanted to send his senses to the same height he was sending hers.

Yet when he rolled her onto her back and his mouth made a slow descent up her thigh, she was so lost in sensation that all she could do was grip the quilt in her two fists and wait with an anticipation that was nigh to painful.

"Let me taste you, Ileana," he murmured hoarsely. "Let me taste your sweetness."

Stunned at what he was about to do, she had no strength to protest, and then when his tongue gently probed at the intimate petals of her womanhood, any protest she might have had evaporated.

"Oh! Oh, Mac! Mac, I need you!"

She'd barely uttered the garbled words when wave after wave of incredible sensations began to wash over her. Her upper body strained toward him, and then her control slipped. Mindlessly her fingers dug into the flesh of his shoulders while she splintered into a thousand shards of glittering crystal.

Moments later, as she floated back to reality she was certain her body was incapable of feeling more, but Mac instantly proved that wrong as he shifted his position so that his mouth was back on hers, scorching her senses, stirring the simmering fire in her loins.

"I can't keep going, honey," he muttered. "I have to get inside you."

Wordlessly, she wound her arms around his back and urged him down to her. "I want us to be together, Mac. Like this. As one."

Mac's desire was already near the breaking point. But something about her voice caused him to rein in his needs. This wasn't just about him. Ileana was rewarding him with everything she had to give, and he wanted this time for her to be even more glorious than her dreams.

Cupping his hands along the sides of her face, he bent his head and kissed her trembling lips.

"Hang on to me, my darling," he whispered against her mouth. "Hang on and don't let go."

He entered her as slowly and gently as was humanly possible. During the process he could feel her flinch and draw back. When that happened, he focused his attention on her lips, teasing and tugging with his teeth and tongue, while at the same time giving her time to adjust to having him inside of her.

When a moan of need finally sounded deep in her throat and her hips began to thrust upward toward his, he was sure the bed rocked beneath them. Stars exploded behind his eyes, and the only thing that existed at that moment was her soft, pliant body surrounding him, her eager hands racing over him, her lips pressing kisses across his chest.

The more he tried to restrain his thrusts and make it all last for her, the more he pushed them both over the edge. For Mac, time could have stopped or spun even faster. All he knew was that he suddenly felt her body tightening, convulsing, and then he had no choice but to fly straight toward the sky and burst through the clouds.

Mac was still trying to gather his breath and his dazed senses when he felt her faint stirrings beneath him. At some point his weight had collapsed on her, and now it took all the strength he could muster to roll to one side.

Even opening his eyes took great effort, and as he glanced over at Ileana he wondered what she'd done to him. Sex had never drained him like this before.

That wasn't just sex, Mac. You poured out a part of your heart to her. And you might as well get used to being weak because you're never going to be whole again.

He tried to push the thoughts away, tried to convince himself that this encounter with Ileana was nothing different. Yet as she opened her eyes and looked at him, he knew he was lying to himself. Everything about being with Ileana had felt new and earth-shattering.

"Mac."

As she breathed his name, the corners of her mouth tilted upward in a gentle smile, and Mac felt his heart melt like snow beneath a hot sun.

Her hand fell weakly toward him. He picked it up and hauled it to his mouth where he kissed each finger, then the middle of her palm.

"Ileana. Oh, Ileana." It was all he could say as he reached for her and pulled her body alongside his.

Ileana shyly nestled her head in the crook of his arm and closed her eyes. She'd never felt so utterly satiated, so completely content in her life. Mac had made love to her, and their union had been more than she could have ever dreamed or hoped that it would be.

"I'm so happy," she murmured.

His fingers meshed in the crown of her hair, then stroked down the long strands. "I'm glad that you're happy."

"Was I…terribly awkward?"

Her question must have caught him off guard because he didn't answer immediately. But then his brown eyes looked tenderly into hers.

"Awkward? Oh, honey, you couldn't have been more perfect."

She chuckled softly. "You don't have to overdo it, Mac."

Smiling seductively, his hand slid from her shoulder, down the slope of her rib cage and onto the rise of her hip. "You're one spicy doctor. And as soon as you give me a few minutes to recoup, I'm going to show you there's no such thing as overdoing it."

By the time they emerged from the house later that evening, the sun had melted at least half of the snow. Mac drove his truck up the hill and parked it in Ileana's driveway, but neither of them mentioned him going back to the Bar M. Although, as he shoveled snow off the front deck of the house and tossed it over the railing, the notion was following Mac around like a giant elephant.

What the hell did he think he was doing? He couldn't just camp here with Ileana and then in a few days walk away as though nothing had happened.

Why not? You've done it plenty of times before.

Damn it, why was he suddenly developing such a conscience? Ever since his giant mistake with Brenna, love 'em and leave 'em had been his motto. He didn't break promises because he didn't make them in the first place. He didn't expect a woman to love him. And he didn't want a woman to love him. His rules made everything easy.

But nothing felt easy when he looked at Ileana, when

he took her into his arms and kissed her. Why did it feel so good, so right? Why did the sky and everything around him seem a bit brighter?

A few minutes later, when Ileana came out of the house carrying an armful of crumpled papers and a box of matches, Mac was still asking himself those questions. But they weren't nearly as important as watching a smile spread across her face or enjoying this short time he had to spend with her.

"Do you like hot dogs?" she asked cheerfully.

"Sure. Why, are you getting hungry?"

"Famished." She gestured over to an iron fire pit sitting in one corner of the deck. "I thought we might build a fire out here on the deck and roast hot dogs for our supper. Unless you're too cold."

"Too cold! Are you kidding? This Texan is getting used to thirty-degree weather," he teased.

She laughed. "Okay, tough guy, if you'll pull the pit over here in the center of the deck, we'll get the fire going."

Mac positioned the large, bowl-shaped fire pit, then fetched wood from the lean-to at the back of the house. While he got the fire roaring, Ileana went to the kitchen and gathered the makings of the hot dogs.

Before long they were sitting on camp stools, roasting hot dogs over the warm campfire, while in front of them the evening sun was quickly dipping behind the mountains. Purple shadows were spreading across the deck, enveloping them in soft shadows. As Mac watched firelight flicker across Ileana's face, he couldn't remember doing anything so simple or pleasant.

"Do you do this often?" Mac asked.

She shook her head. "No. Adam gave me the fire

pit as a Christmas gift one year, but I rarely use it. Sitting out here alone isn't—well, it isn't enjoyable unless someone is with me."

God, how many times had he sat on his front porch at home, looked out at his cattle grazing and wondered why it all didn't make him happier? Ileana had stated it simply and perfectly. It took two to make a place mean something.

"Yeah. I know what you mean," he said, then before he could stop himself, he reached over and clasped her free hand with his. "Ileana, we haven't talked about this. But now that some of the snow has melted I can drive back down the mountain to the ranch house tonight—if you want me to."

Her fingers tightened around his as she looked at him. "That's true. You can leave now if you want. But I…hope you want to stay."

Emotions totally strange to Mac suddenly swelled in the middle of his chest. "I want to stay."

Her shy smile was all it took to make him feel like the most special man on earth.

Chapter 10

By Sunday evening it had sunk in on Mac that in the past twenty-four hours he'd done two things he'd not done since he and Brenna had divorced nearly fifteen years ago. He'd stayed all night in a woman's bed. And he'd gone to church with her.

Maybe to most men those things didn't sound like life-changing events, but the more Mac chewed on it, the more he recognized that Ileana was changing him. *Had* changed him. Where was it all going to lead? How was he going to go back to Texas and be the Mac he used to be? Could he go back to being that man?

There couldn't be any question about that, he thought, as he sat at Ileana's dining table, sipping at a cup of coffee that had grown cool while he waited for her to finish a few business calls. He had to go back to Bee County, and the sooner he did, the sooner he'd remember who he was, what he was. He'd get his life back to normal.

"I'm sorry about that, Mac," Ileana said a moment later as she stepped into the kitchen. "Dr. Vickers had several things to go over with me."

After church this morning, Ileana had changed into a pair of jeans and a striped shirt. Now as she moved over to the cabinet counter, Mac's gaze traveled appreciatively over the thrust of her breasts, the curve of her bottom and the shape of her thighs. Just looking at her filled him with visions of creamy skin and rosy nipples, teased his senses with the scent of lilac and the warmth of her soft body.

He clutched the cold cup while wondering why his desire for the woman never seemed to be quenched. "Problems?"

Smiling, she said, "No. In fact, he says that over the past two days Frankie has made a big stride toward getting well. Once she was finally able to sit up for an extended time, it's greatly helped her lungs."

Frankie was getting better. That meant he would soon be able to visit with the woman. And no matter how that visit turned out, his time here in New Mexico would end. Only moments earlier, he'd been telling himself he needed to go home. So Ileana's news should have thrilled him. Instead, his insides felt like lead weights.

"That's good. And your other patients?"

She poured herself a cup of coffee and joined him at the table. "I'll be able to release two of them tomorrow. The rest are coming along nicely."

He tried to smile, tried to hide the warring emotions inside him. "It must make you feel great to know that you're getting people back on their feet," he said.

With a modest smile, she reached across the table and covered his hand with hers. Everything in Mac wanted to turn his hand over and snatch a hold on her wrist. He wanted to lead her to the bedroom, make love to her and block out the notion that it would be the very last time.

Gently, she said, "And it must make you feel good to keep people safe."

He shrugged. "What I do isn't nearly as important as your job."

She frowned. "How do you think life would be for the citizens in your county if there was no law enforcement there? It would be dangerous and violent, that's how. People would have to alter their lives just to remain safe." A smile chased away her frown. "We all have a purpose, Mac."

Sighing heavily, he pulled his hand away and rose from the table. Looking at her hurt. Touching her hurt. Everything inside him was twisting with agony. It shouldn't be this way, he thought. Being with Ileana, no matter how short the time, should be making him happy.

Blindly, he moved over to the patio door and pretended an interest in the view of the mountain. "I guess you're right. And right now my purpose is to find my mother. Have you decided when I might see her?" he asked dully.

A long stretch of silence passed, and Mac figured he'd caught her off guard. For the past two days they'd not been discussing Frankie or the reason Mac had come to Lincoln County. They'd simply been enjoying the moment, taking pleasure in each other. But now his question had jerked them both back to reality.

"I hadn't thought about it, Mac. But if things are still okay by tomorrow, I suppose you can see her then."

Her answer was like an electrical jolt, and his head jerked around just in time to see her rising from her chair and moving toward him.

"Tomorrow? Are you serious?"

"Yes."

Pausing in front of him, Mac could see her features were pinched, and when she placed her hand on his arm, he felt his heart crack.

"Are you that desperate to leave?" she asked.

He swallowed at the strange tightening in his throat. "No. Not exactly. I just…well…time has been marching on, and I'm…expected back at my deputy duties soon."

That was only a partial truth. But Mac didn't want to admit to this woman that he was a coward, that he was afraid to stay much longer, afraid if he remained in her presence he would end up doing something stupid. Like fall in love with her.

She appeared to be weighing his every word as her gaze wandered over his face. Mac could only wonder what she was thinking. That he'd been using her? Oh, God, nothing could be further from the truth. Somehow he had to make her understand that.

"I see. I'm sorry, Mac. I wasn't thinking. I guess I was being selfish and thinking—" She paused, then released a long, shaky breath. "I've been…this time with you has been so special for me. It was easy to forget that you have a life back in Texas."

Summoning all the strength he could find, he made himself play it light. After all, there was nothing serious between them, just mutual attraction and respect. She wasn't expecting more and neither was he, he assured himself.

"It's been special for me, too, Ileana."

Her fingers tightened on his arm and like a man gripping a lifeline, he felt his strength slipping, his resistance collapsing.

"You are going to stay with me tonight, aren't you?"

The sweet innocence to her question, the gentle plea on her face was more than Mac could bear. Emitting a groan of surrender, he drew her into the circle of his arms and buried his face in the side of her silky hair.

"Of course I'm going to stay," he said in a muffled voice.

"I'll have to get up very early to leave for work," she warned him.

His hands roamed her back, treasured the feel of her warm body. "Then I'll get up very early and make breakfast. The least I can do is see that the doctor maintains her nutrition."

Tilting her head back, she smiled at him. "I'm holding you to that promise."

By midmorning the next day, Ileana was knee-deep in work yet having a heck of a time trying to concentrate on anything. Minutes ago she'd called Mac's cell phone and informed him that Frankie would be in her room and that he could go in to see her as long as he kept the meeting limited to ten minutes.

The realization that Mac was finally going to get answers to questions about his mother had left Ileana more than anxious. Several times this morning she'd dropped things, missed words in conversations and forgotten to return phone calls. If it hadn't been for Ada following her around, taking care of her missteps, she'd be in a mess.

Actually, Ileana was already in a mess, she just didn't

want to admit it to herself or anyone else. She'd blindly stepped into Mac's arms because she'd been attracted to him, drawn to him in a way that she'd never been drawn to any man. She'd known their time together was temporary yet she'd plowed ahead, eager to snatch a taste of womanhood.

She'd not expected his lovemaking to make such an incredible change in her life. She felt different. She was different. Now, all she could think was that their time together was narrowing down and by allowing him to see Frankie she was speeding up the process.

Oh, God, what was it going to be like once Mac went back to Texas? Her house, her life was going to be so empty. Could she live on just the memories he left behind?

"Doc, are you coming down with something?" Ada asked.

Pulling her hand away from her forehead, Ileana looked up to see the nurse walking into her office. As Ada frowned with concern, Ileana straightened her slumped shoulders.

"Not at all. I'm just a bit distracted this morning."

"A bit!" Ada exclaimed as she rested a hip on the corner of Ileana's desk. "I've never seen you like this!"

Thrusting a hand through her hair, Ileana looked at the other woman. "Mac is going to visit with Frankie this morning. And I'm worried about both of them."

Ileana had given the nurse a brief account of why Mac had come to Ruidoso and why he believed Frankie might be his mother. Since then Ileana hadn't given the woman any hint that she'd gotten close to the man. Even though the nurse hadn't said as much to her, Ileana somehow sensed that Ada believed she was falling for the Texan.

"What do you think might come of this meeting?" Ada asked.

Ileana picked up a pen and began twisting it between her fingers. "I honestly don't know. I just fear that both of them might be hurt."

"Well, you can order the man not to see her."

"No. That wouldn't help matters. This meeting has to happen—for both of their sakes. I only wish—" Pausing, she let out a heavy sigh. "That I could see a happy ending out of this. For both of them."

Ada studied her keenly. "You've changed since he came to town, Doc."

Ada couldn't imagine just how much she had changed, Ileana thought. She was now a woman who understood what it meant to make love to a man, experience the rush of pleasure, the ecstasy of being wanted. Oh, yes, she'd changed. She just hadn't realized it showed.

"Just because I've worn a few dresses and put on some lipstick?" she lightly teased. "Come on, Ada, I'm still the same boring doctor you've always known."

"You're not boring. You never were. But you're more interesting now, and it's obvious the change has a great deal to do with your tall Texan."

"He's hardly mine," Ileana muttered, but even as she said the words her cheeks turned bright pink. "And we'd better get back to work."

Rising from her seat, she expected Ada to follow her out of the office. When the nurse failed to make a move, Ileana looked back at her.

"Are you stuck to that desk?"

Shaking her head, Ada smiled. "We've seen the last patient for this morning. It's almost time for lunch, or hadn't you noticed."

Amazed that she'd been in such a fog, Ileana glanced at her watch. "I guess time got away from me," she mumbled.

"Why don't you go over to Sierra General?" Ada suggested. "Maybe Mac is still there."

Ileana's eyes widened. "Mr. Hampton was the last patient?"

Ada nodded. "I told you that when we left the examining room, but I guess you weren't listening."

"Sorry, Ada. I've not been myself this morning." She hurried over to a hall tree where her coat and muffler were hanging. "I think I will go to the hospital. I'll see you after lunch."

Across town, Mac didn't know what to expect when he walked into Frankie Cantrell's hospital room, but one thing was for sure, he didn't expect to find the beautiful, fragile woman sitting in an armchair.

Her image was framed by a picture window, and the sunlight illuminated her face. As he grew nearer, Mac decided she looked much younger than he imagined, but much older than the woman who'd walked away from the McCleod farm nearly thirty years ago.

"Ms. Cantrell?"

The faint smile on her face told him that she didn't have a clue who he was. The fact hit him almost as hard as the sight of her. Yet he told himself that there was no way she could connect his image with that of a ten-year-old boy. One that she'd not seen in years.

"Yes. Are you the visitor that the nurse told me about?"

"I am." Bending forward, he offered her his hand. "I've been here in Lincoln County for the past several days, waiting for you to get better. Ileana—I mean—Dr. Sanders tells me that you've been very ill."

"Yes. But I'm much better now."

She politely shook his hand, and Mac noticed her fingers were cool, the skin as delicate as a rose petal. The blue of her eyes was deep, and while they curiously scanned his face, Mac could only think how her brow and the shape of her mouth resembled his brother. Dear God, if there had been any question before, there wasn't now. This was their mother! His mother!

"You say you've been waiting for me to get well? I'm sorry but you have the advantage on me. Should I know you, young man?"

His nostrils flared as he drew in a deep breath, and unexpected pain burned in the middle of his chest.

"I think so. My name is Phineas. Phineas McCleod. But I used to be Mac to you."

All these years Mac had dreamed of this moment. He'd imagined finding his mother and how she would look once he confronted her. He'd believed that shocking her would give him pleasure. It didn't.

Her face not only appeared ashen but it looked wounded. As though he'd physically struck her with his open hand.

"Mac."

She repeated his name in childlike wonder, as though she'd just stepped into a dream world.

"Yes."

Her mouth fell open, and one hand clutched her

throat. For a moment he feared the shock was going to give her a heart attack, but then she seemed to gather herself, and he was relieved to see a bit of color flood back into her cheeks.

"How did you find me?" she finally asked.

"Betty Jo Andrews. She died. Or did you know?"

Her expression sober, she nodded. "Yes," she said hoarsely. "I keep up with Goliad County obits."

Then obviously she knew that her first husband had died nearly seven years ago. Yet she'd not shown her face to her sons. Not bothered to acknowledge their father's death. What had happened to this woman? he wondered incredulously. How could she have gone from a loving, devoted mother, to denying her own sons?

"Oscar, her son, gave the correspondence you'd exchanged with Betty Jo to Ripp."

"Ripp. How is he?"

"He's fine. He's married now. With a family."

"That's good." A faint light flickered in her eyes. "Then you two have read my letters?"

Mac felt as cold as the snow piled outside the window. "No. We've not read them. But Oscar told us that our names were mentioned. That's how I came to be here. We figured it had to be you."

Her head bent forward, and as Mac watched her bring her hand up to her eyes, he told himself if she cried he wouldn't allow her tears to get to him. No. As a child he'd cried plenty of his own, but she'd never been around to console him or his little brother.

"I can't imagine what you must be thinking now. I—"

The remainder of her words was cut off with a racking cough, reminding Mac of her fragile health. He didn't want the woman to be ill. Nor did he want to cause her emotional pain. He honestly didn't know what he wanted. He felt dead inside.

After the coughing stopped, she regained her breath, then looked up at him. Clearly, this time there was anguish in her eyes, but Mac could only guess what was causing it. If she'd suddenly developed a conscience it had taken her a hell of a time to do it.

"Whatever you're thinking, Mac, I never stopped loving you and Ripp. I never stopped wishing that you were in my life."

The cold indifference that had settled over him was scaring Mac. He had finally found his mother! She was saying a tiny portion of what he needed to hear her say. Yet it all seemed so insignificant now. Words couldn't replace years of desertion.

Not bothering to reply, he walked away from her and stood staring out the window. He should have let Ripp come here, he thought miserably. He should have let his brother try to come up with the right words to say to a mother who'd chosen to quit being their mother a long time ago.

But then, he couldn't wish that entirely, Mac realized. Otherwise he would have never met Ileana. Never had the chance to hold her in his arms.

"I honestly don't know what to say to that," he finally spoke.

His words were met with silence, and he glanced over his shoulder to see that she'd closed her eyes and her hand was pressed to her bosom.

Concerned now, he walked back over to her. "Are you all right?"

"No," she answered faintly. "I—I'm very, very tired. If you'll excuse me, I need to get back in bed."

He needed answers. Answers that had haunted him and his brother for years. But those were apparently going to have to wait until another time.

"I'll get a nurse to come help you," he told her, then quickly left the room.

Moments later, at the nurses' station, he was relaying Frankie's need to one of the nurses, when he spotted Ileana hurrying toward him. The sight of her was like a ray of sunshine after a violent storm.

He walked to meet her, and she took him by the arm and led him toward the waiting area.

"You've already seen Frankie, haven't you?" she asked as her eyes continued to scan his strained features.

He nodded. "She's my mother, Ileana. That—that part of it wasn't much of a surprise, I guess. The evidence had already pretty much told us that. But I—" Pausing, he shook his head with dismay. "Seeing her was a surprise. I didn't expect her to still resemble the mother I remembered. I thought she'd be different somehow."

Aching to comfort him, Ileana clasped her hands around his. "How did she react?"

He shook his head again, and Ileana could see he was dazed.

"She was— Let me put it this way—she wasn't ever expecting to see me in her lifetime," he said bitterly.

"Oh, Mac," she said gently. "Did she explain anything?"

"We didn't get to that. I'd only been in the room for

a few short minutes when she said she was tired and needed to go back to bed."

Ileana nodded. "I'm sure she wasn't lying about that. She's in a very weak condition, and the shock of seeing you probably drained her rather quickly."

Jerking off his hat, he raked a hand roughly through his hair. "I'm sorry about that, Ileana. I'm sorry about a lot of things!" He slapped the hat back on his head. "I've got to get out of here," he muttered. "Maybe you'd better go check on her."

Frankie was her patient, but her first concern was Mac. "What are you going to do?"

"I'm going back to the Bar M. And I'm going to talk with my brother."

Ileana was greatly relieved to hear he was planning on going home to the ranch, but she was worried about his state of mind. For the first time in her life, she wished it wasn't imperative that she return to the clinic this afternoon. But her patients' welfare had to be considered, and they were all counting on her.

"I won't be home until late this evening," she said with a troubled frown. "Why don't you stop by the ranch house and visit with my parents or the hands in the barn? You shouldn't be alone, Mac."

His expression grave, he bent his head and brushed a kiss on her cheek. "I'll be okay, Ileana. Don't worry about me. I'll see you later."

He pulled away from her and walked briskly toward the exit. As Ileana watched him disappear beyond the revolving door, she realized that his happiness had become very important to her, even more important than her own.

Once Mac pulled onto the main highway and headed his truck toward the Bar M, he punched in Ripp's cell number and hoped his brother was available to take his call.

After three rings without an answer, Mac was about to hang up when he heard Ripp's voice.

"Hey, brother! You finally decided to call me and let me know you're still alive?"

Mac squinted at the curving highway ahead. "You have my number. You could have called."

"Yeah. Sorry, brother. I was only teasing. It's been heck around here. We've had several car accidents to work. Not to mention a rash of robberies. Plus Marti got sick with the flu, and I've been taking care of Elizabeth as much as I can while Luci tends to him."

"You don't need to apologize to me. We're brothers, remember." He swallowed as the image of their mother's frail image swam before his eyes. "Are you sitting down?"

"No. Why?"

"Maybe you ought to," he said grimly. "I just saw Frankie a few minutes ago."

There was a long pregnant pause, then Ripp asked, "And?"

"She didn't recognize me. Not until I told her my name. Guess it had been too long for her to know her own kid."

He could hear Ripp blow out a heavy breath.

"God, I can't believe you've found our mother! What did she say? Did she have any sort of explanation?"

"She knew Betty Jo had passed away. Apparently she keeps up with Goliad County news. But as for anything about her leaving the family—we didn't get to that. She's still very weak. I've had to save all that for another time."

"Oh," Ripp said with obvious disappointment. "So what are your plans now? To see her again?"

"I have to, Ripp. We can't just leave things dangling like this. I've come all this way to find her. Now we need to know why, don't we?"

"Yeah. The why is the thing that's always tormented me," Ripp huskily replied.

"Me, too." Mac let out a heavy breath. "Seeing her wasn't easy, Ripp."

"No. I don't expect it was. How did she look?"

The dead feeling that had come over him in the hospital room was now evaporating, leaving pain in its wake. "You remember that one picture we have of her? Well, she looked just like that. Beautiful—only older."

There was another long pause, and then Ripp said, "I think that's why Dad destroyed every picture he could find of her. He didn't want them around, reminding him of the beauty he'd lost."

"We lost her, too, Ripp."

"Yeah, but we kept her picture," he pointed out. "Don't forget that, Mac."

"I haven't forgotten anything, little brother."

Later that evening, long after dark, Ileana found Mac at her mother's horse barn, helping the grooms blanket the horses that had been worked earlier in the day. Once he and the other men finished the chore, Mac climbed in his truck and followed Ileana up the mountain to her house.

In the kitchen, he helped her lay out plates and utensils so they could eat the take-out meal she'd brought home with her.

"Why don't you sit and let me do this, Ileana," he said as she pulled out a container of fried chicken. "You've had a long day."

"It couldn't have been as nearly as long as yours," she said, then turning away from the cabinet, she walked over to him and placed her palms against his chest. "I've hardly been able to work due to worrying about you."

When had any woman ever worried about him or expressed their concern about him in any way? He couldn't remember a one and the fact that Ileana's thoughts were on him rather than herself totally amazed him.

Lifting his hand, he stroked his fingers through the hair at her temple. "Sweet girl, I'm not anything to worry over."

Her palms moved up and down against his chest. "That's not the way I see it."

The tenderness in her eyes, the warmth of her hands caused desire to flicker low in his belly. Groaning at the unbidden yearning, he bent his head and nuzzled a kiss against the side of her neck. The honey taste of her was more than a balm to his aching heart. It blanked his mind to everything, but her. "Do you think we could forget about eating for right now?" he murmured.

Her soft sigh skittered against his cheek as she slipped her arms up and around his neck. "We have all night," she whispered.

Chapter 11

The next morning Mac was still sound asleep when Ileana slipped from the bed and quickly readied herself for work. Rather than wake him, she left him a note on her pillow with a promise to call him later in the day, then quietly exited the house.

Throughout the dark drive to Ruidoso, their lovemaking of the night before rolled over and over in Ileana's mind like a sweet, but haunting, refrain. In spite of all the tenderness he'd shown her, she'd felt desperation behind his kisses, a hunger in his hands that she'd not felt before. The change in him had left her heart heavy because she knew, in his own subtle way, he was saying goodbye.

You knew that time would come, Ileana. You can't be sorry about it now. You can only be glad that you've had this much time with the man.

Ileana realized the voice inside her head was right, but that didn't make it any easier to accept the idea that he would soon be gone. Through all her lonely years, she'd never dreamed or imagined that a man as handsome, exciting and loving would ever come into her life. She didn't want to let him go. Yet she didn't have any right to ask him to stay. Their coming together had been without strings, without promises. To try to drag more from him now would be humiliating and meaningless.

A few minutes later Ileana found the halls of the hospital busy as shifts changed, medicine was dispersed and breakfasts served. She slowly made her way from patient to patient, carefully monitoring their condition and making a point to address their questions and concerns.

Purposely, Ileana saved Frankie's visit for her last stop, and as she knocked lightly, then entered the woman's room, she wondered what, if anything, the woman might bring up about Mac.

"Good morning, Frankie." Her patient's breakfast tray had already been pushed aside with two-thirds of the food gone uneaten. She looked pointedly at the tray, then to Frankie. "Aren't you hungry this morning?"

"No. I've been counting the minutes until you got here."

Ileana's brows lifted as she pulled a stethoscope from her white lab coat and reached for the blood pressure cuff hanging over the headboard of the bed. "Oh? Are you feeling worse? Coughing more?"

"My cough is better and I feel stronger." Frankie closed her eyes and pinched the bridge of her nose. "I'm just in turmoil." Groaning with anguish, she opened her eyes and looked up at Ileana. "Did you know about Mac? About his being here?"

Feeling a bit duplicitous, Ileana felt her cheeks fill with color. "Yes, I did, Frankie. He came to me several days ago and—well, he explained the situation and asked to see you. At the time I had to refuse. You were too ill for such a meeting. But now you're better."

Rising up to sitting position in the bed, Frankie looked at her, and Ileana could see haunting shadows in the woman's eyes. Fears and doubts etched every line of her face.

"I have to see him again, Ileana. Yesterday I was so shocked—but there was so much I needed to say. Wanted to say. Is he still here? Can you ask him to come see me this morning?"

With each word that passed her mouth, Frankie was growing more anxious and agitated. Ileana realized it would only cause her more stress if she tried to put the meeting off until a later date.

"Yes, he's still here. And, yes, I'll ask him to come. But first you must calm down, Frankie, or your heart is going to give you even bigger problems."

Shaking her head, Frankie bit down on her lip and turned her watery gaze toward the window. "I don't care about that. My heart's been broken for a long, long time," she said in a stricken voice.

Nearly thirty miles away, Mac was bundled in his coat, sipping coffee on Ileana's deck as he stared out at the surrounding mountains. But the beautiful scenery was not the thing on his mind.

He'd come here to Ruidoso for one thing and one thing only. To see if Frankie Cantrell was his lost mother. He'd done that. Frankie Cantrell had once been Frankie McCleod, the woman who'd given birth to him and Ripp. So now what? There were lots of answers he still didn't have from the woman, but did he really want to stick around and try to pry them from her? What good would that do him or Ripp? All these years she'd clearly known where to find her two sons, yet she'd chosen not to. Wasn't that enough to tell him that she didn't care? That she'd never cared?

Sighing, he rose from the lawn chair and walked over to the railing that bordered the wide deck. Much of the snow had melted yesterday, and now patches of green juniper and sage dotted the slope of land running away from Ileana's house. The landscape and the climate were nothing like South Texas, and he'd not expected to like it. He'd expected to want to get his business done and get back home as quickly as possible, but Ileana had changed all of that. Now when he looked at the desert and mountains, he thought of her, and realized how hard it was going to be to leave them both.

He'd tossed the coffee dregs and was about to head back into the house when his cell phone rang. Seeing Ileana's number filled him with pleasure and concern.

"Ileana, you snuck off without waking me," he gently scolded.

"I didn't see any need to disturb you," she said in a rather hushed voice.

Picking up the cue that she couldn't talk freely, he quickly questioned, "Is anything wrong?"

"Yes and no. Can you come to the hospital right now? I'll explain everything when you get here."

His brows furrowed together. "Does this have anything to do with Frankie?"

"Everything. She's asking for you."

After nearly thirty years, she was asking for him. Bitterness, amazement and curiosity swirled and tangled inside him. "I'll be there as soon as I can," he muttered.

"You can catch me at the nurses' station," she told him, then quickly ended the call.

Thirty minutes later, his mind spinning with all sorts of questions, Mac sprinted across the hospital parking lot and into the building.

Nurse Renae Walker was on duty, and she picked up the phone to page Ileana even before Mac came to a stop at the long desk.

"Dr. Sanders is on her way," she told Mac.

After thanking the nurse, he started toward the waiting area, but in a matter of moments Ileana caught up to him and, taking him by the hand, she pulled him over to one side of the wide corridor.

"I'm so glad that you've come," she said.

"Why wouldn't I?"

She shrugged. "I'm not sure. After seeing her yesterday you seemed so disturbed."

Disturbed was a polite way for Ileana to describe his feelings about Frankie. Just looking at the woman and hearing her voice had caused him to ache in a way he'd never ached before. "Ripp and I deserve answers. That's the only reason I'm doing this."

Ileana nodded grimly. "I understand, Mac. But she was so worked up this morning when I went in to see her that her blood pressure was sky-high. Whatever you've thought about her for all these years—well, I think you at least need to hear her out."

As Mac looked down at her, it struck him that just over a week had passed since he'd first come to Sierra General and met Ileana in this corridor. He'd summed her up as intelligent and qualified in her profession but plain and practical. He'd never expected, or even dreamed, he'd feel sexual attraction for the doctor, much less affection. Now he could only think how blind he'd been, how much he would have missed if he'd not bothered to look at the woman beneath the surface.

"Don't worry, Ileana. I plan to give her that much."

She nodded, and Mac gently brushed his knuckles against her cheek before he turned and headed to Frankie's room.

After a light knock on the door, he stepped in the small space to find his mother in the same armchair she'd been sitting in yesterday. This morning she was dressed in a frilly pink bed jacket, and her shoulder-length hair, still mostly black, was brushed loose around her face. She looked fifty instead of sixty, a fact that would be different, he figured, if she'd chosen to stay on the McCleod farm.

A wobbly smile touched her lips as he moved toward her. "Mac," she said quietly. "Thank you for coming."

His insides felt like coils tightened to near breaking point. "Ileana said you wanted to see me."

The smile on her face turned resigned. "And you're here because of her. Well, that's all right. As long as you're here."

There was a wooden chair sitting against the wall. Mac pulled it closer to hers, and once he'd removed his hat and settled himself in the seat, he said, "To be honest with you I wasn't sure that I wanted to see you again. This isn't easy for me, and I expect it's no better for you. Yesterday you seemed pretty upset, and I don't want to be the reason to give your health a setback."

She made a weak, dismissive gesture with her hand. "We're not going to worry about my health. I'll be fine. And you're wrong about one thing. Seeing you yesterday wasn't hard. It was something I've wanted for a long, long time… To see you—and Ripp."

Shaking his head, Mac desperately tried to hold on to his emotions. "I'm sorry, Frankie, but that's hard to swallow. You knew where your sons lived. All you had to do was fly to Texas. Drive to Texas. Even pick up the phone."

Regret etched her features, and as Mac looked into her eyes he saw something that resembled fear. But what did this woman have to fear? he wondered. For years now, she'd been living an easy, pampered life.

"Every day, for the past thirty years, I've been aware of that, Mac. But things weren't all that easy. For a long time I was afraid to go back to Goliad County. And then later, after I heard that Owen had died—" She drew in a long, ragged breath, then released it. "Well, I figured you and Ripp were better off not knowing about me or what had happened. Betty Jo told me that you'd grown into fine young men and that you'd become respected deputy sheriffs. She made it sound like your lives were good, and I didn't want to mess that up for either of you."

Amazed, Mac stared at her. "Mess us up? What do you think you did when you walked out on us? Ripp and I watched the road for days and days. We kept telling each other that you'd come back, that you wouldn't really leave us behind! Thirty years after the fact is a little late to be worrying about messing up your sons' lives!"

Her eyes turned watery, and as she reached for a napkin, Mac tried to steel himself against her tears. She'd hurt him and his brother in the deepest way a parent could hurt a child. Yet it appeared she'd lost something in the process.

"Yes, I deserve your anger and more," she said with a sniff. "But I really did mean to come back after you, Mac. Things just got—" She looked at him, then with an anguished groan, she covered her face with her hand. "Oh, Mac, my son. My son. I never wanted you or your brother to know any of this. That's why I've stayed away all these years." She removed her hand and looked at him through a wall of tears. "But I can see that you don't understand and you need explanations."

Mac hadn't expected to feel as though his heart, his very insides were being torn out of him. But it did, and he struggled to hide the pain from his voice. "The not knowing has been hell for me and Ripp. Can you understand that?"

She nodded miserably. "Yes. But I believed that hearing disparaging things about your father would be even worse for you both."

Scooting to the edge of his seat, he leaned toward her. "Things about Dad? What things?"

Her jaw suddenly grew rigid, and he could see she was fighting to toughen her resolve. "I have no doubt that Owen was a good father to you boys. He loved you both so much. But our relationship was troubled, Mac. Owen was a hard-nosed, hard-driven man. His sons and the farm were his entire life. I was just something on the side, something to make his family complete."

"If you knew he felt that way, then why did you ever marry him?" Mac questioned.

She momentarily closed her eyes. "Because I loved him. And he wasn't that way when we first married. He was charming and affectionate. He treated me as his partner and cared about my interests and wants. But after you boys were born, he began to change and draw away from me. Planting, harvesting, paying the bills—that's all that mattered."

"We never had much money," Mac reasoned. "That's hard on a man who wants to give his family security."

She sighed. "That's true. But I wanted to help him. I wanted him to include me in his worries, his plans. I wanted him to see that I needed more in my life than feeding livestock and cleaning away the blowing grit of plowed fields. Not monetary things—I just needed him to love me."

"So instead of sticking it out with Dad and trying to make it work, you had an affair with Will Tomlin."

Horrified, she looked at him. "No! Sure, everyone in town believed that's what was going on, but they were wrong! Will was a fine and decent man. All he did was befriend me and give me a place to stay while I tried to talk some sense into Owen. Betty Jo was pregnant, and I didn't know where else to go. I'd left the farm in desperation. I wanted to do something to wake him up, to make him see that we needed to make changes in our marriage. Owen would have nothing of it. He was convinced that I was having an affair, and he wanted a divorce."

Mac felt dead inside. All these years he'd believed his father was above reproach and that his mother was the guilty deserter. Now he had to face the fact that he'd been wrong and misguided about both of his parents.

Wiping a hand across his face, he muttered, "So you agreed to a divorce."

"No! I didn't want a divorce. I loved Owen. I went against my own parents' wishes to marry him. They wanted more for me than being the wife of a farmer. But I didn't care—all I wanted was Owen. But after ten years of marriage, he'd grown into a hard, angry man. When I told him that I wanted to come home, that I didn't want a divorce, he told me that I didn't have a choice in the matter and that if I ever tried to see you boys again he would kill me."

Stunned, Mac stared at her. "Surely you didn't think he was serious?"

She dabbed the napkin at her eyes. "I didn't want to think he would ever hurt me. But one day I got up my courage and drove out to the farm. I'd decided I was going to get you boys and run. Owen met me at the edge of the property and threatened to choke the life out of me. And if you could have seen him that day—" Pausing, she shivered as though she was reliving the moment. "I've never seen such rage or hatred on anyone's face. I didn't have any choice, Mac, but to turn around and leave."

Rising from his seat, Mac began to pace around the small, sterile room. "You could have gone to the police, through the courts," he accused. "Didn't that ever cross your mind?"

"Of course it did. All sorts of plans went through my mind. But was fighting Owen for custody going to make anything better for you boys? My reputation was already shot. The whole town considered me an adulteress. If I dragged Owen through the court system, then even more ugliness would come out. You and

Ripp would have been devastated. I didn't have money or means to care for you. Besides, Owen's threats grew more and more frightening, and I realized if I didn't leave Texas entirely, he would probably take my life. So I signed the divorce papers and left."

The ache in Mac's chest was so deep that it was almost impossible for him to breathe. "How did you happen to settle here?" he asked thickly.

Frankie continued to wipe her eyes. "That happened by chance. My car broke down, and I didn't have the money to go any farther. I found a job at the racetrack and slowly began to start my life over."

"When you left Texas where were you headed? To stay with your folks?"

"I was going to California," she admitted. "But not to them. They wouldn't have welcomed me. I didn't know where I was going. I was scared, and I knew if I tried to contact you and Ripp, Owen would hunt me down." Her head was bent, and she covered her face with both hands. "When I met Lewis, my plans about California changed. I told him the whole story about my marriage. He wanted to get you boys and bring you both back here to live with us. But I knew how much you loved Owen, and by then I figured you hated your mother. I decided you needed to be with your father and that I'd be doing you a favor to stay out of your lives."

"You never told Quint or Alexa," he accused. "Were you ashamed of me and Ripp?"

To his surprise she rose from the chair and steadied herself with a hand on one padded arm. "Never, Mac. I was ashamed of myself. Ashamed of failing my sons. But as time went on, Lewis and I decided it would be harder on Quint and Alexa to hear they had brothers in Texas but would never be able to see them."

Mac had never felt so cold, so utterly drained in his life. Everything he'd believed about his family had just been torn to shreds. Everything he'd imagined his father to be now appeared to be just a larger-than-life lie.

"Dad's been dead for over six years. Were you never going to see us? Never going to tell Quint and Alexa about their brothers?" he asked in a low, accusing voice.

"I honestly don't know, Mac. Ever since Betty Jo told me that Owen had passed away, I've been praying for the courage to face you and Ripp. But Owen discarded me as though I'd been no more to him than a broken-down tractor he no longer wanted. And after all these years I've feared that my sons would reject me, too. I guess God answered my prayers by sending you here."

Wiping a hand over his face, Mac walked back over to his chair and picked up his hat from where he'd placed it on the floor. After he'd levered it onto his head, he turned to face her.

"I'd better be going," he said in a choked voice.

To Mac's surprise, she reached out and touched his forearm. "Is that all you have to say?"

He forced his eyes to meet hers and wondered why he'd never been able to forget the image of her bending down and pressing a kiss to his cheek, of her smile as she'd called him her sweet boy.

"I wish there was something I could say to make it easier for both of us," he said in a low choked voice. "But I can't. There's nothing left in me, I guess."

Pain pinched her features. "I thought… I was hoping you could call me Mother—maybe just once."

His gaze dropped to the floor. "I'm sorry, Frankie, but I haven't had a mother since I was ten years old."

Before she could make any sort of reply, he turned and quickly left the room. Staying wouldn't have helped matters and like he'd told her, there was nothing left for him to say.

Back at the nurses' station he caught Nurse Walker's attention as she hung up the phone.

"Is Ileana still here in the hospital?" he asked.

The blond nurse shook her head. "Sorry, Mr. McCleod. She had an emergency at her clinic. I'm sure you can find her there."

"Yeah. Thanks."

Numbly, Mac walked out of the hospital and climbed into his truck. But once he was sitting behind the wheel, he didn't make a move to start the engine. Instead he sat staring out the windshield trying to make sense of all the things Frankie had told him.

Owen had been a hard-driven man. Mac and his brother had always understood that much about their father. But had he really been the insensitive brute that she'd described? How could the man he'd admired and loved, the man who'd spent fifteen years protecting the citizens of Goliad County, threaten to kill his own wife? If Frankie's story was true, Owen had been too stubborn and selfish to try to mend his family back together. He'd deliberately kept the mother of his children away from her sons.

Oh, God, nothing was ever going to be the same, Mac thought miserably. Everything he'd ever believed in was shattered in pieces at his feet. Who the hell was he? He'd thought he was the son of a tough sheriff, who'd been loved and admired by everyone. But no one, not even his own sons, had known the real Owen McCleod.

There was no way in hell he could relay this news to Ripp over the phone. Whether he was ready or not, he had to go back to Texas and face Ripp with the truth, or at least the truth as Frankie had told it.

Closing his eyes, Mac rested his forehead against the steering wheel. He was going to have to say goodbye to Ileana, and he didn't know where he was going to find the strength.

Ileana's day was so chock-full of patients, she hardly had time to swallow a bite of her sandwich, much less take a minute to call Mac. Renae had sent her a message from the hospital that he'd asked for her, but he'd not shown up at the clinic. Nor had he called.

Now as she headed her old truck across Bar M land, she wondered what had taken place between him and his mother. Had he gotten his answers and was his time here in New Mexico over? Just asking herself the last question sliced her with pain.

She'd passed over the bridge crossing the Hondo and was flying on up the road past the main ranch house when she spotted Mac's black truck parked in front of the pink stucco.

Slamming on the brakes, she turned the truck around in the middle of the road and headed it up the long drive to her parents' home.

When she entered the house through the kitchen, Cesar was at the gas range stirring a pot of pasta.

She walked over and kissed his leathery cheek. "Supper isn't ready yet?"

"Nobody is here, except me and Mac. Wyatt and Chloe went to some kind of drilling conference in El Paso. They won't be back for a couple of days."

"Oh. I wasn't aware that they were leaving." Usually her parents informed her if they were going out of town, but she'd been so involved with Mac for the past few days, she might have missed their call.

"It was a last-minute thing," Cesar explained, then gestured toward the sauce he was stirring. "You going to stay and have some of this?"

"I'm not sure. I need to speak with Mac first."

She left the kitchen and walked out to the living room. When she found it empty, she decided to try the room he'd been using before he'd been stranded at her house.

After knocking lightly on the door, she called his name. "Mac? Are you in there?"

He opened the door almost immediately. "Ileana. I wasn't expecting you to stop by the ranch house."

"I saw your truck parked out front," she explained, then her brow quickly furrowed in confusion. "Why are you here?"

He opened the door wider and gestured for her to enter the room. The moment Ileana stepped inside, she spotted his open bags lying on the bed.

"You're packing?" she asked incredulously. "You're not leaving tonight, are you?"

He looked at her, and Ileana could clearly feel the misery on his face. It matched the horrible pain slicing through her chest.

"Yes," he said flatly. "I don't see any point in putting it off."

Behind her back, her hands gripped tightly together

as she watched him walk over to the bed and begin to stuff the remaining clothes in one of the duffel bags.

"I expected you to be leaving soon, but I—" Her throat began to ache so badly she had to stop and swallow before she could go on. "I didn't think it would be tonight."

He stared down at the bag. "I wasn't planning to leave like this, Ileana, but… Well, after this morning I have to."

Hearing the pain in his voice, she hurried over to him and placed her hand on his arm. "What happened, Mac? I was so swamped with patients today I couldn't call. I've been so worried."

He looked at her. "You didn't see Frankie this evening?"

"No. Dr. Vickers made my hospital rounds for me. What happened when you went to see her?"

A long breath rushed out of him. "She gave me the details of what happened all those years ago."

"And you believed her?"

"I have to," he said grimly. "She has no reason to lie about it now. And when a good lawman hears the truth, he usually knows it."

Ileana waited for him to explain more and just when she'd decided he wasn't going to share anything with her, he spoke again.

"My mother wanted to come home. Dad wouldn't let her. He threatened to kill her if she ever tried to get near her sons."

Ileana gasped. Even though she'd always suspected that it must have taken something dire for Frankie to leave her sons, hearing it spoken out loud was shocking.

"I guess that must have knocked your feet out from under you," she said quietly.

Leaning his head back, he stared helplessly at the ceiling. "I don't know who or what I am anymore, Ileana. My childhood, my young adult life was shaped by a man I didn't know."

"Do you think he really would have been capable of hurting Frankie?"

He dropped his head and shook it back and forth. "At first I didn't want to think so. But now that I've had a bit of time to mull it over, I have to admit that he was capable. He seemed to have an obsessive love/hate for Frankie. He forbade us boys to talk about her. Other than the one Ripp and me hid, he destroyed every photo of her in the house. And after she left the farm, he never looked at another woman."

Ileana shook her head in dismay. "Oh, Mac, I'm so, so sorry. I wish none of this had ever happened to you."

His features softened, and he sadly touched a hand to her face. "At least, out of all this, I got to know you, Ileana."

Tears were suddenly burning her throat and the back of her eyes. "Do you really mean that?"

A wry smile twisted his lips. "I've never meant anything more. Our time together has meant everything to me, Ileana. Everything."

Feeling as though she was dying right before his eyes, she turned her back to him and fought to pull herself together. She'd known all along that his time here would be brief. She'd understood that their affair could only be short-lived. She'd chosen to grab what happiness she could, for however long she could. It was now over, and she couldn't get all clingy and embarrassingly weepy.

"Will I…ever see you again, Mac?"

He was silent for a long time, and while she waited, the urge to turn and fling her arms around his neck was so great that she prayed to God to give her strength to keep from sobbing, begging him to stay.

"That's hard to say, Ileana. Maybe. Someday."

Summoning up all the courage she could find, she turned and gave him a wobbly smile. "Well, if you ever get sick and need a doctor, you know where to find one."

He looked miserable, and she was certain her heart was cracking right down the middle. Quickly, before he could make any sort of reply, she rose on her toes and pressed a kiss on his cheek.

"Goodbye, Mac. Travel safely," she whispered, then fled from the room before he could see her tears begin to fall.

Chapter 12

A month later, as Mac drove home from work, he glanced down at the badge on his chest and wondered why he had the urge to rip the piece of silver off his shirt and toss it out the window.

This wasn't like him. He'd always been proud of his job. He'd always felt it was his purpose in life. But ever since he'd returned from New Mexico, he'd felt little joy in anything.

His father had been an admired sheriff, who'd been elected term after term. Mac had always wanted to follow in Owen's footsteps, to be just as tough and fearless as he'd been. But finding Frankie had changed all that. Now he kept asking himself if he was too much like his father, too obstinate and selfish to ever have a lasting relationship with any woman.

Who the hell was he kidding? He wasn't thinking

about a relationship with just any woman. He was thinking about Ileana. That's all he'd been thinking about these past four weeks. Walking away from her had been like slicing off his arms, leaving him incapable of reaching for any sort of happiness.

He was losing a battle to push Ileana from his mind, when he turned down the drive to his house and spotted his brother's truck parked near the front gate. Ripp lived thirty miles away. Unless he was here on sheriff's business, it wasn't like him to be out at night and away from his wife and children.

After parking and hurrying into the house, Mac found his younger brother in the kitchen making a pot of coffee.

"What the hell are you doing here? What's happened?" Mac blurted out.

Ripp sauntered over to the cabinet and pulled down two cups. "Nothing's happened. I've just brought you something to eat, that's all."

Slightly relieved, Mac pulled off his hat and began to unbuckle the holstered pistol from his waist. "I usually manage to eat without you driving thirty miles in the dark to feed me."

"That's what I was thinking, too. But Margie says you haven't been going by the Cattle Call, so that tells me you're not eating."

Ripp carried two plates over to a small round table and tossed two forks next to them. "Lucita made a batch of tamales. She thought you might like some, and it was going to disappoint her if I didn't bring them to you. She's worried that we hardly ever hear from you."

Mac washed his hands at the kitchen sink, then grabbed a bottle of beer from the refrigerator. As he twisted off the lid, he looked at his brother. "This sudden concern for me is touching, but I don't get it. There's nothing wrong. If you'd bothered to pick up the phone and call me, I could have told you that and saved you a trip over here."

Ripp frowned. "Damn it, Mac, don't give me that crap. I've called you several times since you've gotten back from New Mexico, and each time you end the conversation before I ever get started."

"I never was much of a phone talker."

Leaning his head back, Ripp chuckled with disbelief. "You, not a phone talker? God, you are messed up."

Mac bit back a sigh. "Ripp, I'm perfectly okay."

"That's not what Sheriff Nichols says."

Mac lowered the beer bottle from his mouth. "You've talked to him about me? You went behind my back?"

Ripp went over to the microwave and pulled out a plate of tamales. "Before you get on your high horse, I didn't do anything behind your back. Sheriff Nichols called me. He's worried about you."

Stunned now, Mac walked over and flopped into one of the dining chairs. "I haven't made any mistakes on the job."

Ripp pulled out a chair and joined his brother at the table. "He never said you did. You're usually the life of the party, Mac. But the whole sheriff's department can see that you're miserable. They don't understand what's happened, and they're concerned."

A curse was on the tip of Mac's tongue, but at the last second he pulled it back. Ripp was right. He wasn't behaving like himself, and it was wrong to be lashing out at his brother.

Propping his elbows on the table, he dropped his

head in his hands. "Sorry, Ripp. I know I've been acting like a miserable bastard. I guess that's because I am."

"Why?"

Mac's head jerked up and he stared absurdly at his brother. "Hell, Ripp, do you have to ask? I've repeated every word to you that Frankie said. Does it make you happy to know that our father was a liar? That he was threatening and abusive?"

Ripp leaned casually back in his chair, and Mac could only wonder how his brother could be so calm and sensible about the whole thing. Even when he'd first come home and given Ripp the news about Frankie and her reasons for leaving, his brother had taken it all in stride.

"Not particularly. But I've come to realize that Dad wasn't a superhero. He was just a man with faults."

"He led us to believe our mother didn't want us."

Ripp nodded. "Yeah. That was wrong. Really wrong. But on the other hand, he loved us and devoted his life to raising us. I'd rather look at his good points than dwell on the bad." Ladling a couple of tamales on his plate, he glanced pointedly at Mac. "But I don't think this stuff about our parents is the thing that's really bothering you. I think something happened to you while you were in New Mexico. Something that's changed you."

Damn it, why was his brother so good at seeing through him? Or had his time with Ileana changed him so much that it showed on the outside?

Trying to make his face a blank mask, Mac tilted the beer to his lips. After downing several swallows, he said, "I found our mother, Ripp. A mother we've not seen in thirty years. Isn't that enough to change a man?"

"I would hope so."

"What does that mean?" he asked dourly.

Picking up his fork, Ripp whacked off a bite of tamale. "It means that you should be feeling better about everything. Hell, Mac, we went for nearly thirty years not knowing whether our mother was alive or dead. You found her. She's alive and she still loves us."

Mac's jaw tightened on Ripp's last words. "How do you know that? You're not the one who faced her! I was! You don't know how the woman feels about us."

Ripp helplessly shook his head. "Lucita and I have plans to visit her in a couple weeks."

Mac looked at him in surprise. "You're going to see her?"

"Of course. She's our mother, and no matter what she's done, nothing will change that." Ripp's gaze leveled pointedly at his brother. "Look, Mac, you need to stop and realize that both our parents made mistakes—stupid mistakes. But they both loved us in their own way. If you can't understand that—if you can't forgive them—then you're never going to be happy about anyone or anything."

Mac's gaze dropped sullenly to his plate. "Dad's gone. I can't talk to him about any of this."

"No. But Frankie is alive and she still matters."

Mac's fingers gripped the neck of the beer bottle. "What makes you think I haven't forgiven her?"

Ripp didn't immediately reply, and Mac looked up to see his brother thoughtfully studying him.

"Have you?" Ripp asked.

"I guess not," Mac admitted with a guilty grimace.

"Don't you think it's about time you made another trip back to New Mexico? Besides seeing our mother, I think there's someone else there who you need to see."

Mac's eyes opened wide. "Why do you say that?"

Ripp chuckled. "You figure it out, big brother."

A week earlier in Ruidoso, Ileana was in her clinic, going over important test results of a ten-year-old patient. The results had turned out to be wonderful news. The child didn't have leukemia as she'd first feared but a simple infection that had altered his blood count. Ileana was greatly relieved. Yet even this little miracle was not enough to push the heavy weight from her heart.

Nearly a month had passed since she'd told Mac goodbye. She'd not heard one word from him since then. But then she'd not expected to. She'd somehow known that once he returned to Texas he would be out of her life for good. Yet even knowing this, her heart still went into overdrive each time her phone rang. And each time it wasn't him on the other end of the line, her heart sank just that much lower.

For those brief few days in February, Mac had changed her life, and deep down she wanted to believe that she'd changed his. With each day that passed, she hoped and prayed that he would come to realize that he cared for her, that he didn't want to live without her. Yet she also realized that was romantic fantasy. Mac was back in his world, a world that she had no part in.

Ileana's miserable thoughts were suddenly interrupted when a light knock sounded on the door and her mother stepped into the room. She was carrying a white paper sack and, guessing from the odor emanating from it, Chloe had just stopped by a local fast-food restaurant.

"Hi, honey," she greeted her with a smile. "Got time for a little lunch?"

Ileana rose from the desk chair and crossed the floor to plant a kiss on her mother's cheek.

"I suppose I could stop for a few minutes. What do you have in the sack?"

"Hamburgers and French fries, what else?" Chloe said with a laugh. "And don't start preaching about the fat and cholesterol. A person has to cheat once in a while."

Smiling wanly, Ileana pulled up a chair to the front of the desk for her mother to use, then followed it with one for herself.

"Okay, I won't scold you today. I'm all out of scoldings anyway. I've seen some very self-negligent patients this morning. They won't do a single thing to improve their health."

Chloe pulled one of the wrapped burgers from the paper sack and handed it to Ileana. "Hmm. Maybe it's a case of monkey see, monkey do."

Ileana took a seat next to her mother. "You're going to have to decipher that for me, Mother."

"That doesn't need explaining. Your patients can see that their own doctor isn't doing anything to improve her health, so why should they bother?"

Rolling her eyes, Ileana shook her head. "Mother, what are you doing in town, anyway? I thought you were taking that mare up to Santa Fe for breeding today?"

"That's tomorrow. I had a few errands to run today. One of them being you."

"Me?"

"That's right. And don't change the subject on me. Why aren't you doing anything to improve your health? A good doctor like you should know better."

Frowning, Ileana bit into the sandwich and began to chew. Chloe groaned with frustration.

"Know better than what?" Ileana asked after she'd swallowed. "I'm perfectly fine."

"Sure you are. You've only fallen into a pit of depression. You've lost weight and your eyes are circled. The few times you've stopped by the house, you say three or four words then leave. I've never seen you like this, and it worries your father and me. It especially worries us because you're not trying to do one damned thing about it."

Ileana sighed. "Mother, I told you I wouldn't scold you, so why are you doing this to me? I've already had a heck of a day. Are you trying to ruin what's left of it?"

"I'm trying to open your eyes, Ivy. You're miserable, and it's high time you do something about it."

Ileana looked down at the burger in her hands. Food was not what she wanted. She didn't want anything, except Mac. To see his face, hear his voice. "There's nothing I can do about it, Mother," she mumbled. "I simply need time."

"Time? For what?"

Ileana glanced over at her mother. The expression on Chloe's face was more than impatient; it was fed up.

"To gather myself together," Ileana answered lamely. "Can't you understand that?"

"Frankly, no. Since Mac went back to Texas you've become a zombie, and I can't see time making anything better."

Plopping the burger down, Ileana rose to her feet and began to walk aimlessly about the room. There wasn't any use in denying her mother's words. It would be silly of her to try to pretend that Mac's leaving hadn't devastated her.

"Mother, Mac has gone home to his life in Texas. His life never was here with me."

"Do you want it to be?"

Pausing in front of the bay window, Ileana looked at her with faint surprise. "I've never let myself think that far," she said in a strained voice. "It was always obvious that he wasn't serious about me, but I fell in love with him in spite of knowing that. What I want doesn't factor into anything."

Rising from her seat, Chloe walked over and gripped Ileana by the shoulders. "What *you* want should factor into *everything,* Ivy! If you love the man, you don't just sit back and wish and wonder and hope that things were different. You've got to take action."

"Action?" Ileana repeated in a dazed voice.

"Yes! Like going to Texas and telling Mac exactly how you feel. Because I have a terrible feeling that you let him go without saying one word about loving him."

Ileana's face turned beet red. "Dear Lord, Mother, how could I have mentioned the word *love* to the man? We hadn't known each other long enough!"

"You knew him long enough to fall in love with him, didn't you?"

Ignoring that question, Ileana countered, "He didn't want to hear anything like that from me. Mac is— He's a true bachelor."

"Your father believed he was a true bachelor, too. Until he met me," Chloe pointed out, then with an understanding smile, she cupped her palm alongside Ileana's face. "Darling, for years now I've watched you stand in the shadows, believing that no worthy man could ever want you. When Mac come along, I was so happy to finally see my lovely daughter come alive. You deserve to be happy, Ileana."

Tears suddenly filled Ileana's eyes. "Oh, Mom, what—what if I go to him and he doesn't care? What if he's just not interested?"

Chloe gave her an encouraging smile. "Then he's not the man you believed he was and you'll find the strength to move on. But asking yourself what-ifs isn't going to solve anything."

Hope tried to flicker in Ileana's heart as she hugged her mother close. "I'll call Dr. Nichols and see if he can run the clinic for a few days."

Two days after Ripp's late-night visit, Mac tossed a suitcase onto his bed and blindly began to toss in underwear and shirts. The afternoon was already growing late and he'd planned to leave for New Mexico this morning, but an emergency had forced him to change his plans. Several days of rain had flooded the Bianco Creek and Mac, along with several other deputies, had been called out to keep the highway clear of traffic, while ranchers drove their cattle to higher ground.

At least the task had gone off without a hitch and he'd even managed to talk Randal into filling in for him for a few extra days. And he just might need it, Mac thought grimly. Once he got to the Bar M, he had no idea how Ileana was going to greet him. These past few weeks since he'd been back in Texas, he'd not heard a word from her.

Hell, Mac, did you really think a woman like her would stop to give a guy like you a second thought? You're just a simple county deputy. Do you think she'll even give a damn when you show back up on her doorstep?

Yes, he shouted back to the nagging voice in his head. Ileana wasn't a snob. Her wealth didn't determine her friends or the life she led. So what if she hadn't told him that she loved him. She'd given him the most private part of herself—something she'd never done with any man before. That had to mean something.

And you never told her you love her, Mac.

Pausing, Mac took a moment from his packing to look around him. For years he'd told himself that this old ranch house and the few cattle he owned were all that he wanted. He'd convinced himself that being a deputy was enough to make his life feel purposeful. And maybe it had been. On the surface he'd been happy enough. But meeting Ileana had changed all that.

Yes, finding his mother had shaken his foundation and made him realize things about his life that he'd not understood before. But Ileana was the one who'd filled his heart, who'd made him see what loving really meant. He didn't know why he'd not recognized how much he loved her before he'd left the Bar M. Walking away from her had been painful, but the empty days afterward had opened his eyes like nothing else ever had. Now he could only hope and pray that he meant something to her, something more than a bed partner.

He carried the two duffel bags into the living room and dropped them near the door, then walked back to the kitchen to make sure all the small appliances were turned off. He was giving the room one last inspection when he heard someone knocking.

Frowning at the interruption, he hurried through the house while wondering who could be showing up at his door in the middle of the afternoon. If he were needed back at the department, his coworkers would call. Ripp and Lucita had left for Fort Worth to purchase a horse for Mingo's birthday, so it couldn't be his brother showing up with another basket of food.

Running a hand through his hair, Mac pulled the wooden door open and was instantly stunned to see Ileana standing on the other side of the threshold.

She was wearing a springtime dress of blue and white flowers that showed off her waist and fluttered at her knees. Her cheeks were flushed, and her long auburn hair was flying in the breeze and teasing her face. As Mac looked at her, he was certain he'd never seen anything more beautiful than she was at that moment.

"Ileana! What are you doing here?"

A hesitant smile plucked at the corners of her pink lips. "I've been waiting for a Texan to show up on my doorstep. When he didn't, I thought I'd better show up on his."

Dazed, his heart pounding, he pushed the door wider. "How did you find this place?"

She stepped past him and into the house. Still stunned, Mac automatically closed the door, then turned to face her.

"I called the sheriff's office," she answered. "They were very helpful about giving me directions."

He watched her glance around the room, and as she did, she spotted the bags sitting a few steps away.

"Oh? Are you going somewhere?" she asked in an awkward rush. "I realize I should have called, but I wanted to surprise you."

Mac could only look at her in amazement, and then he began to laugh with more joy than he'd ever felt in his life.

"I'm sorry, Mac," she said with a pained expression. "I guess this...my coming here was a bad idea."

Seeing that she'd totally misunderstood his reaction, he reached for her. "Oh, Ileana! It was a wonderful idea! I'm laughing because—" He pulled her closer into the circle of his arms and buried his face in her hair. "When you knocked I was about to walk out the door. I was going to the Bar M to see you."

Levering herself away from his chest, she stared up at him in disbelief. "You were coming to see me?"

Mac nodded as hope began to surge inside him. "Yes. I was hoping— Well, I planned to— Oh, hell, Ileana, I can't talk straight. I don't know how else to say it. I love you. I've been miserable without you."

Tears filled her eyes and rolled onto her cheeks. "Mac. I love you, too. I should have told you that before you left the Bar M. But I was afraid you didn't want to hear me say anything like that." Her eyes dropped to the middle of his chest. "I've been humiliated in the past, Mac. I guess I took it for granted that you would put me off, too."

Suddenly love began to fill every crack and scar in his heart, to warm each cold, empty spot inside him. "Ileana, Ileana." His hands delved into her hair, then drew her face up to his. "I couldn't say anything before now. Because I don't think I understood how I really felt about you until I got back here and took a long look at my life. It was empty—so, so empty without you."

More tears flowed down her cheeks, and he awkwardly wiped them away with his fingertips. "Will you marry me, Ileana? I realize our homes are far apart, but I can find a job in New Mexico—"

Her forefinger suddenly pressed against his lips to stop his words. "Does that really matter, Mac?"

A wide smile spread across his face. "No. Nothing matters except that we're together."

She brought her lips up to his and after a long, promising kiss, she said, "I've always wanted to live where palm trees grow."

With a finger under her chin, his doubtful gaze met hers. "But your clinic, Ileana, and your beautiful house and—"

"There are other doctors just ready and waiting to run my clinic for me. As for my house, I'm thinking it would be great for a summer vacation place." Turning in his arms, she gestured to the living room they were standing in. The furnishings didn't match, the flooring was old and the windows were bare, but to Ileana it was the most beautiful place she'd ever seen. "This house is where we need to raise our children. This little ranch will be our home."

With his hands on her shoulders, he gently turned her back to face him. "But, darling, what about you being a doctor?"

Happiness bubbled inside Ileana, and for the first time in her life she knew she could dance and laugh and shout. The same way her mother did when one of her Thoroughbreds was first to fly across the finish line.

"I've been a doctor, Mac. Now it's time for me to be a wife. A mother. A lover."

He studied her and then a smile crept across his face. "In that order?" he teased.

Rising on tiptoes, she brought her lips up to his. "Maybe we could switch them around—just for tonight," she whispered suggestively.

With a soft chuckle, he brought his arms around her. "This is one time I'm happy to follow the doctor's orders."

Epilogue

Two months later, on a bright spring day, Ileana and Mac entered Sierra General and rode the elevator up to the surgery wing. While they waited for the cubicle to stop and the doors to swish open, Ileana squeezed her husband's hand.

"Your mother is going to love the roses."

Mac glanced down at the basket of yellow roses cradled in his right arm. He'd particularly chosen the flowers because they'd reminded him of the yellow roses his mother had once grown long ago on the McCleod farm. He doubted she would make the connection, but that no longer mattered to Mac. He'd forgiven Frankie, and their relationship was growing stronger and deeper every day.

Oddly enough, after Frankie's secret life was out and her four children were finally together, they'd been able to persuade her to have the heart surgery that she'd needed for so long. The procedure had been a complete success, and Frankie would be able to go home to the Chaparral Ranch tomorrow.

"I hope the roses cheer her," Mac said.

Ileana's eyes glowed warmly as she looked up at him. "Seeing you will cheer her, Mac. Now that I've seen you two together, I get the feeling that you were especially close to each other."

Smiling wryly, Mac said, "Ripp was always a daddy's boy. Before she left, I spent a lot of time with Mother. I guess that's why it was much harder for me to forgive and forget."

The doors to the elevator slid open, and as they automatically stepped forward, Ileana curled her arm around the back of his waist. "She's going to be just fine now, Mac. And you'll have many years to be with her. In fact," she added as they strolled down the corridor toward Frankie's room, "I was thinking it might be nice to have her come to Texas for a visit soon. We have plenty of room…for now."

Stopping in the middle of the hallway, he looked at her with an odd little frown. "What do you mean…for now? Are you trying to tell me—?"

A coy smile touched her lips. "Maybe."

"Maybe?" He looked incredulous and hopeful at the same time. "For God's sake, Ileana, you're a doctor! You should know!"

An impish smile dimpled her cheeks. "Okay, darling. I'm trying to tell you that I'm pregnant. I was going to wait until tonight when we were alone, but—" She gestured to the sterile walls around them. "We first met in this hospital, so I guess it's a fitting place to tell you that you're going to be a father."

He shook his head in happy amazement. "A father!" he softly exclaimed. "Me, a father!"

Love glowed in her blue eyes as she watched a myriad of emotions cross his face. "Does that frighten you?"

Curling his free arm around her shoulders, he pulled her close against him. "Maybe it should. But it doesn't. See, I've already learned everything not to do. And I'm going to love you and this baby, and hopefully more babies, for the rest of my life."

Bending his head, he kissed her until both of them nearly forgot that they were standing in a very public place.

Laughing, Ileana grabbed him by the hand and hurried him toward Frankie's room. "We'll take this up tonight," she promised. "Right now, let's go give your mother our news!"

Minutes later, after Mac had given Frankie the roses and told her about the coming baby, the woman hugged them both, then dabbed at the emotional tears blurring her eyes.

"You know, Mac, when you married Ileana I lost a fine doctor. But I gained a wonderful daughter-in-law. And I couldn't be happier."

Bending his head, Mac placed a kiss on top of his mother's head. "We're all happy, Mom. And that's the way it's going to stay."

* * * * *

USA TODAY bestselling author **Barb Han** lives in north Texas with her very own hero-worthy husband, three beautiful children, a spunky golden retriever/standard poodle mix and too many books in her to-read pile. In her downtime, she plays video games and spends much of her time on or around a basketball court. She loves interacting with readers and is grateful for their support. You can reach her at barbhan.com.

Books by Barb Han

Harlequin Intrigue

Cattlemen Crime Club

Stockyard Snatching
Delivering Justice
One Tough Texan
Texas-Sized Trouble
Texas Witness

Mason Ridge

Texas Prey
Texas Takedown
Texas Hunt
Texan's Baby

The Campbells of Creek Bend

Witness Protection
Gut Instinct
Hard Target

Rancher Rescue

Harlequin Intrigue Noir

Atomic Beauty

Visit the Author Profile page at Harlequin.com for more titles.

RANCHER RESCUE

BARB HAN

The chance to work with the incredibly talented Allison Lyons is a thrill beyond measure. Thank you for sharing your editing brilliance and giving me the chance to learn from you.

To my agent, Jill Marsal, for all your guidance, encouragement and patience.

To Jerrie Alexander, my brave friend and critique partner.

To Brandon, who is strength personified; Jacob, who is the most courageous person I know; and Tori, who is brilliant and funny, I love you.

This one is for you, babe.

Chapter 1

Katherine Harper pushed up on all fours and spit dirt. "Don't take him. I'll do whatever you say."

The tangle of barbed wire squeezed around her calf. Pain seared her leg.

"She got herself caught." The man glared down at her. He glanced toward the thicket, sized up the situation and turned to his partner. "She's not going anywhere."

The first man whirled around. His lip curled. Hate filled his eyes. "Leave her. We have the boy."

"Kane won't like it. He wants them both."

"No. Please. My nephew has nothing to do with any of this." She kicked. Burning, throbbing flames scorched her ankle to her thigh. "I'll give you whatever you want. I'll find the file."

"We know you will. Involve the police and he's dead," the second man warned. "We'll be in touch."

Noah screamed for her. She heard the terror in his voice. A wave of hopelessness crashed through her as she struggled against the barbs, watching the men disappear into the woods with her nephew. *Oh. God. No.*

"He's sick. He needs medicine," she screamed through burning lungs.

They disappeared without looking back.

Shards of pain shot up her leg. Fear seized her. The thick trees closed in on her. Noah had been kidnapped, and she was trapped and helpless.

"Please. Somebody."

The thunder of hooves roared from somewhere in the distance. She sucked in a quick breath and scanned the area. Were more men out there?

Everything had happened so fast. How long had they been dragging her? How far into the woods was she?

All visual reminders of the pumpkin patch were long gone. No open fields or bales of hay. No bursts of orange dotting the landscape. No smells of animal fur and warmth. There was nothing familiar in her surroundings now.

Judging from the amount of blood and the relentless razor-sharp barbs digging into her flesh, she would bleed to death.

No. She wouldn't die. Noah needed her to stay alive. *Noah.*

Anger boiled inside her, heating her skin to flames. Katherine had to save him. He had no one else. He was probably terrified, which could bring on an asthma attack. Without his inhaler or medication, the episode could be fatal.

Forcing herself to her feet, she balanced on her good side and hopped. Her foot was slick with blood.

Her shoe squished. Her knees buckled. The cold, hard ground punished her shoulder on impact.

She scrambled on all fours and tried to crawl. The barbed wire tightened like a coil. The ache in her leg was nothing compared to the agony in her heart.

Exertion wasn't good. Could she unwrap the mangled wire? Could she free herself? Could she catch up?

Panic pounded her chest. Her heartbeat echoed in her ears.

The hooves came closer. Had the men sent company? Had her screaming backfired, pinpointing her location?

Autumn foliage blanketed the ground, making it difficult to see if there was anything useful to use against another attacker. She could hide. But where?

The sounds of hooves pounding the unforgiving earth slowed. Near. She swallowed a sob. He could do whatever he wanted to her while she was trapped. Why had she made all that noise?

She fanned her hands across the ground. Was there anything she could use as a weapon? The best one encased her leg, causing a slow bleed. She needed to think. Come up with a plan. Could she use a sharp branch?

Biting back the pain, she scooted behind a tree and palmed a splintered stick.

The thunderous drumming came to a stop. The horse's labored breath broke through the quiet.

An imposing figure dismounted, muttering a curse. His low rumble of a voice sent chills up her neck.

Her pulse raced.

His boots firmly planted on the ground, Katherine got a good look at him. He was nothing like her attackers. They'd worn dark suits and sunglasses when they'd ambushed her and Noah. Everything about this man was different.

He wore jeans, a button-down shirt and a black cowboy hat. He had broad shoulders and lean hips. At his full height, he had to be at least six foot two, maybe more.

A man who looked genuine and strong like him couldn't be there for the wrong reasons, could he? Still, who could she trust? Couldn't murderers be magnetic?

"What in hell is going on?" A shiver raced up her spine as he followed the line of blood that would lead him right to her.

He took a menacing step toward her. Friend or enemy, she was about to come face-to-face with him.

Katherine said a silent protection prayer.

Her equilibrium was off. Her head light. She closed her fingers around the tree trunk tighter. Could she hold on long enough to make her move?

A dimpled chin on a carved-from-granite face leaned toward her. Brown eyes stared at her. She faltered.

Nope. Not a hallucination. This cowboy was real, and she was getting weak. Her vision blurred. She had to act fast.

With a final push, Katherine stepped forward. Her knees buckled and she stumbled.

In one quick motion Caleb Snow seized the stick being jabbed at his ribs and pinned the woman to the ground.

She was gorgeous in her lacy white shirt. Her sea-green skirt hiked up her thigh far enough to reveal a peek of her panties. Pale blue. He swallowed hard. Tried not to think about his favorite color caressing her sweet little bottom as he wrestled to keep her from stabbing him. The rest of her was golden skin and long legs. She had just enough curves to make her feel like a real woman, sensual and soft. "What's wrong with you?"

The tangle of chestnut hair and limbs didn't speak.

Was she afraid? Of him? Hell no. He took the stick and tossed it. She kicked and punched.

"Hold still. I'm trying to help."

"No. You're not."

"I will as soon as I'm sure you won't try to poke me with that stick."

He'd turned his horse the moment he'd heard the screams that sounded half wild banshee, half horror-film victim expecting to help, not be attacked.

"You're hurting me," she yelped.

The tremor in her voice sliced through his frustration. Her admission tore through him. The thought he added to her pain hit him hard. "Stop trying to slap me, and I'll get up."

Her lips trembled. She looked at him—all big fearful eyes and cherry lips—and his heart squeezed.

Those violet eyes stared up at him, sending a painful recollection splintering through his chest. She had the same look of terror his mother always had right before his father'd raised a hand to her. Caleb buried the memory before it could take hold.

"Listen to me. I'm not going to hurt you." Her almond-shaped face, olive skin and soft features stirred an inappropriate sexual reaction. Skin-to-skin contact was a bad idea. He shifted more of his weight onto his bent knee.

Her breaths came out in short gasps. "Then let me go. I have to find him before they get away."

"As soon as I know you're not gonna do something

stupid, I will. You're not going anywhere until I get this off your leg. You want to tell me what the hell's going on? Who's getting away?" Her actions were that of a wounded animal, not a crazed murderer. He eased more weight off her, scanning her for other injuries.

She recoiled. "Who are you?"

"Caleb Snow and this is my ranch." He picked up the wire to untangle her. Her pained cry pierced right through him. "Sorry about that." He eased the cable down carefully. "Didn't mean to hurt you."

She'd seriously tangled her long, silky leg in barbed wire. She'd lost a lot of blood. He couldn't have her going into shock. "The more you fight, the worse it'll get. You've done a number on yourself already."

Her eyelids fluttered.

Based on her pallor, she could lose consciousness if she didn't hold still. He stood and muttered a curse.

Her wild eyes looked up at him, pleading. "Some men took my nephew. I don't know who. They went that way." She motioned toward the McGrath ranch. Her voice cracked and he could see she was struggling not to cry. Tears fell anyway.

"The wire has to come off first. Then we'll take a look. Don't watch me. It'll only hurt worse. Tell me your name." A stab of guilt pierced him at the pain he was about to cause. The weight of her body had impaled the rusty steel barbs deep into her flesh.

Her head tilted back as she winced. She gasped but didn't scream, her eyes still radiating distrust.

"Hold on. I have something that can help." He pulled wire cutters and antibiotic wipes from his saddlebag. He tied a handkerchief below her knee to stem the bleeding.

"Promise you won't leave me here?"

"Now why would I do that?" One by one, he pulled the barbs out of her skin, giving her time to breathe in between. "Tell me more about the men."

"They. Were. Big." The words came through quick bursts of breath.

He pulled the last barb and stuck his hand out, offering a help up.

Hers felt soft and small. A jolt of electricity shot up Caleb's arm. Normally he'd enjoy feeling a sexual spark. This wasn't the time or place.

"I need to go that way." She pointed north, grasping at the tree.

"You're hurt. On my property, that means you don't go anywhere until I know you're okay. Besides, you still haven't told me why you're out here to begin with."

"Where is here?" she asked, dodging his question.

"The TorJake Ranch." How did she not know where she was? A dozen scenarios came to mind. None he liked. He took a step toward her. She was too weak to put up a fight. He wrapped his arm around her waist for support. "You aren't going anywhere like this. Start talking and I might be able to help. I have medical supplies at the house. But you'll explain why you're on my land or I'll call the sheriff. We clear?"

"Please. Don't. I'll tell you everything." He'd struck a nerve.

He should call Sheriff Coleman. No good ever came from a woman caught in a situation like this. But something about her made Caleb wait.

"My name is Katherine Harper. I took my nephew to a pumpkin patch." She glanced around. "I'm not sure which way."

"The Reynolds' place." Was it the fear in her eyes,

or the tremble to her lips that hit him somewhere deep? He didn't care. He was intrigued.

"Sounds right. Anyway, two men in suits came from nowhere and grabbed us. They dragged us through the woods…here…until I got caught up. Then…"

Tears streaked her cheeks. "They took off with him."

The barbed wire had been cut. The McGrath ranch was on the other side of the fence. He'd have to ask about that. Of course, he preferred to deal with creatures of the four-legged variety or something with a motor.

"We'll figure this out."

Caleb assessed her carefully.

Her vulnerable state had his instincts sounding alarm bells.

Chapter 2

Noah was gone. Katherine was hurt. Her only chance to see her nephew again stood next to her. The cowboy's actions showed he wanted to help. He needed to know the truth. She couldn't pinpoint the other reason she felt an undeniable urge to confide in the cowboy. But she did.

"My nephew was kidnapped for a reason." *Oh. God.* It was almost unbearable to say those words out loud.

His thick brow arched. "Do you know these men?"

She shook her head. "They wanted me to give them a file. Said they knew I had it, but I don't. I have no idea what they're talking about."

The cowboy's comforting arm tightened around her. Could he really help? Noah was gone and she was desperate.

He pulled out his cell phone.

"I'm calling my foreman, then the sheriff. We'll cover more ground that way."

"No police. They insisted. Besides, there's no time. Let's use your horse. We might be able to catch them. Noah needs medicine." She moved to step forward. Pain nearly buckled her knees. Her vision blurred.

"Hold on there," he said, righting her again with a firm hand. "We'll find him, but I'm bringing in the law."

"They'll hurt—"

"I doubt it. Think about it. They'd say anything to back you off. There's no chance to find him otherwise." He turned to his call. "Matt, grab a few men and some horses. We have a situation. A boy's been taken. Looks like they might've crossed over to the McGrath place with him. I want every square inch of both properties scoured. And call the sheriff." His gaze met Katherine's, and her heart clutched. He was right. They were most likely bluffing.

She nodded.

"There are two men dressed in suits. Could be dangerous." His attention shifted to her. "How old is your nephew?"

"Four." With reinforcements on the way, she dared to think she could get Noah back safely before the sun went down.

A muscle in the cowboy's jaw ticked. "You heard that, right?" A beat later came, "Somebody cut the fence on the north corner. Jimmy's been running this side. Ask him how things were the other day when he came this way."

Katherine looked at the barbed wire. The last bit of hope this could have been a bad dream shriveled and died.

"Tell the men to be careful." Caleb took more of her weight as he pocketed his phone. "I've got you."

"I'm fine." Katherine struggled to break free from his grip. Her brain was scrambled. She'd been dragged through this area thinking it had been a random trail, but how could it be? They'd cut the fence in advance. Everything about them seemed professional and planned. But what kind of file could she possibly have for men like them?

The cowboy's strong grip tightened around her as she fought another wave of nausea. "I think I'll be fine once I get on your horse."

"My men are all over this. Matt's phoning the sheriff as we speak. I need to get you home where I can take care of your injuries. The sheriff will need to speak to you for his report."

"The longer I wait, the farther away Noah will be." She had no purse, no ID and no money. Those had been discarded along with his medicine. Everything she'd had with her was scattered between here and the pumpkin patch.

His brow arched. "You won't make it a mile in your condition."

"I can. I have to." Katherine tried to put weight on her foot. Her knee buckled. He pulled her upright again with strong arms. He was powerful, male and looked as though he could handle himself against just about any threat.

Caleb shook his head. "Hell, I'd move heaven and earth if I were in your situation. But you're hurt."

"He needs me. He's little and scared. You can't possibly understand." Her voice hitched.

The lines in the cowboy's forehead deepened. "We'll

cut through the McGraths' on the way to the house. How's that?"

His arms banded around her hips. Arms like his would be capable of handling anyone or anything they came across. He lifted her onto the saddle with no effort and then swung up behind her.

"I need to make sure you're going to be around long enough to greet him. You let infection set in and that leg will be no use to you anymore."

She didn't argue. Fatigue weighted her limbs, drained her energy. If he could fix her leg, she could find Noah.

Taking the long way around didn't unearth any clues about Noah's whereabouts. The sky was darkening. Night would fall soon.

The house coming into view was a white two-story Colonial with a wraparound porch and dark green shutters. An impressive set of barns sat behind the house. There was a detached garage with a basketball hoop off to the side. This was a great place for kids.

Katherine hadn't stopped once to realize this man probably had a family of his own. The image of him cradling a baby edged its way into her thoughts. The contrast between something so tiny and vulnerable against his bare steel chest brought shivers up her arms.

Did he have a son? His reaction to Noah's age made more sense.

She prayed Noah would be home in bed before the sun vanished. Was he still panicked? Could he breathe? Did he have time before the next attack? Did she?

What would happen when the men came after her again if she couldn't produce the file?

She shrugged off the ice trickling down her spine. Police would need a description of the attackers. She had to think. The last thing she remembered was being hauled through the woods. She ran so long her lungs burned. The next thing she knew, she was facedown in the dirt. The men had disappeared. She'd lost everything.

"Lean toward me. I'll catch you." Caleb stood next to the horse.

One of his calloused but gentle hands splayed on the small of her back. He carried her inside as if she weighed nothing and placed her on the sofa in the front room. He lifted her bloody leg to rest on top of the polished knotty-pine coffee table.

The smell of spices and food warming sent a rumble through her stomach. How long had she been dragged? She wouldn't be able to eat, but how long could Noah go without food? Was he hungry?

"Margaret, grab my emergency bag," Caleb shouted before turning to Katherine. "Margaret helps me out with cleaning and cooking. Keeps me and my boys fed."

So he did have children. Katherine figured a place with this kind of space had to have little ones running around. Noah would have loved it here.

A round woman padded into the room. A salt-of-the-earth type with a kind face, she looked to be in her late fifties. Her expression dropped. "What happened?"

Caleb gave her a quick rundown before introducing them. "I'll need clean towels, a bowl of warm water and something for Katherine to drink. Some of these gashes are deep."

Margaret returned with supplies. "If anyone can find your nephew, it's this man."

Margaret's sympathetic expression melted some of Katherine's resolve. "Thank you."

"You look like you're in pain. Tell me where it hurts."

"My head. Stomach." Her hand pressed against her midsection to stave off another round of nausea. "But I'll be fine."

"Of course you will. You're in good hands." She set a cup of tea next to Katherine. "This'll help."

She thanked the housekeeper, smiled and took a sip. "Tastes good."

"Would you mind grabbing the keys to my truck? Call the barn, too. I rode Dawn again. Ask Teddy to put her up for the night." Caleb patted one of Katherine's gashes with antibiotic ointment.

She gasped, biting back a scream. "Now that I'm okay, we're going to find them ourselves, right?"

"I'm taking you to the E.R."

"No." Shaking her head made everything hurt that much worse. "I can't leave. Your guys will find Noah and bring him here, right?"

"Yes."

"Then the only reason I'd walk out that door is to help search for him. I won't leave here without him. He needs me and his meds."

She expected a fight but got a nod of agreement instead.

Caleb went back to work carefully blotting each gash without saying another word. Trying to distract herself from the pain, Katherine studied the room. The decor was simple. Substantial, hand-carved wood furniture surrounded the fireplace, which had a rust-colored star above the mantel. The cushions were soft. The place was more masculine than she figured it would be. There had to be a woman somewhere in the picture. A protective, gorgeous man like Caleb had to have a beautiful wife. And kids. She'd already envisioned him holding his child. She could easily see him with two or three more.

There was one problem. Nothing was out of place. She knew from spending the past week with Noah, kids left messes everywhere. "I hope your wife doesn't get the wrong impression when she sees a strange woman on your sofa."

Caleb didn't look up. "I'm single."

Had she met him under other circumstances, the admission would've caused a thousand tiny butterflies to flutter in her stomach. But now she could only think about Noah.

"Do you want to call Noah's parents and let them know what's going down?"

"No. There's no one else. His mother died. I'm all he's got." *The poor kid.*

Her sister, Leann, had always been the reckless one. Everything had been fun and games and risk for her. Now she was gone and Noah was in trouble.

A hundred questions danced across Caleb's intense brown eyes. To his credit, he didn't ask any of them.

Katherine figured he deserved to know the truth. "She died in a climbing accident at Enchanted Rock a week ago. She was 'bouldering,' which apparently means you don't use safety equipment. You're supposed to have people spot you, but she didn't."

Caleb's jaw did that tick thing again. She'd seen it before when he'd seemed upset and held his tongue. Did he have something he wanted to say now?

"Sorry for your loss. This must be devastating for you. What about Noah's father?"

"She…the two of them…lived in Austin alone. She

never told me who his father was. As far as I know, no one else has a clue, either. My sister may have been reckless with her actions but she could keep a secret." Katherine wondered what else she didn't know about Leann.

"Be easy enough to check out the birth certificate."

A half-laughed, half-exacerbated sigh slipped out. "She put down George Clooney."

If Caleb thought it funny, he didn't laugh.

Katherine cleared her throat. "I doubt if the father knows about Noah. Leann never told anyone who she dated. Not even me. I never knew the names of her boyfriends. When she spoke about them, they all had movie-star nicknames."

"There must've been a pattern to it."

Katherine shrugged. "Never gave it much thought before. Figured it was just for fun."

His reassuring nod comforted her.

"You two were close?"

"Our relationship was complicated, but I'm...was... fiercely protective of her." Katherine squeezed her elbows, not wanting to say what she really feared. Her sister had shucked responsibility and become involved with something or someone bad, and now both Katherine and Noah were in danger. Things had been turning around for Leann. Why would she do it?

Katherine tamped down the panic rising in her chest.

No one could hurt Noah.

She had to believe he would come home safely. Even though every fiber in her being feared he was already panicked, struggling to breathe. What if she found him and couldn't help? Her purse was lost along with his medicine.

One of Caleb's eyebrows lifted. "What about her friends?"

"I don't have the first idea who they were. My sister was a free spirit. She moved around a lot. Took odd jobs. I don't know much about her life before Noah. It wasn't until recently she contacted me at all." Had Leann known something was about to happen? Was she connected to the file?

Caleb didn't look at her. He just went back to work on her leg, cleaning blood and blotting on ointment.

Oh, God. Bile rose in her throat. Acid burned a trail to her mouth. "No news is definitely not good news."

"There aren't a lot of places to hide. If your nephew's around here, we'll find him. My men know this property better than they know their own mothers."

His comfort was hollow. A wave of desperation washed through her. If the men got off the property with Noah, how would she ever locate him?

"You hungry?"

"You know, I'm starting to feel much better." She tried to push up, but her arms gave out.

"Eat. Rest. The pain in your leg is only beginning. You must've twisted your ankle when you fell. It's swelling. Stay here. Keep it elevated. I'll check in with my men."

Caleb disappeared down the hall, returning a moment later with a steaming bowl in one hand and a bag of ice in the other. He'd removed his cowboy hat, revealing sandy-blond hair that was cut tight but long and loose enough to curl at the ends.

He set down the bowl before placing a pillow behind her head and ice on her ankle. He pulled out his cell while she ate the vegetable soup Margaret had prepared.

There was a knock at the front door. Katherine gasped. Her pulse raced.

* * *

Caleb's eyes met Katherine's and the power of that one look shot straight to his core. Her on his couch, helpless, with those big eyes—a shade of violet that bordered on purple in this light—made him wish he could erase her pain.

He let Sheriff Coleman in. The officer's tense expression reflected Caleb's emotions. "Your coming by on short notice is much appreciated."

Coleman tipped his hat, a nod to the mutual respect they'd built for one another in the years Caleb had owned the ranch.

"My men are out looking as we speak. I'll need more details to file the report."

Caleb introduced Coleman to Katherine. "This is the boy's aunt. He was with her at the Reynolds' pumpkin patch when it happened."

Sheriff Coleman tilted his head toward Katherine. His lips formed a grim line. "Start from the beginning and tell me everything you remember."

She talked about the pumpkin patch.

"Do you have a picture we can work with?" he asked, looking up from his notepad.

Her head shook, her lips trembled, but she didn't cry. "No. I don't. Lost them along with my purse and everything else I had with me. Not that it would do any good. He's only been living with me for a week. We haven't been down to clean his mother's apartment yet. I don't have many of his things. A few toys. His favorite stuffed animal."

She rambled a little. Not many women could hold it together under this much duress. Her strength radiated a flicker of light in the darkest shadows of Caleb. Places buried long ago, which were best left alone.

"Let's go over the description then," Coleman suggested.

"Black hair. Big brown eyes. Three and a half feet tall. About forty pounds. He's beautiful. Round face. Full cheeks. Curly hair. Features of an angel."

"And the men who took him?" he pressed.

"One of them had gray eyes and a jagged scar from the left side of his lip. He had a dark tan."

"How big was the scar?"

"Not more than a couple of inches. It was in the shape of a crescent moon." She sobbed, but quickly straightened her shoulders and shook it off.

The sheriff glanced away, giving her a moment of space. Caleb dropped his gaze to the floor, respecting her tenacity even more.

"He mentioned the name Kane. He said 'Kane wouldn't like it.'"

"We'll run the name against the database."

"I'm sorry. It's not much to go on. My nephew is alone. Sick. Scared. If he gets too upset, he could have an attack. Without his inhaler or medication, he won't be able to breathe."

Silence sat in the air for a beat.

Coleman cleared his throat. If Caleb didn't know any better, he'd say the sheriff had moisture in his eyes. In this small town, they didn't deal with a lot of violent crime.

"We'll do everything we can to bring him back to you safe and sound. That's a promise," Coleman said.

"Thank you."

"What's Noah's last name?"

"Foster."

"You said you haven't had a chance to clean out his mother's place. Where's that?"

"Austin."

"That where you're from?"

She shook her head. "I live in Dallas."

Caleb could've told the sheriff that. She had a polished, city look. The jeweled sandals on her feet were one of the most impractical shoes she could wear to the country aside from spiked heels.

"When's his birthday?"

"March. The seventeenth."

Caleb looked at her. He could see the tension in her face muscles and the stress threatening to crack, but to her credit, she kept her composure. Probably needed to be strong more than she needed air. Caleb knew the feeling for reasons he didn't want to talk about, either.

He'd known she was different from any other woman he'd met when he'd showed up to help her and she'd thanked him with a makeshift knife to his ribs. Hell, he respected her for it now that he knew the circumstances. She'd probably believed he was working with whoever had taken Noah and that he'd showed up to finish the job. She'd bucked up for a fight.

When she pushed herself up, it took everything in him not to close the distance between them and pull her into his arms for comfort. No one should have to go through this alone.

If Katherine Harper wanted to do this her way, he wouldn't block her path.

The sheriff asked a few more routine-sounding questions, listening intently to her answers. "You fight with anyone lately? A boyfriend?"

Caleb tried not to look as though he cared about the answer to that question. He had no right to care.

Katherine looked down. "Nope. No boyfriend."

"What about other family?"

"None. My parents died during my freshman year of college."

He didn't want to think about what that would do to a person.

Coleman asked a few more questions about family. Katherine looked uncomfortable answering.

"I'll notify my men to keep an eye out for your belongings. What were you doing out here with your nephew?"

"I wanted to take his mind off things. Get him out of the city. We planned our trip all day yesterday. He'd never seen a pumpkin patch. He loved the open space. I didn't think much about letting him run around. We've been in my small apartment all week. Didn't look to be anything or anyone else around for miles. He followed a duck out to the tree line. When I went over to take pictures, two men came from nowhere and snatched us. I panicked. Couldn't believe what was happening. I remember thinking, 'This can't be.' I fought back. That's when I ended up tangled in the barbed wire and they took off. If only I hadn't been so stubborn. If I hadn't fought."

"Don't blame yourself for this," Coleman said quickly.

"They told me if I came any closer or called the police, they'd kill him."

The sheriff nodded, but Caleb caught a flash behind Coleman's eyes. Caleb made a mental note to ask about that when they were alone.

"Ever see them before or hear their voices?" Coleman's gaze was trained on his notepad as he scribbled.

"No. Nothing about them was familiar. They asked for a file, but I don't have the first clue what they were talking about. Wondered if they'd confused us with someone else."

Katherine continued, "I don't remember tossing my purse or jacket, but I must've ditched them both somewhere along the way. Noah needs his medicine."

"We'll check between here and the Reynolds' place." The sheriff glanced at his watch. "Should have another half hour of daylight to work with."

"My car's still over there. Can't move it until I find my keys." She made a move to stand.

Caleb took a step toward her. The real estate between them disappeared in two strides. "You're too weak. Matt can get your car as soon as we find your purse. For now, I'll give the Reynolds a call. Make sure they don't have it towed."

Caleb phoned his neighbor and gave a quick rundown of the situation. He asked if anyone had reported anything or found a purse.

They hadn't.

Caleb finished the call solemnly. There wasn't much to go on, and time ticked away.

"I feel like I should be doing something besides sitting here," Katherine said to the sheriff.

"Best thing you can do is wait it out. Let my men do their work. I'll put out an AMBER Alert." Sheriff Coleman shook her hand and then walked to the door. "In the meantime, sit tight right here in case I have more questions. Let me know if anything else suspicious happens or you remember anything that might be important."

If Caleb heard things right, he'd just picked up a houseguest. Couldn't say he was especially disappointed. "You'll call as soon as you hear anything, right?"

"You bet."

Caleb thanked the sheriff and walked him out the door.

Outside, Caleb folded his arms. "What do you think?"

Coleman scanned his notes. He rocked back on his heels. "Not sure. Kids are most often taken by a family member. Don't see many kidnappings. Especially not out here."

"Doesn't sound good."

The sheriff dropped his gaze for a second and shook his head.

"What are the chances of finding him alive?"

"The odds are better if he was taken by a relative. Doesn't sound like the case here." Coleman broke eye contact. "That's a whole different ball game."

The words were a sucker punch to Caleb's chest.

"I'd appreciate hearing any news or leads you come across firsthand." Last thing Caleb wanted was for Katherine to learn what had happened to her nephew over the internet or on the news.

"Of course. There's always the possibility he got away and will turn up here. The first twenty-four hours are the most critical."

The thought of a little boy wandering around lost and alone in the dark woods clenched Caleb's gut. "Why'd they threaten to kill him if she called the police?"

"They probably want to keep this quiet. To scare her. Who knows? She's not a celebrity or politician. Why would someone target her? We need to find her phone.

In the meantime, have her make a list of enemies. Ask her if she's gotten into a fight with anyone lately. Could someone have a problem with her or her sister? Without her cell, we don't know if anyone's trying to contact her to make demands."

Caleb shook Coleman's hand before he got in his cruiser and pulled away.

He stood on the porch for a long moment, looking out at the landscape that had kept him from getting too restless for years. He couldn't imagine living anywhere else. This was home. And yet, an uneasy feeling crept over him.

Chapter 3

Matt's black pickup roared down the drive. Caleb walked to meet his foreman. "Find anything?"

"There's nothing around for miles. Whoever did this got away fast."

The whole scenario seemed calculated, ruling out the slight possibility this was a case of mistaken identity. "You checked with the McGraths?"

Matt nodded. "They haven't seen or heard anything all day. Gave us the okay to search their property and barn. I sent Jimmy and Greg over to the Reynolds', too. Not a trace. No one saw anything, either. There's nothing but her word to go on." Worry showed in the tight muscles of his face. "I gotta ask. You think it's possible she could be making this up?"

Caleb ground his back teeth. "This is real. She has the bumps and bruises to prove it."

"It was a crappy question but needed to be asked. There's no trail to follow. No other signs she's telling the truth. Could the marks be from something else?"

"You didn't see her. The terror in her eyes. The blood. I had to cut her free from the fencing. Dig barbs out of her leg."

"Stay with me for a minute. I'm just sayin'. Where's the proof she even has a nephew? How do we know all the mechanical stuff upstairs is oiled and the cranks are working with her?"

The point was valid. If he hadn't been the one to find her, he might wonder if she was crazy, too. But he had been the one. Her tortured expression might haunt him for the rest of his life. She'd faced the hell in front of her with her chin up. He didn't doubt her. "I hear you and I understand your concerns. I do. But you're off base."

"How can you be so sure?"

"I just know."

Matt cocked one eyebrow. "Okay…how?"

"Call it gut instinct."

"Then I'll take your word for it. I'll give her a ride wherever she wants to go." He took a step toward the house.

"Sheriff wants her to stick around."

Matt hesitated. His doubt about the situation was written all over his face. To his credit, he seemed to know when to hold his tongue. He turned toward the barn. "Be careful. You have a tendency to get too involved with creatures that need saving. I'll check on the boys out back."

It would be dark before too long. The sun, a bright orange glow on the horizon, was retreating. "I'll put on a pot of coffee."

As soon as Caleb walked inside, Katherine hit him with the first question.

"What did the sheriff say?" She stroked the little yellow tabby who had made herself at home in her lap.

"How'd you manage that?" He inclined his chin toward the kitty.

She shrugged. "She hopped on the couch and curled up. She's a sweet girl. Why?"

"Claws has been afraid of people ever since I brought her into the house."

"How'd she lose her leg?"

"Found her like that when I was riding fences one day. She was in pretty bad shape. Vet fixed her up, and she's been my little shadow ever since. Scratched the heck out of Matt the first time he picked her up. Usually hides when I have company."

Claws purred as Katherine scratched under her chin. "Can't imagine who would hurt such a sweet girl." She paused, and then locked gazes. "You were going to tell me what the sheriff said."

"That he'd contact me if they found anything. Do you remember what else you were doing before the men showed up?"

"We'd bought a jar of local honey. We were picking out pumpkins to take home with us."

"Anything else?"

"That's it. That's all I remember."

Caleb moved to the side table and picked up the empty soup bowl. "You drink coffee?"

"Yes."

"Give me five minutes. In the meantime, sheriff wants a list of names. Anyone who might've been out to hurt your sister. Or you."

He put down the bowl, took a pen and paper from a side table drawer and placed it next to her before moving into the kitchen.

She was making scribbles on the sheet of paper when he returned and handed her a cup. "Wasn't sure how you took yours."

"Black is fine." She gripped the mug. "What's next? How long does the sheriff expect me to sit here and do nothing?"

"Waiting's hard. Believe me, everything that can be done is happening. The authorities have all their resources on this. My men are filling the gaps. It's best to stay put until the sheriff calls. Give yourself a chance to heal. How's your leg?"

"Better. Thank you."

His bandage job looked to be holding. "What was the last thing you remembered before Noah was..." Damn. He hated saying the word *taken* out loud.

"I don't know. After the pumpkins, we were going on a hayride. I'd gone over to tell him. He was playing with the really big ones on the edge of the patch. Near the woods. I took pictures of him climbing on them. If we can find my phone, I can supply the sheriff with a recent photo."

"Think you might have captured the guys on your camera?"

"It's possible."

"I'll notify the sheriff."

Caleb phoned Coleman and provided an update. The hunt for her belongings intensified. They might find answers. At the very least, Matt would believe her if she could produce a picture of her nephew. Why did that seem so important?

"Think they saw you snapping shots?"

She shrugged. "Don't know."

"Did Noah scream?"

"They covered his mouth at the same time they grabbed him around the waist. Didn't bother once we got out of range." Sadness, desperation, fear played out across her features. "Please tell me we'll find him. I don't know what they want. If I can't produce a file, I'm afraid they'll take it out on him."

Caleb moved from his spot on the love seat to the couch and draped an arm around her. "We won't allow it. We'll figure it out."

"I wish I'd been thinking more clearly. I panicked. Dropped everything. If I had those pics now, we might have a direction."

Five raps on the door—Matt's signature knock—came before the door sprang open. His foreman rushed in holding a black purse.

Claws darted under the sofa.

Katherine strained to push off the couch. "You found it."

"The boys did." Matt's gaze moved from Caleb to Katherine. His brow furrowed and a muscle along his jaw twitched.

"Any luck with my phone?"

"This is all we got before we ran out of daylight. All the men in the county are involved. A few want to keep going. The rest will pick up the search tomorrow."

Matt handed the bag to Katherine. She immediately dumped out the contents, palming Noah's pill bottle and inhaler.

"Did you let Coleman know?" Caleb asked.

Matt nodded. "Sure did. There's something else you

should know. Thanks to that little bit of rain we got the other day, one of the boys located four-wheeler tracks on the McGrath farm on the other side of the fence near where you said you found her."

Matt couldn't deny she'd told the truth now.

Katherine was already digging around the large tote, tossing snack bags and juice boxes onto the sofa. "It all happened so fast. I can't even remember where I put my phone. I just remember taking photographs one minute, then the world spinning out of control the next. I wouldn't even believe any of this myself if it hadn't happened to me. I keep feeling like all of this is some kind of bad dream, and I'll wake up any second to find everything back to normal. Noah will be here with me. My sister will be alive."

As if shaking off the heavy thoughts, Katherine jammed her hand back inside her bag. Blood soaked through one section of the gauze on her leg.

"If you won't let me take you to the hospital, you'll have to listen to what I say. We have to keep this elevated." Caleb curled his fingers around her calf and lifted, watching for any signs he hurt her. Based on her grimace, her darkening eyes, she was winning the fight against the pain. When the shock and adrenaline wore off later, she'd be in for it. He didn't like the idea of her being home alone in Dallas when it happened.

"You're right. I'm sorry. I'm not thinking clearly. This whole ordeal has me scattered. Waiting it out will drive me insane."

Caleb didn't even want to think about the possibility of not finding her nephew.

Big violet eyes stared at him. "It's gone. I must've

still been holding it. They have no way to contact me. What if they've called already? What if they've..."

"Sleep here tonight." Caleb ignored Matt's sharp intake of breath. He hadn't planned to make the offer. It just came out.

"I'd get in your way. Besides, you have plenty to do to keep busy without me underfoot," Katherine argued without conviction.

"If you stay here, I'll be able to keep an eye on your leg and get some work done."

Going back to her one-bedroom apartment was about as appealing as sleeping alone in a cave. Her keys were in her purse, but she doubted she could drive. Even though Noah had only been there a week, she couldn't face going home without him. Staying at the ranch, being this near Caleb, provided a measure of strength and comfort.

His warm brown eyes darkened. "I can have Margaret turn down the bed in the guest room. Doesn't make sense for you to go anywhere."

"I don't want to be rude. I just..."

Frustration, exhaustion was taking hold. It had been three long hours since the ordeal began.

"No reason to leave. This is best place to be for now."

Caleb seemed the type of guy who took care of anyone and everyone he came across. Cowboy code or something. Still, she didn't want to abuse his goodwill. "Thank you for everything you've done so far, but—"

"It's no trouble."

Matt ran the toe of his boot along the floor. "Think they'll call her house?"

"I saw no need for a landline."

The cowboy sat on the edge of the coffee table. "Then it's settled. You stay. Agreed?"

"For tonight."

Matt quickly excused himself and disappeared down the hall. What was that all about?

The cowboy followed.

Her heart gave a little skip at the satisfied smile on his face. She refocused on the sheet of paper. Who would want something from Leann? What file could she possibly have? A manila folder? Computer file?

Why on earth would they think Katherine had it? If they knew Leann at all, they'd realize she could keep a secret. The last thing she would do was confide in her sister.

Maybe a trip to Austin would help? She could start with Leann's computer.

She rubbed her temples to ease the pounding between her eyes. Other than playing with the pumpkins, had Noah spoken to anyone? Had she?

There had to have been at least a dozen other people around. Were any of them in on it? A chill raced up her spine.

Caleb reappeared, holding a crutch. "I should take another look at that ankle before you put any weight on it."

"I just remembered something. There was a man talking to me while I was in line to buy tickets for the hayride."

His rich brown eyes lifted to meet hers and her heart faltered.

"He could've been there to distract you."

Panic at reliving the memory gripped her. She buried her face in her hands. "I'm so scared. What will they do to him?"

He cupped her chin, lifting her face until her eyes met his. "You can't think like that."

"He has to be terrified. He's so vulnerable and alone. I'm praying they haven't hurt him. He's been through so much already. I was supposed to take care of him. Protect him. Keep him safe."

"If he's half as strong as his aunt, he'll be all right." She could tell by his set jaw he meant it.

She almost laughed out loud. Little did he know how weak and miserable she felt, and her heart was fluttering with him so close, which could not be more inappropriate under the circumstances. "I promised on my sister's grave I would look after him. Look what I did."

The weight of those words sat heavier than a block of granite. Panic squeezed her chest. Her breath labored.

Brown eyes, rich, the color of newly turned fall leaves, set in an almost overwhelmingly attractive face stared at her. Before she could protest, his hand guided her face toward his shoulder.

"Don't blame yourself," he soothed. "Talk like that won't bring him back." His voice was a low rumble.

This close she could breathe in his scent. He smelled of fresh air and outdoors, masculine and virile. His mouth was so close to hers she could feel his cinnamon-scented breath on her skin.

She'd felt so alone, so guilty, and then suddenly this handsome cowboy was offering comfort.

Caleb pulled away too soon. Her mind was still trying to wrap itself around the fact a room could be charged with so much tension in less than a second, and in the next she could feel so guilty for allowing herself to get caught up in it.

The sounds of boots scuffling across tiles came from the other room. He inclined his chin toward the kitchen. "Sounds like we have company."

He stood and held out his hand.

By the time Katherine limped into the kitchen with Caleb's help, the table was filled with men. As soon as they saw her, chatter stopped and they stood. There were half a dozen cowboys surrounding the table.

"Ma'am." Matt tipped his hat.

She smiled, nodded.

Caleb led her to the sink to wash her hands and blot her face with a cool, wet towel.

"Take my seat," he said, urging her toward the head of the table.

Matt leaned forward, staring, lips pinched together.

As soon as she thanked the cowboy and sat, conversation resumed.

He handed her a plate of ribs and beans. She smiled up at him to show her gratitude.

He brought her fresh iced tea before making his own fixings and seating himself at the breakfast bar.

She looked down the table at the few guys. These must be the boys he'd referred to earlier.

Yep, he took care of everyone around him, including her.

When dinner was over, Caleb excused himself and moved to the back porch. Remnants of Katherine's unique smell, a mix of spring flowers and vanilla, filled his senses when he was anywhere near her. He had to detach and analyze the situation. He needed a clear head. He could think outside.

Katherine had clearly been through hell. An unexpected death and a kidnapping within a week?

Before he could get too deep into that thought, the screen door creaked open and Matt walked out.

"Tough situation in there," he said, nodding toward the house.

"You believe her now?"

"Hard to dispute the evidence." He held his toothpick up to the light. "I didn't mean to insult her before. I didn't know what to believe."

"Can't say I wouldn't be suspicious, too, if I hadn't seen her moments after the fact."

"I know you're planning to help, and it's the right thing to do, but is there something going on between you two?"

He clamped his mouth shut. Shock momentarily robbed his voice.

"No. Of course not. I met her five minutes ago. What makes you think otherwise?"

"You have a history of getting involved with women in crisis."

"I'd help anyone who needed it."

"True."

Matt didn't have to remind him of what he already knew. He had a knack for attracting women in trouble. Did he feel an attraction to Katherine? Yes. Was she beautiful? Yes. But he knew better than to act on it. The last time he'd rescued a woman, she'd returned the favor by breaking his heart. She'd let him help her, but then deserted him. He needed to keep his defenses up and not get involved with Katherine the way he did with the others. Period.

That being said, he wouldn't turn away a woman in trouble. Did this have something to do with his twisted-up childhood? He was pretty damn sure Freud would think so.

Tension tightened Matt's face. "Just be careful. When the last one walked out, she took a piece of you with her. You haven't been the same since."

"Not going to happen again."

Matt arched his brow. "If I'm honest, I'm also bothered by the fact there's a kid involved."

Figured. Caleb knew exactly what his friend was talking about. "My ex and her little girl have nothing to do with this."

"No? You sure about that?"

"I don't see how Katherine's nephew being kidnapped has anything to do with my past," Caleb said. Impatience edged his tone.

"A woman shows up at your door with a kid in crisis and you can't see anything familiar about it? I've known you a long time—"

"You don't have to remind me."

"Then you realize I wouldn't come out of the blue with something. I think your judgment's clouded." Matt's earnest eyes stared into Caleb. His buddy had had a ringside seat to the pain Cissy had caused when she'd walked out, taking Savannah with her. Matt's intentions were pure gold, if not his reasoning.

"I disagree." He couldn't deny or explain his attraction to Katherine. It was more than helping out a random person in need. He could be honest with himself. He probably felt a certain amount of pull toward her because of the child involved. No doubt, the situation tugged at his heart. But he'd only just met her. He'd help her. She'd leave. Whether she was wearing his favorite color on her underwear or not, they'd both move on. He had no intention of finding out if the pale blue lace circled her tiny waist. He was stubborn, not stupid. "Nothing else matters until we find that little guy."

"Saw the sheriff earlier." Matt's hands clenched. "Heard about the boy having a medical condition. What kind of person would snatch a little kid like that?"

Matt didn't use the word *monster,* but Caleb knew his buddy well enough to know he thought it.

"That's what I plan to find out."

"You know I'll help in any way I can. Then she can go home, and you can get on with your life."

Caleb chewed on a toothpick. "How are the men taking everything?"

"Hard. Especially with Jimmy's situation. He's still out searching."

"Meant to ask how his little girl's doing when I saw him tonight."

Matt shook his head. "Not good."

Damn. "Send 'em home. They need to be with their families."

"I think most of them want to be here to keep searching. Jimmy made up flyers. A few men headed into town to put the word out. Everyone wants to help with the search. They're working out shifts to sleep."

"Tell 'em how much I appreciate their efforts. We'll do everything we can to make sure this boy comes home safe. And we won't stop looking for him until we do."

Matt nodded, his solemn expression intensifying when he said, "You be careful with yourself, too."

"This is not like the others."

"You don't know that yet," Matt said, deadpan.

Caleb bit back his response. Matt's heart was in the right place. "Tell Gus I can't meet tomorrow. I know the buyer wants to stop by, but I can't."

"This is the third time he's set up a meeting. You haven't liked anyone he's found so far."

"Can't dump my mare on the first person that strolls in."

"Or the second…or third apparently. Every time we breed her, the same thing happens. It's been three years and not one of her foals has lived."

"Which is exactly the reason I don't want to sell her. What will end up happening to her when they realize she can't produce? Besides, she's useful around here."

"How so? The men use four-wheelers so it won't do any good to assign her to one of them. I have my horse and you have yours."

"I'll find more for her to do. Dawn's getting older. I'll use both. Not all lost causes are lost causes."

Matt's eyebrow rose as he turned toward the barn. "We'll see."

Caleb had been buried in paperwork for a couple hours when Katherine appeared in his office doorway, leaning on the crutch.

"Mind some company?"

She wore an oversize sleep shirt and loose-fitting shorts cinched above the hips. Even clothes two sizes too big couldn't cloak her sexy figure. Her soft curves would certainly get a man fantasizing about what was beneath those thin threads.

"Sure. Where'd you get the clothes?"

"Margaret put these on the bed with a note saying they belonged to her daughter. Even said I could borrow them as long as I needed to. I managed to clean up without getting my leg wet. I took a nap. I'm feeling much better."

Katherine sat in the oversize leather chair Caleb loved. It was big enough for two. Claws hopped up a second later, curling in her lap.

"Any word from the sheriff yet?"

"No. I put in a call to him. Should hear back any minute. If your leg is feeling better in the morning, I thought we could head to Austin."

"I want to stay here and search for my phone."

"We'll look first. Then we'll head out. Any chance you have a copy of your sister's keys?"

"Afraid not."

"We'll get in anyway."

She cocked her head and pursed her lips. "Tell me not to ask why you know how to break in someone's house."

Caleb cracked a smile as he rubbed his temples. "Misspent youth. Besides, some secrets a man takes to his grave." He chuckled. "I've been thinking. You have any idea if Noah's father knew about him?"

Katherine heaved a sigh, twirling her fingers through Claws's fur. "I should but don't. My sister's relationships were complicated. Especially ours."

"Families can be tricky," Caleb agreed.

"When our parents got in the car crash my freshman year of college, I resented having to come home to take care of her." Katherine dropped her gaze. "I probably made everything worse. Did everything wrong."

"Not an easy situation to be thrown into."

Katherine's lips trembled but no tears came.

"Leann had always been something of a free spirit. Her life was lived without a care in the world. I was the one who stressed over grades and stayed home on Friday nights to study or to help out around the house. My parents owned a small business and worked long hours. I was used to being alone. Leann, on the other hand, was always out with friends. The two of us couldn't have been more opposite. Sometimes I wished I could have been more like her. Instead, I came down on her hard. Tried to force her to be more like me."

"You had no choice but to be serious. Sounds like you were the one who had to grow up." She was a survivor who coped the best way she could.

"What about your parents?" She turned the tables.

"My mom was a saint. The man who donated sperm? A jerk. Dad, if you can call him that, didn't treat my mother very well before he decided to run out." Caleb's story was the same one being played out in every honky-tonk from there to the border. "I rebelled. I was angry at her for allowing him to hurt her when he was here. Angry with myself for not jumping in to save her. Mom worked herself too hard to pay the bills. Didn't have insurance. Didn't take care of her diabetes. Died when I was fifteen." The familiar stab of anger and regret punctured him.

"Did you blame yourself?"

"I know a thing or two about feeling like you let someone down. Only hurt yourself with that kind of thinking, though. I found the past is better left there. Best to focus on the here and now. Do that well and the future will take care of itself."

"Is that your way of saying I should let go?"

"I did plenty of things wrong when I was a child.

You could say I was a handful. Dwelling on it doesn't change what was."

She studied the room. "Looks like you're making up for it now."

Pride filled his chest. "Never felt like I belonged anywhere before here." He'd been restless lately, though. Matt had said Caleb missed having little feet running around. The wounds were still raw from Cissy leaving. Another reason he should keep a safe distance from the woman curled up on his favorite chair. She looked as though she belonged there. "TorJake is a great home."

"I love the name. How'd you come up with it?"

"My first big sale was a beautiful paint horse. The man who'd sold him to me when he was a pony said he tore up the ground like no other. He'd been calling him Speedy Jake. I joked that I should enter him over at Lone Star Park as ToreUpTheEarthJake. Somehow, his nickname got shortened to TorJake, and it stuck. Had to geld him early on to keep his temperament under control. He had the most interesting, well-defined markings I've ever seen. Sold him to a bigwig movie producer in Hollywood to use filming a Western. The sale allowed me to buy neighboring farms and eventually expand to what I have now."

"Was it always your dream to own a horse ranch?"

"I figured I'd end up in jail or worse. When I landed a job at my first working ranch, I fell in love. A fellow by the name of Hank was an old pro working there. He taught me the ropes. Said he saw something in me. He never had kids of his own. Told me he went to war instead. Became a damn good marine. Special ops. He taught me everything I know about horse ranches and keeping myself out of trouble."

"Where is he now?"

"He passed away last year."

"I'm so sorry." Her moment of distraction faded too fast, and he knew what she was thinking based on the change in her expression. "You don't think they'll hurt him, do you?"

He ground his back teeth. "I hope not. I don't like this situation for more than the obvious reasons. This whole thing feels off. Your sister dies a week ago. Now this with Noah. Could the two be connected somehow?"

Katherine gasped. Her hand came up to cover her mouth. "I didn't think about how odd the timing is."

"Maybe she got in a fight with Noah's father. Was about to reveal who he was. He could be someone prominent. Most missing children are taken by family members or acquaintances, once you rule out runaways, according to the sheriff."

"Then what about the file?"

"I was thinking about that. Could be a paternity test."

"If his father took him, at least Noah will be safe, right?" Katherine threaded her fingers through her hair, pulling it off her face.

"It's possible. I don't mean any disrespect. Do you think it's possible your sister was blackmailing him?"

"He didn't pay child support. That much I know. I paid her tuition. She enrolled in a social program to help with Noah's care. Got him into a great daycare. I was planning to move to Austin in a few months to be closer. I work for a multinational software company scheduling appointments for our trainers to visit customer sites, so it doesn't matter where I live. I wanted to be close so I could help out more. I can't help wondering what kind of person would hurt the mother of his child."

"I'm probably grasping at straws. We'll start with trying to figure out who he is. See what happens there."

"She was reckless before Noah. I thought her life was on track since his diagnosis. She got a part-time job at a coffee shop and enrolled in community college. She reconnected with me."

His ring tone cut into the conversation. "It's Matt." He brought the phone to his ear. "What's the word?"

"Jimmy found two things out at the Reynolds' place. A stuffed rabbit and a cell. I told him to meet me at your place."

"I appreciate the news. We'll keep watch for you."

Caleb hit End and told Katherine what his ranch hand had found.

"I hope I got a shot of someone. They wore dark sunglasses, so their faces might be hard to make out, but maybe I captured someone else involved. Like the man who distracted me."

"Either way, we'll know in a minute." Wouldn't do any good to set false expectations. And yet, hope was all she had.

Looking into her violet eyes, damned if he wasn't the one who wanted to put it there.

A knock at the door had him to his feet faster than he could tack a horse, and tossing a throw blanket toward Katherine.

Caleb led Jimmy and Matt into the study. After a quick introduction, Jimmy advanced toward Katherine, carrying a phone. "Found this along the tree line by the Reynolds' place. Look familiar?"

"Yes, thank you. That looks like mine." Katherine's eyes sparkled with the first sign of optimism since

Caleb had found her in the woods. She checked the screen. “Seven missed calls and a voice mail.”

Another knock sounded at the door. Caleb walked Sheriff Coleman into the study a moment later, before moving to her side. The hope in her eyes was another hint of light in the middle of darkness and blackness, and every worst fear realized.

“Put it on speaker.”

“I’m praying the message is from the kidnappers, but I’m scared it’s them, too.”

Caleb tensed. “Whatever’s on that phone, we’ll deal with it.”

Her gaze locked on to his as she held up the cell and listened.

“What’s wrong with the boy? You have twenty-four hours to help me figure it out and get me the file. I’ll call back with instructions. No more games. Think about it. Tick. Tock.”

Click.

Caleb took the phone and scanned the log. “Private number.” He looked at Coleman. “There any way to trace this call?”

“Doubt it. They’re probably smart enough to use a throwaway. We’ll check anyway.” Coleman scribbled fresh notes. “You mentioned the file before. Has anything come to mind since we last spoke?”

Katherine shook her head. “I’ve been guessing they mean a computer file, but I’m not positive. It could be anything.”

Outside, gravel spewed underneath tires. Caleb moved to the window. Two dark SUVs with blacked-out windows came barreling down the drive. “Sheriff, you tell anybody you were coming here?”

Coleman shook his head. "Didn't even tell my dispatcher."

Katherine's eyes pleaded. She wrapped the blanket around her tighter, clutching the stuffed rabbit Jimmy had handed her. "I don't have the first clue what file they're talking about. As soon as they realize it, they'll kill us both. Don't let them near me."

"Dammit. They must've followed someone here. The sheriff can cover for us." Caleb pulled Katherine to her feet as she gripped her handbag. He moved to the kitchen door, stopping long enough for her to slip on her sandals before looking back at his men.

"Can you cover me?"

Chapter 4

Caleb's arm, locked like a vise around Katherine's waist, was the only thing holding her upright.

The barn wasn't far but any slip, any yelp, and the men would barrel down on them. The lightest pressure on her leg caused blood to pulse painfully down her calf. She breathed in through her nose and out through her mouth, slowly, trying to keep her breaths equal lengths and her heart rate calm.

Could the darkness cloak them? Hide them from the danger not a hundred yards away?

Katherine squinted.

The glow from lamplight illuminated the parking pad. There were two men. Dark suits. A wave of déjà vu slammed into her like a hard swell.

They weren't close enough to make out facial features. Only stature. They looked like linebackers. Had the man with the jagged scar etched in his overly tanned face come back to kill her? He would haunt her memory forever.

Her pulse hammered at the recollection. "Even if you have a car stashed here somewhere, they'll never let us get past them."

"Don't need to."

"If you have another plan besides trying to barrel through them, or sneak around them, I'm all ears." She glanced at her bad leg and frowned.

"You still have your keys?"

She nodded, tucking the rabbit into her purse.

"Then we'll take your car."

"How will we do that? It's too far. I doubt I could get there unless you carried me." He seemed perfectly able to do just that.

"Won't have to. You'll see why." Caleb leaned her against the side of a tree near the back door of the barn. "Wait here."

She didn't want to be anywhere else but near him.

A moment later he pushed an ATV next to her. A long-barreled gun extended from his hand. A rifle? Katherine wouldn't know a shotgun from an AK-47. She only knew the names of those two from watching TV.

"This'll get us there." He patted the seat.

She glided onto the back with his help.

He slid a powerful leg in front of her and gripped the bars. "I think we're far enough away. The barn should block some of the noise. Hang on tight just in case they hear us."

Katherine clasped her hands around his midsection. His abdominal muscles were rock-solid. Was there a weak spot on his body? She allowed his strength to ease the tension knotting her shoulders. His warmth to calm her shaking arms.

"Why would they come looking for me? They said I had twenty-four hours. Why come after me before that?"

"Might be afraid you'll alert the authorities, or disappear. Plus, they must've figured out your nephew needs medication since they asked what was wrong with him."

"How did they find me?"

"There weren't many places to look other than my ranch."

"Good point." She hated the thought of putting Caleb and his men in danger. At least the sheriff was there to defend them. He would have questions for the men in the SUV. He'd slow the plans of any attackers and keep Caleb's crew safe. A little voice reminded her how the kidnappers had warned her about police involvement. She prayed Sheriff Coleman's presence didn't create a problem for Noah.

The trip was short and bumpy but allowed enough time for her eyes to adjust to the dark. Caleb cut the engine well before the clearing as she dug around in her purse for the keys.

"They might be watching your car, so we'll need to play this the right way." His earnest brown eyes intent on her, radiating confidence, were all she could see clearly in the dark.

A shiver cycled through her nerves, alighting her senses. It was a sensual feeling she was becoming accustomed to being this close to him. It spread warmth through her, and she felt a pull toward him stronger than the bond between nucleons in an atom. His quiet strength made her feel safe.

Caleb's powerful arms wrapped around her, and she wanted to melt into him and disappear. *Not now.* She canceled the thought. Noah needed her. No amount of stress or fear would make her shrink. She would be strong so she could find him. Sheer force of will had her pushing forward.

"Wait here." Caleb moved pantherlike from the tree line. Stealth. Intentional. Deadly. His deliberate movements told her there wasn't much this cowboy had faced he couldn't handle.

Katherine scanned the dark parking lot. She couldn't see far but figured even a second's notice would give Caleb a chance to react.

There was no one.

Nothing.

Except the din of the woods behind her. Around her. Surrounding her. A chilling symphony of chirping and sounds of the night.

Silently she waited for the all-clear or the telltale blast of his gun. For a split second she considered making a run for it. Maybe she could give herself up and beg for mercy before it was too late? Maybe the men would take her to Noah, and she could get his medicine to him now that she had her purse back?

Maybe they would take what they wanted and kill her?

They'd been ruthless so far. She had no doubt they would snap her neck faster than a branch if given the chance. Without his medicine, Noah would be dead, too.

All her hopes were riding on the unexpected hero cowboy, but what if he didn't come back? What if he disappeared into the night and ended up injured, bleeding out or worse?

Caleb was strong and capable, but he had no idea what kind of enemy they were up against. A bullet didn't discriminate between good and evil.

When the interior light of her car clicked on, she realized she'd been holding her breath. Caleb's calm voice coaxed her.

Another wave of relief came when she slid into the passenger side and secured her seat belt. He put the car in Reverse and backed out of the parking space. The sound of gravel spinning under tires had never sounded so much like heaven.

"You did good." His words were like a warm blanket around her frayed nerves.

"Thank you. Think it's safe to call the ranch?"

He nodded, stopping the car at the edge of the lot. The phone was to his ear a second later. He said a few uh-huhs into the receiver before ending the call and getting on the road. "Everyone's fine. Two men showed up, asking questions."

"What did they want?"

"They flashed badges. Said they were government investigators following a lead on a corporate fraud scheme."

A half laugh, half cough slipped out. "Leann? She didn't even have a normal job. She worked at a coffee shop."

"They didn't ask for your sister. They asked if someone matching your description had been seen in the area."

Fear pounded her chest. "Me? Corporate fraud? I don't have the first idea what they're talking about. I'm a scheduler for a software company. That's a far cry from a spy."

"Coleman took their information and plans to follow up through proper channels. Maybe the trail will lead somewhere."

"I hope so. Where do we go in the meantime?"

"Your sister's place. What's the address?"

Katherine scrolled through her contacts and read the details while he programmed the GPS in her car.

"We can check her computer and talk to her friends. Maybe we'll find answers there."

"Or just more questions. I told you. Knowing my sister, this won't be easy. I'm not sure who she hung around with let alone what she might've gotten herself into that could lead to this."

"Maybe the sheriff will come up with something. Good thing he was there. Might make these men think twice before they do anything else."

"Or..." She could've said it might make them kill Noah but didn't. No police. They'd been clear as day about it. Had she just crossed a line and put her nephew in more danger? Damn.

"They won't hurt him," Caleb said as though he read her thoughts.

"How can you be so sure?"

His grip tightened on the steering wheel. His jaw clenched. His gaze remained steady on the road in front of them. "We can't afford to think that way. First things first, let's get to Austin. We'll take the rest as it comes. Send Coleman the photos you took of Noah earlier."

"I almost forgot I had these." She scrolled through the pictures from the pumpkin patch. Noah smiled as he climbed on top of a huge orange gourd and exclaimed himself "king." Tremors vibrated from her chest to her neck. A stab of guilt pierced her. She scrutinized other details in the picture. Nothing but yellow-green grass and brown trees. A frustrated sigh escaped. “No good. I can’t make anything out on the small screen except him and a couple of large pumpkins.”

“Look up the last number I dialed, and send Coleman every shot you took today. He can blow them up and get a better view.”

Her heart lurched as she shared the pictures one by one. When she was finished, she shut her eyes.

Caleb took her hand and squeezed. Warmth filled her, comforting her. When was the last time a man’s touch did that?

She searched her memory but found nothing. No one, aside from Caleb, had ever had that effect on her.

“Think you can get a little shut-eye?”

Katherine was afraid to close her eyes. Feared she’d relive the horror of seeing a screaming Noah being ripped from her arms over and over again. “Probably not.”

“Lean your seat back a little.”

She did as she watched out the window instead. Interstate 35 stretched on forever. Every minute that ticked by was a reminder Noah was slipping away. Waco came and went, as did a few other smaller towns. The exhaustion of the day wore her nerves thin. Sleep would come about as fast as Christmas to June, but she closed her eyes anyway, praying a little rest would rejuvenate her and help her think clearly. Maybe there was something obvious she was overlooking that could help her put the pieces together.

Had Leann said anything recently? Dropped any hints? Given any clue that might foreshadow what was to come?

Nothing popped into Katherine's thoughts. Besides, if she knew one thing about her sister, Leann could keep a secret.

Sadness pressed against her chest, tightening her muscles. Leann must've known something was up. Why hadn't she said anything? Had she been in trouble? Maybe Katherine could've helped.

Katherine tried to remember the exact words her sister had used when she'd asked if Noah could come to Dallas for a week. Katherine could scarcely remember their conversation let alone expect perfect recall. How sad was that?

Her sister was dead, and Katherine couldn't even summon up the final words spoken between them. Guilt and regret ate at her conscience. Wait. There'd been a tornado warning, which was odd for October. When she joked about not being able to trust Texas weather, Leann had issued a sigh.

Katherine sat upright. "She knew something bad was going to happen."

"I figured it was the reason she sent Noah to stay with you."

"That means everything she did was premeditated. Maybe she'd gotten mixed up in a bad deal she didn't know how to get out of. But what?"

"Drugs?"

"No. She might have been a handful, but she didn't even drink alcohol."

Caleb shrugged. "My mind keeps circling back to the father."

"I guess it could be. I can't think of anyone else who would have so much to lose. Then again, I didn't know my sister very well as an adult. I believe she realized something was about to happen. That's as much as I can count on." Would Leann have blackmailed someone? Didn't sound right to Katherine. Her sister had always been a bit reckless, but not mean-spirited.

She was untrustworthy. Katherine had never been able to depend on her sister. A painful memory burst through her thoughts....

Leann was supposed to watch Katherine's dog, Hero, while Katherine had been away on a school trip. Leann had sneaked him to the park off-leash to catch a Frisbee after Katherine had said no. He'd followed the round disc far into the brush and never come back out. The whole time Katherine had been gone, she'd had no idea her dog was missing.

He'd been gone for three days by the time Katherine returned home. She hadn't cared. She'd looked for him anyway. She'd searched the park, the area surrounding the open field, and the woods, but he was nowhere to be found.

Losing Hero had delivered a crushing blow to Katherine.

It was the last time she'd allowed her sister around anything she cared about.

She sighed. When it came to Leann, just about anything was possible.

"We don't have any other leads. It's a good place to start."

She wanted—no, needed—to believe her sister wasn't capable of spite. Leann had always been a free thinker. She was Bohemian, a little eccentric, not a calculated criminal. Especially not the type to hold on to hate or to try to hurt someone else.

Desperation nearly caved Katherine.

"We'll find the connection and put this behind you." Caleb's words were meant to comfort her. They didn't.

They would be at Leann's place soon and there had to be something there to help them. Get to the apartment. Find whatever it is the men want. Exchange the file for Noah. Mourn her sister. Try to forget this whole ordeal happened. *If only life were so easy.*

The hum of the tires on the highway coupled with the safety of being with someone who had her back for once allowed her to relax a little. Maybe she could lay her head back and drift off. Adrenaline had faded, draining her reserves.

She closed her eyes for at least an hour before the GPS told them to turn left. "Destination is on the right."

Katherine's heart skipped. In two hundred feet, a murderer might be waiting. Or the ticket to saving her nephew. Oh, God, it had to be there. Otherwise, she had nothing.

Caleb pulled his gun from the floorboard as he drove past the white two-story apartment building.

The GPS recalculated. "Make the next legal U-turn."

He pressed Stop. "We better not risk walking in the front door. We don't know who might be waiting on the other side."

Good point. "There's a back stairwell. We can go through the kitchen entrance."

Even long past midnight on a weekday, the streets and sidewalks teamed with college students milling around. Activity buzzed as groups of twos and threes crisscrossed the road into the night. Music thumped from backyards. Lights were strung outside. It would be easy to blend into this environment.

He put the car in Park a few buildings down from

Leann's place. "We can walk from here. But first, I want to check in with Matt."

Katherine agreed. She had no idea what waited for her at her sister's. Her stomach was tied in knots.

"Matt's voice mail picked up." Caleb closed the phone. "I'm setting my phone to vibrate. You might want to do the same."

"Great idea." Katherine numbly palmed her phone. She stared at the metal rectangle for a long moment, half afraid, half daring it to ring. In one second, it had the power to change her life forever and she knew it. *Think of something else. Anything.*

Caleb took her hand. She followed him through the dark shadows, fighting against the pain shooting through her leg.

He stopped at the bottom of the stairwell and mouthed, "Stay here."

"No." Katherine shook her head for emphasis.

"Let me check it out first. I'll signal when it's okay."

"What if someone's out here watching?" Katherine didn't want to let her cowboy out of her sight. She'd never been this scared, and if he broke the link between them, she was certain all her confidence would dissipate. "I want to go with you. Besides, you don't know what you're looking for."

His eyes were intense. Dark. Pleading. "I don't like taking risks with you."

She couldn't let herself be swayed. They might not have much time inside, and she wouldn't wait out here while he did all the heavy lifting. "Either way, I'm coming."

Looking resigned, Caleb's jaw tightened. "You always this stubborn?"

"Determined. And I've never had this much on the line before."

His tense stance didn't ease. Instead, he looked poised for battle. His grip tightened on her hand. His other hand was clenched around the barrel of a gun.

"Then let's go," he said.

Katherine stayed as close behind as she could manage, ignoring the thumping pain in her leg.

Caleb turned at the back door and mouthed, "No lights."

The streetlight provided enough illumination to see clearly. He turned the handle and the door opened. It should have been locked.

Hope of finding anything useful dwindled. Of course, the men would have come here first.

If there was anything useful around, wouldn't they have found it already? They couldn't have, she reminded herself. Or she and Noah would be dead.

She moved to the dining space. The small corner desk was stacked with papers. A photo of Leann holding baby Noah brought tears to her eyes. She blinked them back, tucking the keepsake in her purse. The laptop Katherine had bought Leann for school was nowhere in sight.

Caleb's sure, steady movements radiated calm Katherine wanted to cling to. She dug through the pile of papers neatly stacked on the dining-room table while Caleb worked through the room, examining papers and objects.

Luck had never smiled on Katherine. She had no idea why this capable cowboy appeared. She needed him. The feeling was foreign to her and yet it felt nice to lean on someone else for a change. He looked every bit the man who could hold her up, too.

The realization startled her.

She knew very little about him, and yet he'd become her lifeline in a matter of hours. She could scarcely think about doing this without him and she wasn't sure which thought scared her the most. Katherine got through life depending on herself.

"Find anything useful?" he asked from across the room.

"No. It's hard to see in the dark though. You think whoever was here got what they wanted?"

Caleb moved to her. "Hard to say. You haven't been here since before the funeral, right?"

Katherine nodded. "I offered to pick up Noah, but she said no. Come to think of it, she's the one who mentioned meeting halfway. She'd never suggested that before. She wanted to meet in Waco this time in a restaurant that was way off the interstate. I figured it was just Leann being herself. Wanting to try something new."

"Looking back, did she act strange or say anything else that sticks out?"

"When we met she looked stressed. Cagey. I thought the responsibility of caring for Noah might be getting to her. Don't get me wrong, she loved that little boy. But caring for any kid, let alone one with medical needs, is stressful. Even so, she was a better parent than I ever would be."

She could feel his physical presence next to her before his arm slipped around her shoulders. "You would have been fine. And you will be, once we get Noah back safely."

Easy for him to say. He didn't know her. She didn't want to dwell on her shortcomings. Not now. She'd have time enough to examine those later when this was all over and her nephew was safe. "I thought she needed a break. The responsibility was becoming a burden. And then I didn't even think twice when I found out she'd had an accident climbing. I just assumed she'd been reckless." A sob escaped. "What does that say about me?"

"That you're human."

"Or I'm clueless. No wonder she didn't trust me with the truth. She must've known how little faith I had in her."

He guided her chin up until her gaze lifted to meet his.

"When people tell you who they are, it's best to believe them."

"What if they change?"

"Only time can tell that. Besides, it never does any good chasing what-if. You have to go on the information you have. Move from there."

"I guess."

"Look. You're strong. Brave. Determined. You were doing right by your sister. She trusted you or she never would have sent Noah to stay with you. As for the restaurant, she might've been worried she was being followed. She might've had a hunch there'd be trouble. I'm guessing she didn't bet on anything of this magnitude. She must've thought with Noah safe, she could handle whatever came her way."

His words were like a bonfire on a cold night. Warm. Soothing. Comforting.

Katherine reached up on her tiptoes and kissed his cheek.

* * *

A light touch from those silky lips and a hot trail lit from the point of contact. Caleb's fingers itched to get lost in that chestnut mane of hers. She slicked her tongue over those lips and his body reacted with a mind of its own. His blood heated to boiling. He swallowed hard. Damn.

One look into Katherine's eyes and he could see she was hurt and alone. He wouldn't take advantage of the situation even though every muscle in his body begged to lay her down right then and give her all the comfort and pleasure she could handle. Another time. Another place. Might be a different story?

Then again, he'd never been known for his timing. He'd taken Becca in when she'd showed up at his door in trouble. Anger still flared through him when he thought about the bruises on her face and her busted lip. No way would he turn away a woman who looked as though she'd been abused. Caring for her and giving her a place to stay until she got on her feet had been the right thing to do. Having a relationship was a bad idea.

He'd opened his home and developed feelings for her. *Look how that turned out,* a little voice in his head said. She'd left after a year, saying she needed time to figure herself out.

Katherine faced a different problem. She was being brave as hell facing it rather than running and hiding. "Let's see what else is here."

"While I'm here, I should find some clothes and change."

Caleb walked away. If he hadn't, he couldn't have been held responsible for his actions. His body wanted Katherine. He was a man. She lit fires in him with a slight touch. A spark that intense couldn't lead to anything good. He could end up in a raging wildfire of passion. Weren't wildfires all-consuming? And what did they leave in their wake? Devastation and tragedy.

The image of walking into the kitchen and finding Becca's Dear John on the counter wound back through his thoughts as Katherine entered the room.

Caleb refocused and searched for something that might be significant. A medical file. A sealed envelope. A scribble on a piece of paper. He kept an eye on Katherine. Her tightly held emotions were admirable. Pride he had no right to own filled a small space inside him.

An hour into the search, her expression told the story. Eyes, dark from exhaustion. Lips, thin from anger. Muscles, tense from frustration.

He moved behind her and pressed his palms to the knots in her neck, ignoring his own rising pulse.

"I know I haven't painted a good picture of my sister, but I can't imagine what she could've gotten herself into that would cause this. She could be irresponsible, but she had a good heart. Whatever she did would have to have been an accident. Something she fell into. She wouldn't have caused this much damage on purpose. She was sweet. Harmless. She isn't—wasn't—the type of person who'd do something malicious."

"What happened between the two of you?" He doubted she'd tell him but he took a chance and asked anyway.

Katherine sat for a moment. She leaned forward, allowing him to deepen the pressure on her neck and move his hands to her shoulders.

"She was fifteen. Rebellious. There was this one time I specifically told her not to go out. I needed her home to let a repairman in. She didn't listen and left anyway. Probably out of spite. We had to go the night without A/C in the middle of a Dallas summer. I'd been in class all day and then worked the afternoon shift as a hostess. I was hot. Miserable. I decided to wait up for her. The minute she waltzed through the door, I blew up. Told her she was a spoiled brat."

"You had every right to ask her to pitch in more. It wasn't like you asked her to gut a hog."

"I didn't 'ask' anything. I demanded she stay home. I thought it was my job to tell her what to do with our parents gone, not that she made it easy. She didn't want to listen and was never there when I needed her. I resented her. I learned pretty fast that I couldn't depend on her and had to learn to do things on my own."

"You should be proud of yourself."

"I could've been more sympathetic. But Leann did what she did best—disappeared. When she came home, I noticed she'd been drinking. I came down on her too hard."

Caleb knew all about self-recrimination. Hadn't he been beating himself up with worry since his last girlfriend left? Hadn't the ache in his chest been a void so large he didn't think he'd ever fill it again?

Caleb increased pressure, working a knot out of Katherine's shoulder.

A self-satisfied smile crossed his lips at the way her silky skin relaxed under his touch, and for the little moan that escaped before she could quash it. "You always this tough on yourself?"

Katherine hugged her knees into her chest. "A week later when she left, she didn't come back. I didn't hear from her for years."

Caleb couldn't imagine how difficult it was for Katherine to say those words out loud. She couldn't be more than twenty-six or twenty-seven, and seemed keenly aware of all her misjudgments now. A few years younger than him, she bore the weight of the world on her shoulders. The knots he'd been working so hard to release tightened. "Your sister was old enough to know better. You were trying to do what was best. I'm sure she knew that on some level."

"No. I had to close myself off because it was too painful repeatedly being disappointed by her. We stopped speaking. I didn't hear from her again until this year. Noah had barely turned four. I didn't even know I had a nephew before then."

Caleb moved to face her and took a knee, reaching out to place her hand in his. Her skin was finer than silk, her body small and delicate. The point where skin made contact sent a jolt of heat coursing through him. "Life threw you for a loop, too. Besides, you did what any good person would. You stepped up to fill impossible shoes and did your best. Because you weren't perfect doesn't mean you failed. You're an amazing woman."

He looked at her, really looked at her. There was enough light to see a red blush crawl up her neck, reaching her cheeks. Her skin glowed, her eyes glittered. The fire in her eyes nothing in comparison to the one she lit inside him.

He studied the soft curves of her lush mouth and then let his gaze lower to the swell of her firm, pointed breasts. All he felt was heat. Heat and need. Her jeans, balanced low on slim hips, teased him with a sliver of skin between the edge and the bottom of her T-shirt. Damn that she was even sexier when she was hurting.

He pulled on all the strength he had so as not to take her lips right there…then her body.

Caleb needed to redirect his thoughts before he allowed his hormones to get out of hand. She made it difficult to focus on anything but thoughts of how good her body would feel moving beneath his. Alter the circumstances and things might have been different. Last thing Caleb needed was to get tangled up with another woman who showed up at his door with a crisis. He pushed all sexual thoughts out of his psyche.

"Since there's nothing here, we'd better go. I'm actually surprised no one's been watching the place."

Her gaze darted around the room. "Where do we go next? We can't go back to your ranch, can we?"

"No. I don't want to put my men at risk any more than we already have. What about your place? Any chance Leann passed a file to you in Noah's things?"

Hope once again brimmed in her shimmering eyes. "I hadn't thought of that. It's a possibility."

Caleb glanced at his watch, ignoring the ache in his chest for her. "If we leave now, we'll make it before daylight."

He preferred to move under the cover of night anyway.

She pulled back as they started toward the door. "Wait."

Caleb eased more of her weight on him, ignoring the pulsing heat on his outer thigh at the point of contact. "What is it?"

"I want to grab more medicine and something from Noah's room first." Katherine pushed off him to regain balance.

Her phone vibrated and she froze.

"Take a deep breath and then pick up," Caleb said.

She exhaled and answered.

"Is he breathing?" She paused. "Good. He has asthma. There's an inhaler he uses and I have medicine. I can bring them wherever—"

The guy on the line must've interrupted because Katherine became quiet again and just listened. "What time?"

Her expression vacillated between anger and panic.

"Where?" She signaled to Caleb for a pen and paper.

He retrieved them and watched as she jotted down "Sculpture at CenterPark" and then ended the call.

Her wide-eyed gaze flew up to him. "They want to meet tomorrow afternoon."

"Did they mention anything about the file we're looking for?"

She shook her head. "They only said to bring it to NorthPark Center."

"Good, it's out in the open. What time?"

"Three o'clock."

Caleb glanced at his watch. "We have plenty of time to check it out first."

"They told me to come alone." Determination thinned her lips before she turned and walked away.

He wouldn't argue as he closely followed her, ready to grab her if she faltered. She was determined to walk on her own; he'd give her that. The way she did "stubborn" was sexy as hell. Now was not the time for the conversation he needed to have with her. The one that said no way in hell was he allowing her to go by herself.

"Before we leave, is there any place we haven't looked? Did she have a secret hiding spot?"

"None she would share with me." As she moved behind the sofa, she stopped suddenly. "I didn't think about this before, but it makes perfect sense. We might not find anything, but it's worth checking out."

Katherine limped down the short hall and into the master bedroom.

She stopped in the middle of the room and looked up at the ceiling fan. "She had a small diary when we were kids that she hid by taping it to the top of one the blades. I found it when I was helping my parents spring clean once." A hint of sadness darkened her features. "Found out just how much she was sick of me when I peeked at the pages."

Caleb righted a chair that had been tossed upside down and settled it in the center of the room. "Let me look."

Even on the chair, he couldn't see the tops of the half-dozen blades.

Puffs of dust floated down when he wiped the first. More of the same on the second. His hand stopped on a small rectangle on the third. "I found something."

"Can you tell what?" Her voice brightened with hope.

"It's secure." He didn't want to take a chance on damaging it by ripping it off. His fingers moved around the smooth surface. Tape? He peeled the sticky layer off the item. "I'll be damned. It's a cell phone."

"Thank God, they missed it."

"I don't recognize the brand," he said as he palmed it.

"Think it works?"

He pressed the power button. "It's dead. If we can find a store that sells these, we can buy a new cable or battery. We'll look up the manufacturer when we get back in the car."

"Okay." She spun around. "Oh, and I need to find something else."

He followed her down the hall to Noah's bedroom.

"I know it's here somewhere," she said, tossing around toys and clothes.

"What are you looking for? I'll help."

"No. I found it." She held up a stuffed reindeer. "It's Prancer. One of Noah's favorites. He apparently used to sleep with it all the time. Now he's into the rabbit. I was just thinking he'll need as many of his things as possible to make my place feel like home." She gathered a few more toys from the mess.

"Prancer? Seems like an interesting choice for a name. I mean, why not Rudolph?" He examined the stuffed animal.

"Noah thinks the other reindeer get overlooked. Said Rudolph gets all the glory," she said, melancholy.

Caleb couldn't help but crack a smile. "How old did you say he is?"

"Four."

"Sounds like a compassionate boy." He tucked the stuffed animal under his arm. "We'll keep Prancer safe until he's back with Noah."

When Caleb looked at her, his heart dropped. A dozen emotions played across her delicate features. Fear. Regret. Anxiety.

He walked to her and took her hand in his.

"We'll find him. I promise."

Before he could debate his actions, he tilted his head forward and pressed his lips to hers gently. The soft kiss intensified when she parted her lips to allow him access. His mouth covered hers as he swallowed her moan.

Both his hands cupped her cheeks, tilting her face until his tongue delved more deeply, tasting her.

She pulled back long enough to look into his eyes.

"I believe you mean that," she said, her voice like silk wrapping around him, easing the ache in his chest.

Caleb always delivered on his commitments. He hoped like hell this time would be no different.

Chapter 5

Exhaustion dulled Katherine's senses, but she managed to follow Caleb back to the car. The visit hadn't produced any real optimism. All their hopes were riding on a dead phone.

And what if there's nothing there? a tiny voice in the back of her mind asked.

What then?

Hot, burning tears blurred Katherine's vision. Her mantra—*Chin Up. Move Forward. Forge Ahead*—had always worked. She'd survived so much of what life had thrown at her repeating those few words. Hadn't she been stronger because of it?

Then how did she explain the hollow ache in her chest? Or the niggling dread she might live out the rest of her days by herself. Everyone let her down eventually. Who could she lean on when times got tough? Who did she really have to help celebrate life's successes?

Before meeting this cowboy, she'd never realized how alone she'd truly been. She gave herself a mental shake as she opened the car door and buckled in.

Caleb found her cable-knit sweater in the back and placed it over her as she clicked the seat belt into place.

She slipped the sweater over her shoulders and closed her eyes, expecting to see the attackers' faces or to hear their threats replaying in her mind. She didn't. Instead, she saw Caleb and relaxed into a deep sleep.

Katherine didn't open her eyes again until she heard Caleb's voice, raspy from lack of sleep, urging her awake. For a split second she imagined being pressed up against him, snuggled against the crook of his arm, in his big bed. She'd already been introduced, and quite intimately, to his broad chest and his long, lean, muscled thighs. He'd left no doubt he was all power, virility and man when his body had blanketed her, pinning her to the ground. Her fists had pounded pure steel abs. Warmth spread from her body to her limbs, heating her thighs.

The reality she was curled up in her car while running for Noah's life brought a slap of sanity.

"Where are we?"

"Dallas. If the address on your license is correct, we're a couple blocks from your house." He glanced at the clock. "Don't worry. We have plenty of time before the drop."

She sat up and rubbed sleep from her eyes. They were at a drive-through for a local coffee shop.

Coffee.

There couldn't be much better at the moment than a good cup of coffee save for finding Noah and having this whole nightmare behind her.

Caleb handed her a cup and took a drink from his while he pulled out of the parking lot.

"I ordered black for you."

"Perfect." Katherine took a sip of the hot liquid. The slight burn woke her senses. A blaze of sunlight appeared from the east. "You've been driving all night. You must be exhausted."

Caleb took another sip from the plastic cup. "I'm more worried about that leg of yours. At some point, we need to take another look. Didn't want to disturb you last night while you looked so peaceful."

"I'm surprised I slept at all." Katherine stretched and yawned. She glanced down at her injuries. Blood had soaked through a few of the bandages and dried. Most were intact and clear. All things considered, they were holding up. "You dressed these well. My ankle feels better already."

She touched one, then two bandages. "I think they'll hold awhile longer. At least the bleeding has stopped."

"That's the best news I've heard all day." He cracked a sexy little smile and winked. "We'd better park here." He cut the engine. "We'll walk the rest of the way."

"Do you think they're watching my apartment?"

"A precaution," he reassured her. His clenched jaw belied his words.

"Why didn't they stop us last night? They could've waited at Leann's and shot us right then."

"I thought about that a lot on the drive. They want you to find what we're looking for. And fast."

"I didn't say anything about the file on the last call.

I was too focused on Noah. They must realize I don't have it." She glanced toward her purse where the cell phone had been stashed.

"Stores don't open until ten o'clock. We have to wait to find a charging cable until then." He took a sip of coffee. "I'm guessing Noah's breathing problems must've forced them to ask for a meeting before they were ready. I think they'd rather let you locate the evidence, and then snatch you. Once they're convinced you have it, I have no doubt the game will change."

He watched over their shoulders a few times too many for Katherine's comfort, as they did their best to blend with pedestrians.

"Wait here while I scout the area." They were a few hundred feet from the front door of her apartment. He pointed toward the row of blooming crepe myrtles. There hadn't been a cold snap yet to kill the flowers. Fall weather didn't come to Dallas until mid-November some years. This was no exception.

"Okay."

A few minutes later he returned. "Looks fine from what I can tell. If they're watching, they're doing a good job of hiding. Either way, keep close to me."

She had no intention of doing anything else as she unlocked the door and followed him inside. "I wish we knew what kind of file we were looking for."

Her office had been temporarily set up in the dining room so Noah could occupy the study. From where she stood, she could see they'd taken her computer. "First Leann's laptop is missing. Now my computer. I'm guessing we're looking for a zip drive or other storage device."

"If it wasn't at your sister's place and it's not here, where else could the file be?"

"I work from home, so there's no office to go to. All I need to schedule appointments for my trainers is a computer and a phone. I keep everything here. I'll check the study where Noah's been sleeping. You might be right about Leann slipping it into his things." Katherine moved to the study that had been overtaken by her nephew. Toys spilled onto the floor. She stepped over them and rummaged through his things. No red flags were raised.

This approach wasn't working. If she were going to get anywhere, she had to figure out a way to think like Leann. Where would she stick something so incredibly valuable? Maybe Noah's suitcase? She could have removed part of the lining and tucked a file inside.

Katherine dug around until she located the small Spider-Man suitcase Noah had had in his hand when she'd met up with them. That and the rabbit he'd tucked under his arm were all the possessions he'd brought.

The Spider-Man suitcase had several pockets with zippers. Katherine checked them first. Empty. The lining was a bit more difficult to rip open but she managed without calling for help. *Sorry, buddy.* She hated to destroy his favorite bag.

Nothing there, either. Katherine tore apart the seams.

Zero.

The clock ticked. The men would expect her to produce the file soon. She had nothing to give them and still no idea what it was she was looking for. Damn.

When she returned to the living room, Caleb stood sentinel.

"No luck," she said. "She might've sent it over email."

Katherine dug around in the back of her coat closet to find her old laptop. She held it up. "This might still work."

"Your sister brought Noah to you. He was the person she most prized. Have you thought she might not have involved you because she was trying to shelter you both?"

Katherine hadn't considered Leann might be protecting her. It softened the blow. "We'll see."

A soft knock at the door kicked up Katherine's pulse.

Caleb checked through the peephole. His expression darkened. His brow arched. "Gray-haired woman. Looks to be in her mid-sixties, carrying a white puff ball."

"Does she look angry?"

"More like sour."

"Annabelle Ranker. She's my landlady, and that's her dog, Max. Big bark, no bite for the both of them." Katherine got to her feet and his strong arm was around her before she could ask for help to walk.

Caleb cracked the door open. Ms. Ranker cocked her eyebrow and looked him up and down. An approving smile quirked the corners of her lips. When Caleb didn't invite her in, the skeptical glare quickly returned.

No doubt, the bandages and blood wouldn't go unnoticed. Nor would the fact Katherine was gripping her old laptop as though it was fine crystal.

"Are you all right?" Her gaze traveled to Katherine's hurt foot.

"I'm fine. Got into some trouble in the woods. Turns out I'm not a nature girl. Caleb owns a nearby ranch where we visited the pumpkin patch yesterday."

"That's right. You said you were taking Noah out of the city for the day."

"We got lost in the woods. Caleb found us and helped me home." Katherine could feel heat rising up her neck. No one would ever accuse her of being a good liar. She'd kept her story as close to the truth as she could so her whole face wouldn't turn beet-red.

Ms. Ranker seemed reassured by the answer. "I wanted to check on you and the little boy. Where's Noah?"

Katherine swallowed a sob. She couldn't afford to show any emotion or to invite unwanted questions. "I'm sorry. He couldn't sleep…nightmares. We were…playing army most of the night. I've been trying to keep him busy since his mother…" Katherine diverted her eyes.

"Such a shame." Ms. Ranker shook her head, obviously moved by Leann's passing. "Is he home? I'd be happy to take him off your hands while you rest that foot."

"He's napping. Tuckered out from our adventure," she said quickly. A little too quickly.

The answer seemed to appease the landlady. She nodded her understanding. "I almost forgot. A package came for you while you were out. I went ahead and signed for it since you didn't answer."

Katherine had scarcely paid attention to the FedEx envelope Ms. Ranker held in one hand. Her other arm pressed her prized six-year-old Havenese, Max, to her chest.

"For me?" Katherine asked, lowering her gaze to the fur ball on Ms. Ranker's arm. "Hey, big guy."

She patted his head, stopping short of inviting them in; Ms. Ranker's arched brow said she noticed. Last thing Katherine needed was a long conversation. Besides, she wasn't prepared to discuss her situation with anyone. Except Caleb. And she'd told him things about her relationship with her sister she'd never spoken aloud to another soul. It was probably the circumstances that had her wanting to tell him everything about her. It was as if she wanted at least one person to really know her. The feeling of danger and the very real possibility she might not be alive tomorrow played tricks on her emotions. "Who's it from?"

The well-meaning Ms. Ranker held out the envelope. No doubt she wanted to know more about the handsome cowboy. Plus, it wasn't like Katherine not to invite her landlady inside or to be so cryptic.

She cleared her throat and tugged at the envelope.

A slight smile was all she could expect by way of apology as the older woman loosened her grip enough for her to take possession.

Katherine's gaze flew from the return address to Caleb. The letter was from Leann. Katherine pressed it against the laptop she was still clutching.

Out of the corner of her eye, she saw the door across the courtyard open. A long metal barrel poked out. A gun?

A shower of bullets descended around them at the same time Katherine opened her mouth to warn them. A bullet slammed into the laptop. Before she could think or move, she felt the impact against her chest.

Ms. Ranker's eyes bulged before she slumped to the ground.

In the next second Caleb was on top of Katherine, covering her, protecting her.

"Are you hit?" he asked.

"I don't think so. Can't say the same for my computer." She'd dropped it the moment a bullet hit and then embedded. The hunk of metal she'd clasped to her chest had just saved her life.

He angled his head toward the kitchen. "Go. I'll fire when they get close enough."

Before she could respond, he'd urged her to keep moving as he pulled the gun to his shoulder.

When bullets exploded from the end of it, her heart hammered her chest.

Didn't matter. No time to look back. If Caleb thought she'd get out through the side window, she was in no position to argue. She clawed her way across the taupe carpet until she reached the cold tiles of the kitchen.

A moment later he was lifting her through the opened window and she was running.

Her heartbeat painfully stabbed her ribs.

Why were they shooting? They must've been watching the whole time. Did they think she'd found what they were looking for?

Oh. God. Noah. What would happen to him?

Her legs moved fast. She barely acknowledged the blood soaking her bandages. She had to run. Get out of there.

Caleb guided her to the sedan. "Get in and stay down."

Katherine curled up in a ball on the floorboard. If the bad guys knew where she lived, wouldn't they recognize her car, too?

What about Ms. Ranker? Katherine had been so busy ducking she didn't even look. "Is my landlady…?" Katherine couldn't finish the sentence.

Caleb shook his head. "I'm sorry."

"Max?"

"I think he got away."

Katherine gripped the envelope, fighting against the tears threatening to overwhelm her. Release the deluge and she wouldn't be able to stop. "Maybe this is what they're looking for." She held up the envelope that had cost Ms. Ranker's life.

His focus shifted from the rearview to the side mirrors. "Might be."

She ripped open the letter and overturned it on the seat.

A CD fell out.

"A file?"

"Sure looks like it." Caleb glanced around. "Stay here and stay low. Do not look up until I get back."

Before she could ask why or argue, he disappeared.

Katherine made herself into the smallest ball she could, praying for his safe return.

She couldn't even think of doing any of this without him. And yet, didn't everyone flake out on her eventually?

Even her parents.

The memory of standing on stage, alone, her senior year of high school pushed through her thoughts. The anticipation of seeing her parents' smiling faces in the crowd as she'd competed in the academic fair filled her. She'd worked hard all year and qualified with the best score her school had ever received. She'd sacrificed dates and socials to stay home and work quiz after quiz. On stage, her pulse had raced and she'd felt tiny beads of sweat trickling down her neck. She remembered thinking that if she could just see someone familiar, she'd be okay.

The curtain had opened and she'd scanned the crowd.

No one.

Disappointment and fear had gripped her. Panic had made the air thin. She'd struggled to breathe.

By the third round, she'd choked and given the wrong answer.

When she'd arrived home that evening, her parents had told her how sorry they were. They'd come home from work, opened a bottle of wine, turned on the TV and forgotten. Again.

Katherine had worked to suppress the memory from then on. She'd learned another important lesson that day. If she was going to get anywhere in life, she had only herself to depend on.

Her heart squeezed when she heard quick footsteps hustling toward her. She held her breath until Caleb's face came into view. He slipped into the driver's seat and handed over Max, his white coat splattered with red dots. He was whimpering and shaking. "Is he hurt?"

"No." Caleb turned the key in the ignition and pressed the gas. "Just scared."

Was Max covered in his owner's blood?

Katherine looked to Caleb. He dropped his right hand to his side. It was covered in blood.

"You're shot?"

"Just a flesh wound. Bullet grazed my shoulder. I'll be fine." Caleb hoped what he said was true. Based on the amount of blood he was losing, he couldn't be certain. He wouldn't tell Katherine though. Didn't need her to panic.

She made a move to get up, and winced.

"I'll pull over in a minute and examine us both."

Caleb glanced through his rearview, checking traffic behind them. The usual mix of sport utilities, Ford F-150s and luxury sedans sped down the North Dallas tollway.

His cell vibrated. He instructed Katherine to retrieve it from his pocket and put the call on speaker.

Matt didn't wait to speak. "My coverage has been spotty. I tried to reach you last night but couldn't."

"Everyone all right?"

"Us? We're fine. I'm concerned as hell about you."

Caleb kept watch on the road. "So far, so good here."

"Has Katherine mentioned anything about being involved in corporate espionage?"

"Of course not. I would've told you something like that. She has no idea what they're looking for."

"I guess she wouldn't tell you," Matt said. "Especially if she's involved from the get-go."

Caleb grunted but didn't speak. He had no plans to repeat himself.

"Well, ask her. The men who showed up yesterday claimed to be government officials. They asked questions about a brown-haired woman who had been seen in the area. Said she was involved in a little family business that stole and sold corporate secrets. They'd been tracking her for days before you helped her get away."

"They knew we were there?" Caleb asked. "And I don't have to ask Katherine. You're on speaker."

The line was quiet. "No. But I'm saying—"

"I already know the answer."

"You can't ignore the possibility she's involved," Matt quickly interjected.

"She's not."

"How do you know, dammit?"

"I just do."

Matt let out a frustrated hiss and a string of cuss words Caleb heard plainly through the phone.

"You just met her yesterday, and you're willing to vouch for her already? What do you know about her? You haven't met any of her people. She could've been hurt while running from the government for all we know."

"I told you once so I won't repeat myself. What else did they say?"

"One thing is sure. She shows up then suddenly we have official-looking men coming out of the woodwork. All we have to go on is her word. She claims there was a kidnapping, but did you actually see the kid?"

No, he hadn't seen the boy. That didn't mean there wasn't one. He'd seen the pictures of him. Had been there moments after Noah had been taken. He'd seen kid toys at her sister's place and at Katherine's. Besides, Caleb had seen the sheer terror on her face. He could still see the agony in her violet eyes. This conversation was going nowhere. He needed to redirect. She most definitely did not make this up, and he hated the fact she had to hear his friend's accusations. "The kid has a name. Noah. Did you speak to Coleman?"

"Sheriff doesn't know what to believe. Said he'd follow up through proper channels to see if the men were legit, but it could take a while. He doesn't exactly have ready access to the kinds of people who can verify something like this. Those men who showed up looked serious to me. They flipped badges, too."

"Doesn't mean anything."

"That's exactly what Coleman said. They looked pretty damn official from where I stood."

"Can Coleman find out if there is a 'Kane' involved in a federal investigation?"

"He's trying but he said not to hold out a lot of hope."

"Anything else?" Caleb tensed against the pain in his shoulder.

"Take her to the nearest government building and turn her in, Caleb. Before this gets even more out of control."

"You know I won't."

"I don't think it's safe for you here at the ranch," Matt said quietly.

"I won't put my men at risk. I won't come home until this is settled."

There was a long silence.

"Then for God's sake, be careful," Matt warned.

"Got it covered."

"I'll keep things working here until you get back."

"Always knew I could count on you." The pressure in Caleb's chest eased. His men would be covered until his return.

"How's Jimmy's little girl?"

"Not good. They scheduled surgery for her in Dallas."

"They found a donor?"

"Seems like it."

"That's good news."

Jimmy's daughter would get the chance she deserved. He'd ensure Katherine did, too.

Caleb asked Katherine to end the call.

She looked at him deadpan. "Why didn't you tell me Matt thinks I'm involved?"

"He's not sure what to believe." Caleb glanced down at her. She looked helpless and small. His protective instincts flared. He wanted to guard her from Matt's accusations as much as from the men chasing her. Those full cherry lips and chestnut hair stirred him sexually. Caleb would swim with caution in the emotional tide.

"What about Jimmy's daughter?"

"She was born with a bad heart. They found a donor. Her surgery is scheduled in a few days." Caleb hoped like hell he'd be around for it.

Katherine frowned. "Children should get to grow up before they have to give up their childhood. They shouldn't have to deal with sickness or death at such young ages. It seems so unfair."

"Agreed."

Her back went rigid as she took in a breath. "Okay. What's next?"

"We need to find a laptop or computer to figure out what's so important on the disk. Coleman's checking into the other. If the men who showed up turn out to be government, there could be anything on that CD."

"And now you don't believe me, either?"

"When did I say that?"

Katherine set the CD down on the seat next to Max. Anger and resentment scored her normally soft features. "You didn't have to. I was putting myself in your shoes."

"Don't."

"What if they do work for the government but whoever's behind this is paying them off?"

"There could be one bad egg. Not this many. Besides, Coleman doesn't think they're legit. He's expecting to find ghosts as he investigates. We can give him a call."

"Would he sit on this kind of information?"

"No. He'd contact me right away."

"Whatever's on this CD caused my nephew to be

kidnapped. I want to find the bastard who did this and make him pay. He deserves to be in jail."

"You're right." Caleb pulled over, and then concentrated on his phone. The map feature produced three coffee shops and an internet café nearby. "There's a place a few blocks from here we might be able to go into."

He'd have a chance to inspect their injuries. Caleb's shirtsleeve was soaked. He needed to stop the bleeding.

Chapter 6

Katherine fumbled for her cell as it buzzed for the second time. The screen read Private.

Caleb parked the car in a crowded lot as she answered before the call transferred to voice mail, hoping she might recognize the voice if she heard it again.

"Did you find what you've been looking for?" His tone was smooth and practiced, and she detected a slight accent. His cool and calm demeanor made the hairs on the back of her neck prickle.

Frustration got the best of her. "What do you think you'll accomplish by hurting me? Not to mention the fact I can't find anything for you if I'm dead. You didn't have to kill an innocent person to get what you want. I'll gladly give it to you when I find it." Could she ask about the government men without giving Caleb away?

"Are you saying you don't have the file?" the even voice said.

"That's not answering my question. Who were those men you sent to kill me?"

"Let's just say I have very loyal employees."

Damn him for being so composed when her world had crumbled around her. She gripped her sister's CD tighter. Anything could be on there. She hoped this was the file they wanted, but she couldn't be sure. Besides, if she said yes and was wrong, she'd be signing a death warrant for Noah. She had to stall them. "Tell me what I'm looking for. I want to help you. I want Noah back and I want this nightmare over."

"What was in the envelope?"

"I don't know what you're talking about." Fire crawled up her neck at the lie. If he could see her now, she'd be exposed.

"Don't play games with me." Anger cracked his voice.

"At least give me a hint. There's a world of possibilities and I have to get this right." Panic made her hands shake. *Breathe.*

Caleb covered her hand with his. His touch calmed her rising pulse.

"Your sister knew exactly what I was talking about. My bet is you do, too."

"Is that why you tried to kill me?" Katherine railed against the urge to scream. She suppressed her need to tell him what he could do with his file. She had to think about Noah. Nothing mattered more than bringing him home safely. "I'm afraid I'm at a disadvantage here. My sister and I weren't that close. She didn't tell me much of anything. Just used me as a free babysitter." Katherine hated playing nice with this guy when she wanted to climb through the phone connection and do horrible things to him. "How's my nephew?"

"Not good if you don't get me what I want."

Katherine's heart pummeled her ribs. "How's his breathing?"

"I won't let anything happen to him. Not unless you don't cooperate."

"Let me speak to him. I won't do anything else until I know he's okay. You won't like it if I disappear," she hedged.

The phone went silent. *Damn.* Anger them more and Noah could pay the ultimate price. She struggled to hold back the tears that were threatening. Let one drop and the avalanche would come.

"Auntie?" His voice sounded small and frail, nothing like his usual boisterous self.

Her heart skipped. "Noah. Baby, listen to me. Everything's going to be okay." He couldn't panic. Not with his condition. "We're going to get your medicine."

"I don't like it here." His sniffles punctured her heart.

"They didn't hurt you, did they?" She struggled to keep her voice calm.

"No. They're nice."

"I need you to be very brave. Can you do that?"

"Uh-huh."

"Be good. Listen to what they say. I promise I'm coming to get you as soon as I can."

Before he could respond, a shuffling noise came through the static on the line.

"Bring the file to the drop alone if you ever want to see him alive again."

Click.

Katherine stared out the window as Max wriggled in her lap.

Caleb took the phone from her and placed it on the console between them. "We'll get him back. He's okay. That's the most important thing right now."

"Why would they call again?"

Caleb shrugged. "Insurance."

"Hearing him...knowing how frightened he is...how brave he's being..." She took a deep breath. "It pains me to sit by like this and feel like I'm doing nothing."

"I understand. He's showing real courage. He got that from you." His words caressed her tired heart. Brought it back to life so that it beat again without painful stabs.

Katherine wanted to cry. To release all the pent-up frustration, anger and worry she'd been holding in throughout this ordeal. *And during her entire life,* she thought as she realized she hadn't really cried in more years than she could count. She'd trained herself to side-step her emotions after her parents died. She'd needed to be the strong one.

At first, she had tried to reach out for help.

Anthony, her first love, had promised to visit every month after she'd had to leave school to go home and care for her sister. His calls were her saving grace. The two jobs she'd worked were barely enough to keep them fed. It was even harder to keep her grades up when she'd lived on little more than a few hours of sleep. But she'd done it. She'd kept her head above water.

His voice, the eye in the storm, had become her lifeline. Without him, she'd feared everything that was still *her* would wash away in the tide and she'd never be the same person again.

With every reassurance he'd given, her confidence

had grown. She could do it. She could make it work. She could take care of her sister and still have something of a life left.

Then the calls stemmed. Excuses about conflicting schedules came. And, eventually, the phone stopped ringing.

She'd learned through the grapevine that he'd been dating someone else.

She'd been devastated.

When she'd needed him the most to lean on, he wasn't there, but she had learned from it. Learned to rely on herself and not to depend on others. Learned that other people were disappointments. Learned to keep her walls high and march on. But had she built walls so high no one could penetrate them?

The men she'd dated since had spent more time at sporting events than with her, and she was fine with it.

Outside the window, the rain started coming down. Big drops fell, making large splotches on the windshield.

"I couldn't put my finger on it before. There's something different about the way the guy speaks. You heard him before when we listened to his message on speaker at your house."

"I don't remember an accent."

"Only certain words." She turned to meet Caleb's gaze, and a well of need sprung inside her.

He stroked the back of her neck, pulling her lips closer to his. He was so strong. Capable.

His dark eyes closed the moment his lips pressed to hers, and she surrendered to the kiss. Completely. Freely. With a need burning so brightly inside her, the flames almost engulfed her.

His tongue pulsed inside her mouth and fire shot straight to the insides of her thighs. How could she want a man so instantly? So absolutely? So thoroughly? Her nipples heightened to pointed peaks, straining for his touch. *More.* She wanted all of him, which was even more reason getting involved with him further would be a bad idea.

Katherine pulled back. "You're hurt. We should check out your injury."

"It's a scratch," he said dismissively, his low gravelly baritone sending another round of sensitized shivers skittering across her nerves.

A pained expression crossed his features, and Katherine knew it was more than from his shoulder. She looked into his gaze and saw something reckless...dangerous... sexy.

Wouldn't he leave when this was all over?

She refused to invest in another relationship, because they didn't work. She'd wind up hurt, and she didn't have it inside her to go through that pain again.

"Let's check it out anyway. I'd feel better if I knew you were going to be okay."

He rolled up his sleeve, revealing a deep gash in solid muscle. He must've caught the panic in her eyes because he quickly said, "It's not as bad as it looks."

"You need to get that checked out."

"I'm not going anywhere until I see this through." His eyes locked on to her as he gripped the steering wheel. "So forget about that."

She clamped her lips shut. Hope filled her chest.

"We should find somewhere we can clean up. I can get supplies. I'm sure people will be suspicious if we stroll into a café looking like this."

"What about the men in suits? I have no idea what my sister got involved in. I don't think she would steal anything, let alone blackmail, but I don't really know. Based on my recent conversation, I think there's some kind of corporation involved."

Caleb started the engine. "We'll get cleaned up and check the CD first." He played around on his phone before putting the gearshift into Drive. "We might have everything we're looking for in our hands already."

He blended into traffic at the next light.

"Whoever those men are, they aren't here to help. They kidnapped your nephew. Tried to take you, too. They've fired at us in broad daylight. They knew where we were, so they've been following us or someone was waiting, watching your place." He issued a grunt. "It'd take one big secret to bring on what we faced today."

"Or one powerful man."

"Your sister made a big enemy out of someone important. The question is who has this much influence? This Kane guy?"

"I have no idea. It'd have to be someone who has the ability to make permanent accidents happen. Send men at a moment's notice to erase people."

Caleb nodded. "Everything's online now. If we had her computer, we might be able to find an electronic trail."

"I'm scared." The admission came when she least expected to voice it.

"I won't let anything happen to you." Even though the set of his jaw said he meant every one of those words, he couldn't guarantee them.

Katherine didn't respond. What could she say?

"The biggest thing he has going for him is that we

don't know who he is. I wish there was some way to flush him out."

"I hope we have everything we need in here to find him." The information she needed *had* to be on that CD or Leann's phone. Anything else was unthinkable.

Caleb parked in front of a hotel and excused himself, returning a few minutes later holding a card key. "Once we clean ourselves up and get supplies, we'll check out that disk. Tuck Max into your sweater."

She hobbled out of the sedan. Her stomach growled, reminding her how long it had been since she'd last eaten. It didn't matter. Food wouldn't go down on her queasy stomach. Her nerves would be fried until she knew what was on that CD.

The room was simple and tasteful. The dark wood furniture was modern with clean lines. Artistically angled framed photos of flowers hung above the king-size bed. There was a desk with chair, a minifridge and microwave.

The card on the bed said it was "Heavenly." Katherine didn't need a note to tell her the fluffy white blanket would feel amazing wrapped around her. Add Caleb's arms to the mix and she could sleep for days in his embrace. She quickly canceled the thought. Didn't need to go there again with thoughts of what Caleb could do for her on a bed.

He held up a towel. "Why don't you clean up first?"

"Okay."

"Do you need help?"

She set Max down. Caleb poured water into a coffee cup and placed it on the floor for the little dog to drink.

"I can handle it," Katherine said as she closed the bathroom door behind her.

"Take care with those cuts. I'll clean Max before I head out to pick up supplies. With any luck, I'll find a charger while I'm out." His voice was so close she could tell he'd stopped at the door. "Keep that foot elevated."

Katherine glanced down at her leg. If she looked anything on the outside like she felt on the inside, she dreaded looking into a mirror. Freshening up suddenly sounded like a good idea.

Caleb returned half an hour later with bags of food and supplies. "I found a big-box store and picked up antibiotic ointment and gauze. I located a battery for the cell phone, too. I popped the CD into one of their laptops. Nothing unusual jumped out at me. All I saw were pictures of Noah."

Her violet eyes went wide. "That's it?"

"Maybe we'll find more when we go downstairs to the business center and have more time to look."

She nodded.

"As for the cell, I found an interesting number. Did she ever talk about Bolden Holdings?"

"No."

"Sebastian Kane's the CEO. I don't know why I didn't connect the dots sooner. I've seen him on the cover of *Forbes* before. Any chance that accent you picked up on is Canadian?"

Her head rocked back and forth. "Very well could be. But why would my sister be involved with him? Seriously? What issue could a man like that possibly have with her? How could she have information about his company?"

"Someone like Kane would care about money and his reputation. I'm betting she somehow got tangled up with him. She could've been dating him. We don't know anything for sure. Maybe that CD will tell us specifically. Maybe there's a picture of them together. I sent a text to Coleman. He's following the lead."

"Before we go downstairs, I should check your shoulder."

"After I take care of your ankle," he insisted. "But first, I've been thinking. Could your sister have had a job you didn't know about? Did she ever talk about her work?"

"She had a part-time job as a barista at Coffee Hut. Said it allowed her to go in early in the morning before Noah was awake. The neighbor sat with him. Then she could take late-morning classes and still be home for him after lunch."

Didn't sound like the kind of person who would go rogue and steal much of anything. Let alone someone who would have the guts to blackmail a major player. Then again, her money was tight. She might have risked it all to be able to spend more time with her son. "I know she didn't mention the father to you, but what kind of guys did she normally date?"

A throaty laugh came from Katherine. "Before Noah? Every kind. She dated smart guys. Athletes. Ones who grew their hair long and ate nothing but kale. I don't think she was seeing anyone lately. She calmed down considerably since she had a baby. Said she couldn't remember the last time she'd had sex."

A blush reddened her cheeks at the admission. Caleb could feel his heartbeat at the base of his throat. She was sexy when she was embarrassed.

Caleb motioned for her to sit on the bed while he positioned the desk chair in front of her and sat on the edge.

"You think she got mixed up dating Kane? Maybe

saw something or found something while she was at his place?"

"Anything's possible. Hard to imagine her in a relationship with the head of a conglomerate. Although, she was beautiful."

"She could've met him at work. Maybe he stopped into the coffee shop where she worked? We could find a way to ask her coworkers."

Katherine had cleaned up and looked even more sexy wrapped in a bath towel. The thought of her naked in the shower sent heat rocketing through him. That was the last thing he *should* be thinking about. But hell, if he were being honest, he'd admit seeing her naked was actually at the top of his list of appealing ideas. He gave in to his appreciation for her body. Looking at those long, lean legs, small waist and smooth hips stirred an immediate reaction. When his gaze slid from the smooth curve of her calves down her slender ankles to her bare feet, his mouth dried.

He forced his gaze to her face.

She slicked her tongue over her lips and damned if the image wasn't even sexier. He lowered his gaze to her neck. Her chest rose and fell with her rapid breathing. He saw her breasts tighten under the thin fabric of the towel.

The need to protect her and kiss her surged. If he didn't get a grip she'd know exactly how badly he wanted to make love to her.

Max's bark crashed him back to reality.

He forced himself to think rationally. She was in trouble. He was there to help.

He'd have to work harder to contain his growing attraction.

"Let's get a look at those." He hated the idea of causing her more pain, but her cuts needed tending to, and she needed antibiotic ointment. He'd have to get her to a clinic soon for a tetanus shot, too.

"What about your injuries? We should make sure you're okay," she said, her lips set in a frown.

"I'll live. Do you always put others first?" He wasn't used to that. Wasn't he always the one saving the day? Rescuing others? Denying himself?

"What if something happens to you? Is there anyone I should notify? Girlfriend?"

"Not now. A few before."

She gifted him with her first real smile of the day.

"I told myself I didn't have time for them when I moved into the Dust Bowl Ranch outside San Antonio as a kid. I was busy working and trying to stay under the radar."

"I'm sure they made time for you."

He shrugged. "I dated around. Couldn't find anyone special enough to marry." Caleb figured he'd rather spend his time building his empire than on an evening out with a woman who made him want to stick toothpicks in his eyes for how dull the conversation was. Waiting for the right girl had taken too long. He'd dated here and there. He'd all but given up when Cissy showed up. "Almost got married once."

"What happened?"

"Didn't work out. She left. Said life on the ranch was boring." He didn't want to get into the details about the little girl she'd taken with her. Savannah had been all smiles and freckles. Her heart was bigger than the land. Caleb still wondered if Cissy was taking good enough care of the little angel.

"How long ago was that?"

"Couple of months, I guess." Caleb tucked the remaining gauze back into the box and closed the lid. "Leg's looking better. Swelling's going down. I thought it might get worse after all the running today. Take these." He handed her a couple of ibuprofen and a bottle of water.

"Not sure if I'll know what to do without pain," she said with a weak smile.

He liked that she was relaxing with him. Her sticking around was an idea he could get used to. He mentally slapped himself. Nothing personal, but the last thing Caleb needed to do was to get romantically involved with another woman who needed rescuing. Even if this did feel…different.

Keeping his feelings in check became a bigger priority. Besides, they needed to get dressed and find the business center.

"Took a guess at your size." He tossed the bag onto the bed. "Think you'll find a few things in there you can wear. Can't promise they'll be fashionable."

Katherine took out the cotton shorts and pink T-shirt, blushing at the underwear and bra. "These will work fine."

Caleb fed Max, and then moved to the sink in the bathroom. He unbuttoned his shirt and shrugged it off.

In the mirror, he saw Katherine, now dressed, approaching. She stopped when she saw his shirt was off. Her gaze drifted across his bare torso.

A lightning bolt of heat spread through him, flowing blood south.

Not one woman had brought instant lust like this before. The closest he'd ever been to this was with Michelle and that still paled in comparison. She'd appeared at his doorway broke, asking for work. She'd had no money and no place to live.

He'd taken her in and helped her find a job. It hadn't taken her long to figure out where his bedroom was.

The sex had been hot. Chemistry outside the bedroom, not.

She'd moved her things in though, and seemed intent on staying for a while.

Caleb had started working longer hours than usual, looking for excuses to stay out of the house. Eventually, she'd left. No note.

He'd learned his lesson. He didn't do sex for sex's sake anymore.

Sex with Katherine would be amazing. No, mind-blowing. He had no doubt they'd sizzle with chemistry under the sheets.

Connecting in the everyday world would be no different than his past relationships. At least that's what he told himself. The thought this could be anything deeper or more real scared the hell out of him.

Katherine cleared her throat. "Here. Let me help you with that."

She moved next to him without making eye contact, took a clean washcloth from the counter, rinsed it under the tap and wrung it out. Dabbing his gash, she pressed her silken fingers to his shoulder. Contact sent his hormones into overdrive. Need for her surged faster than he could restrain. His erection pulsed, reminding him of all the things he'd like to do to her and with her. He wanted to be inside her. Now.

"Get ready. This might hurt," she said with a tentative smile, scooting in front of him.

"I'm fine." But was he? His head might be screwed on straight, but his body had ideas of the sexual variety. Damned if he wasn't thinking about sex with Katherine again.

She rubbed the wound with the washcloth until it was clean. Next, she gently dabbed antibiotic ointment on the cut.

He wasn't used to hands like hers. Soft and tender. It felt like a caress.

A crack appeared in his mind, like light in a small dark tunnel. His exterior armor threatened to splinter. He couldn't figure out why he'd told Katherine about Cissy. Weren't those wounds still fresh? Didn't they sting worse than the exterior cut on his shoulder?

Shouldn't he feel guilty for being this close to a woman in a hotel room given that Cissy had walked out so recently?

He didn't.

Instead he felt the strange sensation of warmth and light that accompanied allowing someone to take care of him for a change.

The whole concept was foreign to him. He'd taken care of himself and everyone around him for as long as he could remember.

Her touch, the way it seemed so natural to have her hands on him, suddenly felt more dangerous than the men with guns. All they could do was end a person's life. A woman like Katherine could make it not worth living without her.

Caleb eradicated the thought.

She was a woman in trouble. He was there to help. When this was all over, she'd go back to her life and he'd return to his.

He backed away and slipped on a new T-shirt.

"Let's see about that CD."

Chapter 7

Katherine tucked Max inside her handbag and followed Caleb downstairs. The business center was a small room adjacent to the lobby. A wall of desks and two computers occupied the space. The wall between the business center and the lobby was made of glass. There wasn't much in the way of privacy, but it would have to do.

Katherine fished the CD out of her bag and handed it to Caleb.

Max squirmed and whimpered.

"Poor little guy. You miss her, don't you?" A wave of melancholy flooded Katherine as she stroked his fur. "He lost his home."

"He can come to the ranch. Unless you want him."

"Might be too sad to go home with me. Although when this ordeal is settled, I'll be looking for a new place to live. Can't imagine going back to my apartment after..."

"Either way, he'll have a new home."

"Poor little guy might need to go out soon after eating and drinking all that water."

"I saw a green space on the side of the building. We can take him there as soon as we see what we're dealing with here."

There was one file on the disk. It was labeled "Katherine."

Caleb's gaze flicked from hers to the computer screen. "Nothing stood out before. Let's see if a closer look tells us what your sister wanted you to know."

Katherine's pulse raced. She took a deep breath. "Okay."

He clicked on her name as she looked over his shoulder.

"I can't help but wonder why she would send snapshots of Noah through FedEx when she was meeting me to hand him off."

"She must've realized she was being followed and wanted to be sure they weren't intercepted. Let's look through 'em. See if we can find a clue." Caleb started the slide show.

Katherine watched, perplexed, as picture after picture of Noah filled the screen. There were photographs of him at Barton Creek. He'd been to the zoo. It looked like a montage of his summer activities.

"Check your email. It's possible she sent you a note. Pull up her last few messages and look for anything that might signal the file's whereabouts. There might be hints. A word out of place in a sentence. A location she mentions more than once. See if there's anything we can go on."

She logged on remotely. There was nothing unusual as she scanned the last couple of notes from Leann. No extra emails from her sister mysteriously appearing posthumously, either. Not a single clue.

From the lobby, the TV volume cranked up.

"An elderly woman has been gunned down in front of her neighbor's apartment in a normally quiet suburb. The news has rocked a small North Dallas community. The name of the deceased is being withheld until family can be notified but two persons of interest, Katherine Harper and an unidentified male, are believed to have information that would assist in the investigation. An eyewitness saw them running from the scene with a weapon, and police are warning citizens not to approach them but to call 9-1-1 if they are spotted..."

Katherine's heart dropped. She glanced around. The man behind the registration desk picked up the phone and stared at her. Was he phoning the police? She nudged Caleb.

He turned around and cursed under his breath.

"How on earth could we be tied to Ms. Ranker's murder?" The feeling of being trapped made her pulse climb. How would they get out of the hotel unseen? And if they did, where would they go? Everyone in the area would be looking for them. If they so much as tried to get coffee or food, they might be spotted. There would be nowhere to hide.

Caleb ejected the CD. "We'll figure this out later. Right now, we've gotta get out of here."

"Do we have time to get back to the room? I left everything in there but my purse and Max."

"I don't know how much time we have, but we need to try. I changed clothes and the car keys are in my old pants."

An uninvited image of Caleb's shirtless chest invaded Katherine's thoughts. Reality crashed fast and hard. She glanced around wildly as Caleb led her out of the business center half afraid the guy working the front desk would give chase.

As soon as they entered the stairwell, he urged her to run. They made it up the couple flights of stairs easily thanks to the ibuprofen tablets she'd taken earlier. The medicine saved her from the pain that would be shooting up her leg otherwise.

Caleb stopped at the door. "I'll grab everything I can. You watch the hall. If anyone darkens that corridor, let me know. A second's notice might be the difference between freedom and jail."

He disappeared.

Not a minute later, the elevator dinged.

Katherine stepped inside the room. "Someone's coming."

"Damn." He threw a bag of supplies over his shoulder and took her hand. His grip was firm as he broke into a full run, leading her to the opposite stairwell.

"Stop!" came from behind.

Katherine glanced back. A man dressed in a suit and wearing dark glasses gave chase. How could they escape? Where would they go?

She and Caleb slipped inside the stairwell. The shuffle of feet coming toward them sounded at the same time Max whimpered. How would they get anywhere quietly with him on board?

"It's okay, boy," she whispered. His big dark eyes

looked up at her from the bag, and she realized the little guy was shaking. Max was in a totally foreign environment without his owner. *Poor thing.* She lifted him and cradled him to her chest to calm him.

The door from the third floor smacked against the wall at almost the same time as the one from the floor below them. With men coming in both directions, they were sandwiched with no way out.

"Stick close to me," Caleb said, squeezing her hand.

He entered the second floor.

Halfway down the hall, the maid's cart framed a door.

"In here," he said, urging her toward it.

"We'll be cornered in there. I don't see another way out."

"Trust me." Caleb darted toward the room as he glanced back.

She saw more than a hint of recklessness in his eyes now—a throwback to his misspent youth? "How did you get so good at evading people?"

"I told you, I had a rough childhood. Learned a lot of things I didn't want to need to know as an adult." Caleb ducked into the room and shooed out the cleaning lady as doors opened from both ends of the hallway. He slid the dead bolt into place.

Shots were fired and Katherine ducked. Oh. God. She was going to die right there.

Before she could scream, Caleb pulled her to the floor and covered her with his body. His broad, masculine chest flush with her back, she felt the steady rhythm of his heartbeat.

More shots were fired; bullets pinged through the walls. She had the split-second fear her life was about to end and all she could think about was her family. The memories brought a melancholy mix of pain and happiness coursing through her.

What did Caleb have?

Other than his mother, hadn't he been alone most of his life? Her heart ached for him. Maybe that's why he'd gotten so good at taking care of others.

Because of her, he'd end up in jail or dead today.

His exterior was tough. Tall, with dark brown eyes she could look into for days. With his broad shoulders, lean hips, stacked muscles, he was physical strength personified. His substantial presence would affect anyone. He was like steel. But what did he have to fortify from within?

Katherine felt herself being pulled to her feet as she held tight to Max. He'd stopped whimpering. "What are we doing?"

He made quick work jimmying the window open. "Escaping."

A bullet pinged near Katherine's head. Caleb pulled her to the floor and covered her again before she had a chance to react.

The bullets stopped as a thump sounded against the door. Could they kick it in?

"From here on out, we've got to stay off the grid." His carved-from-granite features were stone.

Katherine took a moment to absorb his words. He was saying they couldn't show their faces again in public. They'd go into hiding and then what? How would they eat? And worse yet, what would happen to Noah? How would she make it to the drop? The center of a mall was about as public of a place as she could imagine.

The crack of an object slamming into the door wrenched her from her shock.

"You climb out first. I'll hold you as long as I can." He set Max on the floor. "I'll toss him down to you, and then I want you to run. Don't wait for me. You hear?"

Not wait for him? Was he kidding? Katherine wouldn't make it two steps without Caleb.

"But—"

"No time."

She sat on the edge of the window for a second to gather her nerves. Caleb helped her twist onto her belly to ease the impact to her leg. He lowered her.

"Ready?"

She nodded, bracing for the impact on her hurt leg. She landed hard. Her legs gave out. As soon as she turned, Caleb was half hanging out the window, making himself as low to the ground as he could before he made sure she was ready and then he let Max drop.

Catching him with both hands, she breathed a sigh of relief when Caleb followed almost immediately after.

"Aren't we near Mockingbird and 75?" he asked as he broke into a run.

"Yeah, but my car's the other direction." Katherine pointed west.

"We have a better shot of getting lost if we can get to the train."

Then what?

Before Katherine could wind up a good anxiety attack, a flurry of men in dark suits came pouring out of the building.

She powered her legs forward to the edge of the lot with the adrenaline thumping through her, ignoring the throbbing pain coursing up her leg. Caleb pushed them forward until they disappeared into a tree line.

The roar of the train sounded nearby.

"If we can get across the tracks, we can make it." He lifted her as if she weighed nothing and sprinted toward the station.

The train was coming fast. Too fast. They'd never make it in time, especially with him carrying her. "I can run."

"Not a chance." Caleb picked up speed, clearing the rail with seconds to spare.

The train car doors opened and he hopped inside, placing Katherine in the first available seat. She prayed the Dallas Area Rapid Transit police or fare-enforcement officers wouldn't be checking passengers for tickets. The last thing they needed was to give someone a reason to notice them, and she remembered reading the rail had increased security after a series of recent murders.

She tucked Max in her purse and watched out the window as the buildings blurred. "Think they saw us?"

"It's a pretty good bet. We'll jump off at the next stop. Get lost somewhere on the Katy Trail."

The engine slowed and the light rail train stopped. They hopped off.

She didn't want to weigh them down. His shoulder was bleeding again from carrying her. He'd never admit it, but he had to be exhausted by now. He was going on no sleep as it was. "I can make it."

"You sure?"

Katherine nodded. They ran for a few minutes before her leg gave out. "I'm sorry. I need a rest."

He found a small clearing and stopped to catch their

breath. “Squeeze into these bushes. This should provide enough cover to hide us for now.”

Katherine was beginning to wonder if she’d ever feel secure again.

He took Max from her arms. “Better let him stretch his legs.”

Max scuttled to a nearby bush and relieved himself.

“C’mon, boy,” Caleb said, patting his leg. His breathing was hardly accelerated whereas Katherine’s lungs burned.

The sound of pounding footsteps broke the quiet.

Peering through the leaves, Katherine’s heart skittered when she saw the men in suits. They were staring at something in their hands.

Caleb backed out of the underbrush and urged her on the move again as he scooped up Max.

The men seemed to be a few feet behind everywhere they went.

“It’s no use,” she said, panting. The pain in her leg was staggering.

“Dammit. I didn’t even think about this before. It makes sense now.”

“What are you talking about?”

“Give me your phone.” He held out his free hand.

She dug it out of her purse and placed it on his flat palm.

“Hold Max.”

She did.

He pulled out the battery and smashed the phone under the heel of his cowboy boot. Did the same to his own. Then picked up the pieces and tossed them.

Panic gripped her as it felt like icy fingers had closed around her chest and squeezed. All the air sucked out of her lungs in a whooshing sound. "They can't contact me now. What have you done?"

"They can't find us anymore, either." He took her hand in his. "They've been following us using the GPS tracking in the phone. It's the only way they could always be a step behind."

"How can they do that unless they work for the government?"

"It's surprisingly easy. Anyone can buy the program online." He urged her forward as he took Max, and then ran for what seemed like half an hour before stopping. "We should be safe now."

She hobbled a few feet and settled onto a large rock, stroking Max and fighting waves of tears from exhaustion and panic. "Any idea where we are?"

Caleb shook his head.

He sat beside her and braided their fingers together. "You don't have to keep it together all the time."

Yes, she did. He didn't understand. She had to be strong for Noah. She'd had to be strong her entire life. "I have a lot of responsibility, and the last thing I can afford to do is break down." She sniffed back a tear.

"It's okay to cry. I'm right here, and I'm not going anywhere."

Her heart skipped a beat when she realized those words comforted her far more than she should allow. She shivered and raised her gaze to meet his. Warmth spread through her body.

His chest moved up and down rhythmically, whereas her breathing was ragged. And not just because she'd outrun bullets and scary men with guns. Her pulse rose for a different reason. His body was so close she could breathe in his masculinity. Her arms were full of goose bumps. She knew the instant her body shifted from fear to awareness…

Awareness of his strong hands on her. Awareness of the unique scent of woods and outdoors and virility that belonged to him. Awareness of everything that was Caleb. A sensual shiver raced up her spine.

Being close to him, drinking in his powerful scent was a mistake. Katherine needed a clear head. Especially because she could so vividly recall the way his lips tasted. How soft they were when they moved with hers.

Katherine's heart beat somewhere at the base of her throat, thumping wildly.

Wisps of his sandy-blond curls moved in the wind. His rich brown-gold eyes were fixed on her, blazing. In that moment she wanted nothing more than to explore the steel muscles under the cotton fabric of his T-shirt. Her hands itched to trace his jawline to the dimple in his chin.

Guilt slammed into her. How could she allow herself to become distracted? Noah was the only person who mattered. He needed her now more than ever. Nothing could ever happen between her and Caleb. *Not now. Not ever.* She had a family to think about, and a drop spot to get to. *Refocus.*

"I still can't believe my sister would have had anything to do with a man like Kane."

"I've read he has his hand on everything that crosses the borders from Canada to Mexico."

"Which makes even less sense to me. How would my sister be connected to a man like that? She didn't have any money. She worked at a coffee shop, for God's sake. I know she could keep a secret, but she didn't run in circles like that." Katherine gripped the tree branch tighter. "Wish we could've had more time to check out that CD. Maybe there's a hidden file or something? All I could see were pictures of Noah. Which would make a person think that's all she was sending, but we both know it can't be right."

"Especially when she sent them 'signature required.'" Caleb redressed one of her injuries.

"You said you got into trouble when you were young. What happened?"

He didn't look up. He put away supplies as he finished with them and rolled them into a ball, placing them in a backpack. He patted Max on the head. "I told you. I had a few run-ins with the law when I was younger. Gave my mom a hard time. Stopped when I saw what it was doing to her. End of story."

"Did you act out because of your father?"

He scratched behind Max's ears. The little dog had stopped shaking and sat at Caleb's feet.

"He'll need to eat again soon." The subject had been changed.

All she knew about the handsome cowboy was that he saved cats, dogs and women in trouble. Katherine wished he would open up more.

"You hungry, too?" His jaw did that tick thing again.

She figured the subject of his father was closed.

Caleb needed to find safe shelter for Katherine. He needed to protect her from everyone and everything bad more than he needed air. Help her, yes, but where had this burning need to banish all her pain come from? He could feel her anguish as if it were his own.

A crack of thunder in the distance threatened a storm.

By tying them to Ms. Ranker's murder, everyone would be on the lookout for him and Katherine now. No place would be safe. They were wanted. Had no transportation. If they ducked their heads inside the wrong building, they'd be shot at or captured.

The police wouldn't believe their story, so going to them was out.

He and Katherine would need to change their appearance and figure out a place to bed down tonight. But where? He could think of a dozen or so places he could hide her on the ranch.

A lone thought pounded his temples. What would Kane have to gain by getting them arrested?

Dammit. Was there a mole in the police station? A man like Kane could buy a lot of goodwill. Could he ensure they didn't make it out of jail, too?

The DART rail system could get them as far as Plano. The hike back would be dangerous. If anyone spotted them, they would most likely call 9-1-1. How much longer could they outrun a man with Kane's resources?

He had no idea how he'd survive this, let alone keep Katherine and Noah safe. That little boy deserved a life. He had a right to be loved and to have the kind of family she would provide. He deserved Katherine.

She'd be a better mother than she thought. She was risking her life for the child. That kind of dedication and love would ensure Noah had an amazing childhood.

The boy had already lost the one person he was closest to in the world. A pang of regret sliced through Caleb. He knew exactly what it was like to lose a mother. The overwhelming pain that came with realizing he was all alone in the world.

An urge to protect Noah surged so strongly inside he was completely caught off guard.

He refocused on Katherine. Watching her as she tried to be brave would wear down his resolve not to touch her. He fought like hell against the urge to take her in his arms and comfort her already. A little question mark lingered in the back of his mind. Did she want him the way he wanted her?

He could feel her body react to him every time he touched her. Yet she pulled away.

Dammit.

Under another set of circumstances, he would like to take his time to get to know her. Take her out somewhere nice for dinner. Learn about where she went to college and more about the kind of software company she worked for. Date. Like normal people.

Caleb almost laughed out loud.

His life had been anything but *normal.* And this impossible situation was only getting worse. The more time he spent with her, the louder his danger alarms sounded. She was already under his skin, and he wanted to get closer.

His biggest fear was that he wouldn't be able to protect her when the time came, and he would lose her forever. They'd narrowly escaped several times in the past few hours.

Her resolve was weakening.

He could go a few more days without sleep, and his only injury came from his shoulder. He could fix it with a sterile needle and thread. Neither of those was on him at present. He was running out of options for places to hide.

He'd take her to the only place he'd ever truly felt safe, his ranch...and figure out a way to get a message to Matt. Then he'd have to find a way to keep this family safe.

Chapter 8

Katherine's chestnut hair had been pulled up loosely in a ponytail. Caleb's fingers itched from wanting to feel the stray strands that framed her face. The desire to reach out, touch her, be her comfort, was an ache in his chest. But he couldn't be her shelter now and still walk away later when this whole ordeal had passed. No use putting much stock in the emotions occupying his thoughts. He checked the area and deemed it safe. For the moment. "I need to get back to TorJake."

"Why? Won't they be all over the ranch?" Her violet eyes were enormous. "Isn't that the last place we should go?"

"They'll be watching at the very least. And we're out of options."

He glanced around, keeping an eye on a homeless

man curled up near the underbrush. "Out here, there are too many factors outside of my control."

"What if they're already there waiting? With everything that's happened so far, they will be all over the place. If the police don't catch us first."

"It's a big ranch. I know a place we can hide for a while as long as we can get supplies."

"You think they have the police in their pockets?"

Caleb scratched behind Max's ears. "There could be an officer on Kane's payroll, not the entire force. Rich, connected people use any means to get what they want. Doesn't matter. He has his own personal army of security to command. I can't watch our backs out here."

"What if the sheriff is there? What if he's waiting to arrest us?"

"He believes you're being set up, too."

Shock widened her eyes. "He said that?"

"Yes."

"How can we be sure he's telling the truth? I mean, he could set a trap to make us feel safe so he can arrest us. Or Kane might have gotten to him, offering cash."

Caleb paused for a beat. "I believe the sheriff is honest. I've known him long enough to vouch for him." Caleb and Coleman might have had a good relationship in the past. But that was before Caleb was wanted for questioning in a murder. It'd be risky to trust Coleman now that they were on the run and wanted for questioning, but he didn't want to tell her that. They couldn't risk being delayed at the station and losing time in their search for Noah. Her fingers were interlocked. "If this guy is as big as you say he is, who can really protect us? Where can we go? Even if we make it to the ranch by some miracle, how will we survive? We'll be in hiding forever."

"Only until we come up with a better plan. I can connect with Matt and the boys. They'll be able to help."

"And Noah will end up dead. I heard him wheeze on the phone. If these men are as heartless as you say, then they won't take him to the hospital. They'll just let him die and dump him somewhere."

"We'll figure out a way to get medicine to the drop. Then we have to hide. I didn't see anything on the CD that will help us."

She folded her arms across her chest. Her hands gripped her elbows until her knuckles went white. "They can't contact me now, remember? Not after you trashed my cell. If I don't show up to the drop and stay, they will kill him. There's no other way to reach me."

"We don't know that. If you go, they'll shoot you on the spot. Then what?"

She looked as though she needed a moment to digest his words. "Why do you think they went from trying to make contact with us to trying to kill us?"

"My guess is whatever Leann had over them, they think you've seen it."

"Will they hurt Noah now anyway?"

"I believe they'll keep him alive until..."

"They finish the job. Meaning, erase both of us. Then they'll kill him."

Caleb looked into her vivid gaze. The hurt he saw nearly did him in. He leaned toward her and rested his forehead against hers.

Her hand came up to his chin and guided his lips to hers.

Those lips, soft and slick, pushed all rational thought

aside. The bulge in his jeans tightened and strained. The thought of how good she would feel naked and underneath him crashed into his thoughts like a rogue wave, making him harder. He wanted to lay her down and give her all the comfort she could handle.

Was this a bad idea? How could it be when it felt this right? She was almost too much for him. Too beautiful. Too impossible to resist. Were her emotions strapped on a roller coaster she didn't sign up to ride? Was she afraid? Acting on primal instinct?

She needed confirmation of life. Could he hope for more? That she wanted him as badly as he wanted to feel her naked skin against his?

Her tongue dipped in his mouth, and his control obliterated. Blood rushed in his ears, overshadowing rational thought.

His body was tuned to hers. Every vibration. Every quick breath. Every sexy little moan. The thin cotton material of her shirt was the only barrier to bare skin. He slipped his hand up her shirt, sliding under her lacy bra where he found her delicate skin. Her nipple pebbled. A whoosh sounded in his ears. His muscles clenched.

He wanted her. *Now.* He pushed deeper into the vee of her legs. Her legs wrapped around his waist. He was so close to her sweetness, he nearly blew it right there.

She flattened her hands against his back, pulling him closer.

His chest flush with hers sent heat and impulse rocketing through him.

Much more and he couldn't stop himself from ripping her clothes off right then and there.

She needed him to think clearly. Not like some teenager drunk on pheromones. Besides, she already wore the weight of the world on her shoulders. He didn't need to add to her guilt.

With a shudder, he pulled back. "I'm sorry."

"Me, too."

"I don't think this is a good idea."

"Oh." Embarrassment flushed her cheeks.

He hadn't meant for that to happen. "Believe me, I *want* this."

"No. You're right. I should definitely not have done that." Her solemn tone of voice sent a ripple through him.

He stood to face her. "I didn't mean to hurt you. All I want to do is help."

She stalked to a tree, putting distance between them. Her beautiful face, the pout of her lips, stirred another inappropriate sexual reaction. Didn't she realize his restraint took Herculean effort at this point?

Dammit that he wanted nothing more than to lay her down right then and make love to her until she screamed his name aloud over and over again. It was all he could do not to think about the pink cotton panties she wore. He hadn't dared buy her another pale blue silky pair.

Hell, the need to hold her and to protect her surged so strongly, he'd almost blown it. He was trying to be a better person and show self-discipline. Last thing he wanted was to take advantage of her vulnerability and have her regretting anything about the time they spent together.

When they made love—correction, *if* they made love—it would be the best damn thing either of them had ever done. She wouldn't walk out of his life afterward. It wouldn't be temporary. *Where the hell did that come from?* The admission shocked him.

What was he thinking exactly?

That he didn't want a convenient relationship with her. Wouldn't she leave when the heat was off and she could return to her normal life? She was used to living in a busy major metropolitan city. Life on TorJake was simple. Hard work. Long days. Lots of paperwork.

Caleb didn't get out much. He didn't hit the bars or see the need to sit at white-tablecloth restaurants.

He loved a hard day's work. A cool shower. A down-home meal. And to wrap his arms around the woman he loved. Life didn't get any better than that.

Simply put, their worlds were too different and when she got her life back—and she would get her life back—wouldn't she walk out like the others and move on? Just like Cissy had? One look at Katherine made his heart stir. Not to mention other parts of his body.

He grunted.

This time, his heart might not recover. He felt more for Katherine in the few days he'd known her than he'd ever felt for his ex-girlfriend.

And that scared the hell out of him.

Katherine rubbed to ease the chill bumps on her arms. Her attraction to Caleb was a distraction. His square jaw. Those rich brown-gold eyes reminded her why fall was her favorite season. He was so damn sexy. With his body flush to hers, everything tingled and surged.

The wind had picked up and the threat of rain intensified. There was a breeze blowing now with pockets of cooler air blasting her. The temperature between her and Caleb had shifted, too. The question was why?

Not that any of this mattered. Those men would find them. They were going to kill her, Caleb and Noah.

She glanced at her watch. "If we're going to make the drop, we'd better get going."

He shook his head. "Not a good idea."

"I don't have a choice. Noah won't survive without his medicine. I have to get it to him."

"You can't save him if you're dead. You have to know it's a setup. I won't allow them to hurt you."

She bristled. "I have to go."

"I don't like it. They've set a trap."

"At least I'll be in the middle of a busy mall."

"That won't stop them. It's absolutely out of the question. They won't allow anything to happen to Noah as long as you're alive. They know it's the only leverage they have. They let him die and there's no deal."

Katherine had to figure out a way to drop the medicine, especially since she didn't have the file. Didn't he understand she had to take the risk? Those jerks may very well be setting her up. What could she do about it? Bottom line? If she didn't show, what chance did Noah have?

She couldn't allow that to happen. She would have to convince Caleb.

"I need to find a phone so I can make contact with Matt. He'll give me a pulse on the sheriff."

"You can use Leann's."

"Lost the power cord. Besides, they don't know we have it yet. Best leave it that way."

Katherine stood and wobbled. "My ankle hurts. I don't think I can walk anymore." She sat on the nearest rock.

Caleb took a knee in front of her. "Let me see what we have here."

"No. You go on." She glanced around and propped her leg on a big rock. "I need a few minutes."

Trepidation and concern played out over his features. "I guess you'll be okay while I scout the area. I'll leave supplies in case you need anything while I'm gone."

Good. She needed to think. "I'll be fine until you get back. Besides, we have a long journey ahead of us later when we head back to the ranch."

He issued a sharp sigh. "Fine." He looked down at Max. "C'mon, boy."

The little dog scampered to Caleb's feet.

"I'll take him so he doesn't make any noise or draw attention to you. We'll be right back. In the meantime, I want you to stay put. No one can track you here. Stay low and hidden." He motioned toward the thicket. "You'll be safe until I get back."

Safe was a word Katherine figured could be deleted from her vocabulary. Without Caleb, she feared she would never be safe again.

As soon as Caleb was out of sight, she organized supplies.

The sound of Noah wheezing on the phone earlier hammered through her. Time was running out for both of them.

Chapter 9

Caleb tugged the ball cap he'd bought low on his forehead and put on sunglasses, hooding his eyes. An ache had started in his chest the moment he left Katherine. The memory of her kiss burned into his lips.

It was too early to have real feelings for her. Wasn't it? Protectiveness was a given with her circumstances. His desire to help would be strong. She was in serious trouble. But real feelings?

Not this soon.

Katherine was at the right place at the right time. His wounds from Cissy were still too exposed. She'd got him thinking about what it would be like to have little feet running around the TorJake.

Except that he never missed Cissy the way he was missing Katherine.

Even so, Cissy must've primed him for thinking

about having his own family someday and a woman like Katherine by his side. He couldn't deny how right her hands had felt on his body back there.

Hell's bells.

Katherine wasn't interested in a relationship with him. She'd been clear on that.

Maybe this was his twisted way of missing his ex-girlfriend.

Caleb redirected his thoughts as he broke through the tree line and located a phone two blocks away in heavy traffic.

He looked up in time to see a young blonde in tattered jeans and a blouse heading straight toward him. Her backpack had been tossed over her shoulder and her keys were clipped to the strap. A college student? He was most likely in the West Village near the main Southern Methodist University campus. He thought for a second about how close they were to the drop spot and glanced around to see if anyone looked suspicious. Kane could have men stationed anywhere. And they could look like anyone. Even the pretty young woman standing in front of him, stroking the dog, could be a threat. Caleb eyed her.

"Awww. What a cute puppy," she said.

Last thing he wanted was to attract attention. He kept his head low and nodded.

"What's his name?"

"Max." Caleb tensed. His gaze fixed on her, looking for any hint of a weapon. If she had a gun tucked somewhere, he'd see it.

Then again, Kane hadn't exactly been subtle so far.

"He's a sweetie." She bent down and nuzzled Max's nose. "Aren't you?"

Caleb scanned the area, watching for anything that stood out. The street was busy. The sidewalk cafés were full. This section of Dallas teemed with life. It would be so easy to blend in here.

Her gaze came up, stopping on Caleb's face. "You look familiar. Do I know you?"

"Don't think so." He smiled and paused for a beat. "I better get him back to his mom." An image of Katherine waiting in his bed popped into his thoughts. *Not the time. Or the place.*

The girl smiled and walked away.

Caleb picked up the phone and called Matt.

His buddy answered on the first ring.

"I don't have much time to talk, so I'll make this quick—"

"Caleb? What the hell's going on? Where are you?" Matt was silent for a beat. "Never mind. Don't answer that. We probably have company on the line."

Caleb hadn't thought about the line being tapped. It made sense someone would be listening in and trying to locate him by any means possible. Katherine's little sister had done far worse than take a bat to a hornets' nest. She'd written death warrants for everyone she loved and anyone else who tried to help them. Finding a hiding spot was next to impossible when Kane seemed to have so many people in his pockets. "What's happening at the ranch?"

"The men in suits have been here twice. Whatever she stirred up has gone downright crazy."

"Did you catch the news?"

"Sure did. I know you didn't have anything to do with what they're saying. You couldn't have. I don't care what the witness says," Matt said solemnly.

"Thanks for the confidence. It all happened right in front of me."

"You were there?"

"Unfortunately, yes. One minute I was talking to her. The next, bullets were flying. Surely the investigators will be able to figure out which direction the bullets were fired."

"We'll do whatever we have to, to clear your name." Matt issued a sigh. "There's something I should tell you."

"What's that?"

"A man came by the other day. Said he was a U.S. Marshal. He's offering witness protection to her," Matt whispered. "Said he'd already offered it to her sister."

"What else did he say?"

"He can work out a deal for you, too. Put you both in the program."

"You know I won't leave my ranch," Caleb said, steadfast.

"Well, you might have to. This thing has blown up beyond big."

"Did Coleman meet with him?"

"Yes."

He knew the sheriff was honest to a fault. If he trusted the stranger, then Caleb could risk a little faith, too. Not even a man with Kane's pull could persuade Coleman to switch teams. "What did he think?"

"Said the guy checked out. Thinks you should talk to him. And, Caleb, I do, too."

Then again, the guy working for a legitimate agency didn't mean he was clean. Maybe Caleb could get a better feel if he spoke to Coleman directly. "Tell the sheriff I'll be in touch."

"Not a good idea. He has a tail. Besides, you're wanted. He said to warn you if he sees you he'll have to detain you."

Caleb should've seen that coming. "I don't have much time. How's the ranch?"

"To hell with that, how are you?"

"I'm good. Don't worry about me. Just take care of my horses until I return."

"You know I will."

"Make sure you check out the property, too. The teenagers have been hitting the north fence hard. The acreage in the east needs to be checked for coyotes."

"Jimmy's been on it."

"Won't he be off for his daughter's surgery soon?"

"Yeah."

Caleb needed to drop a hint. Tell Matt where he was going. But how? "You better take over for him. And make sure someone's exercising Dawn. Can't have her too restless like before, when Cissy left. No one's been watching that trail she rode and I might not be back for a long time."

"Don't talk like that." He listened carefully for the telltale rise of Matt's voice when he caught on. "We'll get this figured out, and you'll be home before you know it."

Nope. Matt hadn't picked up on the clue. "I wouldn't count on it."

"It will all work out."

Maybe he could send Matt on a mission? "Do me a favor?"

"Name it."

"Find a picture of Sebastian Kane."

"The businessman?"

"Yes. Call the manager of the Coffee Hut in Austin and send him the picture. Find out if he came into the shop much, or spent any time with one of the employees by the name of Leann Foster."

"Consider it done."

"I'll be in touch."

"Be safe, man."

Caleb ended the call. He prayed he'd disconnected before his location had been tagged. Being away from Katherine gave him an uneasy feeling, like dark clouds closing in around him, threatening to take away all that was light and good. He needed to get back and make sure she was all right. With her damaged ankle, she might not be able to run. He'd never forgive himself if anything had happened while he'd been gone.

Keeping his head low, he circled back to the brush where he'd tucked her away.

What the hell?

"Katherine," he called into the nearby shrubbery. He searched branches and bushes. Nothing. No answer.

Fear and anger formed liquid that ran cold in his veins. Had he been careless? Had he left her vulnerable and alone with no way to defend herself? Had the cops picked her up?

The bag of supplies was left leaning against the rock. He checked it. The pain relievers were missing as were several bottled waters.

He called her name again, louder.

"Caleb." Her voice came from his left.

He rushed to the bushes at the edge of the hill. His heart thumped in his throat. "What happened?"

"I slipped on a rock." She was on all fours, climbing up.

He picked her up and carried her to the rock. Relief filled his chest. He didn't want to acknowledge how stressed he'd been a minute ago. "What were you doing over there?"

"Looking for you. My leg gave out and I slipped over the edge."

Glancing at his watch, he swore under his breath. "The drop."

"I'm fine. I can make it."

"You wait here. I'll figure something out."

"No. Please. I can do this." She tugged at his hand. Her eyes pleaded.

Looking into her determined eyes, he knew he couldn't leave her behind. She'd be safer if he kept her within arm's reach until he could get her back to Tor-Jake. "Okay."

Caleb retraced his route to West Village, going as slowly as she needed to.

If memory served, NorthPark Center wasn't far. In fact, it should be on the other side of Highway 75. Easy walk for him. Nothing was easy for Katherine right then.

If they thought she'd showed up alone, and weren't expecting him, the element of surprise would be on his side. The thought of anyone touching her or hurting her sent white-hot anger coursing through him.

Why was she so stubborn?

Didn't she realize she might be walking right into their arms? Being in the open was good. Crowds hid a lot of things.

He didn't know if this was the best play. They were walking into a situation set up by Kane. They didn't have the file. Should he turn and walk away while they still could? Meet with the marshal who'd seemed legit? Because nothing about his current situation was going to turn out the way he wanted. She was far too willing to put herself in harm's way to protect everyone around her. Except this burning desire to help Katherine, to keep her safe, kept his feet moving anyway.

People didn't accidently get mixed up with a man like Kane. What was the connection?

Caleb chewed on that thought as he led Katherine a few blocks, near the meeting site.

"Let me go first. Get a good read." Caleb ran ahead and entered the grassy area, leaving her at the perimeter. He blended in with the noisy lunch crowd.

Scanning the area, he could see at least five shooters in position.

Kane had come prepared to do anything necessary to erase Katherine.

If she took a couple more steps, she'd be right where they wanted her.

An imposing figure made a move toward her.

Caleb crouched low. When she stepped into his sight, he sprang forward and clutched her hand. She was shaking.

He pulled her into the crowd.

Glancing around, the shooters didn't seem to notice the small commotion. He turned to a teen and tapped his shoulder. "Hey, kid."

The teen glanced up, looking annoyed at the interruption. When he saw Caleb, the teen straightened his back and pulled out his earbuds.

"Sorry to bother you while you're listening to your music, buddy. I was wondering if you'd like to make a quick twenty bucks."

The kid eyed Caleb suspiciously.

"I need to deliver this stuff to the bronze statue." Caleb took the medicines from Katherine's tight grip. She stroked Max.

The boy's face twisted, giving the universal teenage sign for, *Have you lost your mind?* "Mister, that's only, like, twenty feet away."

Caleb smiled and winked. "It's a dollar a step basically. You want the job or not?"

"Sure. I'd kiss your mother for twenty bucks."

"Deliver the medicine. And leave my mother out of it."

The teen palmed the pill bottle and inhaler. "That's it?"

Caleb nodded.

"Deal."

"Be inconspicuous and I'll make it forty."

A wide smile broke across the teen's face. "Then I'll be stealth."

He rocked his head back and forth as he walked to the sculpture. His gaze intent on the music device in his hand, he plopped down next to the statue.

Caleb never saw the kid slip the medicine under the bronze, but as soon as he popped to his feet and strolled away the package stood out. Amazing.

"Nice job, kid." Caleb handed him a pair of twenties. He had no idea what Kane and his men would do when they realized there was no file.

"Pleasure doing business with you," he said as he turned and then sauntered off.

With his hand on Katherine's shoulder, he guided her toward a tour group. "Let's get out of here before anyone gets hurt."

"I—I can't. Not without knowing if they got his med—"

"See that baby over there?" He pointed to a mother nursing an infant. "They both could die if we don't leave now."

A mix of emotions played across her features. Worry. Guilt. Her stubborn streak was visible on the surface as her chin lifted. "You're right."

No sooner had the words left her mouth than a scufflelike noise moved toward them. People ran in different directions, parting faster than the Red Sea, as a serious-looking man walked down the middle. Sunglasses hooded his eyes, but his intention was clear. His face didn't veer from Katherine.

Caleb grabbed her by the arm and pushed her ahead of him, placing himself in between her and the suit. If he could get her toward the flagship store, maybe they could get lost in the rows of clothing.

As they neared the wide-open door, two similar-looking men in suits flanked the entrance.

They were trapped. The man from behind was closing in on them fast. Glancing from left to right, Caleb looked for another way out. One side was a brick wall. Nothing there.

A police radio broke the silence from the left-hand side. Not good.

Except.

Wait a minute.

That would work.

Caleb ducked toward the officer and waved his hands wildly. "I'd like to turn myself in."

"What are you doing?" Katherine's expression was mortification personified.

"Trust me," was all he said.

The look she gave him said she thought he'd snapped. Lost his mind. Her concern that this would make Kane kill Noah was written in the worry lines on her face. The thought crossed Caleb's mind, too. He had to take the chance or they would all be dead. Besides, Kane would most likely bide his time. If he killed Noah too soon, he would lose all his leverage.

Caleb squeezed her hand. "I know what I'm doing."

Too late. The officer was next to them in a beat. "Katherine Harper?"

"Yes, sir," Caleb said.

Katherine's bewildered expression must've robbed her of her ability to speak, too.

"I believe we're wanted for questioning." Caleb glanced around.

The men had disappeared.

Caleb didn't realize until that moment that he'd been holding his breath.

Katherine allowed Caleb to lead her outside the police station. Being detained for the past twenty-four hours heightened her fatigue. "You didn't say anything about Noah, did you?"

"No. I didn't figure you wanted me to. Thought about it, though."

"So did I. I actually expected to be arrested."

"That might come next. They're still gathering and analyzing evidence. What did you tell them?"

"That we didn't do anything wrong. I explained exactly how it all happened back at my apartment. Said it must be some mistake. A random act of violence."

"So did I. The crime scene evidence should corroborate our story."

"There's no way they'll let Noah go if I involve the police. Kane will be furious at me for evading him at the drop for sure now. He warned me to come alone."

"Yes. But Noah will be alive and so will you." Caleb's forehead was etched with worry. Lines bracketed his mouth as he set Max down in a patch of grass.

"You're right. I probably haven't seemed very appreciative. I hope you know how very grateful I am. None of this would have happened without you. Noah and I would probably both be dead by now."

He squeezed her hand reassuringly. He didn't speak. His focus shifted from face to face as though he was evaluating threats.

Katherine exhaled deeply.

He wrapped his arms around her. She was flush with his chest before she could blink.

He pressed a kiss to her forehead. "It was stupid of us to walk into Kane's trap. I thought, for a second, I might lose you. Turning ourselves in was a risk I had to take to get us out of there and keep us alive."

Panic came off his frame in palpable waves. Fear dilated his pupils. His dark brown eyes sliced through her pain. Her loneliness. Katherine didn't realize how alone she'd been until Caleb. "I'm here. I'm not going away. Not unless you want me to."

"No. I don't. I want you right here with me."

She felt comforted by his strong presence. One hand slipped up his shirt onto his chest, rubbing against his skin in the hope of calming him.

She pressed her face against his cotton T-shirt before placing a kiss on his chest. "I'm right here."

He smiled. His fingers tangled in her hair, stroking it off her face.

He splayed his hand on her bottom, lighting fires from deep inside her. He lowered his face to hers and kissed her. His lips skimmed across hers and lit nerve endings she didn't know existed. Her body zinged to life, tantalized, pulsing volts of heat. A little piece of her heart wished he'd said forever.

A car alarm sounded.

He took a step back and scanned the parking lot, picking up Max. "I spoke to Matt."

Katherine tried to regain her mental balance because for a moment she got lost…lost in his gaze…lost in all that was Caleb. "What did he say?"

"Apparently your sister was talking to the Feds. There's a guy who seems legit. He's offering witness protection to you."

"What about you?"

Caleb shrugged. "Don't need it."

"You would never leave TorJake, would you?"

"It's the only home I've ever known."

Katherine hadn't felt home in so many years she couldn't count. Except that lately, home felt a lot like wherever Caleb was. But that was ridiculous. They'd only just met. It took years of getting to know someone before a bond like that could be created. Running for her life, trying to beat bullets, defying death probably had toyed with her emotions. No doubt, she had feelings for Caleb. That couldn't be denied. But the kinds of feelings that could last a lifetime? Real love? Wouldn't he let her down like the others had?

"Can't say I know what you mean," she lied. "How do we know this man can be trusted?"

Caleb's expression was weary. "I thought about that, too. I don't know. It might be the best chance we have."

"What about Noah? What will they do for him?"

"Good question. This guy said he was trying to help your sister before her accident. If they safely tuck you away, he can go after Noah."

"What do you think I should do?" Katherine turned the tables.

His pupils dilated for a split second as the muscles in his jaw clenched. It was the look he got when he was holding back what he really wanted to say.

"Whatever it takes to stay alive," he said, deadpan.

"So you think I should just turn myself in. Let the government handle this?" How could he say this to her? Hadn't he just told her to stay with him? Why had his gaze suddenly cooled?

"I didn't say that. You have to make the decision for yourself. I tried to drop a hint to Matt of where we'd be. We won't survive long without supplies and neither one of us knows how many of Kane's men are out there. Matt didn't get it."

"Where can we go? The police aren't looking for us right now. But Kane's men won't let up."

"I still think the ranch is the best place. There's a spot no one checks on the far side of the property."

"Then I want to go with you."

"Does that mean you won't turn yourself over to federal protection?"

She crossed her arms over her chest. "No. And it's not up for discussion right now."

"I told Matt to talk to Leann's boss to see if Kane visited the coffee shop."

"Good idea." As she turned to walk away, she could

feel Caleb's presence right behind her. She was tempted to lean back against his chest and allow him to wrap his arms around her. She didn't.

Whatever Leann had gotten involved with had to have been by accident. No way had her sister known this Kane person. She didn't get involved with known criminals or men with this kind of influence. Leann could keep a secret but she wouldn't drag herself and Noah into a mess like this. "She must've seen something horrible to cause all this."

"I was thinking the same thing. She was a witness to a crime. It's the only reason she'd be offered federal protection that I know of," he said quietly. "We need to make contact with the marshal to figure out what exactly."

Relief and vindication washed over Katherine. The emotions were followed by a deep sense of sadness.

Caleb stroked Max's fur. "I recognized one of the men earlier from photographs in the newspaper at the police station. He was definitely one of Kane's entourage."

"They'll keep coming until they find us, won't they?"

"I believe so."

Tears stung her eyes. What kind of horrible man had her nephew? And yet, Noah had sounded okay on the phone. "Think they picked up his medicine?"

"He's of no value dead. They kill him and you'll go into witness protection. They might have found out Leann was considering the program."

"Do you think they killed her? And they had to get to her before she disappeared with the evidence?" A chill raced up Katherine's arms. "Why not kill me and Noah, too?"

He shrugged. "They think you have evidence. Two

sisters and a little boy dead in a short time would sound alarms."

"I just can't figure out why she didn't go right in. Why would she wait?" A beat passed. "For Noah, I guess. She didn't want him to have that life. Kane must not have known about him before."

"Or she didn't think he did."

Reality dawned on her. "Leann was planning to leave him with me before she disappeared. She wanted to make sure he was safe. I'll bet she was ready to turn herself in."

"She must've figured they wouldn't connect the two of you. But why?"

"Leann changed her name when she left all those years ago, so we had different last names. It was her way of cutting all ties." She paused. "Still want to go to your ranch?"

"Yes."

"Then let's go."

"First, we need to change your appearance," Caleb said solemnly, tugging on his hat.

"Good idea. I almost didn't recognize you when you showed up. Max gave you away." She scratched him behind the ears, grateful the police hadn't taken him from her as she recognized the area as their original hiding spot.

"The ball cap. Small changes can make a big difference." He pulled a scarf from the bag of supplies.

She covered most of her hair and tied a knot in the back to hold the material in place. "How's this?"

He tucked a stray strand inside the fabric. "I wouldn't say better. You'd be beautiful no matter what you wore. This is different. Different is good. We want different."

His touch connected her to the memory of his hands on her before. His urgency. Ecstasy. She had no doubt those big hands could bring her pleasures she'd never known.

She ignored the sensitized shivers skittering across her nerves. "A man like Kane won't give up easily, will he?" She lowered her gaze.

He lifted her chin until she was looking him in the eye again. "Don't be sorry for any of this. I'm not. You didn't ask for this any more than Noah did. I'm sure your parents would be proud of you right now. You're risking your life to save your sister's boy. There's no shame in that."

"Except I feel like a coward."

His rich brown gaze trained on her. "Then you don't see what I do."

"Then what am I?"

"Strong. Brave. Intelligent."

She felt a blush crawl up her neck to her cheeks. "You make me sound like so much more than I feel right now."

"Sometimes the brain plays tricks on us. We don't have to buy into it. That's our choice."

She looked him dead in the eye. "You think we'll be safe at your ranch?"

He nodded. "For a while anyway."

Katherine was certain they'd be caught.

If not by Kane's men, then eventually by the Feds. The government wouldn't give a free pass to fugitives. Murderers. If Kane had his way, that would be the label put on them by everyone. Police. Reporters. Citizens. Anyone and everyone.

Strangers would be afraid of them.

Her life was shattered. There'd be no going back.

A new identity didn't sound like a bad idea. She doubted she'd have a job left to go back to when all this was said and done anyway. Would her friends and boss believe she'd had nothing to do with the murder of her landlady?

Friends? That was a joke. Katherine kept to herself most of the time. She worked and read and kept people at a distance, didn't she?

Except for her cowboy.

How could he push her toward the program? Didn't that mean they'd never see each other again?

Her lip quivered, but she ignored it. "I'm tired of running scared. They always seem a step ahead of me anyway."

A mischievous twinkle intensified his gold-brown eyes. "Are you saying what I think you are?"

"I'm ready to fight back."

Caleb's face brightened with anticipation. His eyes glittered an incredible shade of brown. "It's risky."

Risky didn't cover the half of it to Katherine. And yet, waiting, not knowing what would happen next, giving the other guys all the advantage wasn't an option, either. She'd been letting Kane and his men hold the cards for too long. Time to take control. "I know."

"You're sure about this?"

"I've never been more certain of anything in my life. I'm not sure what the plan is yet. Just that we need one."

"Then let's give 'em hell."

He got a sexy spark in his eye when he was being bad. How could someone become so special to her in such a short time span?

She couldn't imagine doing any of this without Caleb. Her cowboy protector...friend...*lover?*

Chapter 10

Caleb needed transportation. Walking around outside exposed wasn't good, especially after Katherine's fall. Her ankle was swelling again. Kane's men would be all over the place now that they'd managed to get away from them. He was half surprised no one had waited outside the police station earlier. Could he get Katherine out of the city safely before Kane figured out they'd been released?

Even though they'd been questioned and released, being identified by a random person could put them both in danger. Especially if one of Kane's men was around. Attracting attention wasn't good.

He located the nicest restaurant in the area; intently watched where the valet parked cars. He scanned the parking garage for witnesses. A family stepped out of the elevator. He froze. A stab of guilt hit him. He didn't like the idea of taking someone else's property, but there was no other choice. Steal or die.

When the valet parked an SUV with the windows blacked out, he waited for the family to unload their minivan and the valet to jog out of sight.

Caleb figured the owner would be in the restaurant for a good hour. That should give them enough time to get out of the city before anyone knew the sport utility was missing. He could ditch the SUV in a field or alley outside of Allen. If he could get that far, he'd be close enough to get home on foot. The less walking the better for Katherine. Even with a modest amount of pain reliever, she had to be hurting.

He put on a pair of sterile gloves and felt the back tire on the driver's side. Jackpot. The keys were there. A trick he'd learned back in the day before he'd gone on the straight and narrow.

The ignition caught and he drove the SUV to pick up Katherine and Max a minute later.

"I don't want to know where you got this, do I?" She slid into the passenger seat next to him.

"Probably not."

"Then I won't ask." She smiled. Her violet eyes darkened, reflecting her exhaustion. She was putting up a brave front. He could see the fear lurking behind her facade.

He merged the SUV into traffic a few moments later, disappearing onto Highway 75. "Why don't you put the seat back and rest?"

She eyed him warily. "How did you find this so easily?"

There was no use lying to her. "I have a record. Got into trouble as a kid. Had reasons to know how to lift a car quickly." He looked at her more intently, needing to know if his admission bothered her. "I did all that stuff a long time ago. I would never do it now. Hank helped me straighten up."

She didn't blink. "Seems like he also taught you some useful skills for staying alive."

"Any decent man would help a woman in this situation."

"Am I just any woman?"

Was she?

He wanted to continue to compare her to Cissy, the others, needing something to tamp down the out-of-control reaction his body was having. "I never said that."

"Never mind. You've been my knight in shining armor. Which falls into the 'any decent man' category." Her smile didn't reach her eyes.

He wanted to be more to her than "any decent man." But he couldn't ignore the realities. Katherine was a woman in trouble. Cissy had been in dire straits when she'd showed up at his door, too. She'd cried and begged him to help. He would've done anything to save that little girl of hers. Cissy hadn't needed to grovel. And yet, she'd begged to stay at the ranch. Said Savannah loved it out there. When he'd arranged all the doctor visits and taken over her medical care, Cissy had become even more attached.

She'd played a good hand. Turned on the tears when he hadn't immediately returned the sentiment.

Caleb had been convinced her feelings were real. Even though he'd believed getting involved would be a bad idea, she'd eventually worn him down. One thing was certain, he'd do it all again if it meant saving Savannah.

Did he have a deep-down need to save women?

He figured a shrink would have a field day with his psyche. They'd probably say he rescued women because he hadn't been able to save his mom. They'd be right about the last part. Caleb hadn't been able to stop the bastard who'd fathered him from hurting his mother. If Caleb had been older…gotten his bare hands around that man's neck… Caleb would have ripped the guy's head off.

He'd been too young. Too weak. The old man was bigger. Stronger.

Caleb saw too much of the jerk in himself when he looked into the mirror. Let the bastard show his face now. Why did they have to look so much alike?

He couldn't go back and change what made him the man he was today any more than he could stop himself from doing what he thought was right.

Katherine's delicate hand on his arm redirected his attention.

Caleb couldn't ignore the bolt of heat shooting through him from where she touched. She stirred emotions he'd sworn not to feel again. And yet, how could he stop himself?

Cissy hadn't been gone long. She'd left a hole. Was he trying to fill it with Katherine?

"Where'd you go just now?"

"I'm right here."

"You're not getting off that easily, buster. You know all about my situation. Now it's your turn. Talk."

"You don't want to know what I was thinking."

Her violet eyes widened as she sat up. "Why not? Does it have to do with me?"

Katherine was brave and caring. Even when she

was afraid, she faced it. She hadn't asked for his help. In fact, she'd been leery of accepting any aid. Every step of the way, she thought of others, not considering herself during this entire ordeal. When they were both hurt, she wanted to attend to his wounds first. The guilt she carried was a heavy weight on her back. She didn't use tears as a weapon. No, she refused to cry. She held everything on her shoulders and rarely let him in. When he really thought about it, the comparison to Cissy didn't hold water.

Katherine was nothing like Cissy.

He didn't have any plans to tell Katherine how much she occupied his thoughts.

"Maybe I should drive. You haven't slept in a couple of days now. All the adrenaline must be wearing off, too. I'm sure your body's as worn down as mine," she said. "Probably more so since you haven't so much as closed your eyes since this whole ordeal started."

"I'm fine."

"Still, I'd feel much better if you got some rest. You have dark circles under your eyes. Let me take the wheel for a while."

"I appreciate your concern." She had no idea how much he meant those words.

The back of her hand came up to press against the stubble on his face. Desire pounded him, tensing his muscles and demanding release. A dull ache formed at his temples.

No way was he acting on it in the car.

Maybe soon…

"Besides, we have to ditch the sport utility," he said.

She moved to the back seat. He noticed her taut legs and sweet round behind as she climbed over.

"Here, the least I can do is rub your shoulders."

She worked his tense muscles. Having her hands on him created the opposite effect she desired. Instead of relaxing, his body went rigid. His need for her surged, causing his neck muscles to become more tense.

He glanced in the rearview mirror in time to see her frown.

"You're so tense. That can't be good."

A grin tugged at the corners of his mouth. She had no idea the effect she was having on him. "You touch me much more like that and I can't be held responsible for my actions."

Her eyes widened as reality dawned on her.

Was that a smile he just saw cross her features?

"I didn't mean to create an issue for you," Katherine said, quashing the self-satisfied smirk trying to force its way to the surface. She enjoyed the fact a man so strong, so powerful, reacted so intensely to her lightest touch.

"Well, you have," he said with a killer grin.

Damn, he was sexy.

Katherine forced her gaze away from him and climbed into the front seat.

The sexually charged air hung thickly between them, sending her body to crackling embers. Had she ever felt this way for a man before?

No. Never.

And a tiny piece of her couldn't help but wonder if she'd ever feel this way again. Or if she'd live long enough to see where it could go. Noah. Baby. She prayed he had the life-saving medicine he needed by now.

"This looks like a good place to ditch the SUV," he said, pulling into a corn field.

"Then what?"

"We walk from here. Unless we get lucky and find an ATV."

About the last thing Katherine felt was lucky. "What are the chances of that happening?"

"Pretty good actually. When you know where to look." There came that devilish smile again.

It sent Katherine's heart pounding and her thighs burning to have him nestled against her. She sighed. More inappropriate thoughts. They were becoming more difficult to contain. Caleb was one powerful man. His presence had a way of electrifying her senses and causing her to want. She knew better. Her body wanted nothing more than to get into bed with him and allow his strong physical presence to cover her, warm her and protect her.

Her logical mind knew to rail against those primal feminine urges.

She opened the door, but Caleb was already there. He took Max, and let him run free.

"We'll be okay for a minute. Let me check that ankle before you try to walk on it."

He closed his hand around her ankle and she ignored the fires he lit there, focusing instead on the little dog.

Max piddled on a nearby cornstalk and scurried back to Caleb's feet.

Smart dog. He seemed to know on instinct who the alpha male was.

She took in a deep breath to clear her mind but only managed to breathe in his scent. He was outdoors and masculinity and sex personified. *Bad idea.*

Katherine gripped her purse. "How terrible is it?"

"Are you in pain?"

"A little." She blocked out the true wound. The cavern that couldn't be filled in her chest if anything happened to Noah…or if she couldn't be with Caleb. Her ankle was nothing in comparison to those hurts. "I'll be able to walk on it."

"It's pretty swollen. I'd hate to make it worse."

"Not much choice." She smiled. "We can't hide out in a cornfield forever."

"I was trying to decide if I should let you walk or carry you."

"Oh, don't do that." The very thought of his hands on her sent a sensual chill up her back. The feeling of his arms wrapped around her would be nice. No doubt about it. But if her body was pressed to his, he'd read every bit of physical reaction she had to him. That couldn't possibly help matters.

Katherine squared her shoulders. "No can do, captain. I'm ready and willing to walk the plank."

Her attempt at humor fell flat. *Can't blame a girl for trying.* Where had that come from? She was becoming delirious. It would do her good to focus. Walking, painful as it would be, would also keep her on track and feeling alive.

Noah's kidnapping came crashing down on Katherine's thoughts.

I won't let you down, baby.

"You mind staying here while I look for transportation?" Caleb asked, breaking through.

"Not at all." She took out a bottle of water and sipped before pouring a little in her curled hand for Max. "Besides, I have company."

Max ignored the water and followed Caleb as he walked away, leaving the water to run off her palm.

Two-timing little puff ball.

Not that she could blame the dog, really. If she had a choice between being protected by her or Caleb, she'd choose the hunky guy with sex appeal to spare, too.

With Caleb by her side, they'd deflected bullets and escaped crazy killers, and yet he'd managed to keep them both alive. If she had money to put on a horse, that Thoroughbred would be named Caleb Snow.

Katherine opened her bag. The pic of Leann with baby Noah she'd taken from the apartment stared up at her. A lump formed in her throat, making it difficult to swallow. She wanted to cry. To feel the sweet release of tears. To liberate all the bottled-up feelings swelling in her chest and let everything go. Nothing came.

Katherine was the emotional equivalent of a drought.

Caleb's luck improved considerably when he located the ATV at the edge of the field. He roared up with it, enjoying the feeling of making Katherine smile. She looked from Max to Caleb. The little dog had perched its front paws on the steering column and wagged his tail as soon as Katherine came into view.

What could Caleb say? The dog had good taste.

He helped her onto the back and secured her arms around his midsection.

Fifteen minutes into the ride, the ATV stalled. "Out of gas." Going on foot from here would frustrate anyone who was able to follow their tracks.

"Me, too," she said with a brilliant smile. The kind of smile that made a man think she possessed all the stars in the heavens and they reflected like stardust from her face. Wasn't like him to wax poetic.

He made a crutch for her out of a thick tree branch,

urging her to put her weight on him as Max tagged along behind, keeping pace.

"Where are we headed?" Katherine asked as they pushed deeper into the woods.

"There's an old building at the back of my property. It's the original homestead. Not much more than a couple of rooms. Been empty for years. No one ever goes there. Hell, few people even know it exists it's so far to the edge of my property. I like it that way, too. I keep a few basic supplies, blankets and such, in the place in case I get out here riding fences and don't want to come back."

"What could you possibly have to hide from? The world? Why? You have a beautiful ranch. Your life looks perfect to me."

Not exactly. There was no one like her waiting for him when he came home every night.

His adrenaline had faded, and he was running out of juice. Especially with the way his mind kept wandering to thoughts of her. What he'd like to do to her.

The rest of the long walk was quiet.

Relief flooded him as the building came into view. A few more steps and he could get Katherine off her bad leg.

He opened the door, and put a thick blanket on top of the wood platform he'd frequently used as a bed. The place had gotten a fair amount of use when Cissy had left. Plenty of times, Caleb hadn't wanted to be inside the main house. She'd disappeared in such a hurry she hadn't packed. Her things were left in the bedroom. Savannah's toys littered the grounds. Reminders of his life with them had been everywhere. They'd been like land mines to Caleb. Each one had detonated a memory…

brought out the hollow feeling in his chest. He hadn't been able to look at the color purple again without seeing Savannah's stuffed hippo. It went with her everywhere, tucked under her arm. When she'd watch TV, the hippo was her pillow.

"At least tell me why you have so many things out here. And I don't believe it's just in case you get restless. I'm sure there are plenty of places you could find to soothe yourself." Her violet eyes tore through him.

"My ex had a little girl. They both left. It broke my heart."

"I'm sorry. She wasn't yours?"

He shook his head, stuffing regret down somewhere deep. "No."

"What happened?"

"When they left, it felt like my heart had been ripped from my chest."

She covered his heart with her hand, connecting to the pain he felt.

"Thought I would suffocate inside the house for how empty it felt. Like the air was in a vacuum and I couldn't breathe."

"You must've loved her."

He nodded. "I'd take my horse, Dawn, out after supper. At times, I couldn't bring myself to go back inside, so I would come here. Guess everyone worried. Matt followed me one night. Margaret probably made him. So, he knows about this place, too."

"Anyone else aware of this place?"

"Me and Matt. Now you."

He settled her onto the blanket and tended to her cuts. He didn't have ice in any of the supplies. There was no electricity at the place. But he'd bought a compression sock at the big-box store and that should help with the swelling. He slipped off her sandal and slid the sock around her foot and up her silky calf. “This should help.”

He didn’t immediately move his hand. It felt so natural to touch her.

Max circled around a few times before curling up in a ball next to Katherine.

“He lost a lot today. He’s probably exhausted,” she said.

“So are you.” He patted the little puff ball’s head.

“I can’t help but worry about Noah. I’d close my eyes but I’m afraid of the images my mind will conjure up.” The corners of her mouth turned down.

The picture of her when he’d first seen her, all chestnut hair and cherry lips, scared and alone, invaded his thoughts. Her misery was his. He wanted to kiss away her pain. Since he knew he’d never stop there, he went to the small kerosene stove instead and heated water. Margaret had slipped some herbal bags in with his supplies. More of her healing tea no doubt. Caleb was a coffee man, but he was glad for what she’d done. It might provide Katherine with the comfort she needed to relax.

“What’s this?” she asked when he handed her a tin cup full of steaming brew.

“Margaret said something about it calming the mind.”

“You didn’t sleep much after your ex-girlfriend left, did you?” The question caught him off guard.

He shook his head. “I was in bad shape for a while.”

He’d rebounded faster than he believed possible thanks to the love and support he received from his second family. Margaret and Matt had been beside him every step of the way until the pain had faded.

He could recall very little about Cissy in detail. He couldn't for the life of him remember what she smelled like, and yet the spring flower bouquet with a hint of vanilla, Katherine's scent, was etched in his memory. Vivid. If she disappeared right then and he never saw her again, he would remember how she smelled for the rest of his life. "I'm better now."

The sound of branches cracking stopped him.

Glancing around, he realized he had nothing to use as a weapon out there. He'd ditched his rifle long ago when he'd run out of ammunition at Katherine's house.

He moved to Katherine and covered her with his body, pulling dusty blankets on top of them to hide.

Even after the outside noise stopped, Caleb held his breath. Matt might have figured out the hint from their earlier phone call, and he could've brought the sheriff with him for all his good intentions. Or it could be an animal.

Katherine lay beneath him, her soft warm body rising and falling with every breath she took, pressing against him. The memory of the way they'd met etched in his thoughts. The way her body felt underneath him. A perfect fit. Her face was so close; he wouldn't have to move far to skim his lips across her jawline, or the base of her throat where he could see her pulse throb. It wouldn't take much movement to lift his chin and kiss her. But he realized he wanted so much more than her kiss.

More than her body.

He wanted all of her. Mind. Body. Soul—if there was such a thing.

Before any of that could happen, he wanted to be able to trust her.

He needed to know that if he opened his heart, she wouldn't stamp her heels all over it and walk away.

The tricky part? To find out, he had to go out on a limb and give the very thing he avoided…trust. Both his father and Cissy had done a number on him in that department. Since history was the best predictor of the future, believing in someone again felt about as easy as skinning a live rattlesnake with a hairbrush.

He wished like hell he'd told Katherine how he'd felt about her when he'd had the chance.

If he could get beyond the pain of his past, could he have a real future with her?

Or would she leave just like the others?

Chapter 11

The door to the homestead creaked open slowly. "Caleb, you in here?"

Caleb recognized Matt's voice immediately. He threw the covers off and stood. "Come inside and shut the door."

Worry lines bracketed his friend's mouth. "Damn, I've been worried."

Relief eased Caleb's tense muscles. "I didn't think you'd caught on to my hint on the phone."

"It took me a while. Then it finally clicked."

Caleb helped Katherine into a comfortable sitting position, elevating her swollen ankle. He turned to Matt. "What's going on?"

"You tell me. People are coming out of the woodwork looking for you. Margaret's beside herself with worry."

"No doubt they've been expecting me to come home."

Matt nodded.

"What kind of people have been showing up?"

"The marshal for one. He's been checking in every few hours. I didn't tell him you'd made contact, but he seems to know."

"The line must be tapped."

"I guessed as much."

"Speaking of which, you didn't bring your phone with you, did you?"

Matt shook his head. "Figured if they could get to one, they could get to another. Left it in the barn just in case. Sneaked out the back."

"Good thinking. Kane's men followed our movements with the ones we had. I had to ditch them."

"No wonder I kept rolling into voice mail every time I called."

"Who else has been by the ranch?"

"The men in suits have stopped by several times." His lips formed a grim line. "They're staying in town at the Dovetail Inn."

"Did you tell the marshal about them?"

Matt nodded. "He said to ignore them. Truth is I don't know what or who to believe anymore." His gaze traveled from Caleb to Katherine.

"I do," Caleb said firmly. He sensed this whole ordeal would be coming to a head soon, and a big piece of him dreaded the day he would part company with Katherine. It was selfish. He should want everything to be behind them and for normal life to return. Except that she'd imprinted him in ways he could never have imagined a woman could. Being forced to live without her sounded worse than a death sentence. His heart said she wouldn't walk out, but logic forced him to look at his history.

Then again, if the men with guns had their way, he might not live long enough to miss her. And he would. From somewhere deep inside where a little bit of light still lived within him.

"Either way, I can connect with the marshal if you want to go into the program we talked about." Matt shot another weary glance toward Katherine.

Her chin came up proudly, but to her credit she didn't say anything.

She was strong and bold. Another reason Caleb's argument she was just like Cissy didn't hold up. Damn, she was sexy, beautiful and strong. Made him want to kick Matt out and do things to her that would remind her she was all woman and not some errant fugitive destined to die by the hands of some criminal jerk.

"They'll have to take me out of here in a box. I have no plans to leave my ranch again." Closure was coming, one way or another, and Caleb regretted the second he realized it also meant their time together would come to an end. He silently pledged to show her just how appealing she was before that happened. "I won't run anymore."

"Is that such a good idea?" Matt's chin jutted out, and he blew out a breath.

Caleb shrugged. "This is my home."

"I can go. I'll draw them away from you," Katherine said, seeming resigned to her fate.

He was touched but not surprised she'd be willing to put herself in more danger for him. Her current situation had come about because she would give her life to protect her nephew. Yet another difference between her and Cissy. Cissy had only thought about herself.

"I don't mean any disrespect, but she brings up a good point. Maybe if she leaves..."

"It won't matter. I'm still a person of interest in a murder, remember?"

"How could I forget?" Matt said with a disgusted grunt. His gaze intensified on Katherine.

"Enough," Caleb barked to his friend. Frustration was getting the best of him. "Did you have a chance to follow up on the mission we discussed?"

"I did." His face muscles pulled taut. "I called the manager, and asked if I could email him a picture of someone I was looking for. I sent him a photo of Kane from a news article I found. He recognized him right away. Said he came in the coffee shop all the time. Or used to when Leann worked there before the accident."

"I wonder why a man like him would get involved with my sister."

"I already know. The manager put one of her coworkers on the line. She was chatty. Said she and Leann used to go climbing together sometimes. She was with her the day of her accident at Enchanted Rock. They all stood by helplessly when she lost her grip and tumbled...."

Matt fixed his gaze on the floor a second before continuing. "The woman said Leann practically dropped out of sight when her old boyfriend showed up a few months ago."

Katherine gasped. "They dated?"

Caleb closed his hand around hers, looping their fingers together, and offering reassurance so she could hear more. She rewarded him with a weak smile.

"Said they were like two lovebirds. He'd visit her at

the coffee shop and drop off presents, flowers." Matt looked from Katherine to Caleb and back. "She also said he's Noah's dad."

Katherine's fingers went limp.

"No," came out on a whisper. "Can't be."

"If it's true, if Kane's the father, then Noah's safe," Caleb reassured her.

"But he's a monster. Who knows what he's truly capable of?"

"His company ranks are filled with relatives. I read somewhere that he's devoted to family. Noah's his only child. He'd want to keep him close, but he wouldn't hurt his own son."

"No. He'd just use him as a weapon against me." She released a pained sob but gathered herself quickly.

"This is a game changer. Explains why they didn't kill Noah when they didn't get the file." Anger pierced Caleb for not being able to shield her from pain. "The coworker said she was there that day?"

Matt nodded.

"Then we know it was an accident at least." He turned to Matt. "Wait for me outside?"

"Okay."

He settled Katherine onto the makeshift bed and pressed kisses to her forehead, her eyelids, her chin. He held back the new thought plaguing him. That Kane would realize she would never be able to produce the file, and kill her.

"I'll check the area as Matt leaves. Make sure no one followed him."

Katherine's chest rose on harsh breaths. She nodded.

"I want to give him the CD. See if he can find anything. What do you think?"

Those tormented violet eyes looked up at him. She hesitated. "If you trust him, then I agree."

"Good. Try to get some rest. I'll be right back."

She gazed up at him, confused, tired. "He can't be the father. I'll never see Noah again."

"Don't be afraid. When you close your eyes, I want you to picture me. I'll protect you." She couldn't possibly know just how much he meant those words.

Caleb met his friend on the porch and closed the door. "We need to come up with a plan. But first, we've had a long couple of days, and we need rest."

"It'll be dark soon. You should be all right for tonight. They will figure out where you are eventually. And they'll come with guns blazing. Make no mistake about it," Matt said.

"I know."

"Then what's the game plan? How do you expect to get out of this alive?"

He could see that his friend was coming from a place of caring. "We'll be ready for them. Tomorrow morning, I want you to tell the men to stay away. Margaret, too. Tell them not to come back to work for a few days. That should give us enough time to handle things. Also, I want to meet with the marshal. First thing before daylight." Caleb held out the CD. "And take a look at this. See if you can find a hidden file, or anything that seems suspicious."

Matt took it and studied the cover for a minute. "What has that woman gotten you into?"

"She didn't." Caleb's jaw muscle tensed. Friend or not, Matt had crossed the line. "Look. My eyes were wide open when I decided to help her. You need to know I plan to see this through no matter what."

"Why? What is she to you?"

"You don't get it." He didn't have a real answer to that question so he said goodbye, checking to make sure no one was in the woods lurking, waiting to make a move. "Keep things quiet tonight. Set up the meeting in the tack room."

Matt agreed before disappearing into the thicket.

Caleb moved inside to find Katherine awake, eyes wide open.

"What did you mean when you said you wouldn't leave the ranch again?"

"Did you get enough to eat? I can open and heat a can of soup." He changed the subject as he lit a Coleman lantern, allowing the soft flame to illuminate the room as the sun retreated, casting a dark shadow to fill the room.

"I'm fine. But you're not thinking straight. I won't let you risk your life for me anymore."

"We going down that path again?" What Matt said must've hurt her feelings. "Matt means well. He doesn't know what he's saying."

"I agree with him. They'll go easy on you. I'll tell everyone I shot Ms. Ranker if I have to." Desperation had the muscles in her face rigid as she stood in front of him, moving closer. A red heat climbed up her neck.

"I can't let you lie." He smiled. "Besides, you're no good at it. And the evidence will clear us."

Defiance shot from her glare. Her stubborn streak reared its head again. "You don't get to decide."

Her gaze was fiery hot. Her body vibrated with intensity as she stalked toward him.

He readied himself for the argument that was sure to

come, but she pressed a kiss to his lips instead, shocking the hell out of him. More than his spirits rose.

"There's been enough fighting for one day. I need something else from you."

He locked on to her gaze. "Are you sure this is a good idea?"

"No. Not at all. But I need to do it anyway. I want you. I've never wanted a man more. Do you want me?" She tiptoed up and wrapped her arms around his neck. Her eyes darkened, and she was sexy as hell, gazing up at him. A tear fell onto her cheek.

He kissed it away.

"Sorry. I can't remember the last time I cried."

"Don't be." Caleb knew all about holding in emotion. The way it ate at a person's gut until it felt as though there was no stomach lining left. He dropped his other hand to the small of her back. "There's nothing to be ashamed of."

"I'm being stupid. How could anyone want someone who practically cries all over them?"

"I think it's sweet." Rocking his hips, he pressed his erection against her midsection as he cupped her left breast. Heat shot through his body. "This give you any clue as to the question of whether or not I want you?"

Her face lit up with eagerness, and it nearly did him in. "I need to forget about the danger we're in and the fact Noah's been kidnapped, just for a little while." She snuggled against him, shifting her stance to wrap her arms around his waist.

Her sensuality was going to his head faster than a shot of hard liquor. "Hold on there."

"What? You don't think this is a good idea?"

"No. It's been a while for me. And I want this to last."

"Either way there's far too much material between us," she said, stepping back long enough to shrug out of her shirt.

Sight of the delicately laced bra she wore caused a painful spasm in his groin. The light color an interesting contrast to her golden skin.

A second later her shorts fell to the ground, revealing matching cotton panties. The panties he'd picked out for her. Pink.

She stood there, arms at her sides, allowing him a minute to really look at her. "Do you still want me?"

He swallowed a groan. "You're beautiful. You're also determined to end this before it gets started."

"Not exactly. I want long and slow." She unhooked her bra and let it drop before shimmying out of her panties.

Caleb ate up the space between them in one quick stride. His thumb grazed her nipple. It pebbled under his touch and a blast of heat strained his erection. His body needed release. He needed to be inside her where she was warm and wet, moving in rhythm with him until they both exploded and she lay melted in his arms. He needed Katherine.

"You want help with those?" She motioned toward his T-shirt and jeans with a teasing smile that stirred his heart.

His shirt came off in one quick motion and joined her clothing on the floor. She didn't wait for him to unzip his jeans, she was already there, her hands on his zipper. He aided her in their quick removal along with his boxer shorts.

Her eyes widened when they stopped on his full erection. "I want to feel you inside me."

Caleb nearly lost control right there. He needed to think about something else besides the way her honeyed skin would feel wrapped around him. His passion for her hit heights he'd never known with a woman, and he hadn't even entered her yet.

He picked her up and placed her on the bed before retrieving a condom from his wallet. His hands shook as he attempted to sheath himself.

"Here. Let me." She placed it on his tip and rolled her hand down the shaft.

His muscles went so rigid he felt like an overstrung cello. "You're sexy…and beautiful."

She lay back, watching him. "Then make love to me."

Her thighs parted and he positioned himself in the V. In one thrust, he drove inside her warmth. She was so wet, he nearly exploded. Her body fit him perfectly.

"More," she said through a ragged breath. She gripped his shoulders.

He wanted to make her scream his name a thousand times as he rocketed her toward the ultimate release.

He tensed and struggled to maintain self-control. Not what he was used to. "Not if you want this to last any longer."

He commanded his hips not to move as she traced her fingers down his arms, then onto his back. Her hands came up and anchored on his shoulders as he lowered his mouth over hers, marking her as his. Her silken lips parted, and his tongue drove into her mouth, tasting her honeylike sweetness.

Her fingers skimmed along his spine, setting little fires everywhere she touched. His skin burned with desire only she could release.

Caleb kissed her hard, claiming her mouth as her tongue moved with his. He lightened the kiss softly, allowing her to be in control and to take whatever she needed from him.

In that moment he belonged to her completely, and for as long as she needed him.

And what did he need?

Every needy grasp of her fingertips…every possessive fleck of her tongue…every blast of heat she sent firing through him….

All of her.

She was every bit the woman capable of unleashing his tightly gripped emotions and sending him soaring.

Her tongue delved into his mouth as her fingernails gripped his bottom and he shuddered inside her.

Tremors moved up and down his spine as he pumped her silky heat.

"Caleb," she breathed his name.

He pressed his mouth to the soft curve of her right breast, taking her pointed peak inside his mouth. Her moan was like pouring gasoline on the fire inside him.

He pumped harder as his own desire blazed through his veins.

Hold on…not yet…

He wanted her to explode in his arms into a thousand fragments of light.

He covered her lips, swallowing her next moan and delved his tongue as he bucked his hips.

"Oh, Caleb…"

She tensed her muscles around his erection, and he could feel her nearing the edge.

He pumped faster…harder…deeper…needing to find

her core and tantalize her until the mounting fire inside her detonated.

He teased her nipple between his thumb and forefinger, causing her back to arch. Her chestnut hair blazed across the pillow, her body moved in rhythm with his. Her hips wriggled him deeper inside until he thought he might lose all control. She was on the edge, and he felt it.

Her muscles convulsed, and he thrust deeper, again and again, until he felt her completely come undone in his arms. Only then did he allow himself to think about his own release.

Her tight muscles squeezed around his erection and his body reacted, shivering and quaking. In a sensual burst, he let go. Thundered.

In that instant, there was no Caleb or Katherine. They existed together…as the same person…in one body….

She felt so right in his arms. Would she stay?

Until tomorrow, a little voice said.

Pain gripped him. He couldn't contain his growing feelings for her. This would be over soon. She would be gone. He most likely would never see her again.

Chapter 12

The now familiar sounds of the woods, crickets chirping and insects' wings buzzing, broke through the silence in the room. Katherine's sensitized body tingled as Caleb's warm breath moved across her skin. He'd pulled her in tight against him.

Her rapid breathing eventually eased, becoming slow and steady as it found an even tempo. Her heart beat in perfect harmony with his. Everything about the two of them fit together so perfectly. It was so easy to be with Caleb. Being naked with him felt like the most natural thing in the world. She had no insecurities about her body as she lay there. They were like links in a fence, their bond strengthening the whole.

A dumbstruck thought hit her. Their feelings didn't matter anymore. She had Noah to think about. Or did she? She had no idea if he was hurt, or worse. Did Kane even bother to pick up Noah's medication at the drop spot earlier? Would he keep the boy around if he wasn't useful anymore? Logic told her he would, but her heart feared the worst anyway.

If they did survive this nightmare, would she ever see her nephew again? Wouldn't a father trump an aunt? A rich man like Kane could pull strings to ensure she never saw her Noah again.

She recalled the emotions that had drilled through her when she'd found out she'd be responsible for her baby sister. Jealousy. Bitterness. Resentment. They were not the feelings she had about caring for Noah, but she'd known exactly what she was getting into with him. She was older. Ready.

Even though Caleb would never admit it, he would resent her for strapping him down with a ready-made family. If she survived, all her energy had to go toward getting Noah away from Kane.

"Are you sorry?" He broke through her train of thought.

"No. Not for making love. I figured we had to put this attraction behind us so both of us could concentrate. We'll need all our wits about us tomorrow. It was difficult for either one of us to think clearly before."

"And now?" He eyed her suspiciously.

"Everything's crystal clear."

A dark brow lifted. He propped himself up on one elbow. His muscular body glowed in the soft light.

A well of need sprung up inside Katherine so fast and so desperately she had to take a second to catch her breath and allow her pulse to return to normal—whatever "normal" was anymore.

"And what does that mean exactly?" he asked, eyeing her intently.

"It's highly improbable that all three of us will come out of this alive. If what you said about Kane is true, then at least Noah will be safe." If she and Caleb did survive, could they become a family? He'd spoken so fondly of Savannah, could he grow to accept Noah, too? No. Caleb loved Savannah because he loved her mother. He didn't have those feelings for Katherine. Did he?

Her mind was really playing tricks on her. No way could he have fallen in love with her in such a short time. As much as she'd like to believe the possibility, her practical mind brought her back to reality. They'd been running for their lives. Dodging bullets. They'd narrowly escaped death. He'd been her knight in shining armor, showing up at a time when she needed him most. Of course she had strong feelings for her cowboy. But she shouldn't confuse gratitude for keeping her alive with real affection.

"If I have anything to say about it we will." The way he set his jaw said he meant every word, too.

Even a superhero had a weakness. What was the chink in Caleb's veneer?

Women in trouble.

She needed him, just as Cissy had.

Maybe that was the connection.

Katherine shut the thoughts out of her mind. She didn't want to compare what she and Caleb had with his relationship to the other woman. She didn't even want to think about him with another woman.

"What's the plan?" she asked, trying to redirect her internal conversation.

"Our best bet is to make contact with the marshal."

"Why do you think we can trust him?"

He shrugged. "A hunch."

"Why not contact the sheriff?"

"He'll probably put me in jail."

She gasped. "Surely he doesn't believe you had anything to do with the murder."

"Knowing Coleman, he'd detain me to keep me safe until this whole thing blows over."

"You think there's a chance this'll just go away?" Unrealistic hope flickered inside her and then vanished.

"No. I think they'll keep coming until we're both dead."

"Then we should leave. Hide. I'll go with you."

His dark brow arched. "Would you?"

"If it meant you'd be safe."

"And then as soon as I turned my back you'd disappear and try to protect Noah. You're always looking out for those around you, but who looks out for you?"

A tear welled in her eye. "I don't need anyone."

He grunted. "Like hell you don't. I never met anyone who needed people more."

Like Cissy?

Why did the admission hurt so much?

His reasons for helping her were becoming transparent. "Does your cowboy code force you to save all damsels in distress?"

His jaw muscles pulsed and his gaze narrowed. Anger radiated from him. "Being with you has nothing to do with obligation."

"Then what?" She hated feeling so insecure and so vulnerable. Maybe that's why she'd spent so much time blocking out the world? Considering Caleb was about the only true friend she had and they'd just met. She'd been doing a great job of keeping people away to date. Didn't everyone let her down eventually?

He didn't immediately answer.

"I was doing fine by myself before you came along," she lied. She told herself if she could close her eyes, she might even be able to rest.

He pressed a kiss to her forehead. "I know you were. But I wasn't. And I don't know what I'd do without you here."

The thin layer of ice protecting her heart from being broken melted. "We might never know why he's after us." She fell silent. The rock of dread positioned on her chest grew heavier. Her chest walls felt as though they were caving in…as if she was drowning and couldn't get air into her lungs. Leann's secret was a boulder tied around Katherine's neck as she catapulted to the ocean floor.

"Maybe Matt will see something on the CD we overlooked. We didn't exactly have time to dig around on it before they caught up to us," Caleb offered.

"You're sure we can trust him?"

"I'd put my life in his hands."

He just did. And hers, too. Matt didn't hide the fact he didn't have the same dedication to Katherine that he did to Caleb. At least she knew exactly where she stood with him. "He doesn't think you should be around me."

"Just proves he doesn't know what's best for me."

"I can't see a way out of this. Even if you talk to the marshal, you're taking a risk. He might be on Kane's payroll. How can we know he'll be of assistance to us?"

Caleb shrugged his shoulders. The light from the lantern made his face look even more handsome. "Don't see another choice."

"Me, either. You're right. We need help from someone."

"I can leave before the sun comes up to get Matt. I'll be back before the first light with a few answers. For now, I'd like to try to sleep. Unless you can think of something better to do." He quirked a devastating grin.

One look was all it took for him to stir her sexually. "As a matter of fact, I can. And I think we make love quite well."

"All the more reason for us to keep doing it," he said with one of his trademark looks.

"Unless you're too tired." She repositioned herself better to kiss him, enjoying the feel of the perfect fit of their naked bodies. His was like pure silk over finely tuned muscle.

"Are you doubting me?"

She kissed his collarbone. "That wouldn't be a wise move on my part. I've seen your stamina. But even you have to sleep sometime."

"After a while," he said, pressing his erection to her thigh. "Right now, I have something else demanding attention."

This time, their lovemaking was slow and tender. Did they both realize each moment together was a precious gift to be savored and enjoyed?

Caleb rose before the sun and heated water for coffee while Katherine slept. He'd had to force himself away from her to get out of bed. Every bone in his body wanted to curl up with her, hold her. He hadn't wanted to leave a second before he had to. He'd managed a few hours of shut-eye, thanks to her being by his side.

He'd expected coming back to the homestead would evoke a hailstorm of bad memories. It didn't.

Katherine had chased away those demons for him, he thought while he let Max outside to take care of his business.

Caleb kept the door cracked open as he opened a can of beef stew and heated it for the pint-size critter. The little guy had been too stressed to eat last night. He'd curled in the corner and slept until he heard Caleb stir. His little ears had perked up and he'd whined until Caleb went to get him.

Time seemed to drip by as Caleb glanced at his watch for the third time in five minutes. Matt was supposed to meet him in the tack room, providing it was safe. He'd been tasked with making contact with the marshal, and trying to figure out what Caleb had missed on the CD.

The unanswered questions in this case weren't helping matters. If he knew what information Kane was looking for, he could provide a better bluff.

One wrong move and boom.

Caleb had not expected to let himself get involved with another woman so quickly. Hell, he was beginning to doubt if he'd ever find true love. What he'd had with Cissy couldn't be classified as such. Real love meant putting others before yourself.

He'd told himself his entire life he hadn't gotten involved with a woman because of his devotion to making a success out of his life.

Was it?

He'd almost made a full-time job of avoiding relationships, hadn't he?

And how much of it had to do with your screwed-up childhood?

In trying to avoid being like his father, had he closed the door to finding anything real in his life?

He'd told himself he didn't have time for women, that all he could afford to focus on was work in order to have a better life. Money didn't buy happiness, but being poor didn't, either. He'd had a ringside seat to that show throughout his childhood.

If his mother could have afforded insurance, she would have been able to take better care of herself.

If his old man had stuck around, she wouldn't have had to be the sole provider.

If they'd had more money, she wouldn't have had to work so hard.

If. If. If.

Was he the one to blame for his relationships not working out? For Cissy? He could tell himself she'd used him till the cows came home, but had he given her anything to hang on to?

He had his doubts.

All his heartache, all his loving memories, had little to do with her and everything to do with the thought of having a real family. His heart ached for the idea of a family, not his ex-girlfriend. And why didn't he really miss her? Or any of the other dozen women he'd spent time with in the past?

Is it because they weren't Katherine Harper? asked a quiet voice from the back of his mind.

Whether he wanted to acknowledge it or not, if anything happened to her, he would never be the same again.

Chapter 13

Katherine couldn't remember the last time she'd slept so deeply. Dangerous under the circumstances. Caleb's outdoorsy and masculine scent was all over her…the sheets…bringing out a sensual daydream.

She got out of bed, needing to leave this room, this place, as fast as she could. She felt stifled being on his property, in his homestead with reminders of him everywhere, knowing it wouldn't last.

Her ankle tolerated some weight as she hobbled into the makeshift kitchen trying not to think about Caleb's absence.

The possibility he might not come back crossed her mind. Then what?

They hadn't discussed a contingency plan for that.

Katherine struck the thought from her mind. Caleb would return. They would figure out an arrangement.

Somehow, some way, they would find a way out of this mess.

She thought about Leann, wondering if her sister had believed the same thing when she'd decided to take these men on by herself.

What file did Leann have that would make Kane turn on her family?

Did she have any idea what she was up against?

Did Katherine?

Kane's twenty-four-hour deadline to produce the file had come and gone. His men were out there, searching for her, ready and waiting. Something told her they'd never give up until she was dead, file or not.

Caleb was out there somewhere, too, putting himself in harm's way for her again. He'd promised to be back before she woke, before sunrise, and yet the sun was blazing in the east. A little piece of her heart died at the thought of anything happening to him.

She stopped at the door and her gaze went to the bed. They'd made love right there last night again and again until their bodies were zapped of strength and they gave in to sleep.

Being near him had made her feel more connected to him than anyone else on the planet. They'd made love intensely, sweetly, passionately, until their bodies became entwined and she could no longer tell where he stopped and she began.

They became one body, one being.

The idea of losing him, losing one more person she loved, was worse than a dagger through the chest.

She sat on the floor, stroking Max's neck absently. The strong coffee revived her. She redressed the wounds on her leg. Some of the gashes were deeper than others but they all looked to be healing rather quickly given the circumstances. The swelling was going down on her ankle. A few more days of rest and she'd be all better.

The external wounds would heal. As for the internal damage, that would depend on how the events of the day progressed.

She sighed deeply. Where was Caleb?

Caleb didn't like the idea of leaving Katherine alone all morning. Matt had been late and that had pushed back the whole morning's timeline.

During the meeting, all Caleb's danger radar fired on high alert. He couldn't figure out if it was because of the marshal or because he'd left Katherine alone in the homestead unguarded.

The meeting with the marshal ran over and Caleb's pulse hammered every extra second he was there. This whole scenario could be a scam to get Katherine alone. That's exactly what the marshal would do if he was on Kane's payroll.

Matt hadn't found any secret files, either, not that he was a computer guru. Caleb needed to talk to Katherine about handing it over to the marshal. The government would have the necessary resources available to uncover anything on the CD. Problem was, they'd have to be able to trust the Feds first. If there was a leak in the department, turning over evidence could be more than a huge mistake. It could be a fatal one.

The idea burned Caleb's gut. He couldn't decide if he wanted to put these guys behind bars or take them out himself. The idea they would threaten an innocent child to get to Katherine fired instant rage in his belly.

There were too many "ifs" to feel good about a decision one way or the other.

He wouldn't make a call without filling her in first.

Climbing onto the porch step, the knot in his gut tightened. Maybe he should've taken her with him and stashed her somewhere close by during the meeting.

No. She was safest right where she was and a part of him knew it. Damn that he was second-guessing himself.

Maybe it was because of the news he had to deliver. Or that a little voice kept reminding him she would leave him. If not now, then later.

Relief hit him faster than a rain shower in a drought when he stepped inside and saw her on the floor playing with Max.

Her eyes were wide. "Thank God. You're all right."

He moved to her and pressed kisses to her temples. "Matt was late. He thought someone might be following him. I'm sorry you were worried."

"How'd it go?"

"He didn't find anything on the CD. The marshal might be able to if we give him access."

She moved to the counter and then handed him a tin cup filled with coffee. "I can't decide. What's your first instinct?"

"The government can hack into just about anything." He took the disk from his pocket and held it out between them. "If we can trust the bastards, they'll find what we're looking for."

She palmed it. "What if there's nothing on it?"

"We'll have to cross that bridge when we come to it." He paused a beat. "Even if there's enough evidence on this to lock him away forever, there's something else you should know."

Her violet eyes were enormous. "You're scaring me."

"The marshal said Kane has most likely left the United States."

She sat there, looking dumbfounded. "How can that be?"

"It's believed he has a compound across the border in Mexico. The marshal is working on a few leads, gathering more intel."

"What's the use of turning over the CD when everyone, including me, will be dead before they capture him?"

Not if Caleb had anything to say about it. "I know how hopeless this feels."

"Why does he even need the file when he can disappear out of the country with Noah?" She stared blankly at the door. "And I suppose we're just supposed to let the government take its sweet time finding Kane? Meanwhile, he has an assault squad on us."

"They've offered protection."

She blew out a breath. "Like that would do any good. They'd find us eventually."

"Maybe not."

Silence sat between them for a long beat. "I would never see Noah again."

"That's not going to happen."

"Did he say what Kane is after?"

"Said Leann has evidence linking him to a crime."

"I know I haven't painted a great picture of my sister. But she was a good person. I can't imagine why she would get involved with a man like that."

"The marshal said she didn't know. She was young

when they met. He swept her off her feet. Spent lots of money on her. He was a successful businessman. Everything looked legit. By the time she figured out his dark side, she was pregnant. She disappeared and had her baby. Never planned to tell him he was the father. Kept the evidence of his crime stashed away just in case he showed up again. And then, one day, he walked into the coffee shop. There she was. She pretended that she missed him and secretly got in touch with the Feds. She was planning to turn state's evidence to keep him away from Noah."

"Explains why she moved around so much before. With Noah getting close to school age, she wanted to put down roots. Do they know what evidence she had against him?"

"She offered to provide pictures to back up her testimony." He issued a grunt. "I think you should take the deal. Let them tuck you away somewhere safe."

"They'll kill Noah."

"Kane won't hurt his son."

"How am I supposed to do that?" Her response was rapid, shooting flames of accusation.

"It'll keep you alive until they can find Kane and Noah."

"And then what? Live out the rest of my life in fear? Alone? Waiting for him to finally figure out where I am? He won't stop until he finds me. I don't know where the picture is. I can't put him away without it. If this guy is as ruthless as they say, Kane won't let up until I'm dead."

She had a good point and Caleb knew it. "It's just an option."

"And what about you, Caleb? Where will you go?"

"I already said it once. I won't leave my ranch."

An incredulous look crossed her features. "They'll find you and kill you. They won't even have to look far."

"I'll be fine. You're not thinking straight."

"Oh, so what am I now? A crazy lunatic? Can you look me in the eyes and tell me I'm wrong?"

He lowered his gaze. "No."

"What's your plan?"

"I'm going to stay and fight. No matter how many men they send, I'll return them in body bags if I have to," he said, determination welling in his chest.

"I shouldn't have to run and hide. I didn't do anything wrong," she said, pacing.

"They'll use Noah as bait to get to you. And you to get to me. You know that, right?"

"Let them. It's obvious they won't let up until I'm dead or Kane's locked away. I may not be able to change the cards I was dealt, but I can decide how to play them."

Her stubborn streak was infuriating. And damn sexy.

"I hear what you're saying, but if anything happens to you, it's game over. At least with you alive, we have cards left to play. He will have a lingering doubt about the file. He'll have no choice but to hide." Couldn't she see he was trying to save her? Why did she have to be so stubborn?

You'd be the same way, a distant voice said.

Her chin jutted out. "I thought last night meant something. Why would you want me to disappear from your life forever?"

With every part of him, he didn't. But he'd say anything if it meant keeping her safe. "We got caught up in the moment. I think you should go." Damn but it nearly killed him to say those words.

The pure look of hurt in her eyes nearly made him take it back. He couldn't. He wouldn't let her stick around because of him. He told himself she'd be safer in custody.

"Then I will leave. But I'll be damned if you get to tell me where I'll go." Her lips quivered but she didn't cry.

He'd seen that same look of bravery on her how many times now and it still had the same effect on him.

She grabbed her bag and made a start for the door.

Caleb stepped in front of her, blocking passage. "Where exactly are you going?"

"I don't know and you shouldn't care." Katherine was a study in determination.

Katherine's heart had been ripped from her chest. She knew whatever she and Caleb had couldn't last, and yet his words harpooned her. "Get out of my way, I have something to do."

"I shouldn't have pushed you away. I'm sorry. I only said those things because I thought they might influence you to go into protective custody. I didn't mean a word of it. It's killing me that I can't protect you."

Was he lying then or now?

Katherine had no idea. Everything in her heart wanted to believe this was the truth. That whatever they had between them was genuine and real. The physical attraction had to be, she reasoned. No one could fake what had happened between them last night that convincingly. The sex had been complete rapture. No other man had made her feel like that—sexy, beautiful, devoured. He'd drank in every last inch of her and come back for more. Everything about the night was still vivid in her mind. His gorgeous body, bathed in moonlight and the soft glow of the lantern. His cinnamon taste that was still on her lips.

When he'd entered her, she'd felt on top of the world, as though she was soaring above the earth and didn't need air to breathe. She'd felt more alive in that moment than she had her entire life.

Then again, maybe it was purely physical for him.

Sex for sex's sake.

Didn't men view intimacy differently than women?

Maybe the whole experience was food for his sexual appetite. A man like Caleb was surely used to having his way with women. One look at him, his honey-gold skin and brown eyes with their gold flecks, would stir any woman who could see.

The sex had probably been far more special to her than him. Or maybe she refused to acknowledge the possibility he'd love her and could accept her nephew as his own someday. And she would get Noah back.

"I'd like you to move," she said, tears welling in her eyes.

He didn't budge. Instead, he stared at her incredulously.

"Now." How dare he? Hadn't he just told her she meant nothing to him? And now he had the audacity to pretend to care.

"I'm not going anywhere until you believe me."

"Then we'll be here all day."

"I can think of a good way to spend 'all day' here." He got that mischievous look in his eye. The reminder he knew how to take what he wanted.

Katherine's thin veneer was cracking. She folded her arms. "Let me go."

"What's the matter? Afraid you'll run out of excuses to push me away?" He broadened his stance and quirked a devastating smile.

Damn. He knew he was getting to her.

Her hands came up to his chest again to push him away, but he stepped toward her and she ended up gripping his shoulders to steady herself from the physical force that was all Caleb.

Tension crackled in the air between them as he stared at her, his gaze filled with desire. He leaned down and kissed her so tenderly it robbed her ability to breathe.

"I'm sorry I said those things to you. I was a jerk."

The crack expanded like ice defrosting.

"Yes. You were." She leaned into his broad chest.

"Can you forgive me?"

Katherine was startled to realize there wasn't much he could do she wouldn't forgive.

Not that it mattered. Pretty soon, she'd be exactly where Kane wanted her.

Chapter 14

"We need to make contact with Marshal Jones. See if we have anything to work with here." Caleb pointed to the CD.

"How do we do that?"

"Jones gave me this." Caleb pulled a cell from his pocket and held it out. "It's secure."

"Must be. No one has showed up with a gun," she said.

He opened the contacts, touched the name Marshal Jones and then the call button. "Katherine is willing to turn over the CD we discussed," Caleb said, a little weary they were about to hand over their best and only playing card. "But I need some reassurances."

"I'll go with an outside guy to examine it. No one else will see it," Jones said, answering the unasked question.

"I like where you're headed. Go on."

"Served with him in Iraq. He was dishonorably discharged when he punched his sergeant for his stupidity. Let's just say there's no love lost between this guy and the government."

That's exactly what Caleb wanted to hear. "Then he sounds perfect for the job."

"He will be. If there's anything on the CD, you'll know it. We'll catch up to Kane eventually. And we'll have the evidence ready when we do."

Caleb caught Katherine flexing her hands. Was she trying to stop them from shaking? Was she still angry about his harsh words?

He picked up Max and pointed to a wooden chair. When she sat, he handed her the little mutt. The best way to lower her blood pressure was to get her interacting with the dog. It might distract her enough to calm her down. Give her time to think through his actions—actions that would convince her his feelings were real.

"And until then?"

"We need to keep searching. He'll make a mistake, and we'll be there to catch him. He'll know anything we do is most likely a trap. He could just send his minions to do his dirty work, and I can't guarantee anyone's safety if you're not in custody," Jones said.

Caleb walked outside onto the porch. "He'll come for us. This is personal. He'd never planned to hurt his own son. It's always been about taking back evidence and silencing Katherine."

"You may be right. Don't take any chances. I can order extra security."

"Matt will insist on helping, too."

"I don't want to risk any more civilian lives, but I won't stop you. I'll speak to Sheriff Coleman, too. He might be able to provide some assistance. We'll cover all the bases we can," Jones said ominously.

"I feel a lot more comfortable with the odds of keeping her safe at the ranch. It's better than being out there where anything can happen. I can control who has access to the main house. I'll take her there as soon as it's dark. Don't want to move around during the day if I don't have to."

"I'll have the results by morning. If I find what I'm looking for on that CD, we'll arrest him the minute he shows his face in the U.S. again."

"And her nephew?"

"He'll go back to his aunt where he belongs."

"Other than your men, I don't want anyone else knowing we're staying at the ranch," Caleb insisted.

"Agreed. There's no sense inviting more trouble than we already have coming to this party. We'll have our hands full as it is. No additional government agency involvement apart from my men and Coleman. Your location is easy to secure by vehicle with only one road in and out. I'll station someone near the main house and another officer at the mouth of the drive."

"I'll turn over the CD to the officer on duty." Caleb closed the cell, walked back inside and filled Katherine in on the part of the conversation she missed.

Katherine's body language was easy to read. She was curled up with Max in her lap, making herself as small as she could possibly become. She wanted to disappear.

It wasn't cold inside the homestead, but she was shivering slightly. No doubt, she wanted to block out everything that was happening to her.

"It'll be nice for you to sleep in your own bed for a change," Katherine mused, doing her level best to steer the conversation away from anything stressful. She knew on some level that Caleb hadn't meant to hurt her, but her wounds were still fresh. She needed a minute. Something told her Kane was close by. A man like him would want to finish what he started. No chance he'd walk away and leave her alone.

"No argument there. Except I'll give you the soft bed to sleep on while I keep watch." Caleb moved to the food supplies and opened a can of beans. When they were warm, he offered her first dibs.

"No thanks. I ate a protein bar that was stashed here." The ticking clock was a reminder of how little time she had left. How little time either of them had left. "Did Marshal Jones mention anything about Noah?"

Caleb shook his head.

The pressure was stringing her nerves too tight. A half-desperate laugh slipped out. "I'll just keep hoping for the best then."

He moved to her and kissed her. Warmly. She didn't resist. He tasted like coffee.

"Do you want me to make some more of Margaret's calming tea?" he asked with a wink.

She straightened her shoulders. "God, no. I'm a coffee person through and through."

A white-toothed smile broke across Caleb's face. "You really are determined to hold it together, aren't you?"

"Not on the inside. I'm a wreck." That much was true.

"I'd never be able to tell." He kissed her again.

He pulled her down on his lap as he sat, embracing her as though he might never see her again. He held her as though one of them could be gone tomorrow. Or both.

The gravity of what they were facing hit her hard.

A wave of melancholy washed over her. She'd been

so intent on finding a way to bring Kane out into the open, she hadn't really considered the position she was putting herself in or the consequences. "Promise me that if something happens to me, you'll find Noah anyway and get him away from that animal."

His grip tightened around her as his breath warmed her neck. "Don't have to. You'll be around to take care of him yourself."

She turned enough to look into his brown eyes. "Promise me anyway."

His expression was a mix of sadness, regret and sheer grit. "I will not let anything happen to you. That much I can vow."

She could tell from the intensity in his gaze he would take a bullet for her if that was the only way to protect her.

"Drink up." He motioned to her cup. "It'll be dark outside soon. In a short while we can shower and eat a real meal at the main house."

"Both sound almost too good to be true. Although I haven't exactly felt like I've been suffering out here. Not compared to what we've been through." Or the hell she faced at the thought of never seeing Noah again.

Caleb smiled his trademark smile. He rose, let Max out and stood at the open door.

She brought her hand up to his neck. If they survived this ordeal, could the three of them think about a future together? Would he resent having a ready-made family as she had all those years ago?

Or could he love Noah the same way he did Savannah?

Caleb couldn't see. He didn't have time to let his eyes adjust, either. He knew this trail better than the back of his hand. The path from the homestead to the ranch was thick with trees. They provided much-needed shelter from a sweltering August sun and would afford cover for them now.

He fumbled for Katherine's hand and then slipped through the mesquites in the black, moonless night.

Quietly he made his way through the woods he loved so much. Every tree, every stream, felt so much like a part of him, entwined with his soul. He'd memorized and mentally mapped every inch of his property.

Once inside the house, Caleb bolted the lock. Not that it would do much good against the kind of firepower Kane's men would bring to the fight, but it would make Katherine feel better.

Keeping her as calm and relaxed as he could under the circumstances became his marching orders. "Which sounds better right now—a hot shower or a good meal while I take the CD to Jones's guy out front?"

She sighed. "I'll take either. Both. But let me take one more look at that before we turn it over."

"You know where the office is. Password is TorJake." He handed her a couple ibuprofen and a bottle of water, shoving the fear he could lose her down deep. "Then you get cleaned up while I see what's in the fridge."

"Deal." She popped the pills in her mouth and downed them with a gulp of water before disappearing down the hall with the disk.

He showered and brushed his teeth in the guest room before returning to the kitchen. The CD sat on the counter near the coffeepot. He could hear the shower going in the master bathroom.

Caleb trucked outside and waved as he neared the cruiser. "Marshal Jones is expecting this. Said you'd know what to do with it."

"Yes, sir," the officer said, opening the door. When he stood, he wasn't more than five foot ten but had a stocky build. "I'll take it to him. There's an officer stationed at the top of the road. He'll keep watch until I return."

Caleb thanked him and returned to the house.

Margaret had stacked several Tupperware containers filled with food in the fridge with a note on top. "This should keep you from getting too skinny until I get back in a couple of days."

The idea of eating Margaret's food was almost enough to bring a smile to his lips again. She'd made several of his favorite meals. There was a roast with those slow-cooked rosemary potatoes he loved, a tub full of sausage manicotti, and what looked like smoked brisket. There were mashed potatoes in another container and some greens.

Caleb pulled out the roast, fixed two plates and heated them in the microwave.

Katherine stepped into the kitchen wearing one of his T-shirts and a pair of shorts. Seeing her in his clothes, in his house, stirred his heart. God, he needed her.

She was as beautiful as looking at the endless sky on a clear blue day.

He didn't want this moment to end. For them to end. An ominous feeling it wouldn't last plagued him.

She walked over to him, inclined her head and pressed those sweet lips to his.

The second the kiss deepened, Caleb lifted Katherine and carried her to the bedroom, shooing Max away with his foot.

He made love to her so completely, so thoroughly, she fell asleep in his arms. Right where she belonged.

Chapter 15

Caleb's body warmed Katherine's back. Forget sleep tonight. Her leg hurt. Her throat was dry.

Could she move without waking him?

Even if she managed to slip out of bed undetected, there was Max to deal with. Her nerves were banded so tight, she felt as though one might snap.

Slowly, she rolled away from him until she could feel the edge of the bed. The absence of his touch made her skin cold and her heart ache. She ignored the painful stabs in her chest and slipped off the bed.

Thankfully, Max didn't make a sound. It was too dark to see him, but she figured he was sleeping at the foot of the bed.

She tiptoed out of the room. She'd hoped to feel some relief when they'd come back to the ranch. Instead, the hairs on her neck prickled.

Something brushed against her leg. A yelp escaped before she could suppress it.

Claws?

Katherine squinted. Light streamed in from the window in the hallway. "Here, kitty."

Claws stalked away without looking back.

The kitchen was dark save for the light coming in through the window.

She checked the clock and calculated it had been at least four hours since her last dose of pain medication. She palmed a couple of ibuprofen. Turning the spigot, she scanned the yard.

Where was the officer? His sedan was there. Parked. Doors open. Lights on.

Ice trickled down her spine.

She shook it off.

An officer was parked at the top of the lane and another was right outside the door. It was safe here.

She downed the contents of her glass and set it on the sink.

Where was the officer? If he was walking the perimeter, wouldn't he close the door?

She peeked out the screen door. Nothing stuck out as odd.

The crackle of a radio broke through. She stepped out onto the porch. Outside, every chirp seemed amplified.

The pain in her ankle flared despite the compression sock.

She limped to the edge of the porch. Her mind clicked through a few possibilities. Was the other officer at his post?

Maybe they'd met somewhere in the middle?

Her warning systems flared. She should probably turn and run back into the house. Wake Caleb.

"Anyone here?" she whispered.

The place was quiet. She said a silent protection prayer. Her heart thumped in her throat. Her mouth was so dry she couldn't manage enough spit to swallow.

She checked around the corner.

Nothing.

No one.

Frustration impaled her. Caleb needed sleep. Surely the officer was fine.

It might be a false alarm, but better safe than sorry.

She turned to the back door. Before she could hit her stride, a strong hand crashed down on her shoulder, knocking her backward. The icy fingers were like a vise. She tried to scream. A hand covered her mouth.

"I don't think so, honey," said the male voice.

She recognized it immediately. Scarface.

Using all the force she had, Katherine kicked and threw her elbows into him to break free.

A blast of cold metal hit the back of her head. Blackness.

Waking to find Katherine out of bed had disturbed Caleb. He'd already checked the house. Hadn't found her. Desperation railed through him. She wouldn't leave him. Would she?

He checked outside.

The officer wasn't at his post, either.

Noise came from the barn before Caleb reached the doors. His stallion was kicking and snorting.

What had Samson riled up?

Caleb didn't like it.

Then again, there wasn't anything about this situation he remotely *liked* so far. The caution bells sounded louder the closer he got to the barn until he couldn't hear his own thoughts anymore.

Katherine was in grave danger. He could feel it in every one of his bones. He sent a text to Marshal Jones. What had happened to his men?

The closer Caleb moved toward Samson, the more intense his fears became.

Caleb slowed his pace, his steps steady, deliberate. "Whoa, boy."

Katherine was missing. His chest nearly caved in at the thought. *Kane.*

His next call was to his friend.

Matt picked up on the first ring.

Caleb let out the breath he'd been holding. "Katherine's gone. I think Kane has her."

"Damn. What do you need me to do?"

"Where are you?"

"Dallas. At the hospital with Jimmy."

"I don't know," Caleb lowered his tone.

From the north side of the woods, a tall man stalked toward him.

"I gotta go. Don't worry about being here," Caleb said, ending the call.

The guy was big, but Caleb had no doubt he could take him down if need be. As he moved into the light, he recognized Marshal Jones.

"Where are your men?"

"Sent one of my guys to deliver the CD. I've been trying to reach the other stationed at the top of the drive with no luck. I wanted to be close by so I parked up the road in the woods."

"Kane's here. It's the only explanation." Caleb glanced at his watch. "I don't know when he got to her." It could have been hours ago.

"My man was here fifteen minutes ago. They can't have gotten far. I'll radio again. There's no other way out of here by car, is there?" Jones fell into step with Caleb, who pointed his flashlight at the ground.

"One road in. One road out. There's countless ways to reach the house through the woods. None of which a car would fit through." Caleb glanced up. "Think they got to your guy?"

"Must've. He would answer his radio otherwise."

"Bastards." The white dot illuminated the yellow-green grass as Caleb moved closer to the tree line. "They used ATVs before. They're smart. They've studied the terrain."

He trained his flashlight on a spot on the ground.

"Hold on." He dropped to his knees.

"A woman's footprint."

"It's hers." He shone the light east. "The footprint stops here." He glanced around on the ground. "See that?"

"A man's shoe print."

"Which means someone carried her." Caleb followed the imprints to the tree line. "They went this way."

"They most likely have a car stashed somewhere," Jones said as he turned toward the lane. "I'll head to the main road."

"You said you heard from one of your guys fifteen minutes ago?"

"Yes."

"It would take about that long to run to the nearest

place they could've hid a car. You take the road." Caleb ran toward the barn. "I can cut them off on horseback."

Katherine's eyes blurred as she tried to blink them open. The crown of her head felt as though someone had blasted her with a hammer. Her thoughts jumbled. Thinking clearly through her pounding headache would be a challenge.

In a flash, she remembered being outside before someone grabbed her and then the lights went out. Didn't seem like anyone had turned them back on, either. Pitch-black wasn't nearly good enough to describe the darkness surrounding her. Where was she? Where was Caleb? Terror gripped her.

Chill bumps covered her arms. She reached out and hit surface in every direction without extending her arms. Was she in some kind of compartment? Whatever she was in moved fast. She bounced, bumping her head.

She lay on a clothlike material. The whole area couldn't measure more than three or four feet deep and she couldn't stretch out her legs.

Realization dawned. Icy fingers of panic gripped her lungs and squeezed.

She was in the trunk of a car.

Oh, God. How would she get out? Wasn't there a panic lever somewhere?

At least her arms and legs were free. She felt around for something—anything—to pop the trunk. Was there a weapon? A car jack?

Her mind cleared and she recalled more details. Scarface's voice.

Katherine listened carefully to the sounds around

her. The engine revved. Brakes squealed as the car flew side to side.

A thump sounded. A gunshot rang out.

Her throat closed as fear seized her.

The car roared to a stop.

She repositioned herself so her feet faced the lid. She'd be ready to launch an attack at whoever opened the trunk.

Her heart hammered in her chest. She held her breath, fighting off sheer terror. *Patience.*

The trunk lid lifted and she thrust her feet at the body leaning toward her. She made contact at the same time she recognized the face. "Caleb?"

His arms reached for her, encircled her, while her brain tried to catch up. He lifted her and carried her to his horse.

His face was a study in concentration and determination. He didn't speak as he balanced her in his arms and popped her into the saddle. He hopped up from behind just in time for her to see that his jeans were soaked with blood on his right thigh. Her heart skipped a beat. She told herself he'd be fine. He had to be okay. His arms circled her as he gripped the reins.

Scarface hadn't fared so well. He was slumped over the steering wheel. "Is he dead?"

"No." Caleb urged his horse forward as lights and sirens wailed from behind. "But he'll wish he was after the marshal gets hold of him."

The feel of Caleb against her back, warming her, brought a sense of rightness to the crazy world. "You found me."

She could feel every muscle in his chest tense.

Samson kept a steady gallop until they reached the

barn. Caleb took care of his horse, then, keeping Katherine by his side, headed for the house.

"I walked outside to check on the officer. I turned around to come get you when I heard his voice. Then everything went black. I'm so sorry."

"Don't be. I'm just glad I found you." He pressed kisses to her forehead, then her nose before feathering them on her cheeks. "I can't lose you."

His lips pressed to hers with bruising need.

She loved him. There was no questioning that. But what was he offering? A commitment? Her heart gave a little skip at the thought. He'd already proved he would be there for her no matter what. When the chips were down, he'd come through for her, comforting her, saving her. He was the one person in the world she trusted. "I heard a gunshot and panicked. What happened while I was in the trunk?"

"Scarface took aim. There were too many twists in the road for him to be able to steer and shoot, or…"

"Oh, God. Did he hit you?" She scanned his jeans for a bullet hole, panicked when she noticed the blood.

"Grazed my leg. Flesh wound. I'm fine. I caught up to him before he got off another round."

She couldn't hold back the sob that broke free. She couldn't even think about something happening to Caleb.

"I'm okay. I promise."

She buried her face in his chest, her body shaking. His arms tightened around her.

"Let's get you inside."

"We should get back on the road. Follow Scarface. Maybe he can lead us to Noah?"

"I doubt it. Scarface should be in custody by now.

Unless the marshal let him go to follow him. Putting yourself in danger again won't help that little boy."

"This isn't about him anymore, is it?" A chill ran down her spine at the realization. "Kane is after me now."

"For his own freedom. He wants to erase you and the file." Caleb's gaze scanned the trees. "Let's get you inside."

Caleb cleaned his injuries. He dabbed water on his leg, thinking how much he needed to keep his head clear. He dressed the cut on his thigh and changed into clean jeans.

"They might be out there right now," Katherine said as she sat down on his bed. "That's what you were just thinking, wasn't it?"

"Yes."

She glanced at the windows, her tentative smile replaced by a look of apprehension. "What do we do now?"

"I'll reconnect with the marshal and then go after the son of a bitch as soon as we figure out the next step. Until then, we wait here. I won't let him hurt the woman I love again."

"Love?" She rewarded him with a smile. "I love you, too."

By the time Matt eased in the back door, Katherine's nerves were sizzling. "I thought you were in Dallas."

"Came back to help you."

"Why would you do that?"

"When Caleb said he'd found you, I came to stop

them from doing anything else." He excused himself, saying he needed to find Caleb.

She made a pot of coffee in the dim light, having allowed her eyes to adjust to the darkness, surprised Matt would want to come to her aid. She glanced out the window. Were they out there watching? Who else would Kane send?

They could be anywhere right now. Even standing outside, looking right at her. A chill ran up her spine. She had to figure out a way to get Caleb to let her come with him to find Kane.

A noise from behind shattered what was left of her brittle nerves. She turned to find Matt standing there. Her hand came up to her chest.

"Didn't mean to scare you," he said.

"It's fine. I'm jumpy." She held up a mug. "Coffee?"

"I can get it. You should sit down. Caleb said you have to be careful on that ankle."

"Believe it or not, it was much worse yesterday." She eyed him warily. He looked determined to say something. She filled a mug and handed it to him. "How about I let you get your own cream and sugar?"

"I take mine black."

There was another thing to like about him. Under ordinary circumstances, she figured they might actually get along. She reminded herself they weren't really friends and he likely hadn't sought her out to talk about the coffee.

"Me, too," she said anyway, figuring he also didn't want to hear about how much they had in common—such as how much they both cared for Caleb. But that was another common bond between them, whether Matt like it or not.

"I'm not good at this sort of thing…." He paused.

She took a sip, welcoming the burn and the warmth on her throat.

Another beat passed as he shifted his weight onto his other foot.

Whatever he had to say, Katherine figured she wasn't about to be showered with compliments. She braced herself for what would come next. She'd stared down worse bulls than a protective friend.

Didn't he realize she had Caleb's best interests at heart?

When he looked as though saying the words out loud might actually cause him physical pain, she said, "I can save you the trouble. I know you don't like me. But if you gave me half a chance, I think we could be friends."

There. She'd said it. She put it out there between them, and he could do what he wanted with it.

She crossed her arms and readied herself for his response.

"That isn't what I came here to say."

"Okay."

"I need to apologize."

"No, you don't." The tension in her neck muscles eased.

His stance was firm and unmoving. "I appreciate you saying that, but I do."

"If the tables were turned and it was me, I'd probably feel the same way as you. I can see how this looks. A stranger shows up on his property and he puts his life in danger to help her. I wouldn't like it, either."

The corner on one side of his mouth lifted. "There is that."

"You must love him a lot."

"Like the brother I never had."

"But I do, too." Had she just admitted her true feelings for Caleb to the one man who could stand her the least? It was one thing to say it to Caleb. Damn. It had come out so fast and yet sounded so natural. Felt natural. Her heart was so full it might burst that he'd said it to her first. But to make the declaration to a friend? To let everyone else know took the relationship to a new level. Was she ready?

Katherine steadied her nerves. Her admission would probably spark a rebellion anyway. Why couldn't she just leave it alone? Why did she need Matt to understand her feelings for Caleb?

Because Matt was like family to him. He was important.

She secretly wished for his approval.

"I know," Matt said softly. "He feels the same way. I knew it the first time I saw him with you."

Katherine stood stunned. "I had no idea."

"It's half the reason I've been so…worried," Matt said, leaning against the counter.

"I realize you know him best. You must've seen that look before?"

"No. Never. Not with anyone else." His tone was deadpan.

Katherine's heart skipped a beat. Maybe she could believe his love was real. He wasn't confusing his need to help with true feelings. Maybe this was different than the women in his past.

Caleb strolled in before she could thank Matt for telling her. "Not with any what?"

Chapter 16

Katherine held out a mug. "Coffee's fresh."

Caleb arched his brow. The corners of his lips turned up and he winked. He walked to her and wrapped his arms around her waist. "You're not getting out of this so easy. What were the two of you talking about?"

Matt made an excuse about walking the perimeter and slipped outside.

"I remembered something that might help. I'd completely forgotten about Leann's phone. I can contact Kane if we can get another power cord and a battery."

"You brought up a good point, but I don't want you doing anything with that phone. Stay inside the house. No matter what. Promise me?"

She folded her arms. "This is the worst. At least when we were on the run, we had distractions. Waiting around with no way to make contact, doing nothing is killing me."

Caleb's pocket vibrated. He pulled Jones's cell from his pocket and glanced at the screen. "It's Jones."

Katherine's heart went into free fall with anticipation.

As soon as Caleb ended the call, he turned to her. "They found it. They found the proof. Leann had pictures linking Kane to murder. He must've had no idea she had evidence until recently."

"Doesn't do any good if they can't find Kane. Can't he live out the rest of his life in Mexico? With Noah? How will I ever get him back? I can't imagine leaving him to grow up with a monster like that." Panic thumped a fresh course of adrenaline through Katherine's veins. She didn't want to think about never seeing her nephew again.

"We don't know that. Jones has men in Dallas all over it."

His words were meant to be comforting. They weren't. A jagged rock ripped through her chest. Breathing hurt. She'd wait like a sitting duck for how long? Kane's men would never leave her alone. He wouldn't be satisfied until she was dead. "What about Scarface? Did he talk?"

"That's the best part. He did. Kane has been hiding in a warehouse downtown in the garment district. He's believed to be there right now. Jones is going after him. Coleman is on his way with reinforcements."

A myriad of emotions ran through her. Fear for Noah gripped her. Could they get to him in time? A trill of hope rocketed. This whole ordeal could be behind them by morning's light.

A disturbance out front caught their attention.

"Wait here." Caleb moved to the cabinet and pulled out a handgun.

He crossed to her and placed it in her hand. Katherine's hand shook as she recoiled. "Not a good idea. I'm scared to death of those things."

"I won't leave you here without a way to protect yourself. It's a .38. You have to cock it to fire. Like this." He pressed her thumb to the hammer. "Then you point and pull the trigger. Wait here for me, but if someone comes through that door you don't recognize, shoot."

A lump in Katherine's throat made swallowing difficult. Her breathing came in spasms and her chest hurt. *Be strong. Refuse to be defeated.* She gripped the handle tighter. "Okay."

"I better check on Matt." Caleb kissed her forehead. He turned and headed toward the front of the house. "Don't be afraid to use the gun if you need to. Look before you shoot."

All her danger signals were flaring, and she knew on instinct something very bad was about to go down. They'd found her. Fear crippled her, freezing every muscle of her body even though she had the very real sense she was shaking on the outside. Sweat beaded and dripped down her forehead like the trickle of melting ice cream.

She couldn't let Caleb go alone.

Her eyes had already adjusted to the darkness, so finding her way around outside the house wasn't a problem. At the last corner, she crouched low, making herself as small as possible, and moved behind the Japanese boxwoods in the front landscaping. Caleb stepped out the front door with his right arm extended, gun aimed.

Matt was on his knees in front of the house with his

arms and legs bound. A man the size of a linebacker stood behind him, his gun pointed at his head.

Oh. God. No.

She turned away for an instant, unable to look. Guilt this was all her fault gripped her.

"He has nothing to do with this. Let him go." Caleb's voice was surprisingly even. He was calm under pressure whereas Katherine's nerves were fried.

The sound of gravel crunching underneath tires brought her focus to the road where a blacked-out SUV barreled down the path.

"Doesn't seem like your friend here wants to get up," said the linebacker, kicking Matt from behind.

Katherine prayed Caleb wouldn't react to the taunting.

A thousand ideas ran through her head. Should she slip into the house and call 9-1-1? Wasn't Coleman on his way? She crouched low, rooted to her spot as two men stepped out of the SUV. One she recognized from Noah's kidnapping, the other was new. He was smaller than the others, but wore an expensive suit. His hair was dark, curly and slicked back. Kane?

"Put your gun down on the porch, and we'll consider sparing your life," the familiar one said.

Caleb didn't budge.

"Fine. Then your buddy here gets a bullet in the head." He lowered the barrel toward Matt.

Caleb put up both hands in the universal sign for surrender. "No need to do that." He lowered his gun to the porch and kicked it forward with the toe of his boot.

"Where is she?" the man with the slicked-back dark hair asked, his tone clipped; there was that telltale albeit subtle difference in the way he pronounced his vowels.

Katherine knew exactly who he was. Kane.

"I'm afraid it's just us guys here," Caleb responded.

"Don't insult me. I happen to know you were with her. She must be here somewhere." Kane glanced around. "Come out. Come out. Wherever you are."

Kane walked closer to Caleb, eyeing him up and down. He turned to his henchmen and pointed to Matt. "Show them we're serious."

The crack of a bullet split the night air.

Katherine's heart plummeted. A gasp escaped before she could squash it. She fought the urge to vomit. Make a noise and Kane had what he wanted. *Her.* Game over.

She forced herself to peer through the bushes at him, expecting to see blood splattered on the men. There was none. If they hadn't shot Matt, what had they hit?

The bullet must've pinged the ground instead. Thank God. No one was hurt.

A wicked grin crossed Kane's attractive features. Authority and power radiated from him. Underneath that good-looking exterior, this man was the devil reincarnate. How horrible was he? Leann was a good person. How could she have gotten involved with such evil?

Katherine remembered the practiced, cool voice she'd first heard on the phone. Was that the one he'd used to lure Leann? If she'd seen the other side to him, no wonder she'd wanted to escape. She must've innocently believed she could keep him away from Noah. That definitely had to be why she'd moved around so much. It all made sense now. She'd kept the evidence quiet, waiting until the day he showed up again. And when he'd found her? She'd decided to play him while she'd gone to the Feds for help. A new life. A new identity. She and Noah would be hidden forever.

The cost?

She would have to cross the father of her child.

That couldn't have been easy. Sadness and anger burned Katherine's chest, firing heat through her veins. Why hadn't Leann confided in her?

She didn't want to bring you down with her, a little voice said.

Oh, sister.

Kane glanced around wildly. "Still not wanting to come out and play. Well let's see if this changes your mind." He opened the back door to the SUV and lifted a small figure into his arms.

Noah?

Katherine's heart faltered. She feared it would stop beating altogether if her nephew was dead. Kane was a horrible man. Would he hurt his own son?

No. A man who made sure the boy had his medicine wouldn't harm him.

But he would kill Matt. Possibly even Caleb.

She had to stop him.

Without thinking, she tucked the gun into the band of her shorts and stepped out of the boxwoods. There was no way she could hit him from this far. Not with the way her hands were shaking. If she could get close enough, she'd take that bastard out with one shot. His henchmen might retaliate, but at least Kane would die. "I'm right here, you son of a bitch. You don't have to hurt any more innocent people."

Caleb made a move toward her but backed off when Kane aimed his gun at Noah's temple.

"Don't be a hero, cowboy," Kane said, smooth and practiced. "I've been waiting for this day for a long time. You won't ruin it for me, will you? No one's going to wreck my plans. No one sends me to jail." He turned to face Katherine. "Not that bitch sister of yours. And sure as hell not you. She said she loved me. All the time she was sneaking around behind my back. Talking to the Feds. How could she love me when she stabbed me in the back? What about you? Will you betray him, too? Let's see how much you care about your cowboy." He nodded toward his henchman, who moved behind Caleb and pressed a gun to his back.

"Hurt him if you want. It won't bother me," Katherine lied.

She needed Kane to believe those words even though she could feel warmth traveling up her neck to her cheeks. She ignored it.

Convincing Kane she didn't love Caleb might be his only chance to live.

If she could distract Kane long enough to pull the gun, and then fire, she'd stop him from hurting anyone else. He wasn't more than five feet away. So close she could smell his musky aftershave. Too far to make a move before Kane's guy had a chance to pull the trigger and end Caleb's life.

She couldn't get a clear shot while Kane held Noah anyway. Thank God he was sleeping. She had to get that monster away from her nephew and focused on her.

"Besides, he doesn't know anything. But I do. And I'll testify. You'll rot in jail with all the other scum who think they're above the law."

"Scum?" Kane's voice raised another octave. "That's what your sister said about me?" The pained look on his face said he still loved Leann.

"Don't believe her. I know exactly what you did. I

can point authorities to the evidence, too, and she can't," Caleb said quickly.

Damn him. Didn't he see what she was trying to do? He was going to get himself killed.

"He's wrong. This is between you and me. Let Noah get out of here. Matt can take him. And I'll do anything you want." Noah blinked up at her. Fear filled his brown eyes. He couldn't possibly know how much she loved him. And if they saw how important Caleb was to her, he'd be dead, too.

"Let my son go? My son? Your sister tried to keep him from me. No one will ever keep me from my boy again." Kane's voice bordered on hysteria. The high-pitch sound echoed in the night. "Do something to the friend."

The linebacker hit Matt with the butt of his gun.

Matt crumpled forward. Didn't move again.

Was he unconscious? Alive? He had to be.

Tears welled in her eyes. She sniffed them back. She couldn't afford to let her emotions take control.

A bolt of lightning raced sideways across the sky. A clap of thunder followed moments later.

If she were going to stop Kane, she had to act fast.

Caleb spun around and disarmed the man on him. The pair tumbled onto the ground in a twist of arms and legs.

Katherine used the distraction to slip her hand behind her and grip the gun. She fired a shot and the linebacker went down. Before she could locate Kane, he was next to her, his hand gripping her neck, and it felt like her eyes might pop out.

Another shot rang out.

Chapter 17

Katherine forced herself to look at Caleb, expecting her own exploding pain to register at any moment. Everything had happened so fast, her brain almost couldn't catalog the sequence. Both he and the man on him lay still. Blood. There was so much blood. *Please move, Caleb. Get up.*

He didn't.

Hopelessness engulfed her. If he was dead… Oh, God… She couldn't even think what she would do without him.

Tears sprang from her eyes. She doubled over. Her world imploded around her. She'd finally invested herself and fallen in love. Now he was dead. Just like her parents. Just like her sister.

Leann.

Noah was sick. Would he die, too?

A hand gripped her shoulder, pulling her upright. Cold metal poked her back. She jerked away, spun around and stared into the blackest set of eyes she'd ever seen. "You killed him. This is your fault. You caused me to drop my son, too. That won't be forgiven."

Through blurry eyes she searched for Noah. He'd been placed on a seat in the SUV. The door was open.

Her gaze flew to Matt's lifeless body.

"He's still alive. For the moment. Make another move and he'll be dead, too," Kane said into her ear, disarming her. "You're going to pay for what that bitch sister of yours tried to do to me. I loved her. I treated her like a queen. Look what she did." He waved his gun around, and then pressed the metal barrel against Katherine's temple. "I never would've known if she hadn't gone and gotten herself killed. I pieced it together when I was going through her things. Nobody betrays me and gets away with it."

She squeezed her eyes shut.

"Now move," he growled.

Every muscle in her body stiffened as she forced herself by sheer will to walk. He pushed her toward the barn. The man behind her directed her actions. This was something new to fear. A crazed psychopath who wanted to do more than kill her. He needed to see her suffer.

"You won't get away with this," she said in the dark. His icy fingers gripped her neck. Her body convulsed. She could feel his hot breath on her.

"I'm going send you to meet that bitch sister of yours in death. But first, you're going to watch that boyfriend of yours burn."

Katherine's heart shriveled. The air thinned. She

struggled to take a breath. She refused to believe Caleb was gone and her life would end like this. That Noah would be brought up by this monster. There had to be a way out.

He tossed her into a stall and on top of a bale of hay. She popped up. "The cops are coming. They'll arrest you. Hurting me won't help your case. It'll only make it worse. If you leave now, you can disappear. They won't find you if you stay out of the country."

"Be still, kitten." He knocked her down, forced her hands behind her back and tied them together. "I have no plans to rot in jail. Time to get rid of the evidence."

Her body shuddered at his touch. She kicked as hard as she could, connecting with his shin multiple times.

He flinched and slapped her across the left cheek. Katherine's head jolted. It felt as though her eye would explode. A fresh course of adrenaline pumped through her.

"You're about to learn something." A wicked grin spread across his lips. "Look at me."

He touched her cheek with the back of his hand. "She favored you. So beautiful." He shook his head. "She could have had anything she wanted. I would have given her the world."

His lips thinned. His gaze narrowed. "Now you all die." He shook his head. "What a waste."

Katherine struggled against her bindings. The rope cut through her flesh. She ignored the pain, trying to loosen the ties.

A hysterical laugh brought her focus back to Kane. "Stay here, little one. I'll be right back."

Maybe Katherine could free herself before he returned. Her body convulsed. Yet she couldn't budge the ropes. Kicking did no good, either.

It felt as though Kane had been gone for eternity when he finally showed up, dragging a bloody lifeless body.

Her heart beat against her ribs in painful stabs.

Caleb.

"One more to go and I'll finally be rid of you all," Kane said before he disappeared again.

Where was the sheriff? His men?

Katherine's gaze frantically searched for any sign of life in Caleb. She knew it was too much to hope he was still alive. Yet she had to be sure. She watched his chest for signs of movement. His broad chest rose and fell.

Or was she seeing what she wanted to?

Was he unconscious?

Katherine could've sworn she just saw Caleb surveying the area. Were his eyes open?

Yes. Definitely so. Her heart soared at the realization Caleb was alive. He brought a finger to his lips, the universal sign to keep quiet.

Matt was dragged in next. Katherine wanted to scream. She fought harder against the ropes.

Kane positioned Matt next to Caleb and threw a few fistfuls of hay on top of them. Her pulse beat in her throat. She was sure a red heat crawled up her neck. She put all her focus toward Caleb.

Kane hovered over Katherine. She kicked and threw her arms at him, trying to fight. He held out a match over the heap.

She looked toward the man she loved one more time. One wrong move and Kane would shoot. She needed to stall. To get his attention. She looked up at him. "Leann wouldn't want this. She never meant to hurt you. The Feds must've forced her to turn against you. I know she loved you."

Kane's laugh was haughty and arrogant. He trailed his finger along her jawline, and she saw Caleb's hands fist. Hope filled her chest.

"You are almost as beautiful as Leann," Kane said. "She was a free spirit. You, on the other hand, are a bit uptight. Even so, I could make you moan. The things I would like to do to you before I watch you burn...."

Allowing him to touch her and talk about her sister in that way nearly killed her.

He smoothed his hand across her red cheek. "I wish you hadn't made me do that to you."

Kane's dark eyes homed in on her. He brought a match to life with a flick of his nail and dropped it next to Caleb.

The moment Katherine moved, Caleb was on top of Kane. With a few quick jabs to the head, Kane's body slumped on top of her, pinning her to the ground. He was unconscious, but for how long?

A scream escaped before she could get her bearings and push him off. "I thought you were..."

"I'll be fine. I took a blow to the head. Scrambled a few things. Took a minute to shake. By the time I got my bearings again, I was being dragged to the barn."

She struggled against the ropes on her wrists, tears falling down her cheeks. When Caleb helped free her, they pulled Matt to his feet. He shook his head. Disoriented, he didn't seem able to hold his own weight.

"Help him outside." Caleb handed over Jones's cell. "Call 9-1-1. I have to put out the fire before it spreads."

Katherine dialed the emergency number as she bore some of Matt's heft, and walked outside the barn.

After giving her location and details to the operator, she helped Matt ease onto the ground.

A moment later, Caleb dashed to her side, a fire extinguisher in his hands. "It was contained. Didn't take much to put it out."

"The police are on their way." Katherine looked to Matt. "He's hurt, but conscious."

Max was at the door to the tack room. He stood sentinel, barking wildly.

Caleb's autumn-brown eyes pierced through her as he set the extinguisher down and told her to wait for him.

"No. I'm going with you," she insisted with a glance toward Matt.

He motioned for her to go.

Kane was moving toward the back of the tack room, trying to escape. He rounded on them.

Caleb shielded her with his body, pulling a gun from his waistband. Kane launched himself toward them. The gun fired as the two landed on the ground.

In a quick motion, Caleb straddled Kane. Blood was everywhere.

Panic momentarily stopped her heart. "Are you shot?"

He shook his head.

Kane gurgled blood before his gaze fixed and his expression turned vacant.

She dropped to her knees. Max ran to her. She cradled him. "It's over."

Caleb guided her to her feet where the little dog followed. "Let's get Noah."

His hand closed on hers as he led her outside.

Matt stood, still weak, and Caleb took some of his weight.

Another bolt of lightning cut across the sky as a droplet of rain fell.

An SUV was gone. Only the man who'd been shot remained, lifeless on the ground.

By the time they reached Noah, his face was pale. Katherine picked him up and hugged him. He let out a yelp.

Katherine embraced him tighter. "Oh, baby. You're safe."

His brown eyes were wide and tearful.

Caleb stood next to her. "Okay, little man. We're going to get you to the hospital."

Noah nodded. His bottom lip quivered as tears welled. He was too tired to cry. Not a good sign.

"Did the men bring your medicine, baby?"

He shook his head.

His breathing was shallow, and Katherine realized it was probably the reason he wasn't bawling. He didn't have the energy, which meant he needed medicine right away.

"You're safe," she repeated over and over again, hugging him tightly into her chest. He was fading, and she knew it. "Can you check the car for his medicine, Caleb?"

They searched the vehicle, pulling out the contents of the console and glove box, looking for the life-saving drugs.

Rain starting coming down in a steady rhythm as Katherine held on to her nephew, whispering quiet reassurances that he would be okay.

He *had* to be fine.

She glanced at Caleb and tensed at his worried expression. Noah's eyes rolled back in their sockets; he was losing his grip on consciousness.

"An ambulance is on its way. So is Coleman," Caleb said.

Katherine's tears mixed with rain, sending streaks down her face. "Come on, baby. Stay with me."

Her shoulders rocked as she released the tears she'd been holding far too long. They came out full force now. "When will that damn ambulance be here?"

She kissed Noah's forehead. His face was paler than before. His skin was cool and moist to the touch. Her heart thudded in her chest. "Caleb. Oh, God. Nothing can happen to him. Not now."

"The keys are still in the ignition." He hopped in the driver's side and motioned for her to climb in the passenger seat.

The SUV started on the first try. He glanced back at Matt. "Wait here for the sheriff?"

"Yes. Now go," Matt said.

Caleb glanced at his friend again.

"I'm fine. Get out of here."

The engine roared as Caleb gunned it.

Sirens and lights brought the first spark of hope.

Caleb flashed the headlamps as they cut off the ambulance at the top of the drive.

He hopped out of the driver's seat and crossed his arms over his head to signal they needed help. A paramedic scrambled out of the passenger seat as Katherine ran toward him with Noah in her arms. "Help him, please. He's not breathing. He has asthma and may not have had medicine in a few days."

A paramedic took him from her arms and ran to the back of the ambulance as she followed. His hands worked quickly and efficiently.

"Has the patient been to the emergency room or used EMS in the past twenty-four to forty-eight hours?" he asked, not looking up.

"No. He was kidnapped. His skin was pale and his breathing shallow when I found him." A flood of tears spilled out of Katherine's eyes and into the rain.

Caleb's arm came around her, reassuring her. Protecting her.

The paramedic shot a sympathetic look toward her. "I'm going to administer a dose of epinephrine."

Another ambulance whirred past. *Matt.*

She turned to Caleb. "Go. Be with your friend. I have this covered. I know how worried you are about him."

Caleb's head shook emphatically. "I won't leave you to deal with this all by yourself."

There was that cowboy code again. "He's your best friend. And I need to know if he's going to be okay. I want you to check on him for both of us."

She could almost see the arguments clicking through his mind. How torn he had to be. "I'm serious. Go. I'm safe and Noah's getting the help he needs."

The paramedic started an IV and bagged him. "We've got to get the boy to the hospital. You can ride in the front," he said to Katherine before turning to Caleb. "You can follow behind in your vehicle."

"I'll go with Noah. You stay with Matt. I'll meet you at the hospital," Katherine said, determined. She was fine with Noah and he needed to make sure his friend was okay.

"I know that stubborn look. I'd rather stay with you

but I won't argue," Caleb agreed, looking more than reluctant.

She gave him a quick kiss as he helped her into the passenger seat.

Caleb drove like a bat out of hell down the drive. He parked the SUV and went to his friend.

Matt had an oxygen tube under his nose, and his forehead had been cleaned up from all the blood. His cut wasn't as bad as it had first looked.

Matt blinked up at Caleb. "What the hell are you doing here?"

"Checking on you."

Matt issued a grunt. "I'm not the one who needs you."

"Try telling her that," Caleb quipped.

Sheriff Coleman roared up and jogged toward them. "Sorry I'm late. I got called away to another county on an emergency. Got there and they said they never made the call."

"I'm sure you'll need a statement, but I have to get to the hospital and check on the little boy," Caleb said.

Coleman took Caleb's outstretched hand and shook it. "I can always drop by tomorrow if you'd like. Sounds like you guys have had one hell of a night already."

He nodded.

"I spoke to Dallas PD to make sure you were no longer a person of interest in their murder investigation," Coleman said with a tip of his hat. "You're fine. I'll get this mess cleaned up and be out of here before you return."

"Much obliged, Sheriff." The last thing Caleb wanted

to do was to bring Katherine home to reminders of the horrors she and Noah had endured.

Coleman patted Caleb on the back. “You need a ride to the hospital?”

“No, thanks.” He said goodbye and climbed into the cab of his pickup.

He made it to the hospital in record time and found Katherine sitting next to Noah’s bed.

She looked up at him with those expressive eyes. “He’s going to be fine. His skin is already pink and dry.”

Relief flooded him as he pulled up a chair next to her. “Did they say when he’ll be released?”

“Could be as early as tomorrow. They want to keep him overnight for observation.”

“That’s the best news I’ve heard today.”

“It is.”

He cupped her cheek. “Then why the sad face?”

“Nothing. How’s Matt?”

“He’ll be fine. They’re bringing him in. Not that he likes the idea.”

A knock at the door interrupted their conversation. Marshal Jones poked his head inside. “Katherine Harper?”

“Yes. That’s me.”

“Marshal,” Caleb said, nodding.

Jones returned the acknowledgment.

“Could I have a word with Ms. Harper in the hallway?”

“As long as he can come with me.” She moved to the door alongside Caleb who was already in motion.

“Not a problem,” Jones said.

"Is everything all right, Marshal?" Her hand was moist from nerves.

Caleb gave it a reassuring squeeze.

"I didn't mean to worry you," Jones said. "I wanted to let you know what we found on the CD." He glanced from her to Caleb.

Katherine's hand came up to her chest. "What?"

"Turns out your sister videotaped Kane murdering a business associate. We've been watching him for years trying to gather evidence against him for other crimes. He was slick. Anytime we got close, witnesses disappeared."

Katherine's head bowed.

"Your sister outsmarted him. She went to great lengths to hide the evidence. She disappeared. Then he found her."

"I wonder why she didn't run straight to the police or you guys," Katherine said, wiping a tear from her eye.

Caleb pulled her close.

"She'd been on the run, trying to keep her son safe. She was young and scared," Jones said. "All she wanted was to give her son a life. When I finally made contact with her, she told me that if anything happened, she wanted Noah to be with you. Said you'd be the best mother he could possibly have."

Tears rolled down Katherine's cheeks.

"For what it's worth, I'm sorry. She was brave to do what she did," he said. "If not for the accident, she would've brought Kane to justice."

Katherine's gaze lifted, her chin came up. "Thanks. It means a lot to hear you say that."

He inclined his chin. "Emergency personnel tried to revive Kane at the scene. You should know he didn't survive. He'll never be able to hurt you or Noah again. We apprehended an SUV with his associates, and they'll be locked away for a long time."

"Thank you." Relief washed through her.

Jones excused himself as Caleb walked her back into Noah's room.

Katherine checked on her nephew before taking a seat next to Caleb on the sofa.

"You need anything? Coffee?" he asked.

"No. I want to be right here in case Noah wakes in this strange place." Her eyes were rimmed with tears when she said, "I'm sorry you couldn't stay with your friend."

"Are you kidding? He was pissed at me for leaving you."

Confusion knitted her eyebrows. "I didn't want you to have to choose between us and him. He's your best friend."

"And he always will be. Did you think you were doing me some kind of favor pushing me away like that?"

"Yes. Noah was fine, and I needed to know how Matt was doing."

"That so?"

"Yes." She looked at him as if he had three eyes. "Besides, you don't know what it's like to have a family thrust on you before you're ready."

"As a matter of fact, I do. And guess what? It doesn't scare me. You make a decision and then adjust your life to adapt to it. I'm a grown man." He pulled her into his arms and felt her melt into his chest. "And I want you."

Tears spilled from her eyes, dotting his T-shirt. "I want you, too," she admitted.

"Let's make a deal."

She arched an eyebrow. "I'm listening."

"Let me tell you what I can and can't handle when we go home."

"Okay." Her smile didn't reach her eyes.

"You gonna explain the long face?"

"You have the ranch. Where's *home* for me and Noah? We can't go back to my apartment. Not after what happened."

"I was getting to that. I want you both to come to live with me. I love you. My life was empty until you came along. If you don't like the ranch, we'll buy a new place. I belong wherever you are."

"Are you serious?" She looked as though she needed a minute to let his words sink in. Her head shook. "You love that place."

"Not as much as I love you."

"I love you, too. Believe me. I do. But what about Noah? I'm the only family he's got and I don't want to confuse him."

"Then let's change that."

Her expression made him think the three eyes she'd seen on his forehead had grown wings. "All I'm saying is let's make it permanent. *Us*. I want to become a family."

She looked up at him wide-eyed as he stood.

He got down on one knee. "If I live another hundred years, I know in my heart I won't meet anyone else like you. You fit me in every possible way that matters. I don't want you to leave. Ever. I want to spend my life chasing away your fears and seeing every one of your smiles. I'm asking you to be my wife."

Tears fell from her eyes.

He leaned forward and thumbed one away as it stained her cheek, and he waited for her answer.

She kissed him. Deep. Passionate. And it stirred his desire. "Keep that up, and I'll show you what we can do with the bed on the other side of that curtain while little man sleeps."

She smiled up at him and his heart squeezed.

"You haven't answered my question."

"Yes, Caleb, I will marry you."

"Good, because I want to start working on a new project."

"A project?" she echoed, raising her brow.

He pulled her into his chest and crushed his lips against hers. "I want Noah to have a little brother or sister running around soon."

She smiled. "I want that, too."

"And I'm going to spend the rest of my life loving you."

* * * * *

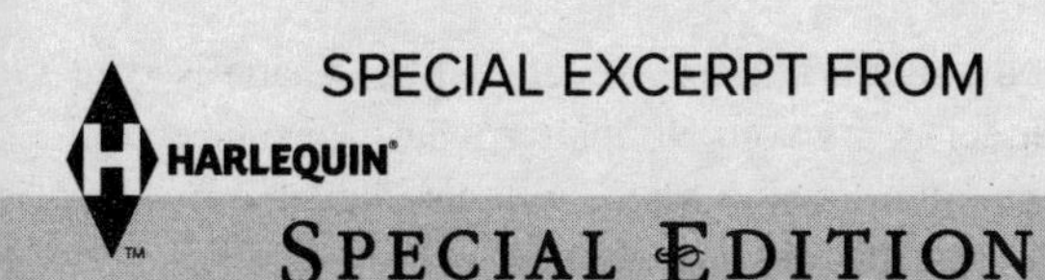

Single parents Liam Mercer and Shelby Ingalls just found out their little boys were switched in the hospital six months ago! Will they find a way to stay in the lives of both boys they've come to love?

Read on for a sneak preview of
THE BABY SWITCH!
the first book in the brand-new series
THE WYOMING MULTIPLES
by Melissa Senate, *also known as Meg Maxwell!*

"Are you going to switch the babies back?"

Shelby froze.

Liam felt momentarily sick.

It was the first time anyone had actually asked that question.

"No, ma'am," Liam said. "I have a better idea."

Shelby glanced at him, questions in her eyes.

"Where is my soup!" Kate's mother called again.

"You go ahead, Kate," Shelby said, stepping out onto the porch. "Thanks for talking to us."

Kate nodded and shut the door behind them.

Liam leaned his head back and he started down the porch steps. "I need about ten cups of coffee or a bottle of scotch."

"I thought I might fall over when she asked about switching the babies back," Shelby said, her face pale, her green eyes troubled. She stared at him. "You said you had a better idea. What is it? I sure need to hear it. Because switching the babies is not an option. Right?"

HSEEXP0318

"Damned straight it's not. Never will be. Shane is your son. Alexander is my son. No matter what. Alexander will also become your son and Shane will also become my son as the days pass and all this sinks in."

"I think so, too," she said. "Right now it's like we can't even process that babies we didn't know until Friday are ours biologically. But as we begin to accept it, I'll start to feel a connection to Alexander. Same with you and Shane."

He nodded. "Exactly. Which is why on the way here, I started thinking about a way to ease us into that, to give us both what we need and want."

She tilted her head, waiting.

He thought he had the perfect solution. The only solution.

"I called the lab running the DNA tests and threw a bucket of money at them to expedite the results. On Monday," he continued, "we will officially know for absolute certain that our babies were switched. Of course we're not going to switch them back. I'd sooner cut off my arm."

"Me, too," Shelby said, staring at him. "So what's your plan?"

"The plan is for us to get married."

Shelby's mouth dropped open. "What? We've been living together for a day. Now we're getting married. Legally wed? Till death do us part?"

Don't miss
THE BABY SWITCH! by Melissa Senate,
available April 2018 wherever
Harlequin® Special Edition books and ebooks are sold.